James Oswald is the author of the  KT-230-146 ctor
McLean series of detective mysteries, as ~ new Constance
Fair~ ~ Book of
Souls, were both short-listed for the prestigious CWA Debut Dagger
Award. *Nothing to Hide* is the second book in the Constance Fairchild
Series.

James farms Highland cows and Romney sheep by day and writes
disturbing fiction by night.

Praise for the *Inspector McLean* series:

'The new Ian Rankin' *Daily Record*

'Oswald's writing is a class above' *Daily Express*

'Oswald easily outstrips the formulaic work of bigger names' *Guardian*

'Crime fiction's next big thing' *Sunday Telegraph*

'Literary sensation . . . James' overnight success has drawn comparisons
with the meteoric rise of EL James and her *Fifty Shades of Grey* series'
Daily Mail

'Hugely enjoyable' *Mirror*

'The hallmarks of Val McDermid or Ian Rankin: it's dark,
violent, noir-ish' *The Herald*

'Creepy, gritty and gruesome' *Sunday Mirror*

'Oswald is among the leaders in the new batch of excellent
Scottish crime writers' *Daily Mail*

Praise for the *Constance Fairchild* series:

'Pacy, action packed and with a really rather fabulous heroine'
Sunday Mirror

'A cracking story beautifully told' *Daily Mail*

'A fast-paced crime caper' *Irish Independent*

'Gr~ ~ke this

JAMES OSWALD

NOTHING TO HIDE

WILDFIRE

First published in 2019 by WILDFIRE
An imprint of HEADLINE PUBLISHING GROUP

First published in paperback in 2019 by WILDFIRE
An imprint of HEADLINE PUBLISHING GROUP

1

Cataloguing in Publication Data is available from the British Library

ISBN 978 1 4722 5005 6

Typeset in Aldine 401BT by Avon DataSet Ltd,
Bidford-on-Avon, Warwickshire

Printed and bound in Great Britain by Clays Ltd, Elcograf S.p.A.

HEADLINE PUBLISHING GROUP
An Hachette UK Company
Carmelite House
50 Victoria Embankment
London EC4Y 0DZ

www.headline.co.uk
www.hachette.co.uk

For Barbara

1

I always thought I'd miss London more.

Time was, the lights and bustle and sheer busyness of the place gave me a buzz as good as any drug. Growing up in the countryside, with parents still happily living in an earlier century, I leapt at the chance to come to the big city. Even Edinburgh, where I spent four glorious student years, felt small and provincial in comparison. Which is why I joined the Met rather than what was then Lothian and Borders police, I guess. London's been my home for long enough that I might even kid myself I'm a local, but lately the shine's gone off its attraction.

There's the endless, unmoving traffic, for one thing. I never had a car before. Never needed one. Now I remember why that was, as I sit and watch the engine temperature gauge on my old Volvo creep slowly towards the red. Every so often a fan somewhere under the bonnet roars into life like a jumbo jet hauling itself into the air from Heathrow.

It's dark by the time I pull into my street, my trusty car still holding on. Against all the odds, I manage to find a parking space too. Someone up there must be smiling on me. There's a familiarity to the block, the concrete stairs climbing up to my floor, the open walkway that is almost a communal balcony for all the flats on this level. Light spills from some of the windows, but the curtains are closed on whatever lives are being lived behind them.

My front door's a little grubbier than it was when I last closed it, although still cleaner than a year ago. I smile at the realisation that it was Roger DeVilliers who had it repainted and a new lock fitted, but the amusement is short lived. He's the reason I've been away, and the reason I glance over my shoulder as I slide the key into the lock. The press have had a field day with what will likely be the trial of the decade, and I'm right in the middle of it. If I'd wanted to be photographed wherever I went, I'd have been a model or something. Not an undercover police officer.

The flat is dark as I step over the threshold and a massive pile of mail, then close the door behind me. For a moment it's just as I remember it, and then the smell hits. Something sour and rotten, as if the drains have backed up while I've been away. Has it been long enough for the toilet bowl to dry out? Do London sewers smell that bad?

I work my way swiftly through the rooms, opening windows despite the chill and damp outside. There's still a little water in the toilet, but I flush it anyway. Then run the taps to fill the U-bends in the basin and shower. It doesn't help.

Whatever it is, it's worst in the tiny kitchen. The bin's empty, I did that before I left, remember it well enough. Then I spot the dark stain on the floor tile beneath the fridge door. Shit. Did I leave something in there?

It's only as I open the door that I realise what a dumb idea that is. There's a magnetic seal all around it keeping the worst of what's in there inside. No light comes on, confirming my suspicion that the damn thing's broken down. Even so, I knew I'd be away a while, didn't think I'd left anything to go off. Something brown and unidentifiable lurks in the salad box at the bottom, though, emitting a smell so noxious I have to run to the front door and open it wide, paparazzi be damned. Saliva fills my mouth and I can feel the bile rising, but I fight back the urge to vomit. That would be some headline in the *Daily Mail*.

The first trip back inside I can hold my breath just long enough to find a roll of bin liners under the kitchen sink before I have to rush out again. I steel myself for the second trip, cursing that I've no police-issue latex gloves to pull on as I take out the entire salad box and shove it into the bag. I leave it by the door and lean out over the parapet for fresh air, gulping down lungfuls of London's finest until the worst of the nausea has passed.

I figure there's no way anyone's going to go in and nick stuff with the flat the way it smells, and besides, I've nothing in there worth stealing. So I leave the front door propped open to let a breeze blow through while I take the stinking bag down to the communal wheelie bins at the back of the building. The narrow space is poorly lit, and I'm a bit dazed from the smell. It's been a long day, too, with a lot of driving. As ever, most people have just piled their rubbish alongside the bins, too lazy to lift up the lid. I'm tempted to do the same just to get rid of the stench, but I was raised better than that. Which is why I'm standing close enough to hear the quiet whimper of pain.

'The hell?' I've spoken the words before I realise. It could have been a wounded animal, but there was an all too human edge to the noise. Something shifts in the pile of abandoned rubbish beside the nearest bin, and I hear that moan again. I pull out my phone, swipe it into torch mode and play the pale light over the bags.

That's when I see the foot, naked and grubby and still very much attached to a leg.

2

'Christ only knows how he's still alive. Poor sod.'
It took less than ten minutes for the ambulance to arrive, half that for the first police officer. Now the little alley at the back of my building is jammed with paramedics and uniform constables. I can't help but notice the sideways glances, whispered conversations. Not to me, about me. They all know who I am, of course. I'm the one who busted open a network of corruption that had been festering in CID for decades. And I'm the one, at least in their eyes, who got a couple of police officers killed.

'He's barely breathing. You say he was moving when you found him?' The first of the paramedics to arrive has moved aside for his more experienced colleagues to attend to the body lying with the discarded trash. I look down at the young man, still a boy really. Dark black skin and short wiry hair, he's barefoot, poorly dressed for the weather. Dried blood flakes from his lips and chin, and there's a stain in his trousers that isn't urine. He smells worse than the inside of my fridge, but he had a pulse when I uncovered him.

'Yeah. Wouldn't have known he was there otherwise. Gave me quite a shock.'

The paramedic looks at me as if he finds that hard to believe. Maybe he knows who I am too, although I don't recognise him.

'Any idea who he is?'

'Not a clue. Don't think he's from the flats, but I've been away a while so he might have moved in recently.' I'm about to tell him all about my fridge and the new life-form I discovered in the salad box, but we're interrupted by a commotion from the far end of the alleyway. Judging by the way the uniforms are behaving, someone from plain clothes has arrived. It surprises me; there's no need for CID to get involved at this stage. The boy's still alive and the priority's going to be stabilising his condition and getting him to hospital. Then a familiar figure emerges into the small circle of light spread by the street lamp overhead, and I'm even more surprised.

'What the fuck are you doing here, Fairchild?'

Not CID. The man walking towards us works for the National Crime Agency, which adds another layer of complication to things. The swearing jars slightly, which is more a reflection of how long I've been away from police officers than his politeness. From what I recall of Detective Chief Inspector Bain, he's no stranger to strong language.

'I found the victim, sir.' I indicate the boy, still surrounded by paramedics, then point up at the building. 'And this is where I live.'

It occurs to me, as I watch the conflicting emotions fight their way across his face, that he should know that. I can't think of any other good reason why he'd have come. I'm due to have a meeting with his team next week to discuss my part in a couple of upcoming trials, but even so it seems odd someone of his seniority would rush to a crime scene like this one.

'Might I ask why *you're* here, sir? Seems a bit below your pay grade, a mugging.'

Bain pauses before answering, and I can see the dismissal coming. Technically I'm still suspended from active duties. If I'm lucky they'll let me start pushing paper around a desk soon, but actually out on the streets investigating stuff? No chance.

Not until the various trials have concluded. Perhaps not even then.

'Depends on whether or not it's actually a mugging.' Bain steps past me, hunkers down beside the two paramedics. One of them glowers at him, the other speaks.

'Just about ready to move him, sir. You might want to give us some room.'

Bain grunts, although whether it's from annoyance or arthritis I can't tell. 'His injuries. What've you found so far?'

The look on the paramedic's face says it all. He wants to get on with his job, doesn't need some interfering busybody detective getting in the way. He doesn't try to hide the annoyance in his voice as he answers.

'Looks like he's lost a lot of blood. That's why he's unconscious and why we need to get him out of here and to hospital as quickly as possible.'

'Where's he bleeding from?' Bain finally seems to get the hint. He stands up and moves out of the way as the paramedic I was talking to steps in to help lift the injured boy onto a waiting stretcher. I don't fail to notice how specific the question is. This is why he's here. It has to do with whatever his team's working on at the moment, and whatever that is, it's just come to my back door. Wonderful.

'Someone's cut out his tongue.' The first paramedic almost wheezes out the words as he works his hands under the boy's shoulders, ready to lift. His colleague is being very gentle with the legs, and I can see they've cut away his shirt and part of his trousers looking for injuries. 'But that's not the worst of it. They've taken his testicles too.'

'Thought you were still up in the Highlands of Scotland.'

I suppress the urge to tell Bain it's usually just referred to as 'The Highlands'. We're standing at the end of the alley behind my building, watching the ambulance wind through the traffic on its careful way to the hospital. Behind us, the uniform constables are busy sealing everything off for later investigation by forensics, which is going to be popular with the other residents and the folk who use that alley as a short cut home from the pub. At least they won't also be using it as a toilet, I suppose. Small mercies and all.

'You ever been there, sir? Perthshire?'

Bain looks at me with a puzzled expression for a moment, then shakes his head.

'Well, take it from me, it's not the best place for a winter holiday. The only thing in its favour is that the gutter press aren't interested enough in me to camp out in the snow. I figured the story had gone cold now so I'd be safe to come back down south.'

'I wouldn't bet on it. Things'll kick off again soon as the trial starts, you mark my words.'

'That's the other reason I'm back here. The CPS want to start getting me prepped for that, and there's still a few things to sort out with Professional Standards, too. Got a meeting next week that'll probably be the first of many.'

Bain shakes his head at that for some reason. I wonder whether I should invite him up to my flat for a cup of tea. Except that I don't have any tea. Or milk for that matter. Given that I've left the place wide open for the best part of an hour, I'll be lucky if I have any possessions at all. The air should have cleared though.

'What's going on, sir?' I jerk my head back to the alleyway.

'What do you mean?' Bain tries to pretend he doesn't know what I'm talking about, but he's not that good at lying. Strange how he managed to climb the greasy pole to DCI without mastering that particular skill.

'That boy. Beaten up, tongue cut out, bollocks off. That's not your typical mugging. And you turning up half an hour after I'd called it in?'

'Like you said, it's a serious assault. CID need to look into these things. The sooner a detective's on scene the less likely it is to have been contaminated too much.'

I open my mouth to protest that there's more to it than he's telling me. He's not CID for one thing. He stops me before I can get started.

'I know you're still suspended, but I want you to come in tomorrow morning. We're working out of your old station still. Call it a debriefing if you like, or a witness statement. I'll fill you in on what details I can then.'

What details he can, not all of the details. It doesn't take a genius to work out what's going on.

'He's not the first, is he.'

Bain shakes his head again. 'Tomorrow. Eight o'clock sharp. I'll tell you what I can.' Then he steps off the pavement and walks away up the road.

Against all expectations, my flat is empty when I finally return to it, a good hour and a half after I left the front door wedged open. The rotten smell has more or less gone, but the temperature is somehow even lower than outside, so I retrace my earlier steps, closing all the windows this time, before cranking up the heating with a silent prayer to the God of gas boilers. There's a lot of noise that sounds like flames burning, and the pipes start gurgling worse than my stomach after a police-canteen lasagne. It'll be at least a couple of hours before any heat works its way into the ancient radiators. In the meantime I dig an old hoodie out of the wardrobe and rifle the kitchen cupboards for anything to eat.

I'm just about to give up my search and go to Shami's for a kebab, like I should have done first, when there's a light knock at the door. My immediate instinct is to hide, which just goes to show how much fun the past few months have been. The lights are on in the front room and hall though, so it's not as if I can pretend there's nobody here. Instead, I approach the front door cautiously, and peer through the little glass peephole to see who's there.

'Con? You in there, child?'

Through the fish-eye lens, I see the distorted form of my downstairs neighbour, Mrs Feltham. She's taken a step back to look in through the window, but I can see she's holding something small and tupperware shaped in her hands. I rattle the chain from its slot and haul open the door to welcome her.

'Mrs F. I wondered who'd drop round first.'

It's a stupid thing to say, really. None of my other neighbours have ever done much more than nod to acknowledge my existence in all the years I've lived in this place. Mrs Feltham, on the other hand, took me under her wing almost the day I arrived. She helped me when I most needed it, and cooks the most fearsome curries you have ever tasted. I've every hope one of them is in the plastic container she's brought with her, although now I think about it, I haven't got anything to go with it.

'There you are. Thought I heard you come back, only then the alley was full of them police officers. What's that all about then?'

It surprises me that she doesn't already know. Maybe she does, and is just asking because to say nothing would be odd. I tell her about the boy, skipping over the exact nature of his injuries. After a minute or so I realise I should have asked her in, both because it's polite and because what little heat the wheezy old boiler had begun to generate is now tumbling out into the winter night.

'And you've no idea who he is?' Mrs F asks before I can suggest she steps inside.

'No. Not yet. My boss – well, sort of boss – was here. He didn't say much, but I get the impression this isn't the first time something like this has happened on his patch.' It sounds a bit corny even as I say it. DCI Bain's team are part of the National Crime Agency. Their patch is the whole of the UK – further afield if necessary. If I'm lucky I might even get to join them. That's if I decide I want to. Still a work in progress, that.

'Sounds like you right back in the thick of it, girl. Here.' Mrs F thrusts both hands towards me, the tupperware box held between them. 'Made it fresh this morning. My boys are coming round later, but they won't miss a little bit, and you look like you need feeding up.'

I take the curry from her, too grateful to even pretend to protest. It's still warm, and I can smell the spices despite the container. 'Thank you, Mrs F. I'd invite you in, only I've no tea or coffee yet.'

'Don't you worry yourself about that, girl. You go eat your curry now before it gets cold. It's good to see you back. Place has been so dull without you.'

I open my mouth to say something, not quite sure what, but she just smiles, waves me silent, then turns and walks away.

3

I'm early to the station the next morning, yawning from a sleepless night. The flat had warmed up soon enough, and Mrs Feltham's curry had helped in that respect too. But I couldn't stop thinking about the young lad lying beside the bins. Who was he? Why was he there? Who had beaten him up so badly, and why those specific injuries? It wasn't random aggression to cut someone's tongue out and castrate them, after all. These thoughts and the constant worry about having my name plastered over the news again fought with each other as I stared at my bedroom ceiling and tried to tune out the city sounds that had once been such a comfort to me. As dawn had begun to pick out more detail in the room, I'd given up the struggle, showered, dressed and gone in search of coffee. Somehow that quest had turned into a long walk and a bus ride across the city until I found myself back where I used to work.

If I'd thought my absence over the past few months would have cleared the air of hostility in the station, it took no time at all to be disabused of the idea. I probably should have expected it from the way the duty sergeant barely said a word to me as he buzzed me through the security door, but surly duty sergeants are hardly anything new. The few uniformed officers I recognise as I make my way through the station stare at me with undisguised malice. For a moment I worry that I've come a bit too casual, but there are other detectives more scruffy than me.

It's only when I hear a constable I barely know mutter under his breath as he passes me, and distinctly hear the words 'some fucking nerve', that I realise there's a problem that needs attending to.

'You say something, Peterson?' I stop and turn back to face him. Watch as he takes two steps, slowing, deciding whether he's going to answer. Finally he makes up his mind.

'I said, you've got some fucking nerve showing your face in here, Fairchild.' His voice rises as he speaks, the blood flushing his cheeks red. He clearly has anger management issues.

'And why's that, exactly?' I match his growing agitation with studied calm, but I hold my ground as he takes two swift paces up to me, standing too close for comfort.

'Half the bloody unit quit or got fired because of you. Good coppers lost their pensions. Some of them are facing charges. You any idea how short-staffed we are? Knife crime's up, drug dealing's up, everything's going to hell out there, and what little respect we had disappeared the moment you . . .'

He tails off, rage spent. Or his brain's finally caught up with his lack of logic. They always shoot the messenger, never listen to the message. 'You really want someone to shout at, Colin, go find some of those good coppers you're so fond of. If they'd not been on the take, none of this would be happening. If one of our own hadn't shot Pete Copperthwaite right here . . .' I reach out and tap him on the forehead, between the eyes. 'Then maybe your job wouldn't be quite so shitty as it is. You got a problem with that, go take it up with ex-Detective Superintendent Bailey. 'Kay?'

His eyes cross slightly as he looks at my fingertip, then he focuses on my face again. I'd hoped reason might have prevailed, but from the sight of him I fear I may have been too optimistic. He's about to say something else when a voice behind me interrupts us both.

'Fairchild. My office. Now.'

I don't need to turn to know that it's DCI Bain. PC Colin Peterson glowers at me as if to say this isn't over yet, so I give him my best cheery smile, then let him slink off with his tail between his legs. On the outside I'm calmness personified, but inside my gut is churning. I'd not thought much about the reception I'd get when I came back to work, but if this is what I've got to look forward to, I'm not sure I want to come back at all.

'You're early.' Bain checks his watch as he speaks, a slim gold thing that looks expensive but probably isn't. 'I said eight o'clock.'

'Couldn't sleep, sir. After that poor lad last night. Any news on him?'

'He's in intensive care. Lost a lot of blood and his injuries are badly infected. Touch and go whether he'll survive, and even if he does there's no telling what state he'll be in.' Bain walks around a desk that's more clutter than surface, slumps into his seat and runs a hand through his thinning grey hair. I stand not quite at attention, but at least with a straight back. No point pissing him off too much. Not yet.

'His injuries seemed quite specific. Any idea why someone would do that to him?'

Bain picks up a report folder, and for a moment I think he's going to chuck it across the desk for me to read. But I'm still on suspension, nothing more to do with this case than a bystander. The report is just a prop, something for him to fiddle with while he decides how much he's prepared to tell me. I give him the time he needs to make up his mind. It's not as if I've anything better to do right now, and in here I'm not getting hate-filled glares from my so-called colleagues.

'What do you know about muti?' he asks eventually. For a moment I'm surprised, but then it starts to make a horrible sense.

I have to suppress a cold shiver as the implications spider out in my thoughts.

'Tribal medicine. Spirit healing. Practised in large areas of south and west Africa. Mostly rubbish, but then so is homeopathy and you can get that on the NHS these days.'

Bain goes back to playing with his report folder, but he doesn't manage to hide the raised eyebrow.

'That's the harmless side of it, anyway,' I continue. 'There's folk who believe you can gain strength or good fortune by taking it from others. And by taking it, I mean by killing them, drinking their blood, eating other body parts or just having them as trophies. That's what we're dealing with here, isn't it? And I'm guessing he's not the first one either.'

Bain puts the folder back down again, flips it open. The first page is a photograph that I can't see properly from where I'm standing. It looks like a body, dark skin and torn clothing, brown earth strewn with rubbish.

'He's the first one we've found who's been still alive.'

'How many before now?'

'You're not part of this team, Fairchild.' Bain leans his elbows on the desk, hands together almost in prayer. 'The only reason I'm telling you anything at all is because it happened on your doorstep. That said, we've had six bodies turn up in the past three months. Seven including yesterday. All young men – boys really. Mostly black like the one you found last night, but not all of them. Some have been missing eyes, some tongues. A couple of them had been castrated like our survivor. Two had been drained of almost all their blood.' He leafs through the pictures in the folder as he speaks, still keeping them too far away for me to see properly. I'm not about to complain.

'And this is all happening here, in London?'

Bain shakes his head. 'No. It's all over. Manchester, Birmingham, Liverpool. This one was Cardiff.' He finally stops flipping the pages and turns the folder around for me to get a better look. A young man lies on his back, surrounded by garbage and forensic tags. Dried blood cracks on his cheeks in tear stains, but it's the ragged hole in his naked chest that makes me glad I only had coffee for breakfast. 'He's missing his heart.'

The silence that stretches on after this last revelation is uncomfortable to say the least. I'm beginning to wish Bain had offered me a seat, or maybe given me a little less detail. He toys with the corner of the topmost photograph, and I can tell he's not really looking at it.

'Is there anything I can do?' I ask when it feels like someone really should say something. He almost startles at my voice, as if he'd forgotten I was here. When he looks up at me, it's with a puzzled expression.

'Do?' I can see him considering the implications of the question, but he quickly dismisses them. 'No, there's nothing you can do, Fairchild. You're suspended, remember? And your team's been disbanded anyway. You'll be reassigned once the trials are out of the way. Best you can do is go home and keep your head down.'

'But . . .' The word is out before I can stop myself. The past few months have left me out of practice, and I was never that good with authority anyway.

'But nothing.' Bain slaps the folder shut, pushes it away as he stands up. The effect would be more imposing if he were taller than me, but I've got a good few inches on him and I wore boots with heels today. I take a step back anyway. Nobody likes a bollocking.

'I should probably never have told you anything about this,' he continues. 'It's only because you found that young lad and called it in quickly. That and you're a police officer. But that's as far as it goes.'

'Yes, sir.' I nod my understanding, turn and walk to the door.

He waits until I've opened it before speaking, as I knew he would. His words are pretty much what I was expecting too.

'Don't mess with this, Constable. Not if you know what's good for you.'

DCI Bain's parting words stay with me as I leave the station and set off towards home. He had to tell me not to get involved; I can quite understand that. Even if he's working out of that station, he's NCA and this is a nationwide operation. I'm a detective constable in the Met, on suspension while Professional Standards look into last year's fuck-up. And I'm going to stay that way until I've given whatever evidence is necessary in the various trials that are going to come out of that. If – when – I am finally reinstated, who knows what my job will be? I don't seem to be terribly popular in my old nick, judging by the reception I got from Constable Colin Peterson, and I can't help remembering the look the duty sergeant gave me. I've seen folk embrace dog mess on their shoes more fondly.

On the other hand, Bain showed me the details. Six young men, seven now. He didn't have to do that, could just as easily have had me sit in an interview room and give a statement to a junior constable, like any other citizen helping the police with their enquiries. I fully expected to have to give someone a statement anyway, and the fact that I haven't seems odd. Maybe I'll get home to a message on the answering machine telling me to come back in again.

Bemused, I stick my hand in my pocket and pull out my mobile. No new texts from anyone at work, although my aunt wants to know if I've arrived safely. I tap a quick reply, really should have called her last night but circumstances conspired to make me forget.

It's only as I go to put the phone away that I realise where I am. Or where I'm close to, more accurately speaking. I don't know what hospital they took the young lad to last night, but there's a very good chance it was the one I'm just a few hundred metres away from. A quick call to one of the few contacts at work still talking to me confirms it. He's in intensive care and still unconscious. Still unidentified, too.

Standing at the entrance to the hospital, I pause for long enough to know that it's a really bad idea, going inside. I have nothing to gain but sated curiosity, and everything to lose. But I can still see the young man as I found him, half curled up, trash pulled over and around him like dirty sheets and blankets. Was he hiding from whoever had done those horrible things to him? Escaped from their clutches, yet too weak, too badly injured to get help? Or was he simply discarded there by his tormentors, along with the rest of the trash? Were they so confident he wouldn't live long that they didn't feel it necessary to finish him off? Did they think he was already dead? I need to see him again, see his face cleaned up. I need to understand.

4

You can't be an officer in the Met for the best part of a decade and not spend some time in hospitals. London has more than its fair share of them, and quite often the job involves dealing with people who've ended up in Accident and Emergency. I've made friends with a few nurses down the years, and even had a bit of a fling with a junior doctor that's probably the closest thing I've ever had to a serious relationship. He didn't work here, fortunately, and neither of us were big on commitment to anything other than the job, so it didn't last. I could never have been a doctor's wife anyway; it would have pleased my parents too much.

Reception is busy as ever, a handful of harassed admin workers struggling to cope with a workload that twice their number couldn't hope to do properly. That's probably why the young man I speak to takes it on trust that I am a detective, and directs me towards the intensive care ward without asking to see my warrant card. My luck holds out when I reach the corridor leading to the unit itself, in the form of a familiar face complete with welcome smile.

'Hey, Con. It's been a while.'

Maggie Jennings is a nurse I got to know well enough back when I was going out with Dr Andrew Walters. She was part of a group who used to hang out with Drew, possibly had a thing for him although she never said. Of all of that lot, she's the one

18

I got on with the best, and as I see her, the whole uncomfortable unravelling of that relationship comes back to me like a drowning wave.

'Hey, Mags.' I try to smile, but probably look like a lunatic. 'How's things?'

'Oh, you know how it is. Always busy.' She has a clipboard under one arm and isn't wearing a standard nurse's uniform, I notice now. So much for being a trained detective. 'I took you up on your advice, by the way. Jury's still out on whether it was a good idea or not.'

'Advice?' I don't recall giving her any advice, but then it's been a few years.

'Yeah. Applied for med school. See me, I'm a junior doctor now.' She smiles once she's said it, but it's a tired smile. The slump of her shoulders and bags under her eyes tell of too much to do and too little sleep.

'That's great, Mags. Go you.' I'm not sure what else to say, and the silence lingers awkwardly between us.

'I take it you're here about the young lad they brought in yesterday?' she asks after a while. I nod my head just enough for her to go on.

'He's in a bad way, poor kid. Whatever they used to cut out his tongue, it wasn't very sharp. Probably used the same blade down below, too. We've got him stabilised for now, but I'm not holding out too much hope for him ever waking up.'

'Can I see him?'

'I guess so. He's in one of the clean rooms though, so just through the glass. Not as if there's any point getting any closer. He's not going to be telling you anything, after all.'

She points me in the right direction, then darts off with a 'we must catch up sometime.' Part of me thinks it might be nice to have friends again, to do things that aren't entirely tied up with work. But I know the chances of me calling her, or of her meaning it when she suggested I do, are very slim indeed.

True to Maggie's word, I find the young man – boy, really – in an isolation room. I can't go in, don't actually want to, but I can see him well enough. Unconscious, he's propped up in bed, hooked to a saline drip, a tube in one nostril. Wires trail from his body to several machines, blinking their quiet readouts as they stand vigil around him. He's been cleaned up, at least, the blood gone from his face, his tight-curled hair washed of the muck and rubbish from around the back of my apartment block. If anything he looks even younger now than he did at the scene. So small and vulnerable. Who the fuck did this to him? Why?

My eyes lose focus after a while. It's quiet here, just the low hiss of the air conditioning and the background hum of the hospital. It gives me time to think, as if I haven't had plenty of that these past few months.

Except that I haven't. Not really. I've gone through the motions of preparing for the trials. I've had endless interviews with Professional Standards, given my statement over and over again. And I've hidden from the press, waiting for the story to lose its lustre, the frenzy to abate. What I've not really done is considered where I'm going next.

My mind drifts back to the autumn, and DCI Bain trying to return my warrant card to me. I turned him down then, still too traumatised by events to even think about work. I always assumed I would go back to the job though, once things had settled down. But all I can think of right now are the looks on the faces of my former colleagues when I walked the corridors of my old station this morning. Colin Peterson might be a shitty little excuse for a uniform constable, but he's a bellwether for the mood there. I can't work with that. Not for long. Not without punching someone.

So what then? Quit entirely? Sure, I could look for a job doing something vacuous. I've got transferable skills and a degree. Might even earn a bit more than they pay detective constables. But that's not me. As I focus again on the boy lying unconscious on the other side of the glass, I see an injustice and a mystery. I want to solve that puzzle and put things right. He might be a total stranger, this young man, but what happened to him happened on my patch. I can't let that lie.

A flicker of motion to the side drags my attention away. I look around to see a young woman dressed all in black. For the shortest of instants we lock eyes, and then she's gone, her boots echoing on the linoleum floor. I hurry along the corridor just in time to see her disappear at the other end, black coat billowing out behind her as she runs. It doesn't take a genius to realise she knows the young lad I've been staring at, so I set off after her.

The door she stepped through leads to the stairs, and as I peer down, I see a hand on the rail two floors below. I consider shouting to her to stop, but I doubt she will. Speeding up, I take the stairs two at a time. It's not easy in these boots though. The heels may have given me useful inches over DCI Bain, but they threaten to tip me forward with every step. They don't even have the ankle support I'm used to.

I'm still a floor above her when I hear the door clatter open, a brief swell of noise from the ground-floor reception area, and then relative silence as it swings shut again. I'm in good shape after a winter spent yomping through the Scottish highlands, but even so I'm out of breath as I push through the door myself. The hall is busy with patients, visitors, nurses and doctors and all the other folk who have very good reason to be in a hospital. I can't see the mysterious young woman in her black leggings and overcoat. I can see Detective Chief Inspector Bain though, and he doesn't look at all happy about seeing me.

★ ★ ★

'What the actual fuck do you think you're doing here, Fairchild?'

I know better than to try and answer that question. He doesn't want to hear it, anyway. Bain's angry scowl and florid complexion are enough to tell me that. He pushes me back through the door I've just exited, into the relative quiet of the stairwell and away from prying eyes.

'I thought I made myself clear back at the station. You're to have nothing to do with this case, understand? And don't tell me you have a sick relative here. You were visiting the victim, weren't you?'

I nod, but say nothing. Ever the professional, I try to keep eye contact rather than looking away like I'm embarrassed. I *am* embarrassed, of course, but only at being caught. Bain breaks first, running a heavy hand through his receding hair as he turns away from me, then leaning against the beige-painted wall for support.

'Why, for fuck's sake?' He asks the question of the wall, rather than me. 'He's unconscious. Got no tongue left, so he couldn't speak to you even if he wanted to.'

'I didn't want to question him, sir. I wasn't here looking for clues.' It's the first thing I've said since he found me, and it doesn't calm him down much.

'Then why come here at all?' He rounds on me again, but the anger's dissipating now, replaced with exasperation and, surprisingly, confusion.

'I wanted to see him. Just to check he was OK, being looked after properly. I don't know.' I shove my hands in my pockets like a defensive teenager. 'And I wasn't the only one, either.'

Bain opens his mouth to shout at me some more, then his brain catches up with him. 'You . . . what?'

'There was a young woman – or girl. I didn't get too good a look at her. She came looking for the boy, but she scarpered soon as she saw I was there. I was following her down the stairs when I bumped into you.'

To his credit, the DCI doesn't immediately go off on one about me acting like this was an investigation I might be involved in. He slumps back against the wall, says nothing for a moment. He's about to, when a couple of nurses enter the stairwell, their noisy conversation disappearing the instant they see us. One of them scowls, the other raises a quizzical eyebrow, then they carry on up the stairs. Their chatter resumes once they're at the first landing above us, and only then does Bain speak.

'This young woman. What did she look like?'

'I only caught a glimpse. She wasn't tall, maybe one-fifty-five, one-sixty. She had boots on, so that probably made her look taller than she was. Long black coat, black hair about so.' I raise my hands to indicate a point maybe an inch above my shoulders. 'Pale skin. Almost too pale, like she was wearing make-up, goth-style, you know? I think she had a black bag over her right shoulder.'

Bain takes out his phone as I speak, taps it on and flicks around the screen. I think he's going to show me a photograph, as if they already know who the mysterious girl is, but instead he places a call. I wait patiently while he tells someone at the other end of the line to request CCTV footage from the hospital. He puts the phone away once he's done.

'You want me to look at it? See if I can spot her?'

For a moment I almost think he's going to say yes. Then he gives his head the very faintest of shakes. 'No, Fairchild. You're going to come with me.'

We go back through the door and into reception, Bain striding through the milling throng as if there's nobody there. I make best use of his wake, and we're across the wide hall and out of the door in no time. It's started raining, but the DCI ignores it, making for a squad car parked on a double yellow line nearby.

He raps on the driver's window, and it winds down to reveal a female PC I've not met before. Her eyes widen when she sees me following Bain.

'Take DC Fairchild home, will you, Constable? You can call it in when you've dropped her off, eh?' The detective chief inspector opens the rear door and motions with his free hand for me to get in. It's a dressing-down, I know. And it's his way of making sure I do as I'm told. But given the wet squalls gusting between the high buildings on either side of the street, I'm more than happy to be humiliated this time.

5

Apart from asking me where I live, my driver says nothing for the first ten minutes of our journey. She's younger than me, and technically I'm the ranking officer since I'm plain clothes. I'm all too aware that I'm also currently suspended from duties, so don't try to make anything of it. She drives well, coping with London's messy traffic with a confidence I've never mastered. From what little of her accent I've heard, she's from the East End somewhere, so probably learned to drive in these conditions, whereas I had the tricky terrain of rural Northamptonshire to practise on, and many miles of private tracks where the most likely cause of an accident would be an escaped cow. It's only when an idiot in a BMW M3 cuts up our inside that she swears under her breath. Colourful but controlled.

'Would you like me to make a note of his number?' I ask, and see the ghost of a smile as she looks at me in the rear-view mirror.

'Reckon I can remember. Personalised, weren't it. Always think they're so cool, but they forget being memorable works both ways.'

'I'm sorry if you had other plans than babysitting an errant detective constable. You could always drop me at the nearest Tube station. Have an hour to yourself before calling in that I've arrived home.'

'You know Control can monitor the exact position of every squad car, right?'

'And you think Bain will check?'

She shakes her head just the once. 'I know he will. He's like that.'

Given that I may end up working for him, I figure this is as good a time as any to try and find out more about the DCI. 'You known him long?'

'Long enough. He was still DI when I ended up as support for one of his operations – must be what, a couple years back? We've crossed paths every so often since.'

'You're not part of his team though.'

'Do I look like an NCA officer?' The smile's gone from her face, eyes staring at me in the mirror. I've been leaning forward the better to speak to her, wishing I was in the passenger seat beside her and not back here where the criminals go. Now I slump back and stare out of the window as we move slowly up the road.

'Sorry. Didn't mean to pry. I just wanted to find out a bit more about Bain. Heard he was one of the good guys, but he's not exactly cutting me any slack.'

'Why should he? You're not part of this investigation. To be honest, you're way too high profile right now to be any use to him.'

'I found that kid though. He was out the back of my apartment block. All I wanted to do was see if he was OK.'

She doesn't answer this, but I can see the raised eyebrow. We continue the journey in silence, and before too long the squad car is pulling in to the kerb outside my block. My new friend switches off the engine and climbs out, opening the door for me as if I am some kind of visiting dignitary. She has to, of course. The child locks are on to stop miscreants from trying to do a runner. At least I'm not in handcuffs.

'Thanks for the lift. I owe you one.' Standing, the constable and I are much the same height, although my boots have chunky heels so she's probably taller than me. Her dark skin and high cheekbones wouldn't look out of place on a catwalk. I wonder why she joined the Met.

'Reckon you do, yeah.' She nods once, short-cropped black hair bobbing over her shoulders. Then she climbs back into the squad car and slams the door. Bain only told her to drop me off, and that's all she's going to do. I don't even know her name.

It's only as the car is pulling away that my brain registers the clicking noise behind me. Too late, I realise what's going on, idiot that I am.

The paparazzi are here.

'That you helping the police with their enquiries, eh love?'

'Give us a smile, Connie.'

I'm trying to run the gauntlet of the gutter press's finest. God only knows how they found out I was back in London. It's not even been twenty-four hours and the shit show that drove me north to Scotland is back just as bad as it ever was. I shove my way through the pack like a seasoned celebrity, head down and wishing I'd remembered to wear shades. Why are they even interested in me? Christ, have they found out about the boy round the back?

'Any truth to the rumour about you and Nero Genovese?'

That last question pulls me up short. Rookie error. There's maybe a dozen photographers and journalists camped outside the entrance to my apartment block, and I make the mistake of trying to work out which one's asked me about Hollywood's latest heart-throb. I'm fairly certain I've never even met the man, don't think I've even seen one of his movies. On the other hand, if that's the level of questioning, then maybe they don't know about what happened last night. At least, not yet.

'Where on earth do you people get this stuff from?' I round

on the nearest camera-toting idiot, and get an eyeful of flash for my trouble.

'So you're not denying it then?'

'Are you out of your mind? I've never met the man.' I blink away the spots, still not sure which ghoul in the crowd is speaking. They are all men, of course. A range of ages, but every one of them with the same jaded expression. I should probably pay them a bit more attention, try to memorise their features in case they turn up again, but it's hard to tell one from the other. They huddle together at the base of the concrete stairs leading up to my floor, either too lazy to stalk me at my own door or not quite desperate enough for a story.

'Have you really not got anything better to do? For fuck's sake, I'm a police officer, not some airhead celebrity.' I push past them and scurry up the steps to my floor. My keys are in my bag, which is why I don't notice the men on the walkway until I'm already there. Seems the mob downstairs were just the warm-up act.

'Detective Constable Fairchild. Can you tell me, are you ready to face Roger DeVilliers in the witness box?'

I recognise this one. He's been a thorn in my side since the story first broke last autumn. Jonathan Stokes has worked for most of the tabloids during his journalistic career, and is currently hatchet man for one of the worst. I last saw him and his parasitic twin, long-lens embarrassing photographer to the stars Chet Wentworth, in a remote glen in Perthshire. Quite what they were doing there I've no idea. It's not as if I'd be out in a bikini in the snow, and I've hardly got a body worth a double-page spread.

'I've nothing to say to you, Stokes. If you want a statement about the upcoming case, please see the press liaison department at the Met. I'm sure you've got their number.'

I've got my keys now, gripped in my fist with the pointy bits facing out just in case things turn ugly.

'I'm told he's hired a team of the best lawyers in the country. They've been doing a bit of digging about you and your family. Lots of juicy stuff in that file, I'd guess.'

Something about the way he says it makes me pause, tense. It's no great surprise the lawyers for the defence will do everything they can to make me look like an unreliable witness, but would they drag my family through the gutter too? Looking at Stokes, I can see that they would. And I'd lay good odds he's being drip-fed information. Maybe even helping them dig stuff up.

'Smile for the camera, love.' Chet chooses exactly the wrong moment to step forward, something expensive raised to his face as he tries to frame me for a shot. It's not been a good start to my return to London, and this is the final straw. Without thinking, I reach up to grab his camera, jabbing keys into a lens that probably cost more than I earn in a month.

'Careful with the merchandise, love.' He tries to pull away, but I'm not letting go that easily. He tugs a bit harder, I pull back. Something goes crack and I'm left with half of his camera as he stumbles into his colleague and lands on his backside on the concrete.

''Kin hell. That's three grand's worth of lens, you stupid bitch.'

'Maybe you should be more careful where you stick it then.' I lob the lens at him, knowing full well that he'll fumble the catch. It makes a satisfyingly expensive noise as it hits the concrete floor of the walkway. 'Now fuck off out of my way before I call the police.'

'You'll fucking pay for that, Fairchild.' Stokes is in my face as he speaks, anger turning his skin red, flecking spittle from his rancid mouth. He's a boil on the arse of society, but I fear he may be right.

* * *

'These two giving you a hard time?'

Stokes's angry stare flicks past my shoulder, and the fight goes out of him. A flicker of worry narrows those yellow and bloodshot eyes. I don't need to turn to know who's there, but it surprises me all the same.

'You've not heard the last of this, Fairchild.' He grabs his friend, drags him to his feet and pushes him past me. He tries to hold my gaze, but I can see his eyes darting to the uniformed constable who has appeared at the top of the stairs behind me. My driver from earlier, she steps to one side to let them past. If it had been me, I'd probably have tried to trip them up as they went, but she's less prone to giving in to temptation. Instead, she just watches them go, and only once they've muttered their way out of earshot does she finally turn to face me.

'I couldn't help noticing the crowd. Thought you might need a little help.'

'Thanks. I hope they don't decide to turn on you instead.'

For a moment her jaw goes slack at the thought, and she stares at the empty stairwell. 'You think they would? I mean, I'm nobody. Just a PC.'

'I was nobody until they decided I was somebody.' I take a couple of steps, glance down over the edge of the walkway to the pavement below. The group of paparazzi and journalists are in a huddle, talking about something, plotting how best to make my life miserable, at a guess. Wentworth is showing his broken camera to a couple of other photographers, and I can tell they're building up a head of steam, their outrage growing even though it's entirely his own fault. One starts to look upwards, so I step back.

'You might want to come in for a while,' I say to my new friend. 'They'll get bored soon enough, but if they get your picture first, they'll probably try and track you down.'

While she's thinking about it, I walk over to my door, open

it and scoop up the pile of mail. A couple of official-looking envelopes are probably some kind of court summons or similar. Life used to be much simpler.

'I'm putting the kettle on, if you fancy a cuppa.' I step inside, leaving the front door open, and head through to the kitchen. By the time I've filled the kettle and switched it on, I hear the door closing. A moment later she's standing uncertainly in the doorway.

'Bain never did tell me your name.' It's not the best of introductions, but she already knows who I am. She looks at me for a moment with the kind of quizzical expression you often see on spaniels, then shakes it away with an almost imperceptible tremor.

'PC Eve,' she says, then realises how formal that sounds. 'Karen. With a K.'

'Con Fairchild. Ignore the mess, will you? Wasn't expecting visitors.'

'You get a lot of that?' Karen-with-a-K hooks a thumb over her shoulder in the direction of the walkway outside.

'Only since . . . well . . . you know. I'm told Roger DeVilliers is good mates with the owner of the paper Stokes and Wentworth work for. Only a matter of time before they started doing everything they can to paint me as an unreliable witness. That's one reason I've been in Scotland over the winter.' I pour boiling water over teabags, hoping the stench in the fridge isn't too bad when I go for milk. It's still there, the rotting garbage smell reminding me of the boy in the hospital.

'Why'd you come back then?'

'Seriously? You ever spent a winter in Perthshire?'

'Never been north of Watford, innit.'

Looking at her, and hearing her East End accent, I can almost believe it. She'd stick out a mile in the Highlands, too. London might be a multicultural melting pot, but the same can't be said for rural Scotland. There's a ghost of a smile and a glint in her eye that suggests she's winding me up though. I'll take that as a good sign.

'You're not missing much. I need to be down here for the trial, too. Key witness and all that. I've a meeting with a couple of lawyers from the Crown Prosecution Service next week. First of many, I'm sure.'

'Don't envy you that. Never much fun being in the witness box.'

'You done many trials then?' It's not surprising, just another part of the job.

'Enough. Nothing as grand as the Old Bailey though.' Karen finishes her tea quickly, glances at her watch, then out the kitchen window onto the walkway at the front of the flat. There don't seem to be any hack reporters trying to peer through the net curtains. 'Thanks for that, but I should probably be getting back before Bain starts to worry.'

'Don't mention it. I should be the one thanking you. Coming to my rescue like that.'

'Yeah, well. I've heard all the chatter in the station, about what you did and all. Seems most of it's the usual bollocks. You didn't ask to be on suspension, even if it does piss people off when they're having to work extra shifts. The rest of it's just boys being boys, right?'

It's late afternoon when Karen-with-a-K leaves, and I wonder what's happened to the day. I should probably go and check no one's tried to steal my car, but the weather's set in again and I really can't be bothered. At least the rain squalls will have driven the last of the paparazzi away, I hope. Knowing my luck there'll be a couple of them in a flat across the road, just waiting to snap me in my dressing gown taking out the bin bags. Why the fuck are they hounding me? I'm not news. Except that I am. It's not every day an obscenely wealthy man gets locked up for child abuse and attempting to murder a police officer.

I go through to the kitchen, take the empty mugs to the sink and give them a cursory wash. I can't make my mind up about Karen. Her initial hostility was understandable enough; nobody likes a troublemaker, and that's what I am. Can't deny it, Con. She wants to be a detective though, and I remember that hunger. I'd do pretty much anything to get onto a decent investigation. Karen's just the same.

It's easy enough to see what Bain's doing, too. He's dangling a juicy transfer to the NCA in front of her, and all she has to do is keep an eye on me. Make sure I don't do anything stupid. It's almost enough to make me behave. Last thing I want is to get another constable in trouble, make another enemy on the force.

I'm staring at nothing, the thoughts tumbling through my mind, wondering how I'm going to manage having an inexperienced shadow. I could just do what Bain wants me to do, of course. Behave, keep a low profile, wait for the trial to be over. The idea makes me chuckle. No chance of that happening.

The day's post is waiting on the little table in the entrance hall where I dumped it when I escaped the paparazzi earlier. Mostly bills, by the look of things, but a thicker, squarer envelope gives me a horrible sense of dread. I knew this was coming, but even so I never wanted it to happen. Never wanted to have to deal with it.

I slip my finger under the flap and tear the envelope open as I walk through to the kitchen. A scent of something expensive wafts up to my nose, temporarily fighting off the malodorous pong from the fridge. How like Charlotte to add a spritz of Chanel N°5 to her wedding invitations. And that's what this is.

Mrs Roger DeVilliers requests the pleasure of your company at the wedding of her daughter Charlotte to Mr Benevolence Fairchild.

I scan the rest of the card, noting idly that Margo still uses her husband's surname. I've not spoken to her since that fateful day, but I'd have thought she'd be looking for a divorce, and a few tens of millions to go with it. More, even. The date for the wedding is sooner than I'd imagined it would be, too. Normal form is to give guests at least six weeks to come up with an excuse. It's the other details that sink me into the nearest chair and fill me with a gloom far deeper than having to deal with the tabloid press. Too much to hope that Charlotte and Ben might elope somewhere. No, they're going to get married in Harston Magna, and the reception will be at the hall. My parents' house.

I'll have to go home.

I'll have to speak to my mother.

6

'**Y**ou're nothing but a trouble magnet, Fairchild. You know that?'

Another morning meeting at the station. At least this time I managed to get to DCI Bain's temporary office without running into any of my old colleagues and their ill-hidden grievances against me. It's a shame that Bain is making up for that with his own.

'I don't know—'

'Of course you don't. You never do.' He's sitting in his chair on the other side of the desk, headmaster-style. Leaning forward, he grabs the first from a small pile of newspapers heaped up in front of him. I'd call them tabloids, but I don't think even the better rags print on broadsheet any more. This one has a red banner at the top though, so I don't expect much. The headline says it all.

'Posh Cop Lashes Out!'

'Posh Cop? Is that the best they can do?' I'm trying to cover my fear with bravado, but Bain's not falling for it.

'Word is you broke one of their cameras. About ten grand's worth, apparently.'

I scan the few words that accompany the photograph, taken of me climbing out of the squad car, one hand up in what looks like an attempt to cover my face. I'm no celebrity, but you wouldn't know that if, like most of the folk buying the paper, you don't actually read.

'Ten grand?' Bain's words finally sink in. 'Like fuck.'

'Normally I'd be sympathetic, Fairchild. Nobody likes these twats.' He picks up the next paper from the stack, unfolding it to reveal an even less flattering image of me. 'But this is exactly the reason why I can't have you poking your nose into any active investigation. However much you might want to. Even if it did happen around the back of your block.'

'Will they ever leave me alone?' I don't think I've ever wanted a member of the Royal Family to fall pregnant more than I do right now. Either that or for some reality TV star to be caught with his pants down. Literally, not metaphorically.

'Once the trial's done they'll lose interest. But you need to keep a low profile until then. It would have been better if you'd stayed in Scotland, to be honest.'

'I can always go back.' I'm not exactly overjoyed at the prospect, although I could try and blag expenses to stay in Edinburgh rather than disappearing into the Highlands.

'No. Annoying though it is, you need to be here. There's too much to go over, and the CPS won't send lawyers up to speak to you in the middle of nowhere. Better if you're here. Just keep your head down, OK?'

'I'll do my best, sir.' But it's not even forty-eight hours since I got back and I've already stumbled on a crime scene, been accosted by the paparazzi and I haven't even told him about the big society wedding that's coming up soon. My brother getting married to the daughter of the man I'm testifying against. The press will just love that. I open my mouth to break the bad news, but Bain interrupts me.

'They reckon he'll live. The lad you found. Still don't know who he is, mind you, but we're working on that.'

'About the hospital yesterday, sir. I'm sorry. I know I shouldn't have gone there.'

'With your press?' Bain chucks the paper back onto the pile. 'Too bloody right you shouldn't. We've managed to keep a lid on it for now. Just another gangland beating as far as they're concerned, and that's not as worthy of a front page as some twenty-something model slipping out of her dress in public. Won't last though, if they find out we discovered the body outside your apartment block.'

'Yeah, well. Not much I can do about that if I'm staying in London. Not unless you've got a safe house going spare.'

I meant it as a joke, but something about the expression on the DCI's face makes me think he's taking the idea more seriously. There's still two months to go until the trial though. No way I'm going to let them confine me to some shitty apartment in Peckham, with an ever-changing rota of bored detectives for company. I'd rather run the gauntlet of the press.

'It's a possibility. If they start making life difficult. Meantime I'll make sure there's a uniform somewhere nearby you can call in if you're being harassed.'

I can imagine that will go down well with Karen-with-a-K. But at least it shows Bain is on my side. Nobody else has done anything for me except complain that I've made their lives difficult. As if I was the one who'd been running a protection racket from within the department for the past thirty years.

I'm still half an hour's walk from home, still fuming at the way I'm being treated by people who are meant to be my colleagues, when I get the feeling I'm being followed. Walking across London's not quite the same as yomping through the glens of Perthshire, but it helps to calm my rage and focus my thoughts on how to deal with the problem. It also lets my subconscious notice things, apparently.

My first thought is to stop walking, look around. Training keeps me moving, but I begin to study my surroundings a bit more closely. Knowing my luck it's another bloody reporter or paparazzi photographer. I can't understand what the interest is, but then I've never understood why people buy tabloids and those weird magazines at the checkout in the supermarket. Maybe I'm just old before my time, but I'd rather watch a film on TV than some reality show or soap opera, rather lose myself in a book than spend hours on social media. And I'd rather pay attention to what's going on around me than stare at my phone as the bus bears down on me.

Which is why I spot her before she knows.

She's on the other side of the road, so she's put a bit of thought into following me. She's not particularly skilled at tailing though, and I recognise her too. There's no reason why the girl from the hospital should be in this part of London at exactly the same time as me unless she's following me. What I can't understand is why.

A little further up the street there's a café. It's too cold for sitting outside, but they've set out a couple of hopeful chairs and a table anyway. I guess some people still like a cigarette with their espresso. It's a little later for coffee than I'd like, but I go in anyway, order a latte and tell them I'll be outside.

The girl's staring blankly at a shop window almost directly over the road and partly obscured by one of London's many plane trees when I step outside. The chairs have been tipped forward to keep the seats dry, but there's still enough moisture clinging to the metal surface that I can feel it through my jeans when I tilt one back and sit down on it. I drop my bag onto the table and search around inside it for my phone, all the while keeping one eye on the girl. Whatever's in that shop is clearly fascinating, which is odd since all I can see is a 'Closing Down Sale' banner and emptiness beyond.

My coffee arrives with a light shower of rain, what I'd call a Scotch mist if I was being pretentious and wasn't in England. The nice lady serving me asks if I wouldn't rather be inside, as she shivers in her white T-shirt and coffee-stained apron. It takes a moment to explain to her that no, I'm fine out here, and when I look back across the road the girl is gone. For a second or two I consider leaving the coffee I've just paid a king's ransom for and going to look for her. Then she appears on my side of the road, not more than ten metres away. She makes no pretence about staring straight at me, so I push the other chair out with my foot.

'Want a drink?'

'You fuzz?'

The girl eyes me with the kind of deep suspicion only teenagers can manage. This is the first time I've mustered a half decent look at her, and I reckon she's not much older than sixteen, if that. Small, her face is very pale, features more Asian than Caucasian. Her heavy black coat drops almost to the ground, and glistens with damp. Little droplets of rain cling to her tangles of black hair too. She looks dishevelled, but in a manner that's more cultivated than due to circumstance.

'Does it matter? You're the one following me, not the other way round.'

'You was at the hospital. Place was crawling with filth.' She takes a few steps closer, but still doesn't sit.

'And you went there anyway. Went to see that poor boy. You know him?'

'Sort of.' She's got a rucksack slung over one shoulder, hands in her coat pockets, but shrugs anyway. 'Not really.'

'You know his name?' One question too many, I see her eyes narrow, the slight tension in her body as the flight response starts to kick in.

'You are a cop, aren't you.' It's not a question.

'Detective constable. Currently on suspension, so I can't show you my warrant card.' I pick up my coffee, lean back in my seat. Not the most comfortable place for a meeting, but it's better than nothing.

'Wot you do then?' She pulls out the chair and perches on the edge of it. Still wary, still ready to run at the slightest hint of trouble.

'What did I do? Where to start.' I take another sip of my coffee. It's not bad, but not as good as Mrs Feltham's.

'I used to work undercover. My boss got killed and they tried to blame that on me. Turns out it was his boss who was bent all along. Never trust a copper, right? And the whole thing got really interesting when an old friend of my dad found out about it and tried to take over. Only he had a bit of a thing for young children.'

I can see her eyes glazing over as I speak, perhaps not the effect I was looking for, but at least she's not running away. Then she snaps out of it, thin painted-on eyebrows shooting up towards her scraggly hairline.

'You're her. I seen you in the papers, right? Sent that old kiddie fiddler down. Remember them talking about you.'

'Them?' The word is barely out of my mouth before I can see it's the wrong thing to ask. Her enthusiasm had been growing, and with it the chance of finding out some more information about the young boy in the hospital. She shuts down almost as quickly as she lit up in the first place. Stands up and shoulders her rucksack.

'Be seeing you, copper.' She turns away from me and starts to walk away. I consider trying to stop her, but it would be a waste of time. She's younger and fitter than me. Street smart. It doesn't stop me calling out to her though.

'Hey. You got a name?'

She stops, turns back to face me. Starts to say something, then corrects herself. 'Anna. And his name's Dan. The boy you found. Daniel Jones. He was OK. Wasn't fair what they did to him. Wasn't right.'

I open my mouth to ask more, but she's already walking away.

7

The local park's not somewhere I'd consider visiting for a picnic. It's not really what I think of when someone mentions that word anyway. Park, to me, means a place of grass and trees and watching where you tread in case of dog mess. This is more of an open square of cracked and weedy paving slabs, arranged around a small children's play area that never seems to have any children playing in it. There's a frame where a couple of swings used to hang, but the swings themselves are long gone. As is the merry-go-round, just a lump of pipe sticking out of the ground that would have been its axle and is surely much more of a safety hazard than the rotating platform that sat on it. In the summer this place is full of homeless people huddling under cardboard sheets and eking out their meagre supplies of cheap booze. In the winter it's full of homeless people trying their best not to die of the cold. A little island of despair, cut off from the surrounding houses and shops by arterial roads feeding the city centre, it's best avoided if at all possible.

It is, however, on my way back home, and I make a habit of walking through whenever my route takes me that way, if only to see what's going on with the local addicts. Having a regular police presence, even if it's only an off-duty detective constable, tends to discourage the dealers too. A shame I've been away for so long.

The first thing I notice is the man, slumped forward on one

41

of the bird-shit-spattered benches. My immediate thought is that he's dead, so awkward is his posture and total his stillness. Where others would probably give him a wide berth, hope that ignoring the problem will make it go away, I approach. I've already pulled out my phone, ready to call this in, when he sits up with a lurching movement more spasm than coordinated. For a moment he looks at me with unseeing eyes, and then he slumps again, a thin line of drool escaping from the side of his mouth. Judging by the state of his trousers, this has been happening for a while.

I'm about to call it in anyway when I notice another body, propped up against a concrete litter bin as if left there by someone because it wouldn't fit through the little slot at the top where you put your rubbish. Leaving the first man, I approach this one more slowly. He looks just as immobile, but I know what this is now, and how it can develop. Spice is a big problem in Manchester, and some of the country's smaller cities and industrial towns. I'd not heard of it being so much of a thing in London, but it was only a matter of time, I suppose. Synthetic cannabis, basically. Hugely addictive, far more potent than the real stuff, oblivion for anyone who can't cope any more with the utter hopelessness of modern life. The drug of choice for austerity-hit Britain.

As I look around the park, I see more bodies. It's a small space that I can't quite believe hasn't been snapped up by some unscrupulous property developer already, but dotted around it like the discarded dolls of some giant infant, I count seven addicts in various states of uncomfortable repose. I'm surprised the authorities don't know about this, and yet somehow they've been left here.

And then a figure appears from the far side of the park, followed by another, two more. A crowd of them, they're all dressed alike, although it's not a uniform so much as something about the choice of clothes, the sameness of the colour scheme. There's an earnestness about them that suggests charity, and the way they split into pairs, each heading for a comatose addict, confirms it for me. Soon all of the addicts are being tended to, gently roused or covered with shiny blankets like they hand out after marathons.

'Who the hell are you people?' The words are out of my mouth before I've considered them, but far from taking offence, the nearest to me looks up and smiles. She's maybe twenty years old, awkward teeth, hair that looks like something from a seventies folk band. Acne scars dot her pale cheeks and forehead.

'We're administering to the needy, the ones who have fallen through the cracks. These poor unfortunates deserve better than to lie here unloved and forgotten.'

OK, so not answering the question. 'Do you do this often?'

'As often as is necessary.' The young woman stands, hands clasped together over her stomach. 'Times are hard, and the temptation to lose oneself is ever present.'

Behind her, the recumbent addict is being helped to unsteady feet. Around the park the rest of them are being led – or in one case carried – away.

'Where are you taking them? You're not paramedics. Not police.'

She smiles as if our ages are reversed and she finds my naivety amusing. 'We are the Church of the Coming Light. This is our mission.'

Again not answering the question, although at least she's now answered my earlier one. 'So where are you taking them, then? Hospital?'

'Our shelter is on the high street, not far from the Danes Estate. We'll care for these poor souls there, try to get them back on their feet. And should any require further treatment we can take them to hospital.'

Mention of the Danes Estate has me glancing up and into the distance, where the squat towers at its centre loom over this part of the city. It's only a moment, but when I turn back to the young woman she is walking away. As swiftly as they arrived, the group depart, taking the addicts with them. By the time I've followed them to the edge of the park, they've loaded everyone into a minibus and are pulling away into the traffic.

I take the back way to my flat, peeking round the corner like a kid playing hide-and-seek to see whether there are any paparazzi waiting for me. A couple of shadowy figures are huddled in a car just across the road from the block, so I guess that answers that question.

'Bin there all day, Con. Gotta give them credit, that's dedication.'

Mrs Feltham's a big lady, taller than me and with a bulk about her that you wouldn't want to argue with. For someone her size, she can move with impressive stealth. I almost jump out of my skin when she speaks, whirling around like I've been caught by the headmistress doing something I know I shouldn't.

'Mrs F. You gave me quite a shock there.'

'You so wrapped up in your little world I could ride past on an elephant and you'd hear nothing, child. Come.'

The old lady beckons me in the direction of her front door, and since it doesn't look like I can slip up to mine right now, I follow. Besides, she makes the best coffee in London and I need something to take away the taste of the latte I had in that café. So I won't get a wink of sleep tonight, but who cares? It's not as if I've got a job to go to tomorrow.

'When did Spice become a thing round here?' I ask after the beans have been ground, the little pot set to bubble on the stovetop and a box of fiery home-made ginger snaps laid out for me to eat.

'Spice?' An angry scowl wrinkles Mrs Feltham's face. She takes her time fetching out two little porcelain cups, then brings the pot to the kitchen table before saying any more on the matter.

'It's the worst thing. You see them, like zombies. Time was we had to deal with heroin round here, but most of that moved farther out. Still a few dealers, mind. But Spice.' Mrs Feltham shakes her head, almost spitting out the word. She pours two cups of thick dark coffee far more addictive than any drug.

'Thank you.' I take the proffered cup, lift it to my nose and inhale the perfect aroma. 'You any idea who's pushing it?'

'Never the same face for more than a few days. My boys, they don't take kindly to folk peddling that kind of thing, see? A bit of weed never done a man no harm, but this poison, it rots your brain. It takes away your will.'

In all the years I've known her, I don't think I've ever seen Mrs Feltham angry. Maybe the occasional short-lived curse at a useless politician or a quiet tut at whatever vacuous celebrity is hogging the news cycle, but now I can see that I've struck a nerve with my question.

'It's worse up north, I've heard. Parts of Manchester you can't walk without tripping over folk just lying about like they're dead.'

'They are dead, girl. Just don't know it. They the forgotten ones. No job, no hope of a job, no education worth nothing. All those opportunities they was promised by the man, come to nothing at all. It any surprise they want to make it all go away? Only it never goes away. It haunts you, nags at you, keeps you coming back for more. And these folk who sell them that? They are worse than any devil I've ever met.'

'Least someone seems to be looking after them.' I take a sip of coffee so bitter it makes my toes curl, but in a good way. 'Saw a busload of charity do-gooders take the whole lot of them to a shelter. Church of the Shining Light? Think that's what they said.'

'Church. Tcha! They not much better than the dealers, only it's a different kind of drug them selling.'

'You know them, then?'

'Know of them, Con. Know the type. Sure the work they do is mostly helpful, but it shouldn't be necessary at all.'

There's nothing I can say to that, so I say nothing. We sit in companionable silence for a while, sipping coffee and chewing on those excellent biscuits. My stomach growls at the food like a neglected dog, and I realise I've not eaten properly in too long.

'You don't look after yourself. Going to waste away if you don't eat proper. Then who's going to want you, eh? A man likes a woman to have a bit of meat on her bones.'

I know she's teasing me, same as she always does, but it hits a nerve nonetheless.

'A man likes a woman who's not being hounded by the press, too. Not that I ever cared much about what a man likes.'

'They'll get bored of chasing you soon enough. Give it time.'

I wonder whether she's talking about the press, or men. Hopefully both. I drink the last of my coffee and reluctantly decline the offer of a refill, even more so another biscuit.

'I'd better be getting on. I should be able to slip past them now, if they're still there. It's getting dark.'

Mrs F doesn't argue, bless her. I can see her thinking about pressing the entire tub of biscuits on me, but I know there'll be hell to pay when her boys come round for their supper later and find them all gone. She levers her large frame out of her chair as I stand more easily, and together we walk the short distance to the front door.

'You be careful out there, Con girl. I seen that look in your eyes before. You go turning over this muck heap you going to get bitten.'

And then she opens the door and ushers me out into the gathering dark.

8

Night has fully fallen when I slip out of my flat some hours and the reheated leftovers of Mrs Feltham's goat curry later. The drizzly rain means any reporters have either gone home or are huddled in their cars trying to keep warm and dry. There's nobody camped outside my front door, and nobody on the stairwell either. Dressed in a long black coat I borrowed from my aunt, collar turned up like an amateur-hour spy, I hug the shadows until I'm well away from my block.

Going to my local pub is possibly a risk. Five minutes' walk from the flat, it's exactly the sort of place I'd stake out if I were a reporter hoping to catch the local unwilling celebrity with her hair down. I need to get out of the flat though, if only to escape the pong still emanating from the fridge, so I'll have to take my chances.

I scan the midweek crowd from the doorway, looking out for anyone who might have noticed me. It's not busy, but not empty either. No band tonight, which is a relief, and as the seconds tick by, the faces ignoring me completely, I begin to relax. There's nobody here looking to give me a hard time.

'Connie! I had no idea you were back in town!'

Too late I remember who else might recognise me here other than the gentlemen of the press. Charlotte DeVilliers appears completely unaffected by the fact that her father is in prison awaiting trial for attempted murder, child abuse and countless other crimes. That I'm in no small part responsible for his fall from grace hasn't even occurred to her, but then she never was the brightest of us, even at school. And of course she's engaged to my brother now, so we're practically family.

'Charlotte.' I nod my head once as she weaves her way through the tables towards me from the direction of the toilets. If I'd been hoping to keep the greeting minimal, I'm disappointed as she fairly throws herself at me, enveloping me in a rib-crushing hug. The best part of a head shorter than me, I get a mouthful of her blonde hair and a whiff of that same expensive perfume that was liberally sprayed over the wedding invitation.

'When did you get back?' she asks when she's finally let me go, or at least almost let me go. She grabs my hand and drags me to the bar, where a drink is waiting. 'What are you having?'

'It's a beer kind of day.' I point at one of the taps lined along the bar. 'Pint, I think.'

Charlotte wrinkles her nose in mock disgust, but orders anyway. She rounds on me while the barman is doing his bit.

'You got the invitation, yah? To the wedding? Sorry it's such short notice, but we just wanted to get hitched as soon as possible. Thought about just jumping in the car and driving up to Gretna, but mother's so fragile at the moment I think the shock would kill her.'

It's easy enough to have a conversation with Charlotte. All you need to do is keep your mouth closed and listen. Actually, that's not true. You don't really have to listen at all. I do, though. It's something I picked up at school. Politeness and all that.

'There you go, Connie. Can't see how you can drink that stuff, but anyway. Let's get a seat in the corner there.'

'Ben not with you?' I scan the room, wondering where my brother might be hiding.

'No, he's in Tokyo, the lucky sod. Something to do with

business. Least that's what he said. Not sure he didn't just do a runner so he didn't have to deal with the wedding plans. Must remember to give him a call in a mo. Never can get the time difference right.'

I take my beer before she can turn it upside down while checking her watch, guide her to a small booth away from the bar. 'About the wedding. I couldn't help noticing it's happening at Saint Thom's, and the reception at the hall.' I wait until we've sat down before making the observation, timing it just as Charlotte's about to launch into her own monologue. Her blinking astonishment lasts for a good fifteen seconds.

'Well, yah. I mean, where else would I get married? And the hall's just right there next to the church so it's perfect. And Earnest's being so brave, what with Izzy being his daughter. I mean, talk about embarrassing family mealtimes.'

I let it wash over me again, stripping out the salient details as best I can from a stream-of-consciousness word soup. It's only when she's blathered on for a good few minutes and a quarter of my pint's gone that I interrupt.

'And what about Mother? How does she feel about all this?'

'What, Margo's mum?' Charlotte's confusion would do an actor proud, but the slow realisation dawns eventually. 'Oh, Lady Angela. Your mum.'

I don't need to be a detective to see that there's something off about the situation. Charlotte's holding something back, and I'm fairly sure I know what it is.

'She doesn't approve, does she.' As if she's ever approved of anything in her life that didn't have a cross attached to it.

'It's not that. Actually, she's been OK with most of the arrangements. But she wanted to get some strange pastor friend of hers to bless us. I wasn't all that fussed. It's just words, yah? But Ben wasn't having any of it. I think that's one of the reasons he went off on his own.'

'Pastor?' I'm not sure whether Charlotte's just being Charlotte when she uses the word. Then I remember it's my mother we're talking about. 'She's not found herself some charismatic preacher again, has she? Some new church to throw her money at?'

'Yah, apparently he's with some missionary outfit or something. African fellow. Sounds a bit do-goody to me. Not like proper church at all. Doesn't matter though. Ben said no, so it'll be the vicar of Saint Thom's. We've had the banns and stuff read out already. You will be there, right, Connie?'

'Course I will, Char. Wouldn't miss it for the world.' I smile as sweetly as I can manage, then hide my discomfort behind my pint glass. Up until the moment she asked me that question it hadn't occurred to me that I might not go to my brother's wedding. So why am I thinking it now?

Charlotte's words weigh on me as I walk back home, not least the news that my mother is associating with some unknown pastor. It's not the first time she's adopted a fringe sect of Christianity, mind you. It bothers me that she wastes money on charlatans, falls for their promises and lies. But it's her money to spend how she likes. I almost feel sorry for my father, but then I remember everything else about him and swiftly change my mind.

'Give us a smile, Connie.'

The shout comes as a surprise, and too late I realise I've let my mind wander, my guard down. I shove my hands into my pockets, feeling the weight of the key ring in my right hand. It's not the best weapon, but it will do at a pinch. Whirling around, hand up ready to punch, I'm greeted by a dazzling flash that temporarily blinds me, at the same time as reassuring me the threat is at least not violent.

'The fuck?' I blink away the spots to see a couple of men with cameras standing close by. A third is hurrying across the road towards us. Bloody paparazzi, I thought they'd had enough of me earlier. But then maybe that was just wishful thinking.

'Come on, Connie. Be a sport.' One of the photographers lifts his camera to his face, and this time I have enough warning to close my eyes before the flash goes off. No doubt the resulting photograph will be as flattering as it's unwanted.

'Fuck off and leave me alone, right?' I take a couple of steps towards the photographers, pleased when they back away from me. 'Haven't you got some celebrity bimbo to go hunting? Maybe a wayward royal or some overpaid footballer?'

'Be a sport, won't you? Not every day a lone copper takes on the richest man in the world and brings him down.'

I'm about to say 'I didn't', but actually when they put it like that, I did. It's never a good idea to engage with the press though, certainly not when they come at you in the dark like hyena.

'Hey, Constance – what's it like, eh? All alone with the whole world out to get you?' The third photographer has caught up now, slightly breathless from the exertion of trotting a dozen or so steps across the road. He swings his camera up from where it's hanging by his side, clicking off a slew of pictures that can't possibly be in focus but will show my gaping mouth if they are.

'I was never all alone.' Again, not exactly true, but I'm damned if I'll give this lot any satisfaction.

'Where you been hiding, then?'

'Come on, Connie. Give us a smile for the front page.'

Maybe it's the slight alcohol buzz I still have from the couple of beers in the pub with Charlotte, maybe it's a bad combination of tiredness and adrenaline jitters, but for whatever reason I can't explain, I stop at the bottom of the steps leading up to my flat and turn to face them. I don't even get the chance to speak before the flashes engulf me in painful light again. Idiot, Con, giving them just what they want.

'Fuck off now, won't you?' I flip them the bird, and somehow I just know that's going to be the picture they use. This is why I left London in the first place, but now there's trial prep work to be done, and the small matter of my job. I don't care what these ghouls say about me any more. Bring it on.

My hot-headed anger cools with each step upwards. Unwelcome though their attention is, this is a lot less intrusive than straight after last year's news broke. They'll get bored of the story soon enough, maybe concentrate more on the man in the dock than the police officer who put him there. Yeah, who am I kidding? DeVilliers is an easy mark; there's no sport in stripping him down. By the time I reach my front door, slide in the key that's still clasped in my hand, I begin to realise exactly what this renewed press attention means.

Tomorrow's going to be a really crap day.

9

At first I think the pounding is in my head, and I groan at the memory of the night before. Then it occurs to me that I didn't drink all that much. A couple of beers in the pub with Charlotte aren't nearly enough to give me a hangover, even if I'm out of practice drinking. Outside it's still London dark, and there's a rhythm to the pounding, a voice to go with it, too.

'Fairchild? You in there?'

It's a man speaking, shouting really. I don't recognise him, but something in the urgency wakes me enough that the memories start to come back. The press. Fuck's sake, will they never leave me alone?

'Oi! Fairchild!' This voice is different, I'm pretty sure of it. I swing my legs out of bed and lower them to the floor, stretch and yawn and rub the sleep from my eyes. Checking the bedside clock, I see that it's only half past six, which hardly seems fair. No active duties should mean no early starts, surely?

'Come on, Connie. Open up and talk to us, why don't you?'

That voice sparks a memory, even though it's muffled by the closed front door and the distance of the hallway. What's with these bloody leeches?

I'm sorely tempted to call my new friend, PC Karen-with-a-K Eve, and ask her to send a couple of uniforms round to clear the reporters from my front door. I've even grabbed my phone, but before I thumb the screen awake my brain starts to work. The paparazzi were hassling me yesterday, but not like this. There must have been some development overnight that's brought them scurrying back again, early and insistent.

'We need to speak to you, Miss Fairchild. Can you come to the door, please?'

That's a first from a reporter, saying please. I pull on clothes – it's never a good idea to confront the press in your undies – and splash a bit of water over my face to try and stop myself looking too much like an extra from a horror movie. There's nothing I can do about my hair, but the spiky punk look's all the rage and paparazzi photos are never flattering anyway. As I pick up my phone again, my finger nudges the button and the lock screen lights up, a notification of a text obscuring the photograph of Cat that's my wallpaper image. It's from DCI Bain, and only the first part of the message is visible. It's enough to explain why the press are outside my door, and to wake me up faster than the strongest cup of espresso.

Roger DeVilliers dead. Team meeting 10.00am. Your presence required.

I click through to the BBC News app, and sure enough, it's the headline. The old bastard had a heart attack in his cell while I was drinking with his daughter last night. Well, good riddance. Except that of course his dying is probably the most inconvenient thing that he could do. The trial won't happen, all that work gone to waste. And an army of tabloid journalists outside my door, building themselves up into a feeding frenzy.

Ah well. Better get it over with, then.

'Did you have to talk to the press before speaking to me?'

Bain's angry, I can see that. But he's not really angry with me.

I'm just convenient, someone for him to work out his frustrations on.

'Given how many of them were outside my front door, I'm not sure I had any choice, sir.' I hold his gaze, in that manner girls who have been brought up properly are not supposed to do. He breaks first, stalking across the room to the end of the conference table. He pulls out a seat and drops heavily into it before speaking again.

'Constable Eve not with you?'

Karen-with-a-K brought me here, turning up outside my flat after I'd been explaining to the world's press for the best part of half an hour that I didn't know anything and so couldn't comment. She'd filled me in on a few details as she drove me across the city, but had gone off in search of a coffee once we'd arrived.

'Think she went to the canteen, sir.' I wish I could join her. Anything has to be better than this airless conference room tucked away at the back of the station. It's been taken over by the NCA for the duration, clutter around the walls and scribbles on the whiteboards. But now the table's cleared and set out for a dozen people, with glasses and water bottles placed at intervals, along with jotter pads and pens for taking notes. Either I'm being roped into a fairly serious strategy meeting, or someone in admin needs to get out a bit more.

'Take a seat then. The others should be here soon.'

I do as I'm told, keeping a reasonable distance between myself and the DCI. 'Others?'

Before he can open his mouth to answer, the door swings open without so much as a knock, and a couple of men walk in. I might be forgiven for thinking they were twins, given their identical, expensive suits and haircuts. One has a mole on his left cheek and is a few inches shorter than his companion though. He seems to notice me too, whereas his colleague's gaze slides over me in that oddly reassuring misogynistic way, his features only changing when he sees Bain.

'Detective Chief Inspector. Thank you for seeing us at such short notice. Shocking business, really.'

There isn't an ounce of sincerity in the man's voice, but Bain stands, smiles, extends a hand to be shaken and doesn't even wipe it on his trousers afterwards.

'It's thrown a spanner in the works, that's for sure. You know DC Fairchild?'

The taller one looks at me now, but I can tell he'd rather not. His almost-doppelganger is more friendly though, swapping the briefcase he's been carrying to his left hand so he can extend the right to be shaken.

'Jack Preston. Pleased to meet you. Wish it could be better circumstances, eh?'

Nothing from his colleague except something that might be a barely-concealed eye-roll. He doesn't make any effort to introduce himself, but it's not necessary. I reckon I've worked it out now.

'You're Crown Prosecution, right? Must be a bit of a bugger doing all that work on DeVilliers and now there's nothing to show for it.'

'It happens.' Jack shrugs his shoulders.

'So the case is closed then? I can get back to work?'

This time the taller of the two CPS men shakes his head. He's probably unaware he's doing it, much like he's unaware of being an utter dick.

'We've still got Gordon Bailey to deal with, remember?' Bain settles himself back down in his chair. Dick takes a seat at the table directly opposite him.

'And how long exactly is that going to take?' I ask. I know I'm not going to like the answer by the way Friendly Jack looks at me.

'That's what we're here to discuss. The two cases are closely linked, so the fact DeVilliers will no longer stand trial means we need to reconsider how to deal with Bailey.'

'Not to mention the fact he was supposed to be our key witness against the DCI,' Dick says. I almost miss it, since he's very much directing his conversation away from me. Almost, but not quite.

'You what?'

Dick looks at Bain rather than me, no doubt hoping he will tell me to shut up.

'You did a deal with that piece of shit?' I can't help the anger rising in my voice.

'Miss Fairchild . . .' Dick finally turns to face me, his words dripping with condescension.

'It's Detective Constable Fairchild, actually.' I'm on my feet now, fists clenched to suppress the trembling rage. 'And do I need to remind you that Roger DeVilliers tried to kill me? Have you forgotten that he raped his own daughter, repeatedly? Are you really telling me you did a deal with that monster and didn't even have the decency to let me know?'

'I'm letting you know now, aren't I?'

If he wasn't sitting too far away, I'd probably punch that smug face.

'Months I've been kicking my heels waiting for you lot to do your job, and it turns out you were going to let him go all along. Well, fuck that noise.' I push my chair back, step around a worried-looking Jack. Of all of them, he's the least likely to get thumped, but it's a close thing.

'Where do you think you're going, Fairchild?' Bain stares at me with genuine confusion.

'Out, sir. There's really no point in my being here, is there?' I pause long enough at the open doorway to let anyone in the meeting object. None of them do, and I suspect the twins from the CPS are probably glad to see the back of me. Bain's not happy, but then he wasn't happy to start with, and I'm done bending over backwards to make life easy for others.

'Can you fucking believe it? They were cutting a deal with him. With DeVilliers. Fuck sake.'

I find Karen in the canteen, nursing a mug of coffee. Grabbing one for myself, I go and join her. If she doesn't want my company, she doesn't say so, and now she's stuck with me at least until my fury calms a little. I can't believe the CPS would cut a deal with that man. Except that I can believe it, and I can see his expensive lawyers pushing for it all the way. Probably making sure I was kept out of the loop too. Not hard to predict how much I'd kick up a stink about it. Fuck, was that the real reason they suspended me? Sent me away to Scotland so I was good and out of the way? Bastards.

'Actually, pretty much everyone knew.'

I almost choke on my coffee at her words, put the mug down quickly to stop myself from hurling it at the wall. 'You did?'

'Yeah, well. You know what we're like. Coppers are the worst gossips and that's a juicy rumour to chew, wouldn't you say?'

I don't say anything to that. Slumping back in my seat's about all I can manage right now.

'It kinda makes sense, too.' Karen leans forward, mug between her hands. 'I mean, you're right. That old man was a disgusting monster who should've been locked away and left to rot. But he had all the intel you could want on Bailey and his gang, and more. He'd have handed it all over, pleaded guilty, gone to an open prison somewhere. Sure, he didn't deserve to be comfortable, but he was never going to live long anyway. And it's not as if he could go out in public even if he wasn't locked up. Tabloids would be all over him like a rash.'

Like they're all over me right now. She's got a point, even if I'm not about to concede it.

'Too much to hope the press will leave me alone now.'

Karen laughs, then covers her mouth when she realises it's not really all that funny. 'Are you kidding? They'll hound you twice as badly now. But they'll get bored soon enough. Give it a couple of weeks. After they've buried him and someone else has done something more interesting. Then you'll get your nice quiet life back.'

It's my turn to laugh, but only briefly, and without humour. 'Looks like I'm going to have to leave town again. Shame. It was just getting interesting.'

10

I knew this was going to be a bad idea as soon as I asked for details of when and where. If I'm being honest with myself I can't admit to any other reason for coming than to make sure that the old fucker's actually dead and not part of some elaborate hoax to get him off the hook. Even so, coming to Roger DeVilliers' funeral has to be one of the most foolish things I've ever done.

At least I dressed for the part. Aunt Felicity's long black coat is a godsend, and the wide-brimmed hat helps to hide my face from the legion of reporters who seem to outnumber the mourners. Not that I'm mourning.

I tag on to a group of people who must have been business associates of the old man, judging by their conversation as they walk to the church, find a pew and sit. They don't seem to notice me, or mind as I listen in on their talk of corporate leverage and backflipped options, whatever they might be. They're so wrapped up in disaster capital talk I'm surprised they could take the time out to come here, but then again maybe this is the best place for a board meeting.

It's been a while since I last stepped inside St Thomas's Church. It's far too close to Harston Magna Hall, for one thing, and I really don't need a run-in with my father right now. God forbid my mother would show her face. She's not in the congregation, which is a relief. I'm surprised to see Margo at the front, though. Even more surprised at how frail she looks.

'You've some nerve coming here, Fairchild.'

The voice startles me, but not as much as the man speaking. Of all the people I'd expect to be here, Detective Chief Inspector Bain is not one of them. He was involved in the investigation that put Roger DeVilliers behind bars, true enough. And he's been part of the team building the case for the prosecution. That's not a good reason to come to his funeral though, surely?

'Sir.' It's all I can manage as I shuffle further along the pew to give him and the pair who've come with him room to sit. I don't know who they are, beyond that they're obviously police. The man's young, clean shaven, skin that must take at least an hour a day to keep that fresh. His suit is as sharp as anything I've seen, but instead of looking at me he is fixated on his incredibly shiny shoes.

The woman beside him is in many ways his complete opposite. She's dressed for a funeral, it's true, but only to the point of wearing dark clothes. Her crumpled black trouser suit looks like she's slept in it, and her shoulder-length grey hair has only seen a brush for a few passes and that recently. Unlike her male friend, she's quite happy to stare at me.

She looks like she's about to say something, but then the organ grinds into life, old Mr Ayres the organist playing the funeral march at a pace so slow it's almost painful. Then again, he used to be the same with the Christmas carols, so it's maybe not a reflection of the situation.

The coffin comes in on the shoulders of a half dozen funeral director assistants, no family carrying the old man to his final reckoning here. The wooden box seems too small for the body inside it, and I'm once more hit by that niggling doubt that he's actually dead. Maybe I should have pulled strings, begged favours and done whatever I could to attend the post-mortem. That would have been a more fitting end to my relationship with

Roger DeVilliers, watching as his chest was cut open and his innards removed. Then again, it would have been galling to find that he had a heart after all.

The service is mercifully brief, in that no-nonsense Anglican way. Soon enough the coffin is making its way out again, followed by a crowd of people keen to watch it being lowered into the ground. I remain seated as Bain and his colleagues stand.

'Not going out?' the woman asks. Her voice is deeper than I'd been expecting, a husky edge to it that suggests a familiarity with cigarettes even though I catch no smell of tobacco off her.

'If it's all the same to you, I'd prefer to piss on his grave in private.'

The young man flinches at my words, but the woman merely smiles.

'Too many bloody photographers here, too. Last thing we need is them raking over this story again. Thought you wanted to go back to work.' Bain shakes his head at me as if I've done the most stupid thing in the world, which might well be the case.

'That likely to happen any time soon, sir? Never thought I'd say it, but being suspended on full pay isn't quite as fun as it sounds. Not given the circumstances.'

'That's up to your station commander, Professional Standards, oh, and the commissioner.' The woman butts in to the conversation as if Bain isn't important. That he doesn't complain makes me think she is. 'You might be just a detective constable, but you're high profile, Fairchild. Another reason why showing up here was . . . inadvisable. Just how do you think you're going to get away unnoticed? Planning on spending the next couple of hours praying?'

'I'm sorry. We've not been introduced.' I meet her gaze, trying to work out whether she's joking. It's hard to tell from her deadpan expression, but there was that smile earlier.

'No. Ed's never been good at that.' She holds out a hand to be shaken. 'Diane Shepherd.' She pauses a moment in thought, then adds, 'I guess Superintendent Shepherd to you.'

Superintendent. So she must be Bain's boss at the NCA. I'm surprised I've not met her before, more so that I've never even heard her name.

'This is Detective Sergeant Latham.' She turns to where she must have assumed her young colleague was still standing in the aisle, unaware that he's wandered off to the entrance. He's staring out at the small crowd, and only turns when the superintendent shouts at him. 'Billy. What are you doing?'

He rushes back, red flushing his cheeks. 'Sorry, ma'am. There's loads of press out there. TV crews as well.' He still won't meet my eye.

'Looks like we're all praying for a couple of hours then,' Shepherd says as a nervous verger steps back inside and stares at us. We're the only ones left, and it's clear from the way he glances at his watch that he'd like his church back now. I don't recognise him, but then that's not surprising given how long ago I last came in here. Some things don't change though, and I know the layout of this place better than most.

'Come with me. We can go out through the vestry. There's a private entrance that leads to the grounds of the hall.' I set off without checking to see they're following. This is exactly the situation I might have predicted happening, if I'd thought through the whole thing beyond simply coming to the funeral. I just hope to the hell Roger DeVilliers has gone to that my parents aren't at home. The last thing I need is to bump into my mother.

'You grew up here? Explains a lot.'

I'd hoped that my little group of detectives might somehow understand the need for stealth as I led them through the vestry, out across the oldest, most crowded part of the graveyard, and through the gate into the grounds of Harston Magna Hall. DCI Bain clearly didn't get the message though. His gaze never rests anywhere long, taking in the walled garden, the various out-buildings that would make many a London house look small, the massive sandstone hulk of the hall itself.

'Couldn't get away soon enough. Sure, it's privileged and posh, but it's bleak as hell. I'd have given anything for a house with central heating. Maybe books that weren't more than a hundred years old and written in languages even scholars have forgotten.'

'Can't have been all that bad. The space. The fresh air.' Super-intendent Shepherd moves slowly along the gravel path between elegantly clipped box hedges, admiring it all like a weekend gardener. I almost grab her arm to hurry her along when she stops to fondle the leaves of some ornamental shrub. Only DS Latham seems as anxious to get moving as me.

'Ma'am, sir. We've a meeting in London, remember?' He glances at his watch.

'Don't fret so, Billy. We'll get there in plenty of time.' Shepherd shrugs, no doubt enjoying her moment of peace. 'And if not, then they'll just have to wait for us, won't they.'

I've no idea what's going on any more. All I know is that the longer we stay within the gardens the greater the chance of bumping into someone I'd rather not meet. Already the thought of staying in the church for an hour or so until everyone else had gone is more appealing than this dangerous traipse down memory lane. And yet my future career, if my future has a career in it, is inextricably linked to DCI Bain and Superintendent Shepherd.

'Where exactly did you park before going into the church?' I ask, hoping that it might mean we can go out through another side gate. Before anyone can answer, a wheelbarrow appears at the end of the path. It's wheeled by a man I don't recognise, although his stooped shoulders and resigned expression are hauntingly familiar. The figure immediately behind him is somewhat different. She sees us all too swiftly.

'This is a private garden. You can't come in— Oh. It's you. Of course it is.'

Ten years since we last spoke. More, possibly. Also 'spoke' is being too kind. 'Shouted' would be more accurate.

'Mother.' I try to keep my voice neutral, since she's not bothered keeping the terseness out of hers. I can't help noticing that my companions have all taken shelter behind me. Cowards. 'I was showing my colleagues the back way out of the church. To avoid the press.'

'And what were you all doing in the church anyway? That . . . man should never have been given the respect of a Christian burial.'

As if to mock her words, a lone bell begins to chime its toll from the tower. That should at least mean that the coffin is covered and the mourners are headed back to the Glebe House for whatever manner of wake there might be.

I feel a light touch on my shoulder, glance round to see Diane Shepherd's nervous smile. 'I'll have Billy bring the car around to the courtyard to fetch you.' She shifts her gaze towards my mother. 'I'm very sorry to have disturbed you, Lady Fairchild. Your formal garden is magnificent, but we won't take any more of your time.'

My mother regards us all with equal disdain, but her shoulders square a little at the use of her title. Complimenting her on her garden was a smart move too, which is probably why Shepherd is a superintendent and I'm still a detective constable.

'Fifteen minutes,' she says to me before turning to leave. Perhaps that's how much time it will take them to get back through the graveyard, out to their car and drive around to the courtyard away from the prying eyes and lenses of the press.

Maybe she thinks leaving me here to talk with my mother alone is a kindness. I haven't the heart to tell her it's at least ten minutes more than I'll need.

I can, just about, remember a time when I loved my mother. It's harder to recall a time when she loved me. I have early childhood memories of warmth and smiles, being read stories, bathed in warm bubble-bath water, cosseted. That may have been any one of a dozen nannies, of course, but I'm sure that somewhere back in the long-lost mists of the last millennium my mother actually cared for me.

When it all started to fall apart is much easier to pinpoint. With hindsight I can see that it was the same time my father was busy having an affair with his best friend's wife, but for me it was when I came back from school for the summer holidays to find the laughter gone and the party frocks exchanged for black mourning.

'Mother.' I struggle to think what else to say, all those endless lessons in etiquette wasted. The gardener has wisely disappeared, wheeling his barrow to another distant part of the garden. I hear the clank of metal as the gate back through to the churchyard closes on Shepherd, Bain and Latham, and we are alone.

'Constance.' She speaks the word as if using it to reassure herself, and for the first time in my life it occurs to me this must be just as stressful for her as it is for me.

'How are you?' I ask. She looks at me as if trying to work out whether I'm taking the piss or not. It's true I don't really care, but there are formalities even at times like this. Looking at her is a bit like looking in a mirror that ages me thirty years. I have the Fairchild red hair, but otherwise I take after my mother far more than perhaps I would like. Not that I feel much affinity with my father either, for that matter.

'As well as can be expected, given the circumstances.' A bony hand instinctively reaches for the crucifix hanging on a thin cord around her neck, a motion I saw all too many times before I left home. Christ is her saviour and solace, and she long ago chose to give all her love to him. Nothing to spare for her children or her husband. Certainly not a handshake, not a polite air kiss to either cheek, or, heaven forbid, a hug.

'You've cut your hair,' she says after a moment's awkward pause. 'It suits you.'

I should compliment her on something, but I can think of nothing to say. She's thin to the point of emaciated, her face far more lined than her years. Her hair's as white as a priest's surplice, and just as short as my own.

'Actually I was thinking I might shave it all off and wear a wig.'

She stares at me with narrowed eyes for several seconds longer than would be polite, were our roles reversed. 'Given your new-found notoriety, a wig might not be such a bad idea. I'd suggest a brunette, or possibly a mousy brown with a bit of grey in it. On the shoulders, not too long. No need to shave your head though. Not unless you want to. You should consider spectacles, too. I'm sure I've got an old pair somewhere that are just glass, no prescription.'

I'm taken aback by her sudden helpfulness. This isn't the mother I recall.

'That's very kind of you. I'll pick them up when I'm back for the wedding, maybe.'

A momentary pause, the slightest of flinches perhaps. I only notice it because I'm used to watching people, used to watching my mother. She crosses her hands defensively over her stomach.

'You received your invitation then.'

'Yes. I spoke to Charlotte recently, too. She tells me you wanted some missionary pastor to officiate.'

That twitch at her soon-to-be daughter-in-law's name is

telling. 'The Reverend Doctor Masters is not some "missionary pastor" as you put it. He is a highly regarded religious scholar, working in the full Anglican tradition. Unlike some of the more lax vicars we seem to be getting these days.'

I'm tempted to ask her how much money this reverend doctor has asked her for, but I keep my mouth shut. Our last meeting ended in a shouting match, me walking out of the house, the grounds and all family life. It's not as if I particularly want to return, but I'm older now, perhaps a little wiser. There's no point in looking for an argument with the lady of the manor.

'Well, I'd best be going. Wouldn't want to keep the superintendent waiting.'

That gets me a slightly raised eyebrow, but no more comment than that. My mother nods her head once, slowly, then steps aside to let me pass. It's only as I'm going that she reaches out her hand and grabs my arm. Her grip is weak, but the contact shocks me more than I expect it to.

'Look after yourself, Constance.' I meet her gaze for a moment, and there's something in the look she gives me that's almost concern. And then the mask comes down again, dead eyes and thin mouth. She drops my arm, turns, and walks away.

11

I drove out to Harston Magna for the funeral, and left my car parked at my aunt's cottage on the outskirts of the village. It had been my intention to get her to run me to Kettering station and catch a train back to London, given how little use a car is in the city and how difficult it is to park one. I'm bright enough to understand that Superintendent Shepherd's offer of a lift isn't one I can turn down. DS Billy Latham drives, and Bain sits in the front passenger seat, leaving me and the superintendent with the back all to ourselves.

'Ed told me about how you found the young boy outside your block,' she says as we hit the motorway. I still can't quite get my head around Bain's first name. He's never struck me as an Ed. More a Reginald, or perhaps a Walter. Someone stuck in the 1950s like my father, although if I'm being fair, he's not that old.

'Daniel.' The name pops into my head, and I remember the strange young woman tailing me.

'I beg your pardon?' It's an oddly old-fashioned expression, coming from the otherwise thoroughly modern-looking superintendent.

'Sorry, I just remembered. That's what I was told his name was. Daniel . . .' I rack my brains for a moment, knowing it's there somewhere. I had coffee, a latte that tasted OK to start with, but left an unpleasant chemical flavour in my mouth afterwards. 'Daniel Jones, that's it.'

Shepherd raises a slim eyebrow. 'Really. And you know this how?'

I tell her about the girl, skip the part about the coffee. I can see Bain tilting his head back to listen in. That's fine by me.

'Why didn't you tell us this before?'

'I forgot all about it. It's amazing how being hounded by the press can do that to a person.'

'And this girl – Anna, did you say? She was at the hospital the day you went to visit the boy.'

'Yeah. I'd have caught her, too, but I ran into an old friend.' I nod forward in Bain's direction, but he's not paying attention any more. He's got his phone out and is speaking to someone. Back at HQ, I'd guess, if his repeated mention of the name Daniel Jones is anything to go by. 'I take it the boy's not woken up yet.'

'He's got no tongue, remember. Couldn't tell us his name if he wanted to.' It's the first thing DS Latham has said since we got into the car, and his scathing tone surprises me. If I didn't know better I might think I'd insulted him in a previous life. I've never met him before today though.

'I'd have thought he'd be able to write it down, you know? They teach you your letters in schools now, I'm told.'

Bain's phone ringing kills the argument before it can really get started. My heart's not in it anyway. It's obvious Latham doesn't like me, but I don't care enough to try and find out why.

'Looks like a good ID, Diane. Missing Persons has a Daniel Jones meets the profile. Reported runaway from Edinburgh, disappeared six months ago. Photo's not a bad match.' The DCI twists in his seat, holding up his phone to show an image on the screen. It's a younger boy than the one I saw laid out with the trash, cleaner and less bloodied too, but I'd give good odds on it being the same person.

'OK, so we've got a name and we know where he came from.

Who've we got at Gartcosh these days? I want all the information there is on him in the next twenty-four hours.' Shepherd pulls out her own phone, the car suddenly transforming itself into a mobile incident room. I feel rather left out.

'Do you think that'll help?' I ask, and immediately wish I'd kept my mouth shut. No choice, I'm committed now. 'Look, he's run away from Edinburgh, gone to London to seek his fame and fortune. That's not worked out for him, but whoever cut out his tongue and castrated him, that's local. Finding out why he ran from home won't tell us who picked him up when he got here.'

The silence that follows lasts far longer than I'd like. All eyes are on me, even DS Latham's through the rear-view mirror. I wish he'd keep his on the road.

'I see what you mean about her.' Shepherd grins as she speaks to Bain. 'Very little appreciation for procedure. She's right though. We know when he ran away already. That gives us a timescale to work with. Six months. What's he been doing all that time?'

I want to say 'I'm here, you know?' but the last vestiges of my self-preservation reflex kick in to stop me. I don't want to be abandoned at some motorway service station and told to find my own way home.

'Would it help if I gave you a photofit of the girl? Maybe go through the hospital CCTV and see if I can spot her?' I venture after they've been going back and forth with ideas for a few miles. Bain looks at Shepherd, and I can see the indecision in both of their expressions. They don't want me involved in this investigation if they can help it. Nothing like feeling appreciated.

'It can wait until tomorrow,' Bain says eventually. 'I'll have PC Eve pick you up in the morning.'

My favourite reporter is waiting outside the apartment block when DS Latham pulls in to the side of the road to let me out.

Stokes doesn't recognise the car, which I hope gives Superintendent Shepherd and the others enough time to escape the scene before he realises what's happening.

'Posh motor, Fairchild. Mates of yours?' He nods towards the end of the road where the shiny black Mercedes is turning.

'I've nothing to say to you or any of your ghoulish friends.' I go to walk past him, but he follows anyway.

'Been to a funeral, I see. Anyone I know?'

Too late I remember that I'm still dressed all in black, Aunt Felicity's long overcoat almost but not quite hiding my leather ankle boots. My wide-brimmed hat is in one hand, all-too-ladylike handbag in the other. I ignore the reporter in the vain hope that he'll go away and find someone else to bother. It doesn't work.

'They buried old Roger DeVilliers today, or so I'm told. Not much tabloid interest in that story any more. "Old Man Dies" doesn't really excite the editors these days, even if the old man was a paedo who raped his own daughter.'

He's prodding me for a reaction, I can tell. I wonder where his photographer friend is, even as I realise I don't actually care. If he wants a fight, I'll happily provide him with one.

'If you were half the journalist you claim to be, you'd be out there trying to find out who else DeVilliers knew. He shared her with his friends, the sick bastard. I bet there's a few captains of industry and prominent politicians breathing a sigh of relief now he's dead. But are you interested in them? Course not. You just get off on making life miserable for innocent people.'

'If you know any names . . .' Stokes reaches out and grabs my arm. If my hands weren't already full I'd probably break his fingers. Certainly have him on the ground in an armlock. Instead I shake him off with a shrug and a killing stare.

'Of course I don't know any fucking names. If I did, they'd be locked up right now, and very wary of their fellow inmates.'

'Touchy. Heard that about you.' Stokes takes a step back, much to my relief.

'What is it you actually want? Only I've had a long day and I'd quite like to get home now.'

'Want?' For a moment he looks genuinely puzzled. 'Oh, right. Yeah. I was dropping by to ask why you didn't go to the funeral, but it seems you did. Some of your mates from the NCA too, if I saw right. That was DCI Bain in the front of that car, wasn't it? You back at work then?'

'As if I'd tell you something like that.'

'Yeah, I heard you liked keeping secrets too. Posh girl like you slumming it in the Met just to get back at Daddy. How do your mates down the nick feel about working alongside an aristo-crat, eh?'

'I . . .' No more words come out than that. I can't think of anything else to say.

'Fascinating family, yours. Brother getting married to the daughter of the man you put behind bars. Mum throwing away her inheritance on whatever religious nut job grabs her attention. And your dad, well . . .' Stokes pauses as much to catch his breath as for any kind of dramatic effect. 'An affair with his best mate's wife? An illegitimate daughter? Wonder how many other wild oats the old goat sowed down the years, eh? Reckon that'd be a story worth looking into.'

He takes two paces back and gives me a mock bow. 'Be seeing you, Fairchild. Or should I say Lady Constance?' Then he turns and walks away into the evening gloom. I watch him go, my brain slowly catching up with what he's just said. With DeVilliers dead, I'd naively thought they'd leave me alone now.

Christ, but I can be stupid at times.

12

PC Karen-with-a-K Eve picks me up at half seven in the morning. It's an early start, but I've been up for well over an hour before she arrives, after spending a largely sleepless night fretting about what Stokes said to me. I phoned Aunt Felicity, as much to tell her I was home safe as anything, but I can't fool myself I wasn't trying to find out if she'd spoken to any reporters. Of course she hadn't, but neither had she spoken to my father, her brother, in a while. Christ only knows what he'd do if someone like Jonathan Stokes turned up at the manor. Invite him in for a cup of tea and a chat, probably.

Karen doesn't say much on the drive across the city, and I wonder if I've done something to upset her. Maybe she's read the papers I haven't had the nerve to look at yet. I can't even bring myself to check my phone for newsfeeds, but at least nobody has texted me, not since Bain confirmed when and where I was to help with a photofit ID of the girl Anna.

'DCI's in the conference room on the third floor, along with the rest of the feds,' Karen says as she lets me in through the back door to the station. Time was I had my own pass, and didn't have to sign the register. All that went when they took my warrant card away.

'You not coming up?' I know as soon as I ask it's the wrong question. Her face has a kind of permanent scowl on it anyway, but it deepens in an instant.

'Do I look like someone who works for the NCA?'

She has a point, but there's more to it than just being pissed off at having to do their bidding. She wants to be someone who looks like she works for the NCA, and the fact that they seem to be courting me for a post despite my clearly being a walking disaster zone rankles. Having to act as my personal chauffeur's just rubbing her nose in it.

'I didn't ask for this either, Karen.' I try to keep the annoyance out of my voice. No point winding her up if she's the only ally I've got in Uniform.

'Whatever. I'll be in the canteen.' She heads off, walking straight through the middle of two junior officers deep in conversation. Both look at her, then at me, the question writ large on their faces. I ignore them and set off for the incident room.

'Took your bloody time, didn't you? Some of us have been at work for hours.'

My heart sinks as I enter the room. Not because the only person in there is Detective Sergeant Latham, or because for whatever reason he still hates me, but because I really can't face the aggro any more.

'It's too early in the morning. Can you not keep the snide comments until after coffee time?'

Latham's face reddens, and it occurs to me that this is the first time he's actually looked me in the eye. I'd not appreciated quite how young he was when we met in the church yesterday, but I've got a comfortable couple of years on him, maybe more. Doesn't matter, since he's a DS and I'm just a lowly constable on suspension. He looks like he's going to say something, but then a noise behind me draws his attention. I turn to see DCI Bain and Superintendent Shepherd walk in.

'Ah, you're here, Fairchild. Good.' Shepherd gives me a look that's almost as unsettling as Latham's. 'Sort of.'

'Sort of, ma'am?'

She raises an eyebrow at my question, or my use of the title. 'I was looking for someone to join our team. Someone with a decent track record and experience in plain clothes and undercover ops. You might have fitted the bill, were it not for your rather high profile.'

'It's a temporary thing, I'm sure.'

'Are you?' Bain walks up and holds out his hand. He's clutching a folded newspaper that I really don't want to take from him. When he gives it an impatient shake I know I have no choice. As is usually the case with the tabloids, most of the front page is taken up with a headline in type large enough for the most reluctant of readers.

SLUMMING IT WITH THE BOYS IN BLUE!

The words frame a photograph that I have to stare at for a long time before I realise it's of me. It must have been taken a while ago, as my hair's still down on my shoulders. I've never knowingly worn a tiara though, so that must be photoshopped, along with the uniform now I think about it. There's a bit of text below the headline that I scan only briefly. Even so, I get enough of the gist.

Officers in the Met were surprised recently to find some true blue blood in their ranks. Posh cop Lady Constance Fairchild, who helped expose disgraced financier Roger DeVilliers as a serial sex offender, can trace her family history back to the Norman Conquest, but it's the more recent affairs of the Fairchilds that might raise eyebrows in aristocratic circles.

'It's all bollocks, you know?' Even I can hear the frustration in my voice. Across the room, DS Latham has a sneer on his face that's just waiting for the wind to change. Shepherd's more sympathetic though.

'It is. It's unfair and it's unhelpful. Given what you did last year, and what you were put through, these papers should be praising your courage, not raking through your family history for any muck they can throw around. If life's taught me anything though, it's that nothing is fair.'

She's got that much right. I stare blankly for a moment at the page laid out on the conference table in front of me.

'So, what then? I can't have a job at the NCA. What about my old one back?'

Shepherd shakes her head. 'Not mine to give, I'm afraid. And there's still the matter of ex-Detective Superintendent Bailey. CPS reckon he'll likely try to bargain now that DeVilliers is dead. That'll drag out the hearing for a while longer. Meantime, with your media profile, you're more likely to be a hindrance than a help to any ongoing investigation.'

She's right, of course. Doesn't mean I have to like it.

'So my career's over, then. Can't go back to uniform, not after this.' I slap my hand against the newspaper. 'Can't be a detective. What then – admin? Management? Fuck that.'

Bain winces at my swearing, but Shepherd hardly seems to notice. 'We'll review things in a couple of weeks. You never know, something might come up that distracts the press for long enough to forget about you. Meantime, you'll just have to try and keep your head down.'

'Who actually reads this shit? I mean, who actually cares?'

I'm not really given to flouncing, but I can hear the petulance in my voice as I drop the newspaper onto the table in the station canteen and slump into a seat. Any hope that Roger DeVilliers' death would put a stop to the tabloid press making my life a misery has been squashed by the latest headline. So much for my career.

'Lady Constance?' Karen pulls the paper towards her, unfolding it to reveal the front page. I try to find the sneer in her voice, but it's really not there. Incredulity, yes, and perhaps the edge of a smirk on her face.

'Technically.' Looking around the room, I see no suspicious eyes on me. At least not yet. It won't be long before the wags start up with jokes. Then there'll be pranks and all manner of other shit. Coppers are predictable that way, and relentless.

Karen flips the newspaper closed again, pushes it to the side and concentrates on her mug. I enjoy the silence while it lasts, more than my own coffee. 'Knew you were posh, mind,' she says eventually. 'Didn't realise you were that posh.'

'You've seen where I live. It's not exactly Buckingham Palace, is it.'

'Why d'you live there then?'

'I'm a detective constable. There's only so far a salary goes. You know what London rents are like, right?'

Karen shrugs. 'Still live with me mum, don't I. Council flat. Well "housing association".' She makes little bunny ears with her fingers as she speaks, then shakes her head. 'But yeah, I know what you mean. London housing's a nightmare. And your place isn't all that bad. It's just you, and it's a good location.'

'Don't tell my landlord that.' As I say it, a horrible thought occurs to me. 'Oh crap. He's going to see this and think I'm loaded. Fuck.'

'It'll all blow over soon enough.' Karen knocks back the last of her drink and stands up, leaving the newspaper behind. 'Couple of months, maybe less. They'll get bored and find someone else to bother.'

'Easy for you to say. You're not the one has to live with it.'

Something like annoyance flickers across her face, and too late

I realise what I've said. I begin to apologise, but she's quicker off the mark.

'You reckon?' She flips the paper open again, flicks through it a couple of pages, then slaps her fingers against a picture of me outside my flat. 'Who's that behind you in the photograph then? Who has to drive you around like you're some bleeding aristo? Oh, hang on. You are one. Fuck's sake, Con. This isn't just about you, right?'

'Yeah, I know. Sorry.' I reach out and fold the newspaper again as she walks away, for all the good it will do. Whether she hears me or not, I've no idea.

13

Karen's words sting, but because they're true rather than that they were said in anger. I sit in the canteen for a while after she's gone, partly because I've still got a mug of coffee to finish, and partly because the bustle of officers coming and going gives me enough white noise to think. Nobody seems to notice me, or if they do they give me a wide berth. I'm not sure what to do, and that bothers me more than any threats from the tabloid press.

I never made a secret of my background, but I didn't exactly advertise it either. It wasn't hard to knock the edges off the posh accent when I signed up ten years ago, my time in Edinburgh had softened the worst of it anyway. The fast track to CID meant I didn't spend as much time in uniform as most officers my age, and I guess I missed out on some of the camaraderie walking the beat gives you. I still mucked in though, never shirked my responsibilities.

None of that's going to make a blind bit of difference now. The people who knew about my past will still believe the lies put about by the papers, and the people who didn't won't know any better.

'Didn't know we had royalty visiting. I'd have polished me boots and worn me good uniform if someone had told me.'

And so it begins. I don't even need to look up to know that Police Constable Colin Peterson is standing on the other side of my table. When I do look up, I'm unsurprised to see that he has a small gaggle of friends clustered around him like haemorrhoids on an arsehole. They're young, recent recruits by the state of their uniforms and expectant faces.

'Did you think that joke up all by yourself, or were you given help?' I really shouldn't rise to the bait, but lately I've been finding it hard to care.

'Some nerve showing your face in here anyway.' One of the other constables raises her chin as she speaks, as if trying to look down her nose at me. Either that or she's sniffing the air like a bitch on heat. I can't be bothered with this shit, and besides, I've finished my coffee.

'Some nerve, eh.' I push my chair back with a squeal of metal leg on canteen floor, then stand up slowly. I'm not tall, but I'm above average. My accuser isn't, and has to tilt her head back even further to keep her eyes on mine. I stare at her for a moment, then reach out and grab my coffee mug in a sudden, swift movement that has the lot of them flinching like frightened rabbits. A small victory, but I'll take it.

'Be seeing you around.' I wave the mug at them, then turn and walk away, all too aware that this is just the beginning in what will likely be a long and tiresome war.

Nobody else bothers me as I climb the stairs and walk the corridors from the canteen to the CID room where my desk is. I say my desk, but I've not actually used it in many months. I'm not really sure why I'm drawn to it, except that the station is a safe place, away from the tabloids, even if I'm getting hostility from some of its inmates. There's the small matter of the girl, Anna, too. I'm supposed to be sorting out a photofit of her. I've a passing knowledge of how the software works, but it needs a specialist to get the best out of it. I'm still waiting for the text to tell me they're ready, and this is as good a place to wait as any. Better than the canteen, at least.

There's nobody about when I enter, just a loose formation of desks, each piled high with paperwork. Some have computer screens, others spaces where laptops have been hastily taken away. Case notes and other important stuff are scribbled and pinned to the whiteboards around the walls. Some are so ancient even I know what they're about, others are more recent, crimes that are being investigated now. In a less busy station, a smaller city than London, many of these investigations would have their own teams, dedicated incident rooms on the upper floors, and morning briefings and pep talks from whichever DI or DCI had been unfortunate enough to be put in charge. There would be information to collate and put into the computer, actions generated by the program to sift through and evaluate, a hundred and one other things to do before actually going out into the real world and talking to people. Settling myself down in what I'm fairly sure isn't the chair I used to have, I can't say that I miss much of it.

'Thought I might find you hiding in here.'

I look up with a start, realising as I do that I've been trying to work out what all the folders on my desk are for. It's only as I see Superintendent Shepherd standing in the doorway that I understand this isn't my desk any more. I should have known, of course. The team I worked with was disbanded. I was pretty much the only one not tainted by association with DCI Bailey. Or dead. It's been months since then. Of course my desk would have been reallocated.

'I'm waiting on a call from the photofit tech.' I know it's a poor excuse, but Shepherd doesn't seem to mind. She winds her way through the desks, grabs a chair from the nearest one to me and twirls it around before sitting.

'Chances are we'll pull a better image from the hospital CCTV, actually. You could help by identifying her from that, of course.'

'Sure. Anything I can do to help.' I start to stand, but she waves me down.

'You any idea how difficult it is to get this lot to leave the room?' She waves a hand in the general direction of everywhere, and I begin to understand why nobody is here.

'I'd have thought it would have taken at least a superintendent's strong hint to shift them. Maybe even a chief super.'

Shepherd smiles at that in the same way a teacher might indulge a bright but otherwise insufferable pupil. 'Ed Bain . . . DCI Bain, I should say. What do you think of him?'

Her directness surprises me, but not as much as my immediate answer. 'I trust him. Not sure I want to work with him.'

She raises an eyebrow, but makes no comment. 'And Billy . . . DS Latham?'

'I get the feeling he disapproves. Either of me, or women detectives in general. I don't know him well enough to make up my mind yet.'

'He has a thing about procedure.' Shepherd tilts her head to one side, and I get the feeling she's considering saying more on the matter. Then with the tiniest shake, she decides not to. 'But it's no matter. I know Ed was keen to get you on to our team. He spoke to you about it, I think?'

'A few months back, yes.' Is this a job interview? Do I want one any more?

'I've read your file, Constance.' Shepherd pauses again. 'May I call you Constance?'

'I prefer Con, but sure.'

'Con. Of course. Anyway. I've read your file, and the reports into the DeVilliers and Bailey cases. What you did, how you coped, well, it surprises me that you're still only a DC. Most of your fast-track contemporaries are DIs or higher now.'

Actually, most of my fast-track contemporaries have quit and are making a mint in banking and finance, but I don't think it would be wise to correct her. I think Shepherd meant it as a compliment. I'll take it as one, even if I'm fairly sure I know where this conversation is going. 'I had the offer of a promotion to sergeant a few years ago, but it meant leaving the team and going back to uniform, at least for a short while. I reckon turning them down hurt my prospects going forward. I wasn't really bothered, mind. The pay would've been nice, but I'm not so big on responsibility.'

Shepherd's frown at my explanation suggests she doesn't really believe me. I'm not sure I really believe me either. The lack of promotion has bothered me in the past, just not enough to do anything about it.

'You know the NCA structure's different to the Met, right?'

'Yeah, kind of.'

'We're not all coppers, for one thing. Ed calls me super-intendent, but that's more of a pay grade than a rank. My background's military.'

That surprises me. I'd thought all ex-soldiers were neat freaks, but Shepherd has the look of someone who wouldn't bother with a hairbrush if she really didn't have to.

'The thing is, Const— Con. I think you'd work well in our team.'

'Yeah, I know. But not right now. You said. Can't say it's not frustrating though.'

'Well it'll be even more frustrating to hear I've okayed PC Eve's secondment to the team. She'll be transferring to plain clothes, too.'

'Good for her. She deserves a break.' I say it because it's the right thing to say, but even as the words come out I realise I mean them.

'That doesn't mean there's no place for you with us. Once the media focus is off and everyone's forgotten about you we can see about getting you on board.'

'And in the meantime? I just what? Put up with it and try not to break anyone's face?'

'That would be a start.' Shepherd shrugs. 'But actually I was thinking maybe it would be a good idea to get out of London again. Just for a while.'

I want to say 'But I live here' and jut out my lower lip like a child. Some small measure of sense stops me, and instead I ask, 'But what will I do?'

Shepherd says nothing for a while, just looks at me with an expression I'd expect from a mother to that same child, as if she's waiting for me to think things through and work it out for myself. Finally she deigns to give me a hint.

'That young man you found, Dan Jones. He's still in intensive care, but the doctors reckon he'll survive. Guess they make them tough up there.'

'Anyone spoken to his family? They been to see him?'

'Apparently there's only his mother, and she's not keen to travel. Or speak to the police. She might talk to the woman who saved her son's life, mind.'

It's not an explicit order. Shepherd's not my boss, for one thing, and it's also highly irregular. But it's better than nothing.

'I've always fancied going back to Edinburgh. Not really been since I graduated from uni a while back.'

'And I doubt the tabloids would follow you up there.' Shepherd gives me a businesslike smile that tells me we're on the same wavelength. Or at least I hope that's what it means. She's really not my type.

'Excellent.' She pushes herself up and out of her seat with a fluid motion, interview over. 'Just try not to tread on anyone's toes while you're there, eh?'

14

I sit in the CID room, mulling over what's just happened, until the first detective comes back in. I always hated office politics, but now I'm stuck in the middle of it all again.

'It's Fairchild, isn't it?' The young man raises an eyebrow as he asks the question. I don't recognise him, which goes to show how long it's been since I really worked in this place, how many people have gone only to be replaced by new faces.

'Yeah. Sorry. Know I shouldn't be in here, but I needed to find a quiet place to think.'

He tilts his head in understanding, and I'm grateful to him for that. There's only one way he could know my name, but he's not giving me any vibes of judgement. Unlike the rest of the station.

'I'll get out of your way. Know how busy this place can get.' I stand up from my old desk, strewn with the detritus of another detective's work. What if it's his?

'Sam,' he says as I step past him towards the door. 'Sam Waddington. Detective Sergeant. Seems only fair, since I know all about you.'

I pause a moment, trying my best not to give him the eye the way so many boys have sized me up over the years. He's OK, I guess. Anonymous, which is good in a detective. Average height and build, mousy hair that's maybe thinning a bit on top. His eyes are brown, but piercing.

'All about me?' I shake my head. 'I very much doubt that.'

I can see the start of his reply, the way he edges forward, mouth poised to open. But I'm not in the mood, and before he can say anything I've moved past him and out into the corridor. If I stopped, looked back, maybe there would be something. I'm not looking for something though, and certainly not here. Not him.

It takes me longer to find PC Eve than it should, mostly because I have to deal with snarky comments from anyone I ask. Eventually I find her in one of the interview rooms, alone and with some complicated-looking paperwork strewn across the table in front of her. She glances up as I knock on the half-open door, doesn't smile, but doesn't glower either.

'I hear congratulations are in order. Going to be moving out of uniform soon.'

Now she grimaces at me, then picks up the nearest form. 'Yeah. Thanks. It's not so easy to get excited once you see the paperwork though. I thought it was bad enough filling in overtime sheets. Most of this makes no sense at all.'

It was a nightmare back when I moved from uniform to CID, and that was two parts of the same organisation. Secondment to the NCA means sort-of leaving the Met. I don't want to think what a bureaucratic nightmare that might be.

'You want any help? Can't promise I'll be much use, but I can try.'

For a moment I think she's going to take me up on the offer, but she shakes her head and smooths the form out flat on the table in front of her again. 'No. Reckon I'll get it done by shift end. That is, unless you're needing a lift somewhere?'

It's tempting, but I've never been all that comfortable with being driven places anyway. 'No. I was just going to let you know I'll be flitting out of town soon. I had a chat with your new boss and we decided it was for the best. I can't really do any police work while the press are hassling me, and that's not going to die away anytime soon.'

If she's happy about this, she keeps it from her face.

'Look, Karen. What you said earlier. It's all true. I'm sorry you got roped into this. Wouldn't wish it on anyone, and I've met a few who really deserve it. You've helped me, though, and I appreciate that. I just wanted to wish you good luck in the new post. Who knows? Maybe I'll be joining you, once the heat's off.'

I slip out through the back door of the station, walk swiftly across the car park and then do my best to merge with the crowd in the next street along. It helps that it's market day, the stalls doing a good trade despite the miserable weather. Hoodie up and backpack slung over my shoulder, I'm just another Londoner about her business, but I still keep an eye out for anyone following.

Without Karen to drive me home in a squad car, the journey across the city will take at least a couple of hours. I could save time by catching a bus, or even worse the Tube, but I'm in no great rush to get home. Chances are there'll be at least one reporter and photographer camped outside my flat, although God only knows why. Tomorrow I'll take the train back to Northamptonshire, go stay with my aunt until I've sorted out the next move. I'm beginning to wonder why I even bothered coming back here in the first place, except that I had to be here for the trial.

Much like the last time I walked this way, I realise my route takes me right past the hospital where Dan Jones is still being cared for. I never asked Shepherd if it would be OK to visit him, but then she never explicitly told me not to either. It's not as if he'll be able to tell me anything, but I feel a need to see him again, to remind myself of what's going on, what started all this. Even if I'm not really sure what 'this' is. And it can't hurt to have the most recent update on his prognosis if I'm going to try and speak to his mother.

It's only as I push through the glass doors at the main hospital entrance that I realise I'm not going to be able to just swan up to the ICU. After the incident with the young woman, Anna, there'll be a police guard on Jones, for one thing, and I don't have a warrant card right now, so getting past reception won't be easy either. Fortunately for me the atrium is busy and nobody notices me heading to the door to the stairwell. It has a security lock on it of course, and I don't have the code, so I pretend to be responding to a text on my phone until a cleaner comes past, unlocks it and steps through. No point following right behind him, that would raise suspicion. Instead, I put my foot against the door to stop it from closing. A nervous count of thirty and then I push through.

The cleaner's long gone, but I'm more worried about trying to remember what floor the ICU is on. There's nothing on each landing apart from a number painted next to the door, and the corridors beyond each narrow glass pane all look the same. I'm fairly sure it was either six or seven, and take a chance with six because I'm too out of breath to climb another flight by then.

Luck's on my side, and it only takes a few moments to get my bearings. There's no police guard to be seen, and when I reach the isolation rooms and peer through the glass at Dan Jones, it's as if nothing has changed in the days since I was last here. He's still that sickly grey-brown colour, still swathed in bandages, still hooked up to machines doing most of his living for him, still unconscious.

'Hey, Con. We must stop meeting like this.'

I've only been staring at the young man for a few moments, and yet somehow I've let myself zone out so much I haven't noticed the junior doctor approach from the direction of the lift. Maggie Jennings still looks tired, but her smile's genuine enough.

'Mags. Hi.' I turn to greet her, but stay at my vigil in front of the glass.

'No update on our patient, I'm afraid. Didn't know he was your case though.' She joins me, standing perhaps a little closer than is comfortable, and we both peer through the window.

'He's not. Not really, anyway. I was the one who found him though.'

Maggie takes a while to digest this news, although I'm fairly certain I told her the last time we met.

'Please don't take this the wrong way, but I can't help thinking it would have been better if you'd not.' She doesn't turn to face me as she speaks, and her words are barely a whisper.

'Is it that bad?'

'He's in a deep coma. I'm no expert on neurology, but the chances of him ever regaining consciousness are slim. Given his injuries, and the state of him before they were inflicted, I'd be surprised if he ever wakes up, poor soul.'

Maggie reaches up and places a hand on the glass, fingers splayed. She's a doctor working in the ICU and so presumably allowed to go into the isolation room if she wants to, and yet it feels as if she doesn't dare.

'You say the state of him before the injuries.' My brain catches up with her words more slowly than I would like. Something about this place. 'What do you mean by that?'

'He'd been dosed with some kind of narcotic. Blood toxicology is similar to what we see with synthetic cannabinoid abuse, but there's none of the other outward signs.'

I remember the addicts sprawled out on the benches in the park close by my flat, Mrs Feltham's angry words. 'Spice?'

'Something like that, but nothing I've seen before. The analyst at the lab said it was more like a single dose used to anaesthetise and paralyse him. Probably what kept him alive while they were . . .' She doesn't finish the sentence, goes back to staring through the glass. The thought doesn't bear pursuing, even if my mind wants to go down that horrible path. Numbed to the pain, paralysed as someone cuts you up. Was he conscious when it happened?

'Hey, a bunch of us are getting together at the weekend if you fancy joining us?' The words tumble out of Maggie's mouth in a jumble, almost like a shy boy summoning up the courage to ask someone he fancies out on a date. It's a welcome distraction from my darkest thoughts, and I almost say yes. Then I remember what's happening in my life right now.

'I'd love to, Mags, but I can't. I'm actually just about to leave town again. Too much attention, if you know what I mean.'

'Yeah. I saw the papers. Can't be much fun.'

'Just never piss off a tabloid hack is my advice. Or break a pap's camera.'

'Oh God. You didn't, did you?' Maggie turns to face me, her expression one of such utter horror I can't do anything but laugh. Soon she's laughing too, the both of us a pair of loons, and for an instant it's almost a decade ago. Then just as quickly as the hysteria comes on, it's gone, and we both of us look back through the glass at the comatose Dan Jones.

'You've told the investigating team about the drugs in his system, I take it?' I can't think of anything else to say, the situation is too awkward.

'Not me as such, but it's in the medical report sent to the police, yes.'

'I'll chase it up. See if anyone's looking into the drug angle.' I take one last look at the young man, then finally turn away. 'We'll find out who did this to him, I promise.'

I'm pleasantly surprised to find there are no journalists or photographers camped outside my flat when I make it back to the apartment block. It's almost as if they didn't know I was coming home. The rain came on not long after I left the hospital, and now I'm soaked to the skin. All I want to do is get these dripping clothes off, warm up in the shower and pour myself a stiff drink. Sod the fact that it's not even four in the afternoon yet.

The route to the concrete steps takes me past Mrs Feltham's front door. I try not to be seen, but I've barely stepped past her flat before her voice booms out from behind me.

'Con, girl. You look like you been thrown in the lake. Them fancy folka yours never teach you to find shelter when it's rainin'?'

It's not actually raining any more, just the memory of it keeping the air damp and misting my breath. Even so, I imagine great fat raindrops bouncing off my head, my face and my shoulders as I turn slowly to face her. I don't think it would be possible to get any wetter than I already am.

'Been avoiding people, Mrs F. I get stared at on the bus. Kids point and whisper.'

'I read about it in that rag they try to call a newspaper. I wondered why all them paparazzi were still hounding you after, well, you know.'

A trickle of icy cold water drips from my matted hair. I can feel it work its way down the back of my neck and my spine. All the way to my tailbone.

'I'm surprised they're not still here, actually.'

'They were here. One a' them knocked on my door and asked where you were. Told them you'd gone out for lunch with a friend. Best look for you at the Green Man over on the high street.' Mrs F raises her chin in the general direction. I wouldn't drink in the Green Man if it was the last pub left open in London, and she knows that.

'Thank you, Mrs F. You're a star.'

'They'll be back. Mark my words. You get yourself inside and dried off now, 'fore they do, child. Got something on the stove for my boys. It'll be ready in about an hour. I'll bring you some up.'

I open my mouth to say that I'd be happy to come down and fetch it, but she waves me away with an impatient arm. 'Go, child, before you catch your death!'

I do as I'm told, hearing the laughter in her voice. I can see the smile on her old face in my mind's eye too. Maybe the stiff drink can wait, if there's some of Mrs Feltham's famously hot curry on offer instead.

The flat is cold, heating not set to come on for another couple of hours. I tap the override as soon as I get in, even though I know it'll take a while for anything to happen. At least there's plenty of hot water for a long shower, and soon enough I'm pulling on clean, dry clothes. I've almost finished draping the wet ones over the still-lukewarm radiators when there's a knock at the door. I shove my hand in my pocket for my phone to check the time; surely it's not an hour since I was talking to Mrs F yet? Only then do I realise it's still on the bedside table. Fetching it I see two missed calls from DCI Bain, and a single line of text message.

Where are you? Eve will be at flat in half an hour.

The knock is more insistent this time, and backed up with a 'Con? You in there?' I hurry to the door and open it, unsurprised to see PC Eve standing there. Surprised to see DS Latham with her. He won't actually look me in the eye, but I can see him gazing past me at the hallway with its damp clothes and general untidiness.

'Boss says you need to come with us,' Karen says. 'Something he wants you to see.'

'Something you shouldn't be involved with at all.' Latham's voice drips with loathing. If he's hoping to put me off, it's having the opposite effect.

'I'll grab my coat,' I say, and soon we're down the stairs and climbing into a waiting squad car. I look back at Mrs F's front door with a feeling of deep regret. The curry will have to wait.

15

Nobody tells me what Bain wants, and I'm expecting a drive back to the station across the city I've just walked through. It comes as something of a surprise then to be taken the short distance to the park instead. Darkness is falling now, and the street lights don't help, casting shadows on the areas where I witnessed volunteers from the Church of the Coming Light gathering up the Spice addicts and taking them off to the shelter. It's reassuring to see none of the zombie-like bodies here tonight. Less reassuring is the huddle of police officers and white-suited forensics technicians over by scraggly trees. One of them breaks from the group and comes over as we approach.

'Where the fuck have you been all afternoon, Fairchild?'

I'm getting more used to Bain's occasional brusqueness, but his coarse greeting puts me on edge. On the other hand, he doesn't seem to know that I spent part of that time at the hospital. Should I tell him?

'What's going on? I thought I wasn't meant to be involved in any police operations, sir.'

'You're not, and yet somehow you manage to find a way. Come.' He waves a hand for me to follow him, then leads me to the huddle of police officers. They're standing a bit further into the trees, clustered around something on the ground.

'You called in a report about some junkies here.' Bain puts no inflection into his words, simply reporting it as fact. 'I take it you come through here on your way home.'

'Sometimes, yeah. I spoke to someone at the local station a few days back. Seems like this is the favoured spot for crashing out on Spice.' I hold my hands out, palms up to the damp air. It's not raining any more, but it will start up again soon enough. 'Not exactly the nicest place for it, especially at this time of year. They don't seem to care, mind you.'

'Bloody nightmare stuff. Don't think it's what did for this poor sod though.' Bain taps the shoulder of one of the forensic tech officers, who moves aside without a word. No one's saying anything much, and as I step forward for a look, I can see why.

Hurrying by, you might think the body was just another Spice victim, passed out on the ground. He's young, but then so many of them are. That's the tragedy of it. There's a stillness to this body that's beyond even the addicts I saw earlier, and I can tell instantly that he's dead, even before my eyes begin to process the grisly details. Like the fact that he's naked from the waist up, and there's a gaping hole in his chest where his heart should be.

'Jesus fuck.'

The 'tsk' of disapproval is so loud it breaks the horrific grip this scene has on me. Turning slightly, I see DS Latham glaring in my direction as if he's never heard anything so blasphemous and shocking in his life. Poor wee soul, what's he doing working for the police if a little light swearing upsets him? Maybe he thinks women should be more decorous. Seen but never heard.

'Got a call from some local shelter. Found him when they were doing a sweep for any addicts passed out.' Bain is unmoved by my cussing. 'I take it he wasn't here when you came through.'

'Didn't come this way today, sir. Has the pathologist been? Any idea of a time of death?' Even as I ask it, I know the question is stupid.

'Not yet. He's on his way, and I dare say he'll tell you not to ask. We're going to have to close this area up for forensics. You know this place though, so anything you can remember about it from your last visit will be useful.'

I look back down at the body, focusing beyond the bloody gash in his chest and the white flecks of broken rib and sternum showing through the gore. There's more blood around his mouth, horribly reminiscent of Dan Jones. I don't think this one's had his bollocks cut off though, or he'd be completely naked. The dead grass and wet earth are trampled, used dog ends and other detritus strewn around much like in any open space in the city. Nothing looks very different from when I was here before. Except for the obvious.

'Last time there were a half dozen or so addicts, but it was daytime. Bunch of do-gooders from the local church tipped up out of nowhere and took them off. They'll be the ones called this in, most likely. You'd be better off talking to the local nick. They'll know all the dealers and players in this area better than us.'

'You might be surprised to know that we've already done that, Constable. We know how to carry out an investigation. This isn't our first.'

It's the most words I think I've ever heard DS Latham speak at once. I don't bother turning to face him. I spent more than a decade in a private girls' school; I understand sarcasm and how to deal with it.

'I need everything you can remember about your last visit here, in a report. Soonest.' Bain seems to be ignoring Latham too. 'Karen can run you back to the station. Might as well get it done while the memory's fresh, eh?'

So much for an evening in with a beer or two and some of Mrs Feltham's curry. I take one last reluctant glance at the body on the grass, thrown out like so much garbage. Who would do that? Who is so confident they won't be caught that they can leave so much evidence in plain sight?

★ ★ ★

It's many hours later, Bain's report written and filed, as I ride the bus home, and mull over the events of the day. I try not to convince myself that everyone is staring at me, although it doesn't help that an abandoned copy of one of the free news sheets strewn across the seat opposite shouts the headline 'Posh Cop Lashes Out!' It's folded over, so I can't see any more of the photograph than what I assume is the top of my head, short cropped dark-red hair looking like I've been dragged backwards through a hedge. It's dark outside so I can see my reflection well enough in the window. Probably time to pay a visit to the hairdresser, or maybe even shave my head and invest in a wig. What would I look like as a brunette? Could I get away with Charlotte's long blonde hair? No, it would annoy the hell out of me.

Thinking of Charlotte reminds me that it's not long now until the wedding, and the thought of getting dressed up fills me with dread. Sure, I've got something in a wardrobe that'll do, and it's amazing what a little bit of nail varnish can hide these days. But do I really want to spend a day with the kind of people who are going to be there? They'll all know about me, what I did. Or worse, the version of what I did that the tabloids are spinning now. Christ, the tabloids. They'll be there, of course. There's nothing they love more than a big society wedding. Except possibly a big society wedding with a whiff of scandal about it. Knowing Charlotte she's probably sold the photography rights to some gossip magazine too.

'Hey. This is you, innit.' A male voice breaks through my musing and I realise I've been staring out of the window at nothing. I check his reflection in the glass first, then turn my head slowly to face him. He must have got on at the last stop without my noticing, and now he's sitting across the aisle from me, unfolded free newspaper in his lap. From the way he's staring, I think he's more of a nuisance than a threat. Older than me, maybe late forties, early fifties, he's dressed in jeans, fleece over lumberjack shirt over T-shirt. Dull brown eyes, five-o'clock shadow on his chin and cheeks, hair cut with clippers to hide the grey coming through. I'd not give him a second thought if he hadn't spoken.

'Nah. Not me. Bin gettin' that lots lately. See if I ever meet her I'll give her a piece of my mind.' I try to put on my best Estuary twang, but I can see he's not buying it. Still, he gets the hint and goes back to reading the paper, unlike most of the men in this city.

He gets off at the next stop, one last look at me as he goes, leaving the paper behind. Another man, younger, picks it up and unfolds it. I can feel his eyes on me like there's insects crawling over my skin. Lecherous insects. Doing my best to ignore him, I scan the street outside for any clues as to how much further there is to go. Still a good distance, but it's not raining any more. As the bus slows for a set of lights, I get up, ping the button.

Nobody else gets off when I do. I watch the bus pull out and diesel away. This part of London's far enough from the centre that it's not too busy late at night, the street quiet. I shove my hands in my pockets for warmth, pull my hoodie over my head and set off on the walk home. There are small groups of smokers outside each of the noisy pubs I pass, but they barely notice me, and I begin to hope that I might get away with it. Home, door locked, maybe even that curry Mrs F promised, if her boys haven't eaten it all. My stomach growls at the thought of it, too long since I last ate. Then I remember the body of the young man, thrown under the trees in the park like so much trash, and my hunger evaporates.

Who the hell would do such a thing? And why? Bad enough to kill someone, worse yet to mutilate them, take organs for whatever sick purpose I can't even begin to imagine. But disposing of the victim like that? It makes no sense. There's going to be forensic evidence all over it, surely? I've worked Organised Crime in this city long enough to know that a body can be disposed of with ridiculous ease. A skilled butcher can chop one up in minutes, be it a pig, a cow, or a human being. Sometimes the smaller parts turn up in unexpected places. Bins, washed up on the riverbank, in the stomachs of dead dogs. It's not often there's enough left to confirm an identity.

It's about the same time as I remember this isn't and never will be my case that I also begin to think I'm being followed. That deeply ingrained instinct has the hair on the back of my neck prickling. I've walked this street hundreds of times without incident, but usually during the day when the little shops are open and there's people around. Normal people, going about their normal lives. Now it's late at night and I'm not all that far from the park where the mutilated body was dumped. I'm even closer to the Danes Estate.

I hit the button on the next pedestrian crossing, taking the opportunity to glance around and spot what's got me spooked. Too few cars driving on the road, and I can't see any people closer than a couple of hundred metres away. Am I letting the events of the past few days get to me? Just because you're paranoid doesn't mean they're not out to get you.

Shaking my head at the stupidity of that kind of thinking, I hurry across the road as the little man turns green. It's only as I reach the other side that I realise the mistake I've made.

I sense the punch a fraction before it connects, just enough time to drop and turn so that it misses the side of my head and instead grazes my shoulder. He's come out of the shadows where one of the street lamps has broken, moving swiftly on silent feet. It's not a killing blow, meant only to incapacitate. That's small solace as the pain flashes in my arm.

My senses sharpen in the moment as the adrenaline kicks in, time slowing. I catch a glimpse of his face and think I recognise the younger man from the bus. Not a random mugging, then. He's chosen his spot well, my would-be rapist. A dark narrow alley opens up just beyond the pedestrian crossing. It makes a short cut from the shops here to the estate, the perfect place to drag a semi-conscious woman. Given he's made no attempt to hide his identity, I've no doubt that if he manages to get me in there, my best chance of ever being found is in the guts of dead dogs.

'Heard the posh ones like it rough.' His voice is oddly high-pitched and nasal, his intention as ugly as he is. He lunges for me as he speaks, but I've anticipated that. I drop to the ground in a crouch and lash out with one foot. My boot catches him on the shin, forcing him back with a satisfying pig-squeal of pain.

'You'll pay for that, bitch.' There's a noise like steel on steel, and a wicked knife appears in his hand from nowhere. Christ, I hate knives. No easy way to protect yourself from them. I need to get away, back to the nearest crowd. He's not about to give me the time, striding forward as I roll away and try to get back to my feet.

'Gonna take my time with you. Enjoy myself.' He's full of himself, but his overconfidence works to my advantage. If he'd pressed his advantage while I was still on the ground, I'd stand no chance. As it is, he gives me enough time to stand and face him before he lunges forward, swinging the knife like a maniac.

I flinch backwards, twist to the side and feel the blade rip the fabric of my coat, a sharp sting of pain in my shoulder. We're close enough that I might even be able to pivot, grab his wrist, get him on the ground, except that he's too big and I'm off balance. It's all I can do to keep my momentum, dance a little pirouette away from him as he stamps, turns and comes back for more. I take another step back, feel the edge of the pavement under one boot and have a mad idea all at the same time. A couple of cars are approaching, not that I expect either of them to come to the rescue. I keep my eye on the knife, weaving its unpredictable arc as he presses in on me, ready for the killing blow.

Everything happens in an instant. The attack comes, I feint away from the road and then step back into it and the oncoming traffic. He follows, the weight of his lunge carrying him forward, foot landing exactly where I'd hoped it would, right on the kerb. He yelps as he goes over on his ankle, crumpling to the ground, but it's more surprise than pain. His boots will protect him from any serious damage. It gives me the time I need though. Ignoring the pain in my shoulder, I run out into the road.

The car's nearly on me as I cross its path, arms wide and waving. Lucky for me the driver's awake, and with a screech of brakes it stops with nothing to spare. A woman's face stares at me from behind the wheel, eyes wide with shock. A blare of horn is the car behind, which has also screeched to a halt. In the distance I can see more cars heading this way, and the unmistakable outline of a bus.

'The fuck is wrong with you?' Her shout is loud enough to hear through the glass. I stand up straight, raise my hands.

'Sorry. This guy's trying to kill me.' I point in the direction of the pavement, sure that any moment I'm going to have to leg it down the road. The woman's gaze follows, at the same moment as the car behind toots its horn again and rushes past, engine screaming and its tyres letting out an angry chirp as it goes. Its male driver gives me a raised finger and an angry shout. I open my mouth to warn him, but he's not paying attention to the road ahead. Too much in a hurry to care that there's a man struggling to his feet at the edge of the road, unsteady on a recently turned ankle.

The noise of impact is far louder and far crunchier than I'd have expected it to be. The car wasn't going that fast, but it was fast enough. My would-be attacker falls under its wheels with a scream that's part terror, part pain, cut off all too suddenly. And then with a sickening double bump the car is past and speeding off down the road.

16

'You certainly have a knack for buggering things up, Fairchild.'

I didn't sleep much last night. It took hours for the adrenaline to wear off, and then I was left with the shock. I spent most of the night in the old armchair in my living room, nursing a mug of tea and listening to Karen Eve snoring on the sofa. My guardian angel, bless her. I thought she'd gone home, but not more than twenty minutes after I called in the incident, there she was. Took me back to my flat and insisted on staying just in case anyone else tried to have a go.

'It's OK, sir. I'm fine. He didn't manage to hurt me much.' The words slip out before I can stop them. Or maybe I just don't care any more. I tense for DCI Bain's angry retort, but he stares at me for a moment before slumping into his chair.

'Sorry. I didn't mean . . .' He rubs at his forehead rather than elucidating, and I can see how tired he is. I guess I'm not the only one who didn't sleep a wink. 'What's the status on the bloke who attacked you?'

'He's dead, sir. Having your skull crushed under the wheels of a BMW SUV will do that.' I don't want to, but I hear that crunchy noise all over again, that scream cut horribly short.

'I guess the driver did you a favour, then.'

'Shame he didn't stick around for me to thank him. We'll get him soon enough though.'

'You saw the number?' Bain leans forward, pulls his laptop towards him as if he's about to run it through the database. As it happens, I did get the number, but then forgot it in the jumble of other things going on.

'Luckily for us the other driver had a dash cam. The footage is quite useful.' And no doubt the part of it where I run into the road and wave my arms around like an idiot will make it on to some hilarious compilation video that'll be shown at the station Christmas party. At least I'll not be there to watch it.

'Do we have a name for him, then? The man who attacked you?' Bain pushes his laptop away again and slumps back into his chair. It's a lot more comfortable than the one I'm perched on.

'We do – Garry Chandler. He's a serial sex offender. Just got let out of prison a month ago.'

Bain gives me a startled look. 'Sex offender? I thought this was . . .' He trails off, unsure what he thought it was.

'The joys of having your face spread all over the tabloid papers. People think they're entitled to a piece of you.' I shudder at the thought of it.

'So this was what? A rape attempt that went horribly wrong? Nothing to do with any ongoing investigations at all?'

'I'm currently on suspension, sir. I'm not part of any ongoing investigations. Not in any official capacity.'

Bain's expression is much like one an irate parent would give a child who denies stealing the chocolate despite having it smeared all over their face and hands. 'Do I look like an idiot, Fairchild? I know you've been asking questions about the young boy, Jones. You could no more sit at home and do nothing like you're supposed to than I could. Thought this might've been something to do with that. Might even have been a breakthrough, if you'd stirred up someone enough to come after you.'

That's cold, even by Bain's standards. I let it slide, although there is one point I can't let go. Even if it's none of my business.

'About Jones, sir. Have you seen the doctor's report on him? His tox screening results?'

Bain looks up at me suspiciously. 'How would you even know about that?'

I shake my head. There's no way to tell him without getting Maggie Jennings into trouble. 'It's not important, really. I was just wondering if it fitted with the other bodies. Was he given something to keep him alive while they . . . did that to him?'

'It's a line of enquiry, but you're not on active duty right now, not part of this team. Best leave it to us, eh?'

I know better than to push the point. I can always ask someone else if I really need to know. 'I was going to leave town for a bit, before yesterday's attack. Spoke to Shepherd about it and she thought it was for the best. I can stay here, though, if Professional Standards want to talk to me about Chandler.'

'They'll need to at some point, but given your current media profile it might be better if you're not somewhere you can be easily found. We can come to you.' Bain closes down his laptop as he speaks, my somewhat mild dressing-down over.

'I'll let you know where I am, sir. Just in case. And I'll try to keep out of trouble.'

Bain's sigh is barely audible as he stands up, but it's there.

'You do that, Fairchild.'

Any hope I might have had that the press would forget about me evaporates as the car turns the corner into my street. The road is partly blocked by television vans, and a mob of reporters are crowded around the base of the stairs that lead up to my floor.

'Jesus. Is this what it's like to be a celebrity?' Karen pulls in to the side of the road before anyone notices us, kills the engine. 'What do you want to do? I can call up a squad car, get them all moved on.'

'I'm sure all my friends in uniform will be really happy about that.' I unclip my seat belt, check the mirror to make sure nothing's coming past, then open the door. 'I'll deal with them best I can. Stay here and call an ambulance if it's needed.'

I meant it as a joke, but her worried expression makes me think I may have missed the mark. Closing the door on it, I shoulder my backpack, pull up the hood on my hoodie and set off towards the mêlée.

As I get closer, I realise the collected reporters and cameramen all have their backs to me, their focus on the concrete stairs. Closer still and I begin to make out the unmistakable voice of Mrs Feltham holding court to a rapt audience.

'Shame on you all, pestering a poor girl who done nothin' wrong. You want a story? I tell you a story. You can go see for yourselves just a short walk from here. You know how to walk, right? Well, just head down that way. Turn right at the lights and keep going. You'll know you're there when you see the bodies.'

I'll say this much for Mrs F, she knows how to work a crowd. This lot are hooked, although how much of the footage will make the evening news is anyone's guess.

'Bodies? What bodies?' someone asks.

'The zombies. The good-as-dead. Folk out of their heads on Spice peddled to them by people who should know better, people the likes of Con Fairchild are trying to put in jail, and yet here you are hounding a girl for just doing her job.'

'Is Spice really a problem here? I thought that was more of a north of England thing.'

I lean back against the wall a few paces behind the crowd and listen in as Mrs Feltham conducts an impromptu press conference with a skill that would shame some of my police colleagues. It's a pity that she's standing on the steps, the only way up to my flat. Otherwise I'd be able to slip past unnoticed, grab a few things and get out again without anyone knowing I'd been here.

'Spice is a problem everywhere. Just ask the people who have to deal with it. Ask the doctors and nurses. Ask the council workers.'

A young lad with an old-fashioned spiral-bound notebook and pen, standing near the back of the crowd, starts speaking as he turns to face me.

'She's very good, isn't she. Can't see my editor going for . . . shit.'

Well, I was going to be spotted sooner or later. Not perhaps the reaction I was hoping for though. Apart from anything else it's very rude. I smile at him anyway, then push past and start elbowing my way through the herd.

'Excuse me. Coming through. Come on. Out the way, please. Some of us have got homes to go to.'

Perhaps because they've been hanging on Mrs F's every word, the good – and not so good – gentlemen of the press take longer to realise what's happening than they should. I've broken through their ranks before they recognise me. I'm sorely tempted to press on up the stairs and make a run for my front door, but they'll only follow, possibly knocking my elderly neighbour over in the process, and then I'll be stuck in the flat until they go. So instead I put on my best brave face, smile and meet my foe.

'Gentlemen.' I scan the crowd, seeing that it is almost all men, then notice one woman from the BBC near the front. 'Lady. I'm not sure what I've done to warrant such attention. As my dear friend here has told you, there's far more important things to worry about than the slow crumbling of England's class system. Maybe you really would be better off all going to the park to see what's happening to the folk who've fallen through the cracks in these times of austerity.'

Christ, I sound like a bloody politician. It's put my harassers on the back foot though. Only the woman from the Beeb seems unfazed.

'Miss Fairchild. Can you confirm that you were involved in the death of a Mr Gareth Chandler last night?'

'That's Detective Constable Fairchild, and yes, I was there. As you well know. A press release was issued early this morning and the whole incident is currently under investigation.'

'Did you push him under a bus, Connie?'

There are too many faces, pressed too close together, for me to see who asked the question. It was a man, though, naturally enough.

'Do you think I'd be standing here if I had? I can't go into any further details of what is an ongoing investigation, but I can confirm that I'm not currently under suspicion of any wrongdoing. Quite the opposite.'

'Will this incident delay your return to active duties, Con— Detective Constable? That's the best part of half a year you've been taking a pay cheque and not doing any work. Must be nice, eh?'

This voice I recognise, and sure enough, there's my old friend Jonathan Stokes elbowing his way to the front. His parasitic twin Chet leers at me from behind him, another expensive-looking camera at the ready.

'Nice? That's not quite how it feels from here. First you lot hound me for doing my job and now you're going to hound me for not doing it? Make up your mind, why don't you?'

'Will you be staying in the police force, now that your secret's out?'

This last question comes from the back of the crowd, another male voice. I can't see who it is for all the popping camera flashes, but it doesn't really matter.

'I've never made a secret about my background, despite whatever you might have heard. There's plenty of university-educated men and women in the police force, some from backgrounds much like mine. Quite why you all think it's an interesting story baffles me. Now if you don't mind, I'd like to go home and have a little privacy.'

I don't wait for any more questions. They've had more than I was intending to give them already. As I turn and hurry up the stairs, a quick nervous smile and wave to Mrs Feltham by way of thanks, it occurs to me that all those flashes are going to be photographs in tomorrow's papers, on the web, everywhere. My face, for all the world to see. So much for keeping a low profile.

Karen doesn't say much on the drive across town to Euston station. I guess that's fair enough. We've probably both had enough of each other's company.

'You any idea how long you'll be away?' she finally asks as we park in a space reserved for the Transport Police. I've packed light; barely more than a couple of changes of clothes, a washbag with all the essentials. Most of the weight of my rucksack is my laptop and all its associated cables.

'Not really, no. I'll have to see what Professional Standards have to say about the incident. I'm guessing the dash-cam footage they got will be helpful there.'

She fetches my bag from the back seat, hands it to me, and together we walk into the concourse. I can't suppress the nervous shudder that runs through me being out in public like this, and I glance up at the big screen showing news footage, half expecting my face to appear there magnified to the size of an elephant. I've put an old baseball cap on, but it's too gloomy to wear shades without drawing even more attention.

'Hear the word of the Lord. Take Him into your heart!'

I almost jump out of my skin as a young man fairly leaps in front of me. He's thin, his face pocked with acne scars, ginger hair trimmed with the aid of a pudding bowl. When he speaks, I catch the edge of a northern accent in his voice.

'Have you heard the good news?' he asks, his enthusiasm so

genuine it's heartbreaking. Oh, to be so deliciously innocent and naive.

'Not today, mate.' Karen switches into police officer mode with ease, stepping forward to move the young man on. He darts around with all the agility of an Olympic gymnast, producing a glossily printed leaflet which he presses into my hand before bringing both of his together in the briefest of prayers. Then before either of us can say anything more, he's gone. I watch him work through the crowd, identifying other marks to convert, and as I do so, I see more of his kind. They're not all dressed identically, but there's something of a uniform to them that sets them out from the crowd. Pale colours, beige and white where everyone else is dressed in drab greys, dark suits, jeans. Clean, too. It's obvious once you've seen it that they're a tribe.

'Christ, there's dozens of them.' I realise the irony of my casual blasphemy too late, but the concourse is being worked by a group of young Happy Clappies more professionally than any band of chuggers I've ever seen. I realise I've seen them before, too. In the park near my flat, helping the addicts.

'Bloody nuisance, if you ask me. Preying on the delusional, sucking vulnerable people into their weird cults. Can't stand 'em.'

Karen's tone is so angry I stop and look at her. There's clearly something deeper going on here, but my train's leaving soon and I don't fancy staying in London any longer than strictly necessary.

'You sound like you've got personal experience.'

'Don't ask.' She rolls her eyes, the anger evaporating as quickly as it came. 'Come on. Don't want you missing your train.'

We push through the crowds to the ticket barrier, and then there's an awkward pause. I've only known Karen a week or so, but she's gone from hating me to helping me. I'd probably call her a friend, in time.

'Thanks,' is all I can think to say, and it sounds lame. So I add 'and I'm sorry I dragged you into all this.' Lifting up both hands to indicate the world in general, I see I'm still clutching the leaflet handed to me by the young man. Without thinking, I shove it in my coat pocket.

'It'll die down. The press and everything.' Karen sweeps me into a very unprofessional hug, which is as mercifully brief as it is unexpected. 'See you, Con,' she says, then steps away quickly, turns and disappears into the crowd.

17

I'm idly flicking through news stories on my phone, cringing every time I see my name or photograph, when a strange voice interrupts me.

"'Scuse me, miss. You've dropped something.'

Looking up, I see the ticket inspector leaning towards me with a glossy leaflet. At first I can't understand what he means, but then I realise it's the one I was handed in the station. It must have fallen out of my pocket when I took out my phone. For a moment, I consider denying it's mine, but I've been brought up better than that. With a quiet muttered 'Thanks' I take it off him, then show him my ticket. Once he's moved on to the next passenger, I flip open the leaflet to see what all the fuss was about.

It doesn't tell me much, just a bunch of generic feel-good quotes that claim to be from the Bible, but probably aren't. The Church of the Coming Light rings a bell, definitely the same people who run the shelter close to the Danes Estate and were out helping Spice addicts the other day. I'm sure I've seen its charismatic leader on the telly from time to time. The Reverend Doctor Edward Masters is one of those people who pops up on late-night news and political programmes, an outspoken opinion in an ill-fitting suit. Either he's friends with the right producers, or he has very good PR. I've mostly tuned out his holier-than-thou pontificating. Me and religion parted company long ago. I can thank my mother for that.

The name, Masters, sparks a more recent memory, too, and that's when it hits me. This is the man my mother was talking about. No wonder Ben put his foot down when she suggested he officiate at the wedding. And how like my mother to find someone so completely inappropriate, her not-so-subtle way of showing her disapproval at her son's choice of bride. A bald-headed African telly-evangelist is certainly her style though, and the coincidence piques my curiosity.

My phone's not the best thing for internet searches, and the signal keeps dropping every time the train goes through a tunnel, but I pick up enough information on the church to know that it's a mixture of good and bad. It takes people off the streets, keeps them away from drugs, runs soup kitchens and walk-in shelters, but it also veers dangerously close to the sort of cult mentality that doesn't quite square with my C of E definition of Christianity.

Masters himself is something of an enigma. He claims to be from Uganda originally, brought to London as a small boy and taken into care when his mother died while he was still a child. That's one story, at least. Another has him as a Nigerian prince, run out of the country in his late teens and taking refuge in God and England. Whatever his true background, he seems to have made a success of himself and his church. I find endorsements from many a politician, and a photograph of him shaking hands with the previous Commissioner of the Met. Seems he's popular for the work the church does getting folk off the street, which on the face of it is no bad thing. Even so, my inner cynic is primed to be wary of him and sceptical of the claims made for his organisation.

Perhaps unsurprisingly, there's controversy too, in particular a high-profile case a couple of years ago that ended abruptly and unsatisfactorily when the charges were dropped with no explanation. The family of a young girl took the church to court, claiming it had brainwashed her and she had been sexually abused, leading first to an unwanted pregnancy and then to a back-street abortion that had almost killed her. I vaguely recall the story, snippets falling into place as I read down through the news clippings. She'd been dumped outside the same hospital that Dan Jones is now lying in. Scrolling down further, I can't help but raise an eyebrow as the name of Detective Super-intendent Gordon Bailey appears. One of his cases before I joined his team, it would seem.

By the time the tannoy announces we're approaching Kettering station, I've scribbled down a couple of pages' worth of observations in my notebook, as if this were some investigation. I always did find train journeys dull, but there's something else about the Church of the Coming Light that I find fascinating. It would be useful to speak to the reporter who worked on the story, but the name on the byline surprises me. I'd always thought Jonathan Stokes was a born gutter hack, but apparently he's won awards for his investigative journalism in the past, and worked for some of the more reputable broadsheets. Something must have happened for him to fall so far, but I'm not about to ask him. For one thing, I'd rather have root canal surgery without anaesthetic than talk to the man. For another, the train's arrived at the station and it's time to get off.

Aunt Felicity meets me on the other side of the ticket barrier, her welcoming smile turning to a frown as I approach.

'What?' I ask, after a somewhat less awkward embrace than the one I had from Karen Eve earlier.

'You've got that look on your face, Con dear. Something's bothering you.'

I almost show her the leaflet, come right out and ask her who my mother's new religious friend is. Something stops me though. Talking about family always leads to unnecessary tension.

'Nothing. Just checking there aren't any paparazzi hiding in the car park.'

'In Kettering? I doubt it very much.' Aunt Flick laughs, and the moment passes. We talk of inconsequential things all the way back to Harston Magna and Folds Cottage, skirting around the reason I'm back so soon after leaving. It's not until we're in the kitchen, a pot of tea brewing and some freshly-baked biscuits filling the room with their delicious aroma, that I feel I can say what's been on my mind since I spoke to Charlotte in the pub the night her father died.

'I'm going to stay away. From the wedding. It's for the best. It's their big day, and I'd only ruin it for them.'

If I'd been hoping for any protest from my aunt, it doesn't come. For a while she says nothing at all, and I listen to the ticking clock in the kitchen. Studying her face gives me nothing, but then she always used to beat me at cards, too.

'You're right. It's a shame though. Ben will be very upset not to have his big sister there when he makes his vows.' She reaches out a hand more withered than I remember and places it over my own. Aunt Felicity's smile is warm and genuine, but tired. How much of the wedding has she been organising herself? I can't imagine my parents being much use, especially if Ben told my mother where to shove her pastor. And Charlotte's mother is still a nervous wreck, although no doubt her husband's death will have cheered her up a bit.

'I'll make it up to him somehow.'

'I'm sure you will, dear. But what are you going to do in the meantime? I take it they've not given you your job back yet.'

The way she says it, I know it's not a question. It brings to mind Diane Shepherd's words, and DCI Bain's. I'll never be able to work undercover again, that's for sure. Too many people know who I am. Too many of the wrong kind of people.

'I'm going to have to go away again. Hide out for a bit.' I know I'd accepted it was necessary, but it hurts to say it out loud. Aunt Felicity gives my hand another reassuring pat, then starts pouring the tea.

'Will you go back to Newmore? I'm sure Mrs Robertson would be pleased to have some company. That cat of yours, too.'

'I don't think I can. Not now the press are making a story out of the family. That's why I can't come to the wedding either. The paparazzi will just ruin it for everyone if I'm there.'

'They'll probably do their best even without you. Charlotte's not exactly off their radar. I think that's why Ben's gone abroad for a while, just to get away from them.' She picks up the plate and offers me a biscuit. 'So if not Newmore, where will you go?'

'Thought I might visit Edinburgh. It's been a few years since I went back there.'

'Edinburgh? Of course. What a brilliant idea. And you can stay with Rose. She'd love to have you, I'm sure.'

'Rose . . . Yes.' I remember the strange friend of my aunt who was staying at Newmore when I fled there last summer. What did the card say? Antiquarian Books, Occult Curios. I get the feeling there's a lot more to him – her, I remind myself – than that.

'I was going to stay in a B & B.'

'Nonsense. You'll stay with Rose. I'll give her a call while you're out.'

'Out?' I was just about to bite into a biscuit, but now I put it back down on the plate. 'Why would I go out? *Where* would I go out?'

Aunt Felicity smiles at me in a way that reminds me of earlier times I've sat at this table, drinking tea and eating home-made biscuits, asking stupid questions. She has that schoolmistress expression of patience in the face of extreme foolishness.

'Here's the thing, Con dear. I quite understand you not going to your brother's wedding. In the circumstances I'd probably do the same. But I'm not the one who has to be told. And neither is your father. No, I'm afraid you're going to have to swallow your pride and go tell your mother.'

18

The last time I walked through the woods behind Folds Cottage, I was abducted by two ex-special forces goons and taken down to London against my will, all on the orders of the father of the woman my brother is about to marry. Before that, the trees had been my childhood playground, the undergrowth a tangle of rhododendron bushes whose hollowed-out insides formed cavernous halls far more inviting than the one I lived in. Ben and I would spend hours in here, playing the sort of games my mother would most certainly deem unsuitable for young ladies. And then we'd be called home and scolded for our muddy knees and dirtied clothes. Or at least, I would be scolded. Ben usually got off more lightly.

I don't know when the woods stopped being a playground. Probably about the same time I began to understand that my little brother was destined to get all the good things in life, and I'd have to put up with being somebody's wife. I knew very early on that I didn't want to be somebody's anything, and maybe it was those games and those muddy knees that made me the woman I am.

There's still plenty of light left in the afternoon, the days beginning their slow lengthening towards summer now. The buds are starting to break on the trees too, pushing leaves out that soon will fill this place with dappled shade. For now it's a land of shadows, silent save for the distant roar of the motorway and the occasional startle of deer. I follow a path slick with last autumn's fallen leaves, winding a route towards the village and the hall that is my parents' cold home.

I thought I might feel something, pushing through the old iron gate and stepping from the wilds into the manicured perfection of the garden. There are memories everywhere, of course. I learned to swim, albeit accidentally at first, in the ornamental lake. Skirting round its southern edge, I can see the massive, slow bodies of the carp searching for food. They terrified me as a child, ancient dinosaurs that might strip the flesh from my bones. Or was that a horrific tale made up by my father in a vain attempt to keep me in line?

The formal gardens are much the same as they would have been when Capability Brown designed the whole estate in the eighteenth century. It used to fascinate me that he might have overseen the planting of some of the trees still here. So much time has passed, and yet so little has changed. I took this all for granted growing up, thought everyone had gardens this size, filled with enormous and ancient trees. Didn't everyone have a wild garden where bamboos and other exotic plants grew? A lot of the girls at St Humbert's did, and while I didn't necessarily get on with them, I found some solace in our shared experience. Edinburgh University was something of an eye-opener; the Met doubly so.

It doesn't take a genius with a psychology doctorate to know that I'm wasting time, doing anything I can to avoid the inevitable meeting. I don't want to be here so much it's like the hall is a negative pole on a magnet and I'm the same. We repel each other with a force that only grows as the distance between us shrinks. It weighs a lot more than me, has been here for centuries. And so I circle its golden sandstone walls and lifeless windows, searching for an excuse to flee.

None comes, and finally I find myself at the front door. We

never used this, except at Christmas when the entire village would come round after Midnight Mass, drink the cheap wine my father had bought in for the occasion and maybe sing a carol or two. Our entrance was at the back, through the boot room and into the pantry, then the kitchen. As children we were rarely allowed into the posh part of the house and as teenagers we didn't want to. I don't live here any more though, and I'm not expected. It seems only right I present myself correctly. Clearly someone else has had the same idea, as a shiny Mercedes with blacked out windows sits on the gravel, its engine pinking gently as it cools.

I've heard the doorbell before, pulled the old brass lever many a time. It more than anything brings back memories of happier, more innocent times. The sound jangles away for a few moments somewhere deep within the house, and it's as if the entire world holds its breath awaiting an answer. Or is it just me?

Something shifts in the air, a change in the pressure, the slightest flicker of movement seen through the glass inner doors. And then the lock clacks, the ancient iron door handle drops and the door itself swings open.

'Constance, what a surprise. We were about to have some tea. Do come in.'

With hindsight the car should have been a giveaway. Nobody local would ever park out the front, so whoever it belongs to must be either visiting from afar or important. Or both. I can't see anyone in the hallway, and have no great desire to meet whoever my mother is entertaining.

'I can't stay long. Just needed to have a quick word about the wedding.'

'Nonsense. There's always time for a cup of tea. Isn't that what your aunt Felicity always says?'

There's a hint of chiding in my mother's voice that takes me straight back to my childhood. But then she's always had that effect on me. Reluctantly, I follow her inside.

I've never much liked Harston Magna Hall. It's too big, too draughty. Too damp and cold, especially at this time of year. When Ben and I were growing up, before both of us were parcelled off to boarding school like so much inconvenient baggage, we'd spend most of our time in the attic, where the servants' quarters used to be. No servants any more, unless you count those nannies, and Mrs Grundy the housekeeper. The attic rooms were damp and cold too, but at least they were drawn to a human scale. The grand entrance hall here is so big you could fit a sizeable London terrace house in it and still have room to park the car. Mother walks over to the oak sideboard that sits along one wall. In a normal house it's where you might drop your wallet and keys on stepping inside. Here it's a repository for ancient duelling pistols, a collection of antique silver bowls that should really be in a museum, and a slightly battered spectacle case. It's this that she picks up, popping it open to reveal frames that are almost cool in a retro way. Thin lenses with no prescription; I'd quite forgotten her mentioning them.

'Here. Not as if I need them any more. There was a fashion for them once, but now I need the real thing, these aren't much use to me.'

'I . . . Thank you.' I take them, unable to stop myself from sliding them on. They're heavy, but not uncomfortable.

'Come through. There's someone I'd like you to meet, since you're here.'

The car. I'd almost forgotten. I slip off the spectacles and shove them back in their case. Mother is almost halfway to the drawing-room door, so I have to speak more loudly than I'd like.

'There's something I need to say first. I've decided it will be better if I don't come to the wedding.'

She stops, turns to face me. She looks almost sad more than angry. This isn't what I was expecting.

'I'll be leaving tomorrow morning. First thing.'

'Leaving? But you just got here, girl.' Ah, that's the Mother I remember.

'I know, and the press will find me here quicker than you can say "*Daily Mail*". I've no intention of upstaging my brother at his wedding, or of bringing the wrong kind of attention to it.'

Another long, narrow stare, and this time I can almost hear the thoughts tumbling through her mind.

'Where will you go?'

'Best if I don't say.'

She holds her hands together across her stomach in the way she did the last time I saw her. It's a defensive posture, but it's something else too. A way of hiding the slight tremor that shakes her entire body. It's cold in the hall, always is, and she insists on wearing the thinnest of clothes regardless. Even so I wonder whether there's not more to it than that.

'Very well. It's your decision, even if it will break poor Benevolence's heart. You always were one to think about yourself first. Come now.' She shakes her head once in the direction of the smaller drawing-room door, and I finally have to concede to follow. As these things go, it could have been a lot worse. We've not actually shouted at each other yet.

The temperature inside the room is considerably warmer than the grand hall, thanks to a roaring fire in the grate. I scarcely notice it, distracted by the figure who hauls himself from the depths of one of the sofas as I enter. He is enormous, bulging out of his ill-fitting black suit as if he put it on whilst still a much smaller man. The hand he extends towards me is the size of a toy dog, and just as unfriendly. I can hear my mother making introductions in her horribly formal manner, but I don't need them. I know who he is. I read all about him on the train here this morning. He's the founder and leader of the Church of the Coming Light.

The Reverend Doctor Edward Masters.

'Lady Constance, what a pleasure it is to meet you. I have read much about your exploits in the papers. It would seem you are quite the resourceful young woman.'

Larger than life already, Masters swells as he speaks. He's a great bear of a man, everything about him bulges: his neck squeezing from a collar that must be uncomfortably tight; his hands big enough to crush my head; his eyes popping from a face like a balloon filled with water. Standing to one side, my mother looks tiny in comparison. And frail. Now that I've noticed the slight tremor that shakes her frame from time to time, I can't ignore it. How long has she been ill? Aunt Flick never mentioned anything, and neither did Charlotte. Then again, it would be just like my mother to suffer in silence.

'We do what we can.' I extract my hand from his massive grip, wondering how easily I can escape this room, this house.

'Each of us has our calling, do we not? God has charged me with bringing His word to the masses, showing them the light.' Masters looms over me, and the look on his face changes in an instant. I've had that look before, usually from men sitting on the wrong side of the table in a police interview room, their lawyer by their side. It's a look that women get every day on buses, in the street, at work. An assessment of your worth as an object. In the space of a heartbeat I've gone from person to thing, and I can't understand why.

'It all sounds very worthy.' The words are out, liberally coated in sarcasm, before I can stop them. I hurry to cover my mistake as my mother draws in a sharp breath. 'Actually, I met a group of your . . . what would you call them, acolytes? Followers?' I manage to stop myself from saying 'cult members'. 'Just the other day. They were tending to some drug addicts, taking them off to a shelter for the night.'

'See. This is exactly the kind of good work the reverend doctor does.' My mother clasps her hands together like a little girl as she steps in between us. 'Come, Constance. Sit down. Have some tea.'

I can't think of any good reason why my mother would be hospitable, so there must be some ulterior motive to her show of kindness. She wants something, and it has to do with Masters. Well, if she wants me as an ally to persuade Ben to change his mind, that's not happening.

'I'm really sorry, but I have to go. It was nice to meet you.' I tilt my head a fraction in the direction of the reverend doctor. He mimics the action, perhaps unintentionally, and all the while I have that feeling of being sized up like a piece of meat. Then almost as quickly as it came on, the look is gone, and he is all smiles again.

'That is a shame. I should have liked the opportunity to get to know you better, Lady Constance.' Masters bows slightly. 'I feel sure that we will meet again, and soon.'

I would like to think that he's just being polite, but there's something about the way he says it that feels all too prophetic. I've had run-ins with unpleasant people before, and Masters gives me that same skin-crawling sensation. Or maybe it's just the setting, this house to which I'd hoped never to return. My mother with her slight tremor and judgmental glower. Whatever it is, I don't want to be around it any more.

'I'll be in touch,' I say to them both, and before either can respond I turn and flee.

19

It's been too long since I was last in Edinburgh. I've hurried by on my way further north a couple of times, sure, but never taken the time to stop. I could tell myself that I'm simply taking the opportunity of being on suspension with full pay to go back to some of my old haunts; I studied at the university here for four years, after all. That's what I'll tell the press if they catch up with me, but I'm not fooling anyone, least of all myself.

The city's changed a lot in the past ten years, and yet it's scarcely changed at all. They've finally finished digging up the roads for the trams, but now they seem to be busy demolishing the big shopping centre at the end of Princes Street, no doubt to replace it with an even bigger one. The sky is almost as full of cranes as London.

Scotland is cold, but drier than drizzly London and the Home Counties I've left behind. It's not cold enough to stop my trusty old Volvo's overheating problem whenever it goes slower than forty miles an hour, though, so inching through slow-moving traffic on North Bridge is a strain on my nerves. If the satnav on my phone is right, then I've not far to go, but it's a test to see which will give out first, the engine or my nerves.

I had a boyfriend who shared a tenement flat just off Leith Walk, all those years ago. The area wasn't the best even then, but cheap rent can help you put up with a lot of things. Money seems to be seeping into this part of the city now though, if the expensive cars in the resident permit-holder-only parking bays are anything to go by. It used to be rusty old bangers back when Den lived here, some without all of their wheels. My Volvo would have felt quite at home.

My first thought when I finally arrive at my destination is one of relief that the car is still running, even if the noisy whir of fans working overtime carries on even when I've turned off the ignition. My second thought is that I never realised such big old terraced houses existed in Leith, sandwiched between the tenements and hidden down back streets. My third thought is that I must have got the address wrong. It's true that my aunt's old Edinburgh friend was very strange, although friendly enough on the one occasion I met her before. But surely she can't live in such a grand place as this?

I start to get my bearings as I lock up the car, cross the road and enter the small courtyard. This building must back on to Leith Walk itself, at the bottom end closest to the old docks and warehouses. Chances are it was a merchant's house a couple of hundred years ago, and I expect to find some kind of multiple button entry system at the front door, access to the many flats this place must have been split into. There's only an old brass plate with a single polished button recessed in the middle. No name to suggest who it is that lives here.

The door opens before I even have a chance to hear what kind of bell might announce my arrival, and I'm confronted with the person I've come to visit. I knew deep down who she was, what she was. I've met her before, and that first meeting was a shock too. Even so, I had somehow managed to forget the most obvious thing about Rose, that for all she might be a woman, she had been born in the body of a man.

'Lady Constance, how delightful to see you again. Please, do come in.'

★ ★ ★

Rose's Edinburgh home is undeniably impressive. It rises over three floors, centred around a wide hall that is twice the size of my entire London flat, lit by an overhead skylight. Stone staircases lead to broad landings, and as I follow her up to an enormous living room on the first floor, I lose count of the number of doors. Big though it is, every available space seems to be taken up with what I can only describe as 'stuff'. Old oil paintings on the walls show a few men but mostly women who must be ancestors of the current inhabitant, given the remarkable facial similarities down the generations. Antique side tables are covered in things: lacquered Japanese puzzle boxes; leather-bound books piled haphazardly as if whoever was reading them put them down and forgot where they were; vases that are probably hundreds of years old and certainly priceless; and cats.

I've been to houses where little old ladies live with legions of moggies. One memorable call-out when I was still in uniform was to a north London ground-floor apartment where the single pensioner had died unnoticed. Some months earlier, judging by the condition in which her army of cats had left her. In my experience, houses where the cats outnumber the humans tend to take on a distinctive and not entirely pleasant aroma. Maybe it's the size of this place, or Rose has found a way of controlling her feline army. The scent is there, but it's not overwhelming, competing as it does with dust, woodsmoke and a touch of damp.

'Felicity told me you were coming. I'm so pleased you did. I get so few visitors these days.'

The sitting room, like the rest of the house I've seen so far, is cluttered almost to the point of being claustrophobic, despite its high ceilings with their traditionally Scottish ornate cornice-work. It's getting dark outside, but I wouldn't be able to tell if I'd not just come in, as heavy velvet curtains hang over the huge bay window. Along with the cats and the general air of living somewhere that hasn't changed in over a hundred years, it hardly surprises me that she gets few visitors.

'I was going to check into a B & B, but Aunt Flick wouldn't have anything of it. I don't want to be an imposition.'

'Nonsense, Lady Constance. It's no trouble at all. But I must confess I am intrigued as to why you have chosen to come back to Edinburgh now. Is it really just the scurrilous lies the press are printing about you and your family?'

'That's one reason. Quite a good one, I think.'

'Of course. And I'm sure the heat will die down in time, my dear. Tea?'

I'm trained as a detective. Noticing things is second nature. But even so I could have sworn that the tray with elegant china teapot and cups, sugar bowl and jug of milk had not been sitting on the low table in front of Rose's chair until she mentioned it. And yet, there it is.

'Thank you. And please, call me Con. "Lady Constance" is what those horrible tabloid hacks call me.'

'Of course, Con.' Rose smiles as she pours tea and then offers a slice of cake. I left very early this morning, and drove all the way north without stopping. It's been a hectic few days with minimal sleep and I struggle to hide my yawn.

'Do you have any plans while you're here? Other than hiding away from the press, that is?' Rose asks after she's watched me drink some tea and eat some cake. I consider keeping my real reason for being in Edinburgh to myself, but then it occurs to me that she probably already knows exactly what I'm up to. Either Aunt Felicity has told her, or she's divined it through talking to the spirits or seen it in her crystal ball or something.

'There's someone I need to talk to, if she'll talk to me, that is.' I tell her about Daniel Jones running away from home, about how his mother wouldn't talk to the local police but might speak to me. To give her credit, she doesn't tell me I'm being a fool.

'You may well be right. I have some small knowledge of the

boys in blue.' Rose smiles at some joke only she knows. 'Well, it's the detectives mostly, but you know what I mean. They're not the worst, far from it, but they're overworked and under-staffed like so many. It's hardly surprising they're not going to put their best man on a task like that.'

I can't help noticing that she said 'best man', not 'best men' or even 'best officers', and it occurs to me that she's thinking of someone in particular. Before I can ask who, Rose speaks again.

'But you'll not be heading out to see Mrs Jones this evening, will you.' It's more of a statement than a question.

'No. She lives in Broxburn somewhere. I've got the address. Thought I'd be better off looking for it in daylight.'

'Very wise.' Rose smooths the front of her tweed skirt with hands that could lay bricks all day, then rises effortlessly to her feet. I find myself doing the same.

'I'm afraid something came up this afternoon that I'll have to attend to this evening. Nothing to concern yourself with, but it's a nuisance all the same. I had so wanted to greet you properly, La— Con. And treat you to a welcome supper. Alas, you'll have to fend for yourself tonight, and the feast will have to wait until tomorrow.'

I know that she is being sincere, even as her words sound like someone of advanced age trying to politely tell a youngster that they're a bit of an imposition and had better not expect too much. I'm also secretly relieved, as the thought of spending an entire evening with Rose is a daunting prospect. Nevertheless, they taught us manners at St Humbert's School for Young Ladies, or at least beat a semblance of them into us, so I do my best to hide my lack of disappointment.

'That's such a shame. I do hope it's nothing too serious, but please, you don't need to do anything for me.'

'Are you sure, my dear? That's very gracious.'

'It's nothing, really. I'll be fine. A bed to sleep in is more than

I could hope for. And it's not as if I don't know Edinburgh. I lived her for four years, after all.'

'Well, that's settled then. Let me show you your room, and where everything is.'

And with that she sweeps from the room, leaving me to follow in her wake like a lost, little child.

20

It would be very easy to get used to this kind of lifestyle, even if I know I'm just staying here for a short while. Rose's house in Leith is vast. The guest room she showed me to when I first arrived is sumptuously appointed, like I imagine a suite at the Ritz might have looked in the 1920s. Its large bay window opens out over the tiny courtyard, the street where my elderly Volvo is parked, and then north across the rooftops of Trinity and Newhaven towards the Firth of Forth and Fife. I've set up my laptop on a desk that looks suspiciously like it might once have graced a private room at Versailles, with a surprisingly comfortable chair to match, although as yet I've not done much more than turn it on and surf the net. Despite the entire house looking like a film set from a period drama, there is electricity and even Wi-Fi. And a wonderful absence of any journalists or paparazzi photographers camped outside.

For all her strangeness, Rose is an easy person to get on with. It doesn't take long at all to stop thinking of her as anything other than 'she', despite her appearance. She asks nothing of me, although I can tell she desperately wants to ask what it is I'm up to. Instead, she gives me the space I didn't know I needed and the time to gather my frayed nerves back together.

The first evening, after my long drive north from Harston Magna, I went to bed much earlier than I would even consider in London. I slept so well that night it was gone ten in the morning before I woke, but if Rose thought me lazy she said nothing. When I walked into the kitchen, she was standing at the stove with a pinafore around her ample waist, stirring away at a pot of perfect porridge. Coffee and breakfast and more chat, before she announced she needed to go and meet with some clients of hers, and that I should treat the house as my own while she was out. It was only when she appeared again much later that I realised I'd spent the whole day just lazing around, browsing through her fascinating and extensive library and making endless cups of tea. I hadn't even been outside, and yet when I retired to bed that evening I once more slept like the dead.

And now another day has passed without the worry of being targeted by the media. Another day of wandering the halls, look-ing at the endless strange objects that fill every available space. Another day of being watched by the legion of cats who come and go as if this house is as much theirs as it is Rose's. I came to Edinburgh intending to seek out Dan Jones's mother, to try to find out what kind of person he was and what life he lived before running away to seek his fate in London. And yet for two days now I've not even felt like stepping outside.

'You look much better than when you arrived, my dear.' Rose is sitting at a kitchen table not so different to the one in Aunt Felicity's house four hundred miles south of here. The pot of tea she insists on pouring herself sits between us, jug of milk and bowl of unnecessary sugar beside it. When we have known each other seven years, I'm told, only then will I be allowed to pour the tea myself in her house. It's a quaint little superstition I find easy to accept, since Aunt Flick is exactly the same.

'I hadn't realised quite how on edge I was. This house has a very calming effect. Sometimes I feel like I could sleep for a week.'

Rose tilts her head slightly, a warm smile on her perfectly made-up face. 'You youngsters are all the same. Burning the candle at both ends, bright as you like, and never a thought for what it's doing to you.'

'Youngster? Nobody's called me that since I turned thirty.'

'Nevertheless, you are. And you do. You take the weight of the world on your shoulders. That's admirable, but not always wise. This house likes you. I thought it would. You will always find peace here, sanctuary even. Please, use it whenever you need.'

It's such an odd thing to say, I find myself staring at the old lady for a while. Then I realise my mouth is hanging slightly open, possibly in anticipation of the teacup I'm holding halfway between it and the tabletop, possibly in surprise. I try not to make too much of a clicking sound as I close it.

'I'm teasing. My apologies.' Rose's eyes glint mischievously, much like I remember Aunt Flick's eyes glinting when she urged me and Ben to do things our parents most certainly disapproved of.

'But I mean it when I say you look well. Rested even. Perhaps it's time for you to renew your quest.'

The way she says it makes me think I'm in some kind of Arthurian legend. It wouldn't surprise me to find a spare suit of armour in one of the many cluttered rooms in the house. Possibly an enchanted sword too.

'There were one or two things I was going to look into while I was here,' I concede. 'Might have to wait until tomorrow now.' I glance up at the window and the encroaching darkness outside, unsurprised to find a cat as black as the night staring at me from the windowsill with luminous yellow eyes.

Rose tops up both our teacups even though mine is still mostly full. 'Why don't you get out a bit before then? Stretch your legs a little and remind yourself what the city looks like. Take the air, you know?'

Despite her words, it doesn't sound as if she's trying to get rid of me so much as giving me permission to leave the house unattended. Until then, I'd not even considered stepping outside, and it's only at that moment I realise that the house had trapped me in a strange spell. If Rose hadn't mentioned it, I might happily have stayed inside for weeks. Longer, even. It's unsettling, and yet at the same time I feel very safe here.

'That's not a bad idea. Think I'll do that. Revisit some of my old uni haunts.'

Rose lays her large hands flat on the table, either side of her cup, then levers herself upright as if getting her bulk standing requires more effort than her legs can manage right now. It's almost impossible to tell how old she is, except that she knew my aunt as a little child, was friends with my grandfather and so must be nearer seventy than sixty at the very least. In that moment she seems all of those years and more, but it passes as swiftly as a frown turned into a smile.

'Splendid,' she says. 'And don't worry about coming home late. The door is always open to those who belong here.'

Edinburgh has that sense of crawling slowly out of a long winter about it. The nights are still dark, but it's not too cold as I stroll up Leith Walk towards Princes Street. Cranes tower over the building site that once used to be the St James Centre and New St Andrews House, like mother birds feeding the brood that will grow into whatever new retail experience is planned for the area. I skirt around it swiftly, heading for the Guildford Arms and a proper pint of Scottish ale, but the crowd spilling out of the doorway deters me. Popularity was ever its own worst enemy. A quick glance at my watch confirms the after-work crowd have just arrived, so maybe I'd be better off drinking elsewhere.

Crossing over North Bridge, I take out my phone and flick through the contacts. Ten years since I graduated from the university, there's not many people I know still living here.

Certainly none I feel a great urge to share a drink with. On the other hand, there's nothing wrong with drinking alone, as long as you don't make a habit of it.

I find it good to walk these old streets again. My legs are full of energy, as if I'd rested weeks, not the couple of days spent cooped up in Rose's strange mansion. Even though the city is choked with cars, the air is somehow cleaner than London. The cold clears my head and makes it easier to think. The breeze blowing in off the Forth is strong enough to disperse the pollution, but not so brisk I'd risk losing my hat. If I was wearing one, that is.

I'm almost all the way there before I realise where it is my feet are taking me. My final year at the university, I lived in a tenement in Bruntsfield, sharing with a couple of postgrad students I hardly ever saw. The nearest pub was a bit of a shithole, but it had the twin benefits of being close by and selling half-decent beer. As I get closer, I begin to recognise little things that haven't changed even in the decade since I left. The long-dead houseplant on a windowsill, dry and brown; the frame of a bicycle chained to the railings outside a front door, its wheels and saddle long gone; the broken neon sign in the window of a guest house that reads 'vac ies' at the moment, but sometimes 'o vac ies' if it's feeling festive. The communal bins still take up too much of the pavement, overflowing with rubbish and piled high with seagull-ripped binbags, but there is one difference I can't help but notice. There are cafés and shops where I remember empty windows painted out white. People cluster in groups around the entrances, chatting. There's a vibrancy to the place I don't remember from when I left. The city feels alive.

Even the Rothesay Arms has had a lick of paint, which surprises me. The usual band of die-hard smokers huddle at the front door, wreathed in smoke and silence as they pay their respects to the Gods of tobacco. I dart through quickly, not wanting to breathe their air, and enter a room that's at once familiar and utterly alien.

It was always a bit of a dive, the sort of place where students came to buy weed. I liked its dark corners and the fact that the locals didn't bat an eye at a woman drinking pints. Or indeed a woman drinking at all. The corners are still dark, but the place has been done up. Where once there were old wooden stools and wheelback chairs, now there are more comfortable padded seats in what I think is dark-green velour of some kind. It's hard to tell as the place is rammed. Not quite as bad as the Guildford, but busy for a midweek evening. Still very much a student part of town, judging by the clientele. And this lot clearly didn't get the memo about millennials giving up booze.

'Pint of Deuchars, please,' I shout at the woman behind the bar once I've elbowed my way to the front. She doesn't look old enough to be serving alcohol, but then students started looking young five years ago too. I've taken my drink, handed over a fiver and got a lot more back from it in change than I would in London when the first unwanted attention arrives.

'You looking to score, pet?'

At least, I think that's what he says. It's not easy to hear over the din, and my brain's more attuned to the London accent these days, even if I've spent a few months hidden away in darkest, wettest Perthshire recently. I focus on the young man in front of me, not quite sure what to make of him. He's dressed the same as the rest of the crowd in here, but that doesn't mean much. There's something of the weasel about the way his eyes dart around the room, never settling on me for more than a second at a time. Furtive, suspicious. My well-honed detective instincts don't need much poking to know he's bad news.

'You what?'

'I can hook you up, ken?' He nods in the direction of my pint. 'Beer's fine, but you need something else to take the edge off, no?'

I'm about to tell him to piss off, in the nicest possible way since he doesn't appear to have recognised me. But before I can say anything, a hand lands squarely on his shoulder and he's spun around away from me. Following the arm that's attached to the hand, I see a woman perhaps five years younger and six inches shorter than me. I wouldn't mess with her despite either of those advantages. For one thing she's got 'cop' written all over her plain-clothes face, and my would-be dealer friend can see it as clearly as I can. It's hard to tell over the hubbub, but I swear he actually goes 'meep', before departing at speed and leaving me face to face with my would-be saviour.

'Constance Fairchild, isn't it.'

I can't help but hear the lack of question mark, so I smile, shrug. 'It's a fair cop.'

She frowns at the joke, then half smiles. 'Detective Constable Harrison. I think we should talk.'

21

It's not as if I can really refuse, and so far Detective Constable Harrison has been very understanding, so I follow her through the crowd to a small booth where another young woman sits, jealously guarding a couple of half-drunk pints. She stares up at me with curious eyes, then shuffles to make room for her friend. I take the indicated seat opposite, saying nothing.

'Someone with a suspicious mind might think you were here for less than honest reasons,' Harrison says once she's realised I'm not going to be the first to break. 'How is it you know our old pal Derrick there?' She flicks her head in the direction of the bar and the spotty youth desperately trying to peddle drugs to anyone who stands still for long enough.

'Is that his name? I can honestly say I've never met him before. I only came in here for a drink.'

It occurs to me that DC Harrison hasn't actually shown me a warrant card, and neither has she bothered to introduce me to her friend. I only entertain the thought that they're not police for a couple of seconds though. Harrison might as well be wearing uniform, but I'm less sure about the other one. She's more casually dressed, for one thing, and her blonde hair is too long, even if it is tied back in a neat braid.

'Con Fairchild.' I reach out and offer her my hand. 'Since Harrison here's not going to.'

She looks momentarily surprised, glancing sideways at her

friend. Then she grins and accepts my hand. 'Manda. Manda. Parsons. Thought I recognised you the moment you stepped in. You running away from the papers?'

'Sort of. I kind of hoped nobody would know who I was up here. So much for that plan.'

'Are you staying in the city long?' Harrison asks. I can hear the unspoken 'you should really have reported in with us' in her voice. She's not overtly hostile, but I get the feeling I've spoiled something here. I'm just not sure what.

'A week or so, probably. Depends on whether the tabloids track me down or not. Hopefully they'll find someone else to pester soon enough. I'd quite like to get back to work. Been off too long already.'

'That's got to suck big time, having a camera shoved in your face wherever you go. And it's not as if you're on *Strictly* or anything. Just doing your job.'

I've decided I like Manda. She's much more welcoming than Harrison, whose frown has turned into a scowl. At least it's directed at her drinking companion rather than me. No doubt being friendly wasn't part of the plan.

'Usually more than one camera. It can be a bit of a scrum.' I remember the scene just a couple of days ago on the pavement outside my apartment block. It's hard to believe the frenzy now, but it was all too real when it happened. 'So you're both Police Scotland, then.'

Manda makes a mock horrified face. 'God no. I work in forensics. Janie's the upstanding member of the community.'

I look between the two of them, so different physically, and yet obviously comfortable in each other's company. It's been a while since I lived here, and she's not really said all that much yet, but Harrison has a broader accent than her friend. Local working class. Manda speaks with a more rounded, softer brogue. She's not as defensive, either.

'So you're really just up here to keep a low profile?' Harrison says finally. 'You've nothing else to do? Not planning on poking your nose in anywhere?'

I shrug. 'Might do a bit of sightseeing. Might just revisit old haunts like this place.'

The look on the detective constable's face is one of strained credulity. 'And you're staying where?'

'Place down on Leith Walk. Big old house. It's—'

'You know Madame Rose?' Harrison's entire posture changes in an instant. 'How on earth?'

'Madame' has me a bit perplexed, but I'll take common ground wherever I can find it.

'I was going to say the same thing. She's an old friend of the family, apparently. I only met her briefly, last year. My aunt's known her all her life though.'

It's almost as if I've passed a test I didn't know I was taking. Harrison's stiff shoulders relax, but Manda looks puzzled.

'Madame Rose?' she asks. 'The strange old wifey who does the fortune telling?'

That's a new one on me. 'I thought she dealt in old books and weird antiques.'

'She does both,' Harrison says. 'And has a habit of getting involved in things she shouldn't have anything to do with. The boss seems to like her though, so I guess she's OK. Once you get past the whole transgender thing.'

'It took me by surprise first time I met her, I'll agree. But we're all calling her "she", so that's something. What's all this "Madame", though? I just know her as Rose.' And it hits me as I say so that it's true. I don't even know her surname, and for some unaccountable reason I've never thought to ask.

'That's what she calls herself. Least, that's what the boss told me.' Harrison's puzzled frown suggests she's having much the same thoughts as I am. 'Never really questioned it before.'

'Well, you two can puzzle it out, since you're both detectives.' Manda shuffles to the end of her seat and stands. 'I'm off to the bar. Want another, Con?'

I was only going to spend a half hour or so in the pub. Just long enough for a pint, see the old place, and then probably walk half the way home before opting for a taxi instead. It's much later when I step out into the cold night air, Harrison and her flatmate Manda close behind. I'm glad I worked out they were just flatmates before putting my foot in it by assuming more to their relationship. That could have been embarrassing.

'You want to come up for a coffee?' Manda asks as we all start walking in the same direction. Then she gets the giggles. I suspect she's had more to drink than I have.

'Thanks, but I'd best be getting back. Don't want to find out you're living in my old flat or something either. There's way too much coincidence going on in my life right now.'

'Number thirty. Top floor left.' Harrison points at the side street we're approaching.

'Thirty-two. Top floor right. Thank Christ for a party wall, eh?'

I leave the two of them pondering that, and set off down the hill towards the Meadows. It seems better than drawn-out good-byes. The night has deepened, cooler air condensing into a fog. What was that word for it? Haar, that's right. Rolling in off the Forth and blanketing the city for days on end. Not something I'd missed, to be honest, although the Northamptonshire fogs could be thick enough to bounce off sometimes.

Many thoughts batter around my beer-fuzzed head as I walk back towards Rose's house. Not least the woman herself. I know Edinburgh's a lot smaller than London, but it seems oddly suspicious that the pub I visit just happens to be frequented by someone else who knows her, even though that pub is on the opposite side of the city. Part of me feels like I've been set up for that meeting, but I can't make the logic work. Even I didn't know I was going to go back to my old local, so how could 'Madame' Rose? She's a fortune teller and reader of tarots, apparently, so maybe she consulted the cards. That makes as much sense as anything.

By the time I reach Leith Walk and turn down the side street that will take me to the house, all fuzziness has gone, and I'm starving. There's a good fish and chip shop not far from here, but I don't think my host would be too pleased at me trailing the smell of brown sauce into her elegant home. Much less a pickled egg and haggis supper. Instead, I take my haul back to my car, and sit with the engine running and the heaters turned up to full while I eat. I know I'll regret the can of Irn-Bru, this late in the evening. It's a tradition though.

Rose is waiting for me in the hallway as I enter, and I can't help but wonder if she's not been standing there for hours, perfectly positioned in the shadows to scare the living crap out of me.

'Did you enjoy your evening?' She phrases it as a question, and yet somehow I know it's not meant to be answered. And when she follows up with 'Have you had anything to eat? I can rustle up an omelette if you're hungry,' I know she can smell the vinegar on my breath. I've cleaned my hands with a couple of wet wipes from the car, but even so I wipe them on my front in a manner my mother would describe as most unlady-like.

'I'm fine, thanks. Met a friend of yours, actually. Detective Constable Harrison?'

I'm studying her face for any tell that she knew this would happen, but I'd be as well looking at a mannequin. The make-up conceals all, and even her smile is inscrutable.

'Janie? How wonderful. She's a fine officer.' Rose clasps her hands together over her ample bosom. 'But it's late, is it not? We should both try to get some rest, I think. Tomorrow will be a busy day.'

'It will?' I have things planned, but there's no way my hostess can know about them, surely. And I get the feeling they are not what she's talking about.

'Indeed it will, my dear. I've had word from your aunt, and a short letter from your mother. Lady Angela and I don't often communicate, which makes me think the situation is far more grave than even I had imagined.'

Maybe it's the beer, maybe it's the hastily consumed haggis supper. It could even be the Irn-Bru, but whatever it is, I feel as if I've strayed into some amateur dramatic society melodrama. I am feeling tired though, so the caffeine hasn't kicked in yet, or the sugar.

'Grave?' I ask. 'I'm not sure I understand.'

'The press, my dear. How they are hounding you, making it impossible for you to carry out your duties as an officer of the law. But no matter. I will help you where I can. Here. Your mother sent this.' Rose puts a large hand into the pocket of her tweed jacket and pulls out a battered old spectacle case. I'd quite forgotten about it, must have left it behind when I met Masters. How unlike my mother to be so thoughtful as to send them on. I open up the case, not sure whether to expect a note or not. There isn't one, just those same old spectacles with their clear lenses and timeless lack of fashionability. Sliding them on feels like pulling on a disguise. From Superman to Clark Kent.

'Very fetching.' Rose takes a step back and tilts her head the better to see me. 'Now go get some rest and I'll see you for breakfast tomorrow. Eight o'clock sharp. Then we can both go into town and do some shopping. I know just the place.'

I do as I'm told. I can't not. It's like I'm a little child again, only without the tantrums. Upstairs, my room is tidy, the bed turned down as if this was a posh hotel and even more inviting. Washed and pyjamaed, it's only as I'm reaching over to switch off the light that I realise I never asked Rose about her name.

22

Going to town with Rose reminds me horribly of being taken to London by my mother when I was a little girl. Then it was to buy my uniform and everything else I'd need for my first term at St Humbert's, and we visited a succession of tiny little shops run by elderly ladies who moved very slowly and fetched everything from the back, unpacking boxes, showing their contents, and then meticulously folding them and putting them away again. I remember the early excitement at going to the big city slowly ebbing away until I was simply bored, and embarrassed by the attention. And horrified by the dowdiness of the clothes I was expected to wear, too.

Rose takes me to remarkably similar shops, and the clothes she selects for me would make my teenage self scream and rebel. At least now I can remind myself that this is a disguise. Its entire purpose is to not be me, and these unfashionable clothes are relatively cheap, although nothing seems to have a price tag on it. Rose's presence brings out the philanthropist in each of the shopkeepers we encounter. Either that or we've fallen through a time warp into the early eighties. That might explain some of the fashions, too.

And finally we enter the last place on the list, the wig maker. It's brighter than the other shops, but still feels like something from a bygone era. The lady behind the counter greets Rose like an old friend, and they chat for what feels like an age before finally turning to the matter at hand – me.

'I had in mind something a bit past the shoulders, full and flowing.'

Rose sits me in a chair almost like one in an old-fashioned hairdresser's. There's a mirror directly in front of me, and I watch her reflection and that of the sales assistant as they discuss my short-cropped locks. I've not quite gone the full shaven head yet, although I will if it means I'll not be recognised.

'We could get a good match to this red. Is it natural?' The sales assistant very gingerly takes some strands between her fingers and rubs them together. Of course there's no dye in my hair, but her surprise is amusing to see. 'Oh my. What an unusual shade.'

'I was thinking maybe something to make me look a bit older?' I recall my conversation with my mother. 'Perhaps a mix of brown and grey.'

'Yes, yes. I think we can do something.' The assistant gives my hair a last fondle, which I suspect is quite unconscious, then hurries off to the back of the shop. I listen to the sound of drawers being pulled out and pushed back in again, cupboard doors being opened and closed, and then she's back. Draped over one arm are what look like several dead animals, but with a deftness borne of many years practice, she whips one up into a shape more like what I'm expecting, then brings it down over my head with a flourish.

'Of course, this'll look better with a wig cap on first, but it should give you the idea.' She smooths the locks over my head with firm but gentle fingers, then fluffs up the hair so it spreads over my shoulders. It feels strange, warm on my scalp as if I'm wearing a woolly hat indoors. The weight is reassuring rather than irksome, and the effect in the mirror is amazing. It's like another person staring back at me.

'I'll have to do something with my eyebrows.' I lean forward, focusing on the thin, dark-red strips. 'Shouldn't be too obvious though.'

'Once Jeanette here's done with you, even I won't recognise you, dear.' Madame Rose stands behind me and studies my reflection too, then reaches out and tweaks the long tumbles of hair a little more. 'But then that is the point, isn't it.'

'Well, I think that's all gone rather well, don't you?'

When I left the house with Rose this morning, I expected to return weighed down with bags. Or at the very least carrying something to show for the hammering my credit card was inevitably going to take. As it turns out, the trip has been less expensive than I expected, and I have nothing to show for it. I'm once more reminded of my mother's shopping trip when outfitting me for boarding school. I came away from that with very little to show for the hours of boredom, but over the course of the next few days a number of parcels arrived at Harston Magna Hall with my name on them. I wasn't allowed to open them; instead my mother would spirit them away to the room where she had laid out all the things I would need for my new life. My final humiliation was being made to fold and pack everything into my trunk repeatedly until it was done to a standard befitting someone of my stature. I can still remember the agony of folding blouses, pleating skirts, making everything perfect, when all I wanted to do was run away into the woods.

To this day, I hate packing. Even if I am very good at it.

'You're daydreaming, my dear.' Rose taps me gently on the knee with a black leather gloved hand, breaking into my trip down memory lane. We're on a bus, even though the distance from the wig maker back to the house is not far. I could walk it in ten minutes.

'Just remembering old times.'

'Happy memories, I hope.' Rose doesn't make it a question, so I don't feel any great need to answer.

'Do you have a plan, then?' This time it is a question.

'It's a tricky one. I'm not on active duty, so technically I shouldn't be poking my nose into anything.'

Rose gives me a look that I've seen all too many times before. It's fair enough, even I don't believe myself. I have to say it out loud though, kid myself that I've at least considered my actions and where they might lead.

'I really should go and visit Mrs Jones. The young lad's mother. You know, the one I found round the back of my apartment block in London?'

Rose nods, but says nothing more. Like a rookie, I fall for her silence.

'I figure since I was the one who found him, it's only right I let her know how he's getting on. And if I can find anything out about him, why he ran away, who he hung out with before that? Well, so much the better. The local police haven't had much luck.'

Rose smiles this time, nods, but again says nothing. I'm about to fill the noisy silence once more, but she reaches up and presses the call stop button before I can say anything.

'I think we can walk from here.'

The bus stop is perhaps twenty metres from a line of modern, single-storey shops, behind which much older buildings climb several storeys. It's only when Rose leads me to a door sandwiched between two empty shop fronts that I realise this is the back of her house, a covered stair leading up to the first floor. Faded writing above the doorway reads 'Madame Rose. Fortunes Told, Tarots Read', and I remember Harrison's words from the night before.

'So you really are a fortune teller then?'

Rose pauses a moment, her hand making the motion of

opening over the old brass door handle. Do I hear a click of the lock? I can't be sure over the traffic noise. Certainly when she finally grasps the handle and twists it, the door swings open.

'This is one of many services I perform for the city. Folk need to know what the Fates have in store for them, even if sometimes they wish they didn't.'

I can't really say anything to that, and before I can think of a reply, Rose ushers me inside. We enter a narrow hall, leading directly to a wooden staircase, thin strip of threadbare carpet rising up its centre. There's a stale smell of damp about the place that dissipates the higher we climb. It's not dirty, but it feels grubbier, seedier somehow, than the house beyond.

At the top of the stairs, we pass through a small reception room with an elderly sofa pushed against one wall and an antique reception desk arranged beside the door that opens onto a large, cluttered study. The feel of this room is much more like the house I know, a calm falling over me as if I'd been anxious at being out in the wide world.

'I sometimes carry out readings in here. The occasional seance,' Rose says as we pause for a moment by a low, round table. Two chairs are tucked in under it, opposite each other, and in between them sits a crystal ball fully the size of my head, resting on a dark mahogany stand. Its interior shows only a distorted shape of the far side of the room.

'Perhaps, my dear, I can see what the future holds for you.' Rose places one large hand on the back of a chair, and for a moment I worry she's going to pull it out, sit me down, make me stare into those glassy depths and pretend I can see anything at all. The occultism doesn't surprise me; it's written on her business card and all over her house. Clearly she believes in all this mystic stuff, but that doesn't mean I have to.

'Not now though. Now we have other things to deal with. Come.'

There is a door opposite the one we entered, and it opens onto the first-floor landing. No sooner have we stepped out of the seance room, as I'm now going to call it, than several of Madame Rose's cats appear. They are obviously delighted to see her, and her them, but I'm transfixed by the view over the railing into the hall, over by the inner front door. For there in a neat pile beside the ornate brass gong that is rung before suppertime stands a neat pile of parcels. Some are brown paper, tied with string, but some bear the logos of the shops we have so recently visited. As far as I'm aware, Rose lives here alone. I've never seen a cleaner, or a cook in the kitchen.

So who opened the door for the delivery? Who signed for it? And when did shops in Edinburgh start doing next-hour deliveries anyway?

23

The address I have for Daniel Jones's mother is a grey-harled semi in a forgotten cul-de-sac at the back of a council housing estate in Broxburn that looks ripe for demolition and redevelopment. Given the way the city is expanding outwards at an alarming rate, I can't imagine it will be long before the property speculators arrive.

A chill wind blows through me as I step out of the car. I look up to see a commercial jet struggle into the air from Edinburgh airport, just a few miles to the east. It rumbles like angry thunder, and above it, the low clouds are as grey as the cracked walls of the houses and the uneven paving slabs beneath my feet. For a moment it feels as if all the colour has been sucked out of the world, a monochrome existence guaranteed to crush the soul. Then I spot a couple of weed flowers poking out through a crack in the pavement. Their yellow petals are ragged and tiny, but cheerful all the same.

The houses to either side of Number Fifteen have modern double-glazed windows and mismatched front doors. One has paved over the tiny strip of front garden and now unidentified machines squat on it under patched and faded blue tarpaulins. The other might once have had a lawn, but it's brown and dead now. A wooden kennel leans against the front of the house, chain looping out from a ring set into the wall. There is no dog though, just a collar in the mud.

Number Fifteen itself looks like no one has lived here in decades. Cracks in the harling seep brown, as if the house is bleeding from its wounds. In places the render has fallen off completely to reveal red brick behind, suppurating sores in its acne skin. I approach the door down a short path made of the same slabs as the pavement. The rest of the front garden is covered in gravel chips the colour of despair. The front window has a net curtain stretched across it, no light on inside. I didn't call ahead to say I was coming, and now that I'm here that begins to feel like a rookie error. What if she's gone to work?

I knock anyway. There's no doorbell. The door, like the window, looks as if it was fitted when the estate was built. A lot of these houses are in private hands now, and even the ones still owned by the council have been upgraded with better insulation and double glazing. The story of improvement and persistent salesmen is written across the whole estate, and yet this one semi-detached house has resisted change with an almost religious zeal.

'Who are you?'

The question takes me by surprise, and I realise I'd let my mind wander as I waited for the door to be answered. A short, thin woman with a severe face stands in the open doorway, staring at me with a look of deepest suspicion.

'Mrs Jones?' I'm unsure now. The young lad I found around the back of my block was dark-skinned, whereas this diminutive woman is the pasty white you might more normally associate with Scotland. She looks old enough to be the young man's grandmother, but that might just be the mark of a hard life.

'Who wants tae know?' She cocks her head to one side slightly as she asks, and something about the movement makes me revise her age down twenty years. Definitely a hard life.

'My name's Con. Con Fairchild. It's about Dan.'

Her expression softens for an instant, then the scowl comes

back twice as harsh. 'I tellt the polis already. I'll no go doon to London. Who'd keep an eye on this place?'

'I'm not . . .' I'm about to say that I'm not the police, but strictly speaking that's not true. 'It's not that, Mrs Jones. I was the one who found him and called the ambulance. I really just wanted to let you know how he's doing.'

The scowl drops slowly from her face and her shoulders sag, as if the effort of being angry at the world has exhausted her.

'You didnae have tae do that,' she says. Then her eyes widen as a thought explodes in her mind. 'Och, you didnae come all this way just tae tell me, did youse?'

'No. I was coming this way anyway.' I look around the housing estate briefly. 'Well, Edinburgh. Wasn't much of an effort to come out here.'

She gives me a glance that says she wasn't born yesterday, but something about her stance changes, her face softening just a little, and she stands back, beckoning me in.

'Ach well, youse might as well come in for a cup of tea.'

My first thought is that I've somehow stumbled into a parallel universe where my mother wasn't born to a wealthy banking family and then married into minor aristocracy. This is surely how she would have lived her life even without the benefit of privilege and wealth. The narrow hall of Mrs Jones's semi is as decked with religious symbolism as the corridors of Harston Magna Hall. I count at least a dozen crucifixes hanging from the walls, some carrying the full dead Jesus, some just plain crosses. A small table holds an ancient telephone with a rotary dial that must have been new around the time my father was born, and above it a calendar shows a picture of Arles Cathedral. Saints peer out at me from several small picture frames, hands raised in benediction even though their best efforts at blessing will surely be wasted. It puts me on edge and I have to remind myself that I'm not here to judge.

'It's wicked what happened to my boy. Just wicked.' Mrs Jones leads me through to the front room, no more appealing from the other side of the net curtains than it was from out on the street. She doesn't switch on the lights, directing me to an ancient sofa that looks like it's only rarely been sat on in its many decades.

'I'll away and put the kettle on. Won't be a moment.'

I wait until she's gone before crossing the room to the slab-like, painted mantelpiece. It sits over a gas fire that must be a health and safety nightmare. A small wooden case carved with yet another cross holds a box of matches to light the gas, the built-in ignition having no doubt given up the ghost long ago due to neglect. The room has that deep-set chill and damp-ness about it, the unmistakable scent of a place that is only seldom used.

There's a carriage clock dead centre above the fire, its hands stuck at a quarter to two, most likely in the previous century. Either side of it, two pictures stand one at each end of the mantel-piece, as if the people they depict cannot bear to be near each other. The first I recognise as the same photograph I saw from Missing Persons when I gave DCI Bain a name for the victim. The other picture must be Daniel's father, an older, darker but otherwise perfect copy of his son. There is almost nothing of the mother in the boy at all.

'Reginald worked in the dockyards, away over at Rosyth. Such a kind-hearted man. The Lord brought him to me, and then He took him away again. Ten years it's been now since the cancer, and I pray for him still.'

'I'm sorry for your loss.' The words are almost a reflex, but she takes them as if they're heartfelt. Now that I am in her house, Mrs Jones seems a little more hospitable. She carries a tray with tea things on it that reminds me curiously of Rose across the city. I wonder what the two of them would make of each other. Rose's religion is of an entirely different nature.

'Please, have a seat. You must be exhausted wi' all that travelling.' She points me at the sofa again, and this time I do as I'm told. I don't try to correct her misapprehension that I've come straight from her son's hospital bed to her door. We neither of us say anything for a while as she goes about the process of serving tea. Only once she's handed me a cup and taken her own to a narrow armchair opposite does she speak again.

'Is the Lord a light in your life, Miss Fairchild?'

'I am perhaps not quite as rigorous in my devotion as you, Mrs Jones.' I consider turning my evasion into an outright lie, but it's always best to keep things as simple as possible. She looks at me shrewdly, but decides to let it pass.

'Tell me about my boy. How is Daniel?'

I tell her what I can, about how I found him, how he has been treated and his prospects for recovery. She asks about the injuries he has sustained, and I tell her as kindly as I can about his tongue and his testicles. She takes it all in quietly, sipping from her tea occasionally, and says nothing for a while after I have finished. When she does finally speak, I am not surprised by her words.

'The Lord moves in mysterious ways, his wonders to perform.' She places her cup back on the tray, stands and walks slowly to the mantelpiece to fetch the photograph of her son. 'Daniel and me. It hasn't been easy since his father passed. He was too young when that happened, needed a firm hand to guide him. I thought the church would be that hand, but he opened his heart to evil.' She presses her fingers against the glass, a slight tremor in her arms that might be grief or might be the early onset of some neurodegenerative disease.

'Do you go to a local church? Did Daniel?' I'm not quite sure why I ask the question, except that I'm fairly sure I'm not going to get much of use out of Mrs Jones. Judging by the house, there's every possibility Daniel was an altar boy, which means he likely had the confidence of a priest. That might have been purely innocent, despite what you read in the papers these days. It's still another person who I can talk to, and a way to make my excuses and leave. I place my own cup, still mostly full of bitter tea, back down on the tray, noticing the lack of cake or biscuits. Maybe not so like Rose after all.

'Aye. Normally I would be there for benediction, and I usually clean the church after that. But Father Gregory's taking a group of us into the city this evening. We're going to a prayer meeting at the All Saints Hall. You know, in the city?'

Something about the way Mrs Jones says 'prayer meeting' makes me think it's not an arrangement of which she approves. Her assumption I know all the various churches and meeting halls in Edinburgh is a bit wide of the mark too, if well intentioned. As it happens, I do know the All Saints Hall, but only because it was a popular venue during the Fringe. The last show I saw there was most certainly the sort of thing Mrs Jones would disapprove of.

'Prayer meeting?' I put a little hint of incredulity into my voice as I ask the question, and she picks up on it exactly as I'd hoped.

'Aye, I know. It's shocking, the modern way of things. But Father Gregory speaks well of Father Edward, and he's an African like poor Reginald. I will hear what the Lord has to say through him before making judgement.'

24

'Get anything useful from Mrs Jones?'

I've unlocked the Volvo and opened the door when the voice startles me, much closer than I was expecting anyone to be. When I turn to see who it is, I recognise the young woman from yesterday evening, Detective Constable Harrison. A quick glance around the street shows she's on her own, which is unusual. Coppers usually come in pairs, especially detectives.

'She's very . . .' I search for the right word. 'Devout?'

'Aye, felt that myself when I spoke to her. Looks at you like you're infecting her with your sinful thoughts. I expect she'll be off to church before long.'

'No. She said the local priest was taking her and a group of them into the city. Some prayer meeting, apparently. Reckon she'll hold out on absolution until then.' I lean on the car roof, all too aware that this conversation, this meeting, can't have been an accident. 'You seem to know this place well. I'd have thought it was a bit off your usual beat.'

Harrison shoves her hands into the pockets of her dark-blue Puffa jacket. Not typical plain-clothes officer wear, but a lot better for this weather than my tatty old fleece.

'My family's from these parts. Uncle runs a used-car place over the way.'

'And you just happened to be visiting? Saw me and thought you'd say hello?'

She shrugs. 'No' exactly. It's my day off. I was away seeing my aunt when I noticed that flash car of yours drive past. Didn't take a genius to know where you were going, mind. Thought I'd have a chat.'

'Off your own bat, or did someone tell you to?'

'Bit of both. I mentioned you to the boss and he said to keep an eye out. Said he'd had a call from someone in the NCA to say you might be asking a few questions. Figured there weren't many folk you'd be interested in talking to.'

'Fair enough.' She recognised me in the pub, after all. Just seems a bit too much of a coincidence her being out here at the same time as me, visiting auntie or no. And then it dawns on me what's going on here. Or at least some of it.

'You needing a lift?'

Her dimples deepen as she smiles again and steps up to the passenger door. 'Aye, if you're headed back to the city?'

'Hop in.' I open the door on my side and sink down into the seat, glancing over my shoulder briefly to make sure it's not a complete tip in the back. Harrison's already belting up, like a well-trained child.

'Thanks. I really didn't fancy catching the bus.'

'Never thought I'd get a lift in a celebrity's car.' DC Harrison makes a show of looking around the cabin, glancing over her shoulder at the mess in the back, running one small hand over the faded black vinyl dashboard. 'It's no' exactly what I thought it'd be, mind.'

'Scoff all you like, but this used to be one of Essex Constabulary's finest fast pursuit vehicles.' I blip the throttle as we move onto dual carriageway, feeling a gentle pressure in the small of my back as the car accelerates to the legal limit.

'Aye, I mind my uncle telling me about these things when they were new. Used to race them in the Touring Cars. She's past her prime though.'

She. I'd never really thought of the car as having a gender, but I'll take it.

'No' quite in the same league as the boss's Alfa Romeo though. That fair goes when you press the loud pedal.'

I glance sideways at my passenger again. I don't know much about her at all. She's a detective constable, last name Harrison, first name Janie. It was her flatmate Manda who did most of the talking last night in the pub; this one's more of a listener, which is a good trait in a detective. I get the distinct impression I'm being sized up, evaluated. If the local police think I'm here to cause trouble, they'll want to keep an eye on me. I could play that to my advantage, of course.

'I'm not a celebrity, by the way. Just a detective constable like you.'

Harrison's dimples reappear as she smiles to herself, and she spends a little while looking at her hands. 'Like me. That's funny.'

'It is?'

'Aye, well. See, you come from a posh family, right? Grew up in a big hoose out in the country. I know most of what the papers print is pure shite, but they get some of the facts right, aye?'

I nod, fairly certain I know where this is going next.

'I grew up on a cooncil estate no' all that far from your pal Mrs Jones. Most of the girls I went to school with are mothers now, and some are grannies. No' even thirty years old.'

I open my mouth to say that a fair few of the girls I went to school with are mothers too. Then I close it again without speaking. I need her on my side, so best not to antagonise.

'Why did you go to see her anyway? Mrs Jones?'

I use the upcoming traffic lights and slowing cars as an excuse to not answer straight away. 'You know I found the boy, Dan?'

'Aye, I heard that. He was thrown out wi' the rest o' the trash. Something like that.'

'Actually, I think he was hiding. He must have escaped from whoever was doing . . .' I think of the horrific injuries, the blood loss, the unimaginable pain, shake my head to try and get rid of the image. Something else occurs to me as I do. 'But he must have had help. There's no way he could have got to where he was in that state. Not on his own.'

'I've no' seen any photos. Can't really say.'

I look across at Harrison as she sits in the passenger seat, staring out at the traffic in front of us.

'They didn't send anything up?'

'No. Just asked if we could interview Mrs Jones about her son. Felt like a box-ticking exercise to me, which is why I was surprised when my boss told me you might be turning up.'

'I'm surprised they asked someone in CID to do it. The NCA have an office up here, don't they? Could easily have sent one of their own out.'

'Aye, but it's over at Gartcosh. Can't see them wanting to travel all that way. No' just for a runaway kid. Easier to get someone local to do it.'

Harrison lays on the sarcasm a bit heavy, but I remember well enough the amicable enmity between the east and west of Scotland.

'What about a runaway kid who's had his tongue ripped out and his bollocks cut off in some kind of ritual ceremony? A kid drugged with something strong enough to keep him alive while they're doing it, too. Probably awake as well, otherwise he'd not have been able to escape.'

'Jesus.' Harrison shudders gently as she says the word, and I feel bad for being so graphic.

'You ever come across anything like that up here?'

'The drug, or the ritual mutilation?' From the way she says it, I suspect the answer is she knows of both. I say nothing, concentrating on negotiating the unfamiliar new road layout in the West End of the city, and hoping she'll elaborate.

'There was a drug doing the rounds a couple of years back. Something opium based, I think it was. Doesn't really sound like what you're describing though. Not sure about ritual mutilation. That's the sort of case my boss would end up with though. He always seems to get the weird ones.'

'Your boss sounds like an interesting man. I'd like to meet him some time.'

Harrison shakes her head slowly. 'Aye, I'm no' so sure about that.'

We're crossing the Meadows now, and she suddenly waves towards the pavement as we near Jawbone Walk. 'Here's fine. I can walk the rest of the way.'

For once, there's not much traffic behind me, so I indicate and pull over. 'You sure? I'm not busy. I can drop you at the station if you want.'

'Day off, remember? It's no' far home from here.' She unclips her seat belt and opens the door, then points up at one of the old wych elms that line either side of the walk. 'See that drugs case I was talking about? We found a body right up in the top of that tree.'

I crane my neck, squint through the car windscreen at the branches, still bare but with buds on the cusp of breaking into new leaf. 'Up . . . ? How?'

Harrison climbs out of the car, then leans back. 'That's the thing, aye? There was a wee boy reckons he saw it all happen. Convinced hisself it was a dragon dropped the man. Thanks for the lift.'

And then she slams the door and walks off without another word.

25

I'm not entirely sure why I decide not to go back to Rose's house in Leith but instead carry on across the Meadows and into Newington. Well, that's not strictly true. I know exactly why I take that route, it leads me to the All Saints Hall. What I'm not sure is why I decide to go there.

As a rule, I don't do religion. Yes, I went to Roger DeVilliers' funeral, but that was more to make sure he was properly dead than out of any great belief. I certainly didn't have any respects to pay to him. Part of me's relieved at the thought I won't be going to Ben and Charlotte's wedding now, as that's another service avoided. There was a time when I enjoyed the ceremony, although if I'm being honest it was mostly the hymns. Even then, there was the naughty-schoolgirl thrill of deliberately singing the wrong words, the ruder the better, knowing full well that the teachers who ran St Humbert's could never prove we were doing it.

For all I felt uncomfortable with it, I couldn't help but be intrigued by Mrs Jones's devotion. It reminded me of my mother too much to be ignored. It's easy to see why Daniel might have felt stifled there, and with no father figure growing up, he could easily have gone off the rails enough to run away. It's also possible he fell victim to that unhappy scourge of the Catholic church, the priest a little too fond of his altar boys, and that's why he jumped on a train to London and ended up near death in my bins. But both of those possibilities feel too easy. There's more to this than meets the eye, and I can't help myself from wanting to know the truth. Even as I know I'm going to regret searching for it.

If I remember it correctly, the All Saints is actually a Baptist hall, so an odd choice of venue for a good Catholic like Mrs Jones. Given some of the bands I saw there back when I was a student, it's happy enough to take a booking from anyone. I drive around the back streets of Newington, past the police station where Janie Harrison and her enigmatic boss work, before finding somewhere to park my Volvo, and even then I have to pay a king's ransom for the privilege. Edinburgh's grown busier since I lived here.

The hall's set back from the street, a stone edifice built in a time when religion trumped planning regulations and building control. It looks like it might have been designed by Alexander 'Greek' Thompson's less talented half-brother, the faux-Doric columns framing its entrance all out of proportion to the rest of the frontage. As I approach, I can see a line of people queueing patiently to get in. I'd not thought a prayer meeting would be so popular, but then I've never understood the appeal of religion either.

As I approach the crowd, I hesitate. The dowdy clothes Rose helped me buy this morning would fit right in here, but I'm not wearing any of them yet. And my new wig, the most important part of my disguise, had not yet arrived when I left to visit Broxburn. Nobody's paying me any attention right now, but that could change swiftly enough if anyone recognises me. Hood up, I skirt past the edge of the waiting crowd and head for the side entrance.

And that's when I spot a flier advertising the meeting. From where I'm standing I can't read any but the largest letters, and neither can I make out the picture of the priest, although I'd recognise him easily enough if I could. I sat drinking tea with him not all that long ago, after all.

The Reverend Doctor Edward Masters.

'Are you waiting to go in? Only we'll be starting in a moment.'

I'm staring at the flier from a distance, trying to work out why an African priest, head of his own church, would conduct a prayer meeting in Edinburgh. It doesn't make sense, which is probably why the young man has managed to creep up on me. He reminds me of the chuggers in Euston station, dispensing platitudes and pressing leaflets into unwilling hands. He's better dressed though, and a local lad by his accent.

'I'm sorry?'

'The prayer meeting? The reverend doctor will be here very shortly.'

'Oh, I'm sorry.' I feign ignorance, which isn't as hard as it sounds. 'No. I was just curious. Thought this was a Baptist hall.'

'And so it is.' The young man's smile is as wide and tooth-filled as his sincerity. 'But our faiths have far more in common than that which divides them.'

I think I'm going to be sick a little, but before my new friend can say any more, a commotion in the street draws both of our attentions. That same black Mercedes I saw outside the front door at Harston Magna Hall has drawn up directly outside the church, smaller vehicles in front and behind it like some presidential motorcade. Almost before it stops, a group of people swarm out of the cars. They are all dressed the same, in simple off-white clothes that look like designer uniforms commissioned by a mad supervillain. Some are acolytes, it's clear, but I clock at least four as security, close in to the limo and helping their lord and master. Who knows, they may be true believers in the Church of the Coming Light, but I suspect they're motivated more by a fat pay cheque than any salvation. They're taller and broader than the others, and their eyes are everywhere, sweeping the concourse for any sign of trouble. One focuses on me, his angry frown a worry until I realise he can't see me properly with my hood up. I ignore him and instead concentrate on the man they're protecting.

Once again he's wearing a black suit that might well have been exquisitely and expensively tailored, but only when he was a younger and smaller man. As if the word of the Lord were filling him to bursting, he has expanded outwards over the years until a point where his clothes can barely contain him. He moves with a surprising, fluid grace, working the crowd of people like any rock star or Hollywood darling. Back at Harston Magna Hall, he was impressive but quiet, as if the ancient stones somehow cowed him. Either that or he felt no need to work the crowd when it was only my mother. Now there's power radiating off him. It's something I've noticed with a few men – and they're always men – who have reached the top and know for a certainty it is where they are meant to be.

'I have to go now. The reverend doctor needs me.'

I startle at the young man. Such is Masters' presence, I'd completely forgotten him. With a shudder, I drag my attention away.

'Sure. Thanks.' It's about as much as I can manage.

'Will you be joining us?' he asks, and for a moment I'm almost tempted. I could sit at the back and see what all the fuss is about.

'No.' I shake off the last of the spell. 'Not my cup of tea.'

I turn and walk away, surprised to find that I'm shaking slightly. A cup of tea wouldn't be a bad idea at all. Or maybe something stronger. That and surrounding myself with people who aren't moved by religious fervour. Normal folk. I take a quick look around to remind myself of this part of town, dredge my student memories, and then I make a beeline for the nearest pub.

★ ★ ★

I don't get all that far.

There's hundreds of pubs within shouting distance of where I am, but I've only gone a few dozen metres before I stop. Something about Masters and his entourage put me on edge, drove me away. That blind instinct of flight is hard-wired and difficult to resist when it hits you. I wasn't prepared for it, but I am now. And I'm intrigued.

Turning back towards the main road, I notice a side door to the hall, propped slightly ajar as if to let the air flow. I can't help myself from going to have a closer look. The door opens onto a short, dark corridor, empty save for a small stack of chairs. There are toilets on each side for the congregation, and the far end is closed off from the hall beyond by a heavy black curtain. I know full well I shouldn't be here, but on the other hand I'm not exactly breaking and entering.

As I approach the curtain, I begin to hear voices. I can see a line of light painted across the floor and wall where there's a slit in the fabric. Scarcely daring to breathe, I inch closer and peer through. The main hall is laid out with more of the same chairs that are stacked behind me, most of them occupied, the people in them transfixed by the man doing all the talking. Edward Masters has abandoned the podium set up in the middle of the stage and is pacing back and forth, hand-held microphone to his face like a stand-up comedian. There's nothing funny about his words.

'. . . rain down fire and brimstone on their heads. He will smite the unworthy, and they will burn in the fires of Hell.'

I scan the backs of the assembled heads, then freeze as a figure moves past the curtain right in front of me. For a moment I think I've been rumbled, hope that I can get out of the door and leg it down the street before I'm dragged inside. Then I recognise the off-white material of the uniform worn by Masters' acolytes. This close, I can see the rough weave of it, some kind of sackcloth or similar. And then the figure walks away, white ankle socks on his sandalled feet. Adjusting my position to take in more of the room, I can see others from the entourage circling the audience like teachers at assembly. Like prison guards. Making sure nobody tries to escape while the great man is speaking.

'. . . there will be no hiding from Him, no escaping His wrath. The Lord sees everything. He knows what you keep in your heart. He sees the look you give your neighbour's wife. He measures the minutes you cheat your employer by leaving early. He is watching you at all times. Judging you at all times.'

It's all pretty generic stuff, really. But there's no denying the power in Masters' voice. He has the assembled worshippers mesmerised. I can feel it myself, like a cord trying to pull me out of my hiding place, through the curtains to join the throng.

'. . . only by accepting His word into your hearts can you hope to feel His love. Only by submitting to His will can you hope to be saved. Are you ready to be saved?'

This final question is bellowed out with such force I rock back on my heels, which is probably just as well given that another one of the acolytes chooses that moment to pause with his back to my curtain. His bulk and the heavy material muffle the words that follow, but it sounds like a commotion. Then the sackcloth back moves aside and the acolyte hurries to where the rest of his fellows are already congregating near the front of the audience.

'Do not harm her, my friends. She yearns for salvation.' Masters' voice booms out again now it's not blocked, and as I adjust my position, I see him step down off the stage and approach the group who have surrounded a young woman. It's hard to tell if she's overcome with holy joy or was hurling abuse. Either way, she is forced to her knees as he approaches, one hand clasping a book that is probably a Bible, the other reaching out towards her. When he presses his palm to her forehead,

I can hear the whole room take a collective breath.

'Are you here to be saved?' Even without the microphone his voice fills the hall.

The young woman twitches, either trying to get away or having some kind of fit.

'Are you here to be saved?'

Two of Masters' acolytes hold her by the arms, a third presses down on her shoulders, and yet the twitches are becoming more violent now. I don't know whether to run out and help her or call the police. Instead, I do what any good millennial would do and take out my phone to start filming.

'I can feel the devil in you, child. Don't fight me. Fight it.' Masters pushes harder against her, and her head tilts back so far I fear it might snap. Lifting up his Bible, he shakes it at the gathered audience. 'Pray with me, people. Pray for this poor tortured soul. In the name of Jesus, pray.'

It's a good show, I'll give him that much. The young woman shakes and convulses like the best ham actor, her wails increasingly strident as Masters exhorts the congregation to pray harder. And all the while he bears down on her with his massive hand. It has to be rehearsed; too staged to be anything else. I'm almost as drawn in by the whole thing as everyone, though, which is why I'm taken by surprise when another of the sackcloth-clad acolytes passes my hiding place. His shoulder brushes the curtain, and I almost drop my phone. I don't think I make a noise, but he must hear something. Before I know it, the curtain's jerked aside and I'm staring straight at him.

We stare at each other, motionless, for what feels like minutes but is likely only a few heartbeats. He doesn't make a sound. One of the professional bodyguards, then. I realise my phone camera is still recording video at the same time as he reaches to snatch it away from me. That's not happening.

I palm the phone as I duck and twist, ready to make good my escape. I'm not exactly doing anything wrong here, but the heavy security presence doesn't bode well. Two steps and I reckon I'm away, but then my foot clatters against the pile of chairs.

'Security!' His shout is loud enough to wake the dead, although whether it can be heard over the ecstatic wails of the young woman in the middle of the hall is anyone's guess. I'm too busy smacking my shins against chair legs and struggling to regain my balance to care. Stay classy, Con.

At least the fallen stack slows the bodyguard from following. I'm limping badly as I push through the half-open doorway and hobble into the street. A glance to the far end, where the front of the hall opens up onto a small square, shows three more burly acolytes appearing around the corner. My car is that way, which buggers up my chances of escaping to it. At least they're hesitant, getting their bearings before charging at me. That's the only thing that saves me from being caught.

Behind me, the first bodyguard has made it through the maze of fallen chairs and is shoving his way through the door. I pause just long enough to pull over the nearest wheelie bin to block his route, then half run, half grimace away. My only advantage is that they're none of them locals. I know these streets well enough, and better yet I know where the pubs are. The ones that will be full of people, and which have handy back doors I can escape through.

Heart pounding, I do my best to ignore the pain in my ankle as I dart down a narrow close. It's tempting to pause and pull more obstacles in the way of my pursuers, but speed is more important. I risk a glance backwards and see two people in pursuit, worrying since there should be four. I might know these streets, but it's been a while. Have they doubled back in an attempt to head me off? Or is my infringement not important enough to justify that amount of manpower? Maybe they've gone back to guarding Masters. He pays their wages, after all.

The first pub I reach is closed, which wasn't part of the plan at all. My pursuers are still following me, although they're not running to catch up now, which is reassuring. I've got my hoodie up, and I'm fairly sure the first bodyguard didn't get a good look at me. Maybe that's what this is all about, simply them trying to identify me. It's not as if Masters is heading up some crime syndicate and I just filmed them planning their next drug run. The more I think about it, the more ridiculous it is even to have these two following me. Are they that paranoid about their little prayer meeting? The laying on of hands? The wailing woman who was almost certainly a paid actress? As the initial adrenaline surge wears off, my fear turns to anger. Who the fuck do these people think they are?

I stumble in through the door of the next pub perhaps a little more noisily than is necessary. The barman looks up in surprise, but nobody else seems to notice. It's early evening, and the place isn't as full as I'd have liked. Still, it's enough folk that my pursuers will probably give up now.

'Sorry about the door. Tweaked my ankle coming up the street and it hurts like a bugger.' I slide onto a stool as the bartender approaches, point at one of the taps. 'Pint of Eighty Bob, please.'

He grunts something non-committal, but pulls down a pint glass and begins to pour. I pull down my hood, look around the bar a bit more. Some football match is playing on a telly across the room, even if nobody is watching it. Directly underneath the screen, two old men nurse silent pints, tiny chaser nips alongside them. A young couple are canoodling in a booth near the door, oblivious to anyone's disapproval. There's a group of young women who might be students, huddled over notes and discussing something that occasionally has them breaking into peals of laughter. It's a late-afternoon pub, and a welcome relief after the excitement of the chase.

'Two fifty, love.' The bartender startles me, but only for a moment. I pay half what the same pint would have cost me back home, take a long sip of the cold, bitter brew. A clatter at the door is more punters coming in, and as I glance at them I see into the street beyond. Too late, I notice one of the bodyguards standing there, staring straight at me. He holds his phone high, camera facing me. A short pause before I can reach my hood. Then he gives me a thumbs up, turns away, and walks back towards the church hall.

26

'Ah, Con. You're back.'

Rose greets me in the hall as I let myself in an hour and a half after my close call with the reverend doctor. I have a horrible sensation of déjà vu, and then it hits me that this is very much like being back at St Humbert's, caught sneaking into school late at night after an unauthorised visit to one of the local pubs. Rose has perfected that same expression of deep disappointment, and I feel suitably ashamed for not letting her know where I was.

'Sorry. Thought I'd go check something out, and then I kind of ended up in a bar on West Preston Street. Needed something to calm my nerves.'

Rose's stern expression melts into a mischievous grin, and I know she's been winding me up. 'Did you get anything to eat?' she asks. 'Or are you on the haggis supper and pickled egg diet still?'

'How on earth . . . ?' I don't finish the sentence. She wouldn't tell me anyway.

'There's some stew in the oven if you're hungry. It's not as good as Emily Robertson's, but it is Newmore mutton. I brought some down the last time I was up there.'

The mention of my aunt's lodge up in the Perthshire high-lands reminds me of when I first met Rose, late last summer. I was being hounded out of London then, too. Only that time it was my life on the line, not hassle from the tabloid press.

'Stew sounds wonderful. Thank you. It's been a long day and I may have skipped lunch.'

'You need to look after yourself, my dear. And drinking alone is not healthy, you know.'

I follow Rose through to the kitchen, mostly tuning out her cautions. I'm well used to being alone and fending for myself, but it's nice to be mothered sometimes. My own mother never much bothered, after all. Too busy trying to wash clean her soul of every perceived sin her family committed. As I tuck into an enormous plate of wonderful-smelling mutton stew, complete with squishy carrots and a baked potato oozing melted butter, I can't help wondering what my mother would have made of this evening's prayer meeting. If you'd asked me a week ago, I'd have said the Reverend Doctor Edward Masters and his ostentatious showmanship would have appalled her. And yet she wanted the man to bless her son's wedding. It makes no sense at all.

'Have you ever come across an outfit called the Church of the Coming Light?' I ask when the weight of the stew begins to slow down my eating. I'd not known how hungry I was until I started.

Rose is leaning with her back to the range, and cocks her head to one side at my question. 'There was a breakaway Mennonite sect of that name in New England, back in the 1890s, I think.'

'No, this is a bit more modern.' I tell her about Masters, the prayer meeting, Charlotte and Ben's wedding.

'Strange. I don't know the man, and I've not heard of his so-called church either.' She turns her back on me, but only to reach the kettle, fill it up with water and place it on the hob. When she's facing me again, it's with a frown. 'Something like that I should know about.'

'I'd no idea he was up here, only heard about his church recently. There's something off about it all, though, and not just because my mother seems to like him.'

'Well, I shall make some enquiries in the morning.' Rose

clears my plate to the dishwasher while the tea is brewing, then busies herself with tidying up until she feels it's ready to pour. Only once the cups are full, the milk added and I've refused the sugar does she speak again. 'Besides, we've more important matters right now.'

'We have?' I'd hoped for an early night, even if it's never a good idea to try and sleep on a full stomach. But now my hostess has that mischievous twinkle in her eye that makes her look more like a giddy schoolgirl than a woman of advanced years.

'Indeed we have. Your new wig arrived while you were out. It's time for you to try on your disguise.'

I see the lights outside my window as I'm getting ready for bed, a lazy blue strobing on the ceiling that I somehow know is there for me. Laid out on the two armchairs across the room, my dowdy disguise clothes remind me of an evening spent play-acting. It was easy to forget all about the Reverend Doctor Edward Masters and his prayer meeting as I tried on all the clothes I'd bought in the morning. There seemed to be a lot more of them than I remembered; I suspect Rose might have supplemented the haul, although from where I'm not sure. We are not even remotely the same size. Some of the dresses are vintage, though, even if they look like they've never been worn.

The knock at the door reverberates through the hall, easy to hear in my second floor room. It is only moments before Rose is answering, and moments later that I recognise the voice of our late-night visitor. I quickly pull on my jeans and boots, throw my hoodie over the rather elegant silk blouse I'm still wearing, and hurry out to see what Detective Constable Harrison wants.

'Lady— Con. There's someone here to see you.' I meet Rose on the stairs. The twinkle has gone from her eyes, replaced with something much more worrisome.

'I know. I saw.' I look past her, over the banister and down to where Harrison is standing in the hallway. From here she looks much smaller, not that she was big to begin with. It's as if this house makes her uncomfortable, and I realise that it quite probably does. I'm at ease here, having grown up in Harston Magna Hall. She comes from a council estate in an ex-mining village. This mansion is bound to be a bit overwhelming.

'Everything OK?' I ask, even as I know it's not. Harrison looks up at my voice, as if she hadn't noticed me on the landing.

'I'm probably going to regret this, but.' She doesn't say but what, just shrugs.

'I'm not in any trouble, am I?' It's that strange thing. Even though I'm a police officer myself, I can't help but feel I've done something wrong whenever the flashing blue lights appear.

'Trouble?' Harrison's expression is a picture. 'No. Why'd you think that?'

'I dunno. Just that whenever the police turn up late at night, it's usually to arrest someone.'

'Aye, well, no. It's no' that. Just was hoping you might be able to help us. See, there's been an incident. We've found a body.'

There's only one reason why my input might be required here. Police Scotland have more than enough experts on bodies that they don't need to come calling on off-duty detective constables from the Met. I look briefly at Madame Rose, but she just tilts her head slightly to one side.

'You go, dear. If duty calls, it's what you should do. The house will let you in when you're finished.'

I raise an eyebrow at 'the house', but say nothing more. Rose is strange, and so is the place she lives. Turning back to Harrison, I ask, 'Will I need my coat?'

'Aye,' she says, then reconsiders. 'Mebbe no. We'll get you a Polis Scotland one for now. Hopefully that way nobody will ask too many questions.'

27

The uniform constable driving the squad car says nothing as Harrison opens the back door and ushers me in. I'm expecting her to go round and climb in alongside him, but she shuffles up beside me. That's when I notice the front passenger seat's already taken. An old man in a dark suit twists around in his seat, reaches through the gap with a large hand. 'Bob Laird. Detective Sergeant, but I'll no' pull rank on you, lass.'

He reminds me of someone, but I can't immediately place who. As the squad car pulls away from the kerb, the subdued lighting inside and orange of the streetlamps outside make it hard to tell whether his hair's sandy or grey, but it is most certainly thinning. When I take his hand, it's warm, the grip not too tight, and not held for too long either.

'Con Fairchild. Detective Constable. Sort of.'

'Aye, I know.' His smile is reassuringly slow, but there's a spark in his eyes that suggests there's far more going on than appears on the surface. 'Spoke to a nice lady called Shepherd this afternoon. She told me all about you.'

'You're Ja— Harrison's boss?' That doesn't make sense given what she said to me about getting into trouble with him back in the house.

'In a manner of speaking, aye.'

'Am I in trouble, then? If you've been speaking to Shepherd.'

'No.' DS Laird pauses a moment as if considering something.

I get the feeling he's all about the considered pauses. 'No' unless there's something you've not told us about.'

'Can't think of anything. Not really. The whole point of my being here is to keep a low profile. Last thing I need is to draw attention to myself, right?'

He doesn't answer my question, but turns back to face out through the windscreen as we drive swiftly along car-lined residential streets in the direction of Newhaven. It's not a part of the city I know particularly well, although like so many other cities, the switch from affluent to run-down is abrupt. Large houses give way to industrial units, a mixture of modern steel-clad warehouses and older, stone buildings, all built on reclaimed land lapped by the waters of the Forth. Across the firth, the lights of Fife twinkle in the darkness, and then as we turn down a narrow alley between two roofless stone warehouses, they are blotted out by the flashing blue of multiple squad cars.

'Stay here a moment,' Harrison says once we've parked at the back of the line. She climbs out, trots off to speak to one of the uniform constables manning the tape. A few moments later she comes back holding a dark-blue regular issue raincoat. I can see her scanning the area beyond the tape, dark and lifeless as far as I can see.

Is there a problem?' I ask as I struggle into the coat. It's at least two sizes too big for me, with 'Police Scotland' emblazoned across the back in white letters. It might be the material, but I'm sure I can feel some residual warmth from whichever poor bugger's just had it taken off them.

'It's always the way when we get a call from a member of the public about something. By the time we get here, the press are circling and half the details are already on YouTube and Insta.'

I want to ask details of what, but given the number of squad cars, I know it's serious. Then again, bodies always are. There's only one reason why they would want me involved anyway, and the thought of it makes me shudder despite the coat. 'Lead on.'

Harrison holds the tape up for me to duck under. Beyond it, a team of forensic technicians are already laying out a clear path, arc lights revealing all the dirty secrets of this narrow alley. The cobbled ground is slick with oily moisture from the Firth, and littered with wind-blown rubbish. We only get as far as the first forensics van before a white-suited technician bars our way.

'You'll have to get suited up, Janie. You know better than that.' I know the voice, but before I can place the face, she's turned away, reaching into the van for a couple of fresh white paper overalls. When she hands them over, she's pulled her face mask down, and a stray strand of blonde hair escaping the elasticated hood gives the game away.

'Nobody's told me what "this" is.' I take the overalls, still in their plastic bag, weigh them in my hand. 'Although I'm beginning to suspect I know.'

'Aye, well. Pathologist's pretty much done, and we're hoping to move the body soon, so you'd better hurry up right enough.' Manda Parsons smiles at me, then turns her attention to her flatmate. 'Reckon it's going to be another late one, Janie. Don't stay out all night, mind.'

It's never easy clambering into white paper overalls at a crime scene, but we do our best, then finally Harrison leads me along the clear path to where a pair of bright lights have been set up to flood the scene. I'm reminded of the area around the back of my apartment block down in London. The big steel bins are almost identical, their black rubber lids propped up by overflowing rubbish bags. Clearly irregular collection is as much a problem here as down south. This is somewhere people use to dump all manner of unusual rubbish, too. A couple of small fridges are lined up almost neatly against the nearest wall, and beside them sits an old armchair that's remarkably similar to one I had in my flat across the city ten years ago. Mine hadn't been quite so badly chewed by rats, though. The stains on its arms were more spilled tea than dried blood. And I don't think it ever had a dead body sprawled in it.

'Sorry about the lack of warning. I wanted to get your initial impressions without any kind of prejudice.'

I don't hear Harrison's words at first. Too busy staring at the poor sod in front of me. He's naked, which makes me shiver in sympathy even though he's well past caring about such things. Rain has pasted his thin ginger hair to his scalp, droplets still running down his face like tears. His eyes are closed, which is a relief. I don't like dead bodies at the best of times, but when they stare at you it's hard to break that gaze and take in the important details.

'How long's he been here?' I ask, hearing the professional edge in my tone. 'When did it stop raining?'

'We got the call about two hours ago. Forensics will hopefully give us a better idea of when he was dumped. Fairly sure he wasn't killed here, though. Rain stopped about six. Maybe half past.'

I crouch down, the better to see the body without casting shadows from the arc lights. He's skin and bones, pasty white, though how much of that is due to blood loss and how much his natural pallor, I'd be hard pushed to tell. It's fairly obvious how he died, though, and I can't suppress the shudder as I inspect the gaping wound in his chest. I've seen this before and not all that long ago.

'I take it his heart's missing.' Standing up pops my knee joints, the noise resonating in the narrow alley. Crime scenes are normally quiet, especially if it's a dead body we're dealing with. This one is no exception.

'Aye, that and his tackle.' Harrison tilts her head down towards the dead man's crotch, or what would be his crotch were it not just a grisly mess. Given the nature of the wound, there's remarkably little blood soaked into the seat. What's on the arms of the chair must have washed off him too, the rain doing its best to make life more difficult for us. No, not us. More difficult for Police Scotland and the Scottish Forensics Service. This has nothing to do with me.

'I take it this is much like the body you found in London?' Harrison's voice tips up at the end of the sentence. A question.

'Which one?' I turn away from the gruesome scene to face her. 'My boss . . .' I pause. Bain's not technically my boss, after all. 'DCI Bain's been investigating a string of similar cases. He's NCA, not Met. They've had a half dozen bodies turn up in a similar state to this one. I take it he knows about this?'

A couple of technicians approach as we're speaking, holding a black body bag and a stretcher. Time to vacate the scene and let them get on with it. I take one last look at the poor lad, but there's nothing I can add to make finding whoever did this any easier.

Harrison backs away from the body, leaving room for the technicians to come in. Another woman in full paper suit, hood and booties is right behind them, clutching a camera. I can't see much of her face, but she nods at the detective constable, then raises a quizzical eyebrow at me.

'We'll just get out of your way, aye?' Harrison says to the newcomer. I take the hint, and together we follow the clear path back to the forensics van.

Detective Sergeant Laird is still sitting in the squad car when I climb into the back seat a bit later. Something tells me he's not moved at all. Given the nature of the incident, I can't say I blame him.

'Any thoughts?' he asks once Harrison has joined us and the doors are all closed.

'You know I'm not part of the investigation, right?'

'Aye, but you've seen two of these now. One alive, one dead. Anything you can tell us is going to be a help.'

I stare out through the windscreen for a moment, collecting my thoughts.

'It's almost exactly the same as the last one. The lad in the park. My guess is he'll be hard to identify. Missing Persons'll be your best bet, but he'll have been sleeping rough for a while. He'll have drugs in his system, too. Might be a regular user, or it might just be whatever shit they gave him so they could do that. And I know I'm not going to make any friends for saying it, but the forensic analysis of the scene? Waste of time. Even if the rain hadn't washed most of it away, they'll not find anything. Least, that's how it's been before.'

The detective sergeant nods his head gently. 'Aye, I was afraid of that.'

'You really need to call DCI Bain at the NCA in on this though. They'll need to know there's been a similar case up here. Whoever's doing this, it's all over the country.'

'He's on his way. Meeting up wi' my boss in the morning.' Laird can't quite keep the sigh out of his voice as he speaks. 'Don't mind working wi' another agency, but there's so much paperwork you'd no' believe it.'

28

It's only as I'm standing outside Rose's house watching the squad car turn at the end of the street that I realise I'm still wearing my Police Scotland raincoat. A quick check of the pockets turns up nothing, so whoever it belongs to will only be cold, not locked out of their house. I guess that means it's mine now. Figure I've earned it after this evening.

The door's open, as usual, only a couple of cats standing sentinel. As I cross the hall towards the stairs, thinking it might be a good idea to slip quietly to bed, I notice a light from the kitchen, hear the soft sound of someone moving about. It's late, but when I open the door, Rose is in the process of making tea. As ever, she is dressed for visitors, and there are two cups on the table.

'You're back, then?' She pours freshly boiled water into the pot. 'I expect you'll need something to help settle the nerves before you sleep. Never a good idea to go straight to bed from a grisly crime scene.'

I can't decide whether she's genuinely concerned for my welfare or angling for an opportunity to quiz me about what's going on. Back before my life imploded last year, I always found it helpful to discuss any ongoing investigation with the other members of the team, but it goes against all my training to talk about a crime scene with a civilian not connected to the case. On the other hand, *I'm* technically a civilian not connected to the case, and nobody's told me not to speak to Rose about it. I get the feeling she's been involved with DC Harrison and DS Laird before. Probably their mysterious boss too.

'I've something stronger if that would help?' Rose mistakes my silence for a lack of enthusiasm.

'No, tea's fine. It's a slippery slope if you start leaning on the booze to quiet the demons.'

'That's a wise head on young shoulders.' Rose cocks hers to one side, a half smile ghosting her lips.

'My old boss always used to say it.' Pete. I've not really thought about him in a while. Well, apart from every day. But that's the fact of his death, the nature of it and everything that came afterwards. I can't remember the last time I thought of him alive.

'It's good advice. I've seen far too many seek solace in the bottle. A wee nip now and then never did a body harm, but when you start to rely on it? Well.' Rose says no more, but sets about pouring tea. I know the routine now, and help myself to a splash of milk from the jug that's in the middle of the kitchen table, a biscuit from the plate beside it.

'I'll understand if you don't want to talk about it,' she says once we're both sitting comfortably.

'It's not that. I expect you've come across all manner of nastiness down the years.'

'I'm not that old.' Rose looks at me with mock indignation. 'Well, actually, I suppose I am. But if you feel you can't tell me, that's fine too. Just take your time, enjoy your tea. It'll help you sleep without the dreams.'

'They found the body of a young man, out by Newhaven.' I tell Rose all about it, and about the horrific injuries he had sustained. I pause for a moment before telling her that this body isn't the first, and that the NCA is looking into the possibility all of the deaths are linked. 'They think that someone is taking specific body parts for ritual purposes.'

'Muti.' Rose shakes her head slowly. 'Or rather something dark and evil that grew out of the practice. Something that feeds on the greed and credulity of men.'

'You know about it?' I'm not exactly surprised.

'I do. I have spent time with some well-respected practitioners, learned some of the secrets of their magic. Their healing seeks to bring harmony within the body and between body and land. It's not destructive, quite the opposite.'

'But—'

'That is the true bush medicine, my dear.' Rose interrupts me before I can get my objection out. 'What you have seen today? What has been done to these poor boys? That is not muti. Not true muti.'

'Why, then? What is it meant to achieve?'

'What does sacrifice ever achieve? In this instance I suspect it is an attempt to gain strength and power. Taking the heart of your foe, taking his manhood. These are very potent symbols.'

Rose falls silent, and I can't think of anything to say to that. We both drink our tea for a while, lost in our independent thoughts. Finally, one of many reservations I have with the whole situation rises to the top.

'What I can't understand is why they just dump the bodies like that. Out in the open, thrown out like the trash. It's . . . I don't know. It's as if they're taunting us, whoever's doing this. Rubbing our noses in how powerless we are. How clueless.'

'That is part of their magic, though. That's how it works. You cannot accord your victim any kind of respect in death, or you risk giving up the power you have taken from him. Throwing the body out like, as you say, trash, shows they no longer think anything of it. Even taking trouble to make it disappear would be to admit you are afraid of the consequences of your actions.'

Much as I hate to admit it, Rose makes a good point. 'That's . . . cold?'

'That is the logic of it. If you accept any logic in this at all.'

'So, what about Daniel Jones? He was in the trash, but he was still alive. How come they only cut his balls off? Didn't take his heart?'

'Now that, Con, is a question for your investigative team, not me. You were the one who found him, though. What struck you most about him then?'

'You mean apart from the fact he was alive?' I picture the scene in my mind, the bins overflowing as usual, the piles of rubbish heaped all around, the foot poking out from under a black bin liner. An attempt to hide.

'He wasn't dumped. Which means he must have got himself there.' Bleeding out, in so much agony it's impossible to imagine, mouth filled with blood and pain, every step an impossible feat of endurance. What drug had they put in his system to stop him dying from shock? 'He had to have been anaesthetised, surely?' I can hear the tone of forlorn hope in my question, even as I know the answer isn't going to be reassuring.

'I doubt whoever did this would want their victim unconscious while they were mutilating him,' Rose says. Her calmness is exactly what is needed, but it's unsettling all the same. 'There are, however, many potions and preparations that can render a man insensitive to pain even as he remains conscious. Powerless, paralysed, but lucid. Aware exactly what is being done to him.'

That's less reassuring. I can't help but shudder at the thought of what must be the ultimate nightmare.

'But it is late.' Rose stands up, takes her cup to the sink and places it ready to be washed. 'I imagine tomorrow will be a busy day. You should get some rest now.'

I thought perhaps the tea Rose made for me might have a little something in it to help me sleep. That's how it would work in a novel, at least. As the minutes creep slowly by on the screen of my phone, midnight leaching into one o'clock and on towards two, I wonder whether she didn't use the wrong potion.

The house feels safe, a refuge in a way my flat in London never has. The only other place I've felt so comfortable is Newmore, my aunt's old lodge up in the Perthshire highlands. I fled there last year expecting to hate it as much as I had when I was a bored little girl, but the house welcomed me. I found sanctuary there for the few days I needed to regroup and take control of the madness. My stay with Rose has been much the same, except that I've a horrible feeling things are about to get a lot worse.

I've seen dead bodies before. Too many dead bodies. I've seen mutilation, too. A car crash can do horrendous damage to a person; jumping in front of a train even more so. I've had to deal with both in my career as a police officer. And I found my former boss, Pete Copperthwaite, beaten black and blue, then executed with a single, close-range shot to the forehead. Shot by one of his own colleagues, even now working the system to get himself into a low-security, high-comfort prison. I'll never forget the expression on Pete's face. But it's the memory of the dead young man from earlier this evening that keeps me awake. It's there whenever I close my eyes, so I stare at the ceiling instead until the shadow patterns of the ornate plaster cornicing high overhead begin to swirl and form into strange monsters, murderous creatures hunting me down to carve out my still-beating heart.

And then I wake up again with a start. A glance at the digital clock face shows another few minutes have oozed by. I've had this sort of thing before. Something on my mind that won't let me sleep until I acknowledge it, file it away, slot it into the hole in the puzzle where it belongs. So what is it? The young man, naked, mutilated, cleaned by the evening rain. His face was pale with blood loss, eyes closed so I've no idea what colour they were. The water had pasted his hair to his scalp, but it was thin, cut quite short, though not as short as my own. He had a scrawny look to him, as if food was something that came his way only infrequently, but I don't remember seeing any track marks on his arms. He wasn't an addict. So why does my brain want me to remember what he looked like?

It hits me then. I've seen him before. But how could I have seen him? Where could I have seen him? I can't place him, but at least I know now why my brain wouldn't let me sleep. I can get Harrison or DS Laird to send me a photograph. That'll hopefully jog my memory.

I'm still mulling over who the young man is when my phone goes off. I must have been asleep for some of that time though, as it's gone six in the morning. The screen says DCI Bain, so my brief thought of letting it go to voicemail is swiftly curtailed.

'Sir.' I try to sound awake.

'You're a bloody nuisance, Fairchild. You know that?'

He's in a good mood then. 'I take it this is about the young man.' I pull aside the covers and slide my feet into the wool-lined sheepskin slippers Rose lent me. Staring out of the window shows dawn beginning to pink the cloudy sky, promising what might be a good day for some people. I suspect I'm not one of them.

'I have to get up to speed on what's happening, speak to the local DCI in charge and smooth a few things over. Then we need to talk.'

'You want me to report to local CID, sir?'

Bain makes a strange noise down the line, as if he's trying to suppress a coughing fit. It takes him a while to answer my question. 'I don't want you going anywhere near any kind of police station. Where are you now?'

'A house down Leith Walk. Staying with a family friend.'

Another pause then. 'Anywhere nearby we can meet?'

29

I remember the café on the top floor of John Lewis from my university days. 'The Place To Eat' they call it, but it's just as good a place to sit and stare. The tall windows stretching across one entire wall look out across the rooftops towards Leith and beyond to the Firth of Forth. At the northern corner, I can see to Newhaven, Fife in the far distance, and I wonder whether the forensics team are still hard at work in that dank, narrow alley.

'Fairchild.'

I look round from the window to see DCI Bain walking towards me, mug and a biscuit balanced on a tray he holds with one hand, the other carrying a battered leather satchel. I've already got my own coffee. I suggested this place because it's easy to find and close to the city centre. It's also not too far from Rose's place, which meant I could get here early. Bain suggested ten o'clock, so it's just as well I did. I arrived as the doors opened at nine, and it's still only half past.

'Sir.' I wait for a tense minute or so as he puts down the tray, takes the mug and biscuit from it, then shrugs off his coat and hangs it over the back of his chair. I know what's coming, but he's going to take his time and make me sweat for it. Only once he's settled down and taken a long sip of his drink does he finally get to the point.

'What the actual fuck do you think you're doing visiting a crime scene like that?'

I'm fine, thank you. How are you? 'I didn't actually have much choice, sir. When the local police ask you to do something, it's usually a good idea to comply, is it not?'

He studies me for a moment, maybe trying to work out whether I'm taking the piss. I am, a bit. This whole situation is beginning to make me tetchy. I'm not even sure if he's my boss, although I can't deny he's a superior officer and so I have to do what he tells me.

'OK then.' He holds his mug in both hands, elbows on the table in a manner that would infuriate my mother. 'What did you make of it?'

So now my input is valued? 'It looked almost exactly the same as the body in the park near my flat. Except that he was black and this poor bastard was white. I've only seen those few photos you showed me back when I found Dan Jones, but they were all black too, weren't they?'

'Most of the victims we've linked together are, yes. But not all of them. The body we found in Cardiff was Caucasian, and one of the Manchester ones too. This makes three white, five black.'

I try to remember the conversation in Bain's office, the crime-scene photographs, the geographic spread of the victims. There had been six, he said. So with the one in the park in London and the young man from last night, that makes eight. Plus the one who survived. 'What about Jones?'

'Who?' Bain had been about to take a drink. Trying to coordinate that with countering my question is clearly too much for him, as he spills coffee all over the table. I wait until he's cleaned it up with a paper napkin before answering.

'Dan Jones, sir.'

'What about him?' he asks after a silent count to ten I can see ticking away behind his eyes.

'He wasn't like the others.'

'I know that, Fairchild. He's still alive, for one thing. Heart's still beating, not ripped out of his chest.'

This last bit of sarcasm is spoken perhaps a little too loudly for a public space like the café we're sitting in. A grey-haired lady who's taken the table just behind ours lets out a little squeak of surprise, her teacup rattling in the saucer as she rushes to put it down before she spills any. Seems the DCI isn't the only clumsy drinker in here.

'I mean, he must have escaped, sir. But you saw his injuries. And he wasn't exactly the world's healthiest specimen to start with. That badly hurt, bleeding, he'd be hard pushed to walk more than a few hundred metres, surely. And people must have seen him, right?'

Bain puts his mug down with less clattering than the old lady this time, then rubs at his face with one hand, working finger and thumb into the bridge of his nose before finally looking at me.

'Believe it or not, we actually know how to run an investigation, Detective Constable. I was conducting inquiries while you were still playing Lady of the Manor up in One Horse Northamptonshire, or wherever it is you lived.'

It's a cheap insult, and I manage to stop myself from protesting, but he's not finished anyway.

'As it happens, one of the first things we considered was that Jones must have somehow got himself to the spot where you found him. And it had occurred to both myself and Detective Sergeant Latham that he couldn't have walked far with his bollocks cut off.'

'Oh my word.' The lady at the nearby table has a Morningside accent not unlike Rose's when she's putting on her airs and graces. She has the volume, too, although her words are those of a soprano compared to Rose's deeper, more contralto voice. She's loud enough to get Bain's attention, anyway. He swivels in his seat to look at her with what must be a withering glare if her

191

hurried departure is anything to go by. At least his temper's cooled a little by the time he returns his focus to me.

'Karen Eve has been going through all the CCTV footage we've managed to collect from the area around your apartment block, and believe me when I say that's a fuck of a lot. We've also had your bins and that whole alleyway forensically examined. We are, basically, collating all the information you might expect and doing everything we can to work out where he came from.'

Put like that, I can see that my initial question might have been a bit annoying. Of course they're doing the job properly, but I'm not involved so I can't see it. I can't help, only make useless suggestions.

'Is there—?'

'No, Fairchild, there isn't anything you can do. Unless it involves keeping the fuck out of our way.'

I slump back in my seat, take a swig of not very nice coffee. I'm about to say something more when Bain speaks again.

'And that brings us to the point of this meeting.' The change in his tone is abrupt, switching from the slightly exasperated DCI to something a touch more reasonable. He even puts a little sigh into his voice when he looks straight at me and says, 'It's time for you to leave.'

The Place To Eat is always a bustle of noise, people coming and going, taking a moment out of their busy shopping experience to refuel. And yet in that moment it seems like someone has switched off the sound. There's just me and DCI Bain with our coffees, the rest of the world outside our own protective bubble.

'Leave?' I know what it means, but I can't help myself from asking all the same. 'Why?'

Bain reaches down to the satchel he brought with him, undoes the clasps and retrieves a newspaper from inside. My heart drops as I see the tabloid format. It almost gives out altogether when he unfolds the paper and lays it on the table in front of me. I thought that Police Scotland top was quite fashionable, but it makes me look like a little girl in her big brother's hand-me-downs.

'Detective Sergeant Laird and Detective Constable Harrison are currently explaining to their boss why they took you to the crime scene last night. Would you care to enlighten me as to how they even knew you were in town?'

I open my mouth to say 'Because Shepherd told them,' but then my brain catches up. Bain didn't know they'd been informed of my arrival, and he certainly didn't know I was going to speak to Mrs Jones. I know Shepherd wanted plausible deniability, but that's taking it a bit far, surely?

'Would you believe it if I told you I bumped into DC Harrison and her flatmate a couple of nights ago, sir? Seems her local pub is the same one I used to drink in when I was a student. Some coincidence, eh?'

'It's no bloody wonder Billy Latham can't stand the sight of you.' Bain rubs at his face again, then puts his hand down on the paper, covering up the headline 'Newhaven Murder!' Well, at least they're not talking about me, even if I'm easy enough to spot in the photograph.

'Look, sir. I came here to get away from that kind of attention, remember? I was doing a pretty good job of it, too. But when that body turned up, they needed to know if it was similar to what you've been dealing with already. Janie . . . DC Harrison knew I was in town, where I was staying. It made sense to get me to have a look, if only to confirm what they already suspected.'

'It's still bloody irregular. I was already on my way up.'

'They couldn't leave the body there, and photographs only go so far. It's not that long since you took me to see that poor bastard you found in the park near my flat, anyway. If that was OK, then why not this?'

Bain pulls the paper back towards him, folds it and places it so that I can only see the bottom half of the photograph. 'End of the day, you going to the crime scene's a Police Scotland problem. You could have said no, but then we both know you never would. No, my problem is that you were seen and photographed. They don't seem to have worked out who you are yet, but it's only a matter of time.'

I'm not stupid. I know where this is leading. 'You want me gone.'

'It's for the best. We're going to be up here working this case for a few days at least, probably more if my gut feeling's right. Thanks to some nuisance local reporter making the same connections as us, the media focus is already more than I'd like. No way that's going to get anything but worse.'

I start to protest. I've run away from these leeches far too much already. My instinct is to turn and fight, but I know deep down that you can't win against the tabloids. Not that way. I learned that lesson when I broke Chet Wentworth's expensive camera. If I'm ever going to be able to work again, then I need the press to forget about me, find someone new to pick on. Frustrating as it is, I need to lay low and bide my time.

'Knew you'd understand,' Bain says, taking my silence for compliance. He plays with his mug for a while. 'Meantime, there is actually something you can do. You can help Eve go through the CCTV footage. We've a ton of it from around your park too. Might as well earn that salary you're getting paid, right?'

'Wait. You want me to go back to London? Back to work?' I'm delighted, of course. It's boring as sin going through CCTV footage, but it beats daytime telly any day. The look on Bain's face tells me that's not the main reason he's sending me back though.

'You want the press to see me, don't you? You want their attention focused down south so you can get on with the job up here.' It takes the shine off being reinstated. Bain simply shrugs by way of confirmation.

'You just do what you do, Fairchild. Leave the rest of it to us.'

30

'Such a dreadful shame. There was so much more I wanted to show you.'

It's only a few minutes from John Lewis back down Leith Walk to Rose's place. I almost called a cab once DCI Bain had left anyway. I'd thought myself safe up here in Edinburgh, but the media circus was always there. The newspaper didn't mention me by name, so I've that much going for me. But I'm not so naive as to think that'll be the end of it. Even now, I can feel the long lenses panning across the empty skies like search-lights, seeking me out. Walking down the street, surrounded by people who didn't even give me a second glance, I still felt naked, vulnerable. And Bain wants me to invite that scrutiny in, just so he can pursue his enquiries in peace.

'You've been so kind to me, Rose. I wouldn't want to bring the worst of the country's gutter press to your front door.'

'Nonsense, my dear. They couldn't find this place if I didn't want them to.'

There's something about the way she says it that makes me think she's telling the truth, although I've no idea how that's even possible. No, I know it's not possible.

'They'll find me. I can't stop that from happening. But there's no need for them to make life miserable for everyone else.'

'Well, at least let me help you pack.' Rose has been standing in the bedroom doorway, but now she comes into the room.

I didn't have much with me when I arrived, but we went shopping and now my expanded wardrobe has as much chance of fitting into my bag as Jonathan Stokes has of developing a conscience. Without another word, Rose strides over to the large wardrobe opposite the bed. It leans slightly into the room, tilted by the ancient and gently sloping floorboards, and I haven't dared approach it in the days I've been here for fear of being crushed. She opens it without a care, reaches inside and comes out with the sort of leather Gladstone bag my great-grandfather might have taken to India.

'This should be big enough for everything,' she says, carrying it back to the bed as if it weighs nothing. I can see from the way the mattress sinks that I'd struggle to lift it even when empty, but if there's one thing I've learned from my short stay here it's that there's no point in trying to protest when Rose has an idea in her head. I step back and watch as she folds my new clothes and old with an expertise that would have impressed the matrons at St Humbert's, swiftly and neatly packing the bag.

'I'll let you sort out all your electronic gubbins.' She waves a chubby hand at the Louis XIV dressing table over which I've inelegantly draped my laptop, phone charger and other paraphernalia essential for twenty-first-century living. With all the clothes in the Gladstone bag it will fit in my backpack no problem.

It doesn't take long to collect everything together, and soon enough I'm downstairs standing at the door. Rose places the bag down carefully before giving me a hug that lasts longer than expected.

'You take care of yourself, Con. I'd say don't go getting yourself into trouble, but I know it has a habit of finding you anyway. Just be careful, OK?'

She sounds like I imagine a mother should, sending her daughter off into the world on her own for the first time.

'I'll do my best.' I heave the bag up as she opens the door, half expecting to be greeted by a hailstorm of camera flashes and shouted paparazzi questions. Instead there's just the small court-yard, the gate and my Volvo parked across the road. I'm going to miss this place. It's only as I step outside that I remember my manners. 'And thank you, too. For everything, but especially the wig.'

Leaving Edinburgh is more of a wrench than I thought it would be. I guess I'd hoped my stay might last longer. I feel bad for not saying goodbye to Janie Harrison and her flatmate, Manda. As I hit the bypass, heading for the A1, I can't help thinking about them, which is strange given how little time I spent in their company. Maybe I'll drop them a line when I get home. Not that I'm really sure where home is these days.

The border's flown past and I'm almost at Newcastle before I realise what day it is today. Friday. My brother's wedding is tomorrow. I was going to miss it, should I still stay away? As the thought hits me, I reach for the button to switch on the radio. It's not as if I expect there to be any mention of it; Ben and Charlotte might be newsworthy for the more seedy tabloids, but they're not exactly royalty. It's more a reflex action to hide the awkwardness of not knowing what to do. The radio's as old as the car, not some flash aftermarket thing fitted by whichever street racer bought it when Essex Constabulary were done chasing robbers up the M11. It takes a while to warm up and find a station, then the sound of a newsreader fills the interior.

'. . . *young man found brutally murdered in an Edinburgh suburb. Initial reports say the victim was badly mutilated. Police are asking for anyone who was in the Newhaven area on the night to come forward . . .*'

I hit the button again, plunging the car back into noisy silence as the road rolls away underneath me. I don't need to know what's going on back there, and I don't want to hear my name pop up either. I'd connect my phone, play some music or maybe an audiobook, but I can't do that while driving and I don't want to stop now I'm moving, so I'm left with my thoughts.

I can see all too easily how Bain is using me. I can't even blame him that much. I'd probably do the same to someone else if it meant I could get on with my investigation free from interference by the press. That doesn't mean I'm all that happy about being forced back to London and into the spotlight. On the other hand, at least I'll be doing some actual police work, helping Karen to scroll through all the many hours of CCTV footage. That means the viewing room at the station, with its stench of body odour and farts. It means the disapproving stares and muttered insults of my would-be colleagues, too. But it's work, and it gets me back on active duty of sorts.

But first I have to deal with this weekend. I texted Aunt Felicity to ask if it would be OK to stay a couple of nights and she didn't even mention the wedding when she replied. Maybe she just thinks I've changed my mind about not going. Have I changed my mind? Could I go?

I'm speeding past signs to Pontefract, thinking about whether to stay on the A1 or take the turning to the M1 when I remember the Gladstone bag in the back of the car. Sitting in a sturdy cardboard box on top of my neatly-folded clothes is the mouse-brown and grey wig. I've got my mother's spectacles with their non-prescription lenses, and some of the dresses Rose insisted on packing would be perfectly suitable for a wedding, even if I expect most of the guests will be wearing much higher fashion. What better way to try out my disguise? If I can get past the nation's paparazzi without being recognised, then at the very least I've some control over my situation when I get back to London. And I can't deny there's a certain thrill at the thought of pulling the wool over their eyes.

31

Even with my early start and Rose's help packing, the day's still faded to evening by the time I turn off the A14 and drive down the narrow lanes to Harston Magna. The village itself is decked out as if it were Christmas, with bunting strung between the few lamp-posts, and the pub lit up like a navigation buoy. Past the church, I catch a glimpse of a huge marquee in the gardens of the hall, and a well-made sign a bit further along directs cars to park in the field where once my pony grazed. Not that I had the riding bug for long. Ben was always better in the saddle, and the humiliation of falling off in the arena at my first gymkhana soon dampened my enthusiasm for equestrianism.

My phone flashes up a text as I'm about to turn down the lane to Fold's Cottage. Short and to the point, my aunt redirecting me at exactly the right moment.

Change of plan. Cottage full. Go to Glebe House.

I imagine every spare room in the village is taken, and many of the better hotels in the towns nearby. I'd not anticipated ever going back to Roger DeVilliers' home, though. Of course, technically it belongs to his widow, Margo, now. Assuming he didn't screw over his family in death like he did in life.

It's not far from my aunt's cottage to the Glebe House. Time was I used to walk there through the woods. Night's coming on fast as I turn down the drive, noticing the 'For Sale' sign nailed to a post by the gate. I'm surprised to see very few lights on in the house, and only one car parked outside. Surely more people will be staying here?

The air's cold and slightly damp as I climb out of my Volvo. Stretching pops my back into line after so long sitting, and I realise the coffee I drank at Scotch Corner wants out now. I can't hear any noise, save the plinking of the car engine as it cools and the dull roar of the distant A14. And then the front door clicks open. Light spills out from the hall, the shadow of a lone figure outlined on the gravel. I take a couple of steps forward before I can see who's there.

'Margo?'

She has a glass in her hand, and I remember how she was on the gin in the middle of the afternoon the last time I saw her.

'Constance Fairchild.' It's a statement of fact, and a condemnation at the same time. I sort of understand, although to be honest I was only the bearer of bad news, not the author of it. You'd think she might even be grateful to me for freeing her from the prison of her loveless marriage, but then people aren't always like that. I suspect she resents me airing her dirty laundry in public far more than she appreciates getting rid of the bad smell.

'I had a text from Aunt Felicity. She told me to come here.'

'Of course she did.' Margo doesn't even try to hide the sigh in her voice, but before she can say anything else, she's forced to step to one side as another figure pushes past and rushes out to greet me.

'Con! You came!'

I barely have time to react before I'm swept up in a fierce hug. It's been a month or two since I last saw her, and I swear my half-sister's grown in that time.

'Izzy. How the hell are you?' I squeeze back as tightly as she's squeezing me, then struggle away. There's only so much a full bladder can take.

'Connie. Thought you weren't coming.' Another figure pushes past Margo, stepping into the gathering darkness. Charlotte's holding a glass, like her mother, but it doesn't stop her from hugging me almost as fiercely as Izzy.

'Change of plan.' I'm about to tell them the real reason for my coming back to Harston Magna, but some small sense of self-preservation kicks in at the last minute. 'I couldn't bear to let Ben down. Not on his big day. He here?'

Charlotte looks at me as if I've gone mad. 'Here? Of course not, Connie. Can't see the bride before the wedding.'

I decide it's probably best not to point out that they've been living together for at least a year, and instead fetch my bag from the back of the car. It's heavy enough that I need both hands to lift it, but it gets admiring glances from Charlotte.

'Is that vintage, Connie? Sweet. Must have cost a fortune. I had no idea detectives got paid so much.'

As always with Charlotte it's all about money. 'Actually, I'm just borrowing it from a friend.' I look back to the front door, expecting to see Margo still there, defiantly blocking my entry. She's gone though, and an altogether more welcoming figure has replaced her.

'You got the text then?' Aunt Felicity strides out to greet me, a quick air kiss to either cheek in the French style. Then she takes my luggage as if it weighs no more than a Prada handbag. 'Come on then, children. It's far too cold for dawdling about out here.'

I take a deep breath, the chill air clean in my lungs. Then with a conscious effort to quell the rising sense of doom, I follow everyone inside.

For all its unhappy memories, the Glebe House isn't a bad place. At least not now its lord and master has gone. Not quite on the same vast scale as Harston Magna Hall, it's nevertheless far larger than any family could possibly need. Built in the days when the second sons of landed gentry were expected both to take holy orders and father large families, it has at least eight bedrooms and countless smaller attic rooms that would once have been servants' quarters. Now it has that empty quality I remember so well from my own childhood home, a place no longer fit for purpose.

Aunt Felicity leads me up to one of the guest bedrooms tucked away at the back of the house. Its window would look out over the woods towards the church and the hall, except that it's dark outside and the curtains are drawn. She dumps my borrowed bag on the end of the bed with an audible 'oof', and I can't help wondering why she felt the need to carry it when I'm half her age.

'I was stronger the last time I saw this.' She takes a couple of deep breaths to recover, before speaking again. 'Given that you left a week ago with just that,' she points at my rucksack, slung over my shoulder, 'can I assume you and Rose went shopping?'

Unbuckling the straps on the bag, I take out the box and then the wig from inside it. I've only tried it on a couple of times so far, and make a bit of a mess of fitting it this time. 'What do you think? Mother's old specs and some frumpy dresses. Nobody will recognise me at all.'

Aunt Flick tilts her head to one side, an unconvinced expression on her face. Then she steps closer and rearranges the wig, tucking stray strands of my red hair under its mesh lining. 'Or you could just have stayed in Scotland.'

I go back to the bag, the long hair tumbling over my shoulders an unfamiliar weight. DCI Bain took his newspaper with him after our meeting this morning, but I picked up one of my own on the way back to Rose's house. I unfold it and hand it to my aunt without a word. She stares at it with much the same unconvinced expression she gave the wig.

'Will they ever leave you alone?'

I'm about to answer when a light knock at the door is followed by Charlotte walking in without waiting for an answer. She does a perfect double-take as she sees me; the girl should have been an actress.

'Connie? Is that you?' A little puzzled tilt of the head and then she laughs. 'Oh my God, it's perfect. Just wait till I tell Ben. No, no. Let's not tell him at all. See if he recognises you.'

Her excitement is almost contagious, but I catch motion behind her at the still-open door, and see Izzy standing there. For a moment my half-sister doesn't realise I've seen her, and her face is pure anguish. How must it hurt her to be back here, back in the house where her step father abused her, shared her with his perverted friends? Then she sees my gaze is on her and the mask comes down, all smiles for her big sister. Half-sister.

'Suits you, Con. Always thought your hair was too short.'

'Says the girl with the buzzcut.' I tease the wig off, laying it carefully in its box. One of the first things Izzy did when the dust settled last year was to cut off all her hair, probably her own attempt to keep the gutter press at bay. It's growing back, but she still looks like an extra from *GI Jane*. 'How you doing?'

'Could be worse.' She shrugs, opens her hands up to indicate the bedroom and the house. 'Hoped I'd never have to come back here.'

'Won't be for long though, will it. I saw the For Sale sign on the drive.'

'Just went up this morning. Talk about timing, eh? Had to get the whole house cleaned so the estate agent could photograph it.'

I can tell that she'd rather have seen the place burn to the ground. And all the bad memories with it. I'm amazed that she's as sane as she is, given all that she went through.

'You ready for Charlotte's big day, then?' I do my best to change the subject. Izzy rolls her eyes at the bride-to-be.

'The dress she's got me wearing? Don't think I'll ever be ready for that. Glad you're here for it though. I was a bit pissed off when they told me you weren't coming.'

'I'm still not.' I pick the wig back up. 'Disguise, remember? I don't want the press giving me all the attention when it's meant to be all about your sister.'

'You're so kind, Connie,' Charlotte interrupts. 'But really. We've laid on the best security. Nobody will get in who's not supposed to be there.'

I smile sweetly at her naivety, exchange a more knowing glance with Izzy. 'Still, Char. Best not to take any chances, eh?'

She pouts in that schoolgirl way that doubtless works wonders on my brother but has zero effect on me.

'No chance of persuading you to be a bridesmaid, then?'

32

I've always enjoyed a good wedding. OK, so I'm not big on the whole church thing, and pledging to love, honour and obey is a bit weird, but there's something about two people in love that makes me happy. It's odd, really, given my own patchy record in that department.

I don't think I've ever had a relationship last longer than a few months, and the only proposal of marriage ever made to me was mortifying to say the least. Simon. I wonder whatever happened to him. I wonder what I ever saw in him, for that matter. Bloody idiot should have known better than to pop the question in public, too. He must have worked out by then that I don't like being pressured into things. On the other hand, he did me a favour even if I hated him at the time. If he'd asked me in private, I might be Mrs Geoffrey now.

For once the weather's being kind, which is just as well. St Thomas's might have been built at a time when everyone in the surrounding neighbourhood was expected to attend church on a Sunday, but even so it's not big enough for all Charlotte's guests. The paddock's filled with Range Rovers, Jaguars and the occasional Rolls-Royce. One of the neighbouring farmers has helpfully parked his tractor nearby, to tow out some of the more ridiculous cars that people have turned up in. She has a lot of friends who like Porsches and Ferraris, it seems. Although some of them might be Ben's friends too, I suppose.

He's at the front of the church, slightly shabby even in his best penguin suit and fidgeting nervously as he waits for her to turn up. For an awful moment I can't remember the name of his best man, a tall, strikingly good-looking chap who holds himself with military bearing. His suntanned face suggests an overseas posting recently, probably Afghanistan or somewhere in the Middle East, and he scans the congregation with sharp eyes. That's why he catches my gaze, sees that I'm staring from my pew near the back. Aunt Felicity wanted me to sit at the front with the rest of the family, but my disguise wouldn't be much good then. I didn't come with her to the church, walking through the damp woods instead. Just as well too, given the media scrum camped out in Church Lane. None of them gave me a second glance as I walked past, a couple of steps behind a Premiere League footballer and his impossibly plastic wife.

But now the best man's staring at me, the puzzled frown of half-recognition on his face probably a close mirror of my own, and I can't remember his name. I look away, aware that I've been clocked and before I can be pointed out to Ben. It was Charlotte's idea not to tell him I was here, but to wait until the reception before springing the surprise on him. She'll be livid if he finds out before she's ready, and I don't want to test my new disguise quite so rigorously. At least not yet.

Alex. Alex Fortescue. The name pops into my head at the same moment the bridal march pipes up on the organ. How many years has it been since I snogged him at one of Ben's birthday parties? Ten? Twelve? Wandering hands, if I remember rightly. Had to give him a slap before he got too familiar.

I'd not thought about it until now, but with her father dead, there's no one to lead Charlotte up the aisle. It's not even her first wedding, so technically he gave her away once already. As it is, she walks alone, Izzy looking uncomfortable in a bridesmaid's outfit behind her. There's a slightly strained atmosphere in the church and I realise it's not all that long since Roger DeVilliers lay in his coffin almost exactly where the vicar is now standing. I push the thought aside, and look around the congregation, as I always do when in church. I'm not exactly going to pray, after all.

There's a bit of a commotion at the door just before the organist finishes with a flourish, and I see two unwelcome faces slip in past the ushers. Jonathan Stokes and his parasitic twin Chet Wentworth are almost certainly not on the guest list, but they slink through the shadows at the back of the church and take up position near the baptismal font. If I wasn't trying to avoid all attention, I'd probably see them out. As it is, I keep a wary eye on them as much to make sure they've not recognised me as to check they're not making a nuisance of themselves. Photographs of the back of Charlotte's dress aren't going to make the front pages, although they'll probably be on some of the gossip websites before the champagne's been uncorked.

The wedding service is much like all the others I've been to, longer than I'd like but still over mercifully swiftly. At least we're none of us Catholics. Freshly-kissed bride and groom troop out, friends and family falling in behind them like good soldiers in expectation of a feast. It's only when it comes to my turn to exit the church that I realise the paparazzi are all still outside and manically snapping at everyone. I'd do what I did the last time, duck through the chantry and out the back way to the hall, but Stokes and Wentworth are inside, watching everyone like hawks. The one time I needed the ushers to do their jobs properly, they've all buggered off to throw confetti.

You've got this, Con. You're well disguised, and they're not expecting you to be at the back with the stragglers. Run the gauntlet and get it over with. I slide to the end of the pew, then slot myself into the slow-moving train of people, alongside a young man who I think I might have seen on daytime telly when I was stuck in my flat a couple of months back. He gives me a nervous grin, mutters something about the crowd that I don't quite catch, and then we both step from the darkness of the church out into the bright morning light.

I remember one of my early duties as a uniform constable was to patrol the area around some of London's more swanky night-clubs. The sort of places pop stars and junior royals hang out until three in the morning. That's probably where I first met the likes of Stokes and Wentworth, only then they had no idea who they were talking to when they chatted with us police officers while waiting for the celebs to show up.

The wall of photographers is something like those far-off nights. There's a certain pride to be had in the knowledge that my sister-in-law can draw such attention, but it's tainted by the realisation of exactly why. Charlotte alone might be worth a few column inches in the gossip pages of the weekend editions, but Charlotte after her father's fall from grace is far more news-worthy.

I'm far more newsworthy too, and I find myself tensing as I step into the blinding flashlights, holding my breath in anticipa-tion of the first shout of 'Constance! Connie! Over here, love!'

It doesn't come, and as I follow the slightly disappointed tail-enders in the congregation over towards the hall and waiting marquee, I let out a sigh of genuine relief. My daytime-television friend might be upset at not being recognised, but I'm really quite glad.

'Excuse me. Miss?'

The voice comes from the church door, and I unthinkingly turn to face the man speaking. My heart leaps into my throat as I see Jonathan Stokes walking down the steps towards me. I hadn't realised just how tense this whole situation had made me, but ten years of training almost go out of the window. Then I see what he's carrying.

'You left this behind.' He holds out my handbag. Or more correctly, Aunt Felicity's handbag. It might well have been fashionable in the seventies, but unlike much from that decade it hasn't made a comeback yet.

'Umm . . . Thanks?' I can't make up my mind whether to try an accent, so probably sound like a mad woman. There's no indication in his manner that he's recognised me though.

'You a friend of the bride, or maybe an old flame of the groom?'

'You what?' I slur the last word slightly, taking the bag at the same time.

'Chums with Charlotte, perhaps? You were on her side of the church.'

'Yeah. We was at school, y'know.' Now I'm laying it on too much. Stokes twitches slightly, his attention more focused.

'Saint Humbert's?'

'Naw. Fairchild Primary, like.' I wave hand and bag in the direction of the village school. Even as I do so, I realise my mistake.

'Local girl, eh? You'll know Connie Fairchild, then.'

I peer through my mother's fake spectacles at him, trying to work out if he knows and is taking the piss. This could just be a play for information, of course. If he doesn't know who I am, then the fact that I'm at the wedding service means I'm close enough to the family to have juicy gossip.

'I have to get going. Don't want to miss the confetti.' I turn away, but quick as a flash he grabs my arm. It's fortunate I'm wearing long-sleeved gloves, as his grip rides the sleeve of my jacket up my arm a little, and without them my tattoos would be on show. Not quite in character with the demure woman I'm pretending to be. My every instinct is to thumb-lock him and throw him to the ground, but I fight back the urge. Something in my glare gets through to him though, and he releases me swiftly.

'Sorry. I just wanted to give you this.' His other hand produces a business card. 'I'm always on the lookout for stories, and you never know, it could be worth your while.'

I hesitate for a moment, then take the card from him. He brushes the back of my hand with one finger, and again I am grateful for the gloves. Actual skin-to-skin contact with such an unpleasant individual might make me throw up. It's enough to know he truly doesn't recognise me under this wig, though. As I hurry away, glancing at the scant details on the card, I realise that having his mobile number and email address might come in handy sometime too.

33

I can't kid myself the wedding reception will be fun. No doubt hoping to make more money from an exclusive with one of the gossip magazines, Charlotte has organised security that's surprisingly effective at keeping the unwanted paparazzi away. There's a slightly awkward moment when they don't want to let me in either, but once that's out of the way things settle down.

Ben's face is a picture when I reach him in the line. I wince as he shouts over the noise to his best man, 'Hey, Alex. Look who's here,' and waves him over. Fortescue's a couple of inches taller than me, even in my chunky-heeled boots, and his time in the army has straightened his back from the slouching teenager I remember. He stares at me in confusion for quite a while before my brother leans in close and half whispers, half shouts, 'It's Con, you idiot. She's hiding from the press.' At almost the exact same moment a flash goes off and I glance up to see a chubby-faced photographer giving us all the thumbs up.

'Fuck's sake. You let Chet Wentworth in here?'

'Who?' Ben asks.

'The photographer there. Chet bloody Wentworth. He's one of the worst paps I've ever had the misfortune to meet.'

'There a problem?' Charlotte leans in to the conversation, her dress not allowing her to come any closer than a shout away.

'Him.' I hook a thumb over my shoulder at the photographer,

212

determined to keep my back to him as much as possible. 'How the hell did he get in?'

Charlotte's thoughts play across her perfectly made-up face as she follows the direction I'm pointing in, then focuses back on me. 'It's OK. I get to choose the photos they'll run. Or at least veto the worst of them.'

'But Wentworth?' I'm aware the queue of people waiting to greet the new couple is growing. Time to move on. 'Never mind. Just try to keep me out of it, OK?'

I feel wretched for adding another worry to Charlotte's already heavy load. This is her big day, after all. Well, her second big day. But the last thing I need is to be recognised, and having multiple photographs of me in my new disguise out there isn't exactly the best way of staying incognito.

'Sorry.' I step in as close as I can get, and give her a hug. 'Don't worry about it. I'll just stay out of his way. Be warned though. He's a total shit. Sell his own mother for a celebrity upskirt. Might want to warn some of your more photogenic friends too.'

Alex catches up with me as I walk away from the line before having to confront my parents. His steering hand to my elbow is less unpleasant than Jonathan Stokes's grab outside, but it's an imposition nonetheless. He's quick on the uptake though, letting go of me the moment he sees my scowl.

'You want me to arrange an accident for him?' He nods towards Wentworth, still hanging by the bridal party and snapping everyone as they present themselves. I'm tempted by his offer, consider suggesting instead that Wentworth's camera might be accidentally damaged, but the images will be on a tiny memory card, and they're virtually indestructible. Besides, if he doesn't get any photos, then Charlotte probably won't get paid by whatever magazine's bought the exclusive rights to the bun fight.

'Maybe some other time, Alex. But thanks.'

A waitress passes by with champagne flutes on a tray. Alex

grabs two, but I turn him down when he offers me one. 'Need to keep a clear head, more's the pity.'

'You've changed, Con. Used to be the life and soul of the party. And you could drink any of Ben's friends under the table. Me included.'

'We were young and stupid.' I almost say naive. 'You've changed too. Army life suits you.'

'How'd you . . . ?' He pauses a moment, staring at me with a puzzled expression. Then he laughs. 'I forgot. You're a detective now.'

'That, and I'm sure Ben mentioned it once, a few years back. Light Infantry, wasn't it?'

'It was.' There's a bit of a pause after his answer, then he takes a long swig of champagne. If I was looking for a challenge, I might try to get him to elucidate. The phrase 'special forces' springs to mind, but despite his company being surprisingly pleasant, I've other things to think about. I don't even know if he's married, although I can't see a lost plus one hanging about. Or a ring on his finger, for that matter.

I look around the marquee, seeing a few faces I know. All my family, and Charlotte's, are still in the line welcoming guests. Soon we'll be ordered to our tables though, and then there'll be eating and drinking too much. I'm trying to work out what table I've been relegated to when I spot someone I recognise over by the bar. Someone I recognise, but can't quite believe is here, even if my mother invited him.

'Well, that's just fucking marvellous.'

I thought I said it under my breath, and there's enough noise in this place to drown out an explosion, but somehow Alex hears me.

'Something wrong? Only I can't help noticing you swear a lot.'

I drag my eyes away from the object of my consternation, look up at him to see the smile on his face. 'Does it bother you?'

'Nothing I don't hear from a hundred squaddies every day. Usually there's a reason though.'

'There is.' I point across the marquee to where even now the Reverend Doctor Edward Masters is accepting a glass of something that doesn't look like champagne from a nervous waiter. 'Him.'

I don't know if I'm more relieved or annoyed that the seating arrangements don't put me on the same table as Masters. Had I not decided to duck out of the wedding altogether, I'd be up at the top with the family and bridal party. As it is, Aunt Flick's decided to call me Jennifer Golightly, and I'm tucked away at the back of the marquee. The reverend doctor is closer to the front, although he, like me, appears to have come alone. I'm surprised not to see his security detail, but then I remember the trouble I had getting in. Not just the uninvited paparazzi being kept at bay, it would seem.

Jennifer has only the vaguest of cover stories, so I pretend to be too shy to speak to the other people at the table. I don't know any of them, although I'm fairly sure I've seen at least one in a late-night movie with most of her clothes off. There must be more than two hundred guests in total, and so far I've only seen a couple of dozen I know, half of whom are family in one way or another. Charlotte truly moves in very different circles to a lowly detective constable in the Met.

At least the food is good, and once the waitress assigned to my table works out that I'm not drinking alcohol, she brings me the most divine virgin cocktails. I do my best to make small talk with my new C-list celebrity friends, but once they work out they've as much in common with me as I have with them, they soon give up. Listening in to their unguarded conversations about which director is fucking which actress is at least vaguely entertaining, if only for the novelty value.

And all the while I'm doing my best to keep an eye on Masters. He has his back to me, but his imposing bulk, straining out of his dark suit, is easy enough to spot over the fad-diet waifs between us. As if sensing my gaze on him, at one point he swivels around in his seat and scans the crowd. If he sees me, he makes no sign. That stare is reserved for everyone equally, and I can't help feeling that he's judging us all, even as he tucks into the foie gras.

Only the soft-porn actress is left at the table by the time the speeches are done and the coffee served. For a moment I think she's drunk, but then she turns to me with a fluid, dancer's motion. Leaning across the table, forearms pressed to the thick cotton cloth, she exposes far more of her cleavage than I really want to see, but her smile's genuine enough, along with her conspiratorial wink.

'So, why the disguise then, Jennifer? Who are you really?'

I toy with the idea of pretending I know nothing of what she's talking about, but there's not really any point. She's a professional. Wigs are something she deals with every day, along with pretending to be someone else. Maybe I should ask her for pointers.

'Con.' I hold out my hand for her to shake. 'Con Fairchild.'

Her eyes widen with surprise in an expression that could be seen from the gods. She sits back upright, mouth open as if to shout something. Then she closes it again, clutches the hand I've just shaken to her chest, and starts to chuckle. Her voice is surprisingly pleasant to listen to.

'Well, so you are. Fancy that.' She turns around the nameplate in front of her so I can read it. 'Sue Warner. And before you ask if I "know" your brother,' she makes little rabbit ears with her fingers, 'I worked with Char at the agency. We've been pals for years.'

I don't ask what agency; it's not important. I'm more worried about how easily she penetrated my disguise. 'What gave it away?' I wave a hand in my general direction.

'Honestly, honey? A few things. You play with that hair way too much for someone who's used to the weight of it. And you don't wear glasses normally, do you?' She smiles, leans forward again and points a finger at my hands. 'But it's the tatts that are a dead giveaway. Mousy girls like you don't have tattoos at all, let alone colourful ones on their wrists.'

I can't help myself from pulling down the sleeves on my jacket, which only makes Sue's smile grow wider.

'Trick is to stop being self-conscious about it. Only, if you think too hard about that, it'll just make you self-conscious.'

'Thanks. I'll bear that in mind. This is just to keep the paparazzi off my back though. Seems to be working so far.'

Sue takes a sip of coffee, glances around the room as if looking for the man she came here with. Chances are he's outside having a smoke, or a vape.

'So who's the big guy up near the front?' she says after a moment, nodding her head in the direction of Masters. 'Couldn't help noticing you staring at him for most of the meal.'

'You don't know?' I suppose I shouldn't be all that surprised. 'That's Edward Masters. Founder of the Church of the Coming Light.'

Sue's raised eyebrow confirms that no, she didn't know. 'He some kind of telly evangelist or something? What the hell's he doing here?'

'My mother has something of a history. I'm not sure if "collects" is the right word. Maybe "adopts"? She has a thing about Christian missionaries. Her cult radar is usually better than this though. Masters is only interested in how much money he can squeeze out of her. I'd bet my career on it.'

34

I'm contemplating how early I can leave the party without causing offence when Charlotte appears from the crowd and slumps down into an empty seat at my table. She picks up one of the wine glasses left behind by the men, reaches for the bottle sitting in the middle of the table, and pours herself what's left. Only once she's taken a long drink does she address us both.

'Hey, Sue. You've met Jenny, right?'

My new friend smiles sardonically. *'Jenny,* yeah.'

'It's OK, Char. She knows.' I almost sweep off the wig in a melodramatic manner. Damn thing itches after a while, and my head feels too warm under it. I realise at the last moment how stupid that would be, and settle for simply taking off the spectacles.

'You're not very good at keeping secrets, are you, Connie? For a detective.'

I don't bother answering that, pointing instead to the table where my mother is now sitting, deep in conversation with Masters. 'What on earth is he doing here? I thought Ben said no.'

Charlotte peers somewhat myopically in the direction I'm indicating, a frown furrowing her otherwise perfect brow. 'Who do you mean, Connie? There's loads of people here.'

'Over there, talking to my mother. The Reverend Doctor Edward Masters.'

'Oh God, him. The pastor.' Charlotte takes another swig of

wine. 'Yah. Ben really put his foot down about that. I was so very proud of him.'

I'd forgotten how difficult it was to get a straight answer out of Charlotte if the question is any more complicated than 'Would you like another?'

'But he's here.'

'Lady A was adamant,' Charlotte says after she's been through the rest of the bottles, disappointment growing with each empty one. I'm surprised a waiter hasn't turned up with more, but they're all a bit busy clearing the dining tables from the dance floor right now. 'They almost had a row about it. Me and Earnest hid in the small drawing room, but we could hear them well enough. Think that's why Ben went off to Tokyo, really. He's such a wimp sometimes.'

'Probably not my place to ask, but why does it matter?'

I'd almost forgotten Sue, the actress. I guess that's part of her skill set, fading into the background and observing people.

'My mother wanted Masters to officiate at the wedding, apparently. If she'd insisted on the Bishop of Peterborough, I'd have understood that, but the leader of a pseudo-Christian cult?' I gesture across the room towards the table, only this time Masters is staring at our little group. I look away swiftly, scrabbling for my false spectacles.

'Well, you can ask him yourself. He's coming over here.' Sue pushes back her chair to stand up, grabbing her bag. 'Think I'll go and see what's happened to the boys. Nice meeting you, Jennifer.'

I watch her weave her way through the tables, off towards the exit. Charlotte at least has the decency to stay with me, working through all the empty bottles again in the vain hope one of them might have miraculously refilled. It's only a few moments before a shadow looms across us both, and I feel a hulking presence behind me.

'Mrs Fairchild. May I say you're looking radiant today. That dress is magnificent.'

For a moment I'm confused by the use of my surname, but then it dawns on me he is addressing Charlotte. I've not dared to look at Masters yet, but to avoid his gaze would be more suspicious than meeting it. Sue, damn her for running like that, is right about one thing. The trick to maintaining my disguise is to stop being self-conscious about it. I'm Jennifer Golightly, slightly mousy friend of Charlotte's from . . . where? Primary school? Christ, Con. You're an experienced undercover cop. Least you could do was work up a decent false identity.

'Mr Masters. Or is it Reverend? I'm sorry, I never can remember what to call people.' Charlotte doesn't stand, so I don't either. Masters leans over the table and offers her his hand. He's a large man, broad-shouldered and tall. His head's too big, and the whole effect is made worse by the way his suit strains to contain him. I'd imagine most people would find him intensely intimidating.

'It is your wedding day. You can call me what you please.' He turns his bulk in my direction. 'But will you not introduce me to your friend?'

Charlotte stares at me like a rabbit caught by the hunter's light. I can almost see the hastily concocted name disappearing from her head. She's more pressing things to worry about, so I can't blame her.

'Jennifer.' I stand up and offer my hand, keeping my elbow loose so that my sleeve doesn't ride up my forearm. 'Jennifer Golightly. Charlotte and I were at school together.'

'Really?' He takes my hand, and I'm expecting it to be almost crushed by those massive fingers, but his touch is surprisingly delicate. The contact is swiftly broken, too.

'Are you a priest?' I decide to go for innocence to match my maidenly attire.

'A priest?' he echoes.

'Only Char called you reverend. That's a priest's title, is it not? Church of England?'

'I am a reverend and a doctor, but my ministry is the Church of the Coming Light. We follow the Anglican tradition though.'

'Never heard of it, sorry.'

'We are more focused on people at the . . .' Masters pauses a moment, as if searching for the right word. He looks around the marquee filled with people whose average net worth is probably nearer nine digits than eight, '. . . lower end of society.'

'Bringing the word of God to the streets, isn't it?' Charlotte barely tries to keep the scorn from her voice. 'I'm really not sure what Lady A sees in you, to be honest. But she's my Ben's mother, and she wanted you here.'

If I wasn't used to reading people's expressions, I might have missed the way Masters clenches his jaw, those massive hands forming into fists that are as swiftly again relaxed. He flashes a smile that is all white teeth in his dark face, begins to speak at the exact same moment as the band starts warming up. Another flash of anger across his face, and he seems to swell in his suit, threatening to burst out of it. I have to fight the urge to recoil, then realise that is exactly what poor mousy little Jennifer would do. Before I can move much, he's regained his composure. He nods his head first at me, then a little less convincingly at Charlotte, turns and strides away.

'See what I mean? Dreadful man. Can't think what your mother's doing having him around.'

I can't either, but it seems unlikely I'll have an opportunity to ask her any time soon. The band finish their tuning up, and the call goes out for the bride and groom.

'Oh my God. That's me.' Charlotte struggles to her feet, grabbing lengths of her wedding dress so she can weave back through the tables to find her husband.

'Here, let me.' I take up enough fabric to make a shelter for a family, help guide her back to the top table and the now-empty dance floor. It's only once I get there that I realise I've relinquished my spot in the shadows at the back of the marquee and now I'm almost the centre of attention, and just a few paces away, staring at the both of us with a quizzical expression I don't like the look of, is Chet Wentworth, the paparazzi's paparazzo. I turn away and drop Charlotte's train as he brings up his camera. Flashes pop all over the place as Ben appears and escorts his wife on to the dance floor.

The band starts up, and the two of them waltz slowly round and round, cheers and jeers from the rest of the party making it hard to think straight. I look around for the exit, but there's another cameraman taking posed shots of everyone before they can go outside. Just far enough away to be safe, the Reverend Doctor Edward Masters sits with my mother, their heads bowed together in what is probably conversation but looks like silent prayer. I could sneak out via the catering tent, I suppose. It's not far to walk back to the Glebe House, and I feel I've done enough for the family already today.

Then I feel a presence at my side, look around and up at the best man. He's timed it perfectly, the utter bastard. Just as Ben and Charlotte slide back towards us, beckoning with outstretched arms.

'Miss Golightly.' Alex bows with military precision, winking as his head bobs downwards. 'Would you do me the honour?'

35

My initial terror at being unmasked dissipates once I've worked out how to dance without holding my arms up too high, or shaking my head around too much. The waltz is OK, but when the band starts to strike up something a bit wilder, I make my excuses and head for the nearest table. Alex follows, and when we're far enough from the music to hear ourselves think, he asks if I need a drink.

'Water's fine. Sparkly if they've got it.'

He pauses for just long enough to make me think he's going to query my sobriety, then with a flick of the head he turns and weaves through the bodies to the bar.

'Alex likes you,' Izzy says as I sit beside her. She looks miserable in her bridesmaid's outfit, and I can see why. There are folk the age of my parents here, and lots of people from Charlotte's and my generation. What's missing are any teenagers. Izzy isn't the kind of person to be wowed by celebrity any more than I am, so this must be especially dull for her. I wonder what Charlotte promised to get her to play along.

'Alex's always fancied me. Ever since he first came home from school for half-term with Ben. They must have been, what, twelve?' Which would have been around about the time Izzy was born, now I think about it.

'You fancy him?'

The directness of her question surprises me. Then I

remember how much older than her years she is. All that she's been through.

'Fancy's a bit strong. Difficult not to see the embarrassing teenager in the grown man.'

'He's nice. Doesn't talk down to me like the rest of Ben's friends. I get the feeling they're all a bit scared of him, too. Him being in the SAS or whatever.'

Any further discussion of the best man is curtailed by his arrival at the table, bearing two glasses that look identical. Either he's on gin and tonic or he's decided to keep a clear head too.

'Get you anything, Izzy?' he asks as soon as he realises I'm not alone.

'Nah, I'm good thanks. Just killing time till I can go home. Well, back to the Glebe House, anyway.'

I can hear the mix of anger and frustration in her voice. Understandable given what went on under that roof. She'll hopefully find some peace once it's sold. 'What are you up to these days anyway?'

'International Bac. Thought I might go and study in Europe for a while. If that's not completely fucked up.' Izzy plays with her empty glass, twisting the stem back and forth and staring at the patterns formed in the bowl rather than at me. 'If that falls through I might apply to Edinburgh. Scotland's nice.'

For some reason I think about the dead boy, thrown out like so much trash, his heart missing. It reminds me that there's another world out there beyond the partying, the free booze and people wearing outfits that cost more than the average annual wage. It's a world I'll be returning to on Monday, and I'm not at all sad to be seeing the back of this one.

'You know what time the bride and groom are off?' I ask Alex. He's been sitting silently, staring out at the dancers. Or possibly lost in his own thoughts if the time it takes him to respond to my question is anything to go by.

'Eh? Oh.' He looks at his watch briefly. 'Any time now, I think. I'd better go see if they need anything.' He hauls himself up with surprisingly lithe grace, bows minutely to me and Izzy, then disappears off into the crowd. A moment later, Charlotte appears, changed out of her wedding dress and into something suitable for the short trip to whatever hotel they're spending the night in before heading off to wherever it is they're going. I've not asked, and neither have I been told.

'What a fabulous party.' She grabs the still-full glass that Alex left behind and necks it, before making a sour face. 'Water?'

'You'll need to have words with the best man about that. He went off to find you.'

'Yah. Ben's with him just now. We're heading off in a minute and I wanted to ask a huge favour, Connie.'

It's too much to hope that she'll stop calling me that. And it's her big day after all. Her late father's ill-gotten money has paid for it all, too, so I guess I owe her. 'Sure. What do you need?'

'It's the house. In Earlham Road. I was wondering if you wouldn't mind staying there while we're on our honeymoon. Insurance is a 'mare about it being empty more than a couple of weeks.'

That they're going to be away longer than a fortnight shouldn't surprise me as much as it does, but as requests go, this ranks high on the acceptability scale. 'Happy to. Might actually keep the press off my back, too. Have you got a key, alarm code, that sort of thing?'

Charlotte beams, leaning forward in her chair and giving me a hug. 'Knew you'd help, Connie. Thanks.' She opens her clutch bag and produces a couple of keys on a pink troll key ring, handing them over. 'And Izzy can show you how to set the alarm. It's not difficult. Not if I can use it.'

I look from Charlotte to Izzy, who's not paying attention but sits slumped in her chair fiddling with the frills on her dress.

'Izzy?' I ask, all too aware that Charlotte said 'show', not 'tell'.

'That was the other favour.' She simpers like a B-movie actress trying to win the hero's undying affection. 'You couldn't, like, keep an eye on her, could you?'

This time Izzy looks directly at me and rolls her eyes. She's sixteen years old going on thirty, more than capable of looking after herself.

'Sure,' I say again, and wonder what I'm letting myself in for.

Charlotte and Ben's departure, complete with rattling tin cans tied to the back of the chauffeur-driven Rolls-Royce, barely dampens the spirits of the celebrity partygoers. I stay outside, enjoying the cold air and the sight of actual stars overhead, and listen as the band strikes up again. They're very good, which is only to be expected for Charlotte's wedding, but I'm not in the mood for dancing. Neither, it would seem, are my parents or the Reverend Doctor Edward Masters, all of whom disappeared long before the bride and groom. Only Margo DeVilliers is still here, and it's not long before she and Izzy climb into a taxi for the very short journey home.

I'm contemplating following them, but walking through the woods instead of asking for a lift, when I hear the crunch of footsteps on the gravel. It doesn't surprise me to see Alex Fortescue approaching, his gait that of a man both used to marching and entirely sober.

'Good evening?' It's a question rather than a greeting.

'Better than I was expecting, to be honest. It's been a while since I was able to let my hair down.'

Alex stares at me as if I've said something really funny, then bursts out laughing to prove it. 'That photographer's gone. Left about half an hour ago. You don't need to wear that wig if you don't want to.'

I put my hand to my fake hair, feel the centre parting and the thin mesh beneath it. Tempted though I am, and wonderful though this cool night air would feel on my sweaty scalp, I can't take the chance there aren't any other Chet Wentworths around.

'I'll keep it on for now. Just in case. Not going to be hanging around much longer anyway.'

Alex puts his hand in his pocket and pulls out a phone. 'Want me to call a taxi?'

'From here to the Glebe House? No. Thanks. By the time one got here I could have walked there and back. It's not raining, and I came equipped.' I lift up one of my feet, pointing at the square-heeled leather knee boot.

'Very sensible.'

'Are you kidding? High heels and marquees do not go well together. I'm surprised no one's broken an ankle yet.'

Alex laughs, then turns it into an embarrassed cough. 'Christ, can you imagine the litigation?'

'I'd rather not.' I glance over at his phone, still in his hand, screen lit up with the time. 'Think I'll head off anyway. Back to London tomorrow, then work on Monday.'

'Through the woods at night? You sure that's safe?'

'This is Harston Magna, not Brixton. Worst you might run into is someone from Kettering out dogging, but it's getting a bit late for that now. Still, you can walk with me if you don't think I can look after myself. It's not far.'

He pauses for just long enough to be gentlemanly, which isn't something they teach in public schools these days. 'OK. Show me the way.'

36

Monday morning has a strange feeling of going back to school. It doesn't help that I've woken in a strange bed yet again, although at least Charlotte's place on Earlham Road isn't surrounded by paparazzi. They might turn up when the happy couple get back from their honeymoon, of course, but with any luck they'll have lost interest in me by then.

Izzy's still asleep when I leave, and I'm not about to wake her. I'm not her mother, after all. I can't be bothered with the wig, opting instead for a frumpy coat and a woolly hat to guard against the cold and minimise the stares on the bus. The duty sergeant doesn't recognise me at first either, which is probably a good sign.

'Didn't know you were coming in today,' Karen Eve says once she's been called down to reception and signed me in. I'm starting to wonder whether Bain was taking the piss.

'But you knew I was coming back, right? To help you go through the CCTV footage.'

'Yeah, and thank fuck for that. I thought the NCA was all about travelling the country and seeing new places, but I'm still stuck in the same old station with the same old arsehole constables. And scanning camera footage isn't exactly glamorous either. You've no idea how much shit there is to wade through. You want to get a coffee before we start?'

I try not to laugh at her moaning. If she didn't realise plain-clothes work is ninety-nine per cent sitting on your backside leafing through piles of hay in search of a needle some other bugger's already nicked, then she'll learn it soon enough. The offer of coffee is tempting, but then I think about all the uniform constables down in the canteen, the sneers and disdain. 'Maybe just grab something from the vending machine, yeah?'

Karen gets it in an instant, which bodes well for our future working relationship. I follow her through the station to the makeshift CCTV viewing room, picking up something that's at least an approximation of coffee on the way.

'Council-run cameras are on these two feeds.' She points at a complex arrangement of screens, scroll wheels, keyboard and switchgear that will allow me to search and view the various recordings. 'That's what door-to-door managed to get from the local shopkeepers and suchlike.'

I look at the boxes, piled up with video cartridges for a dozen different security systems. Most places have switched to digital now, storing footage in the Cloud for instant access. My neighbourhood's not exactly rich though, even if you don't have to walk far to find multi million-pound houses like Charlotte's. It's a miracle we've got anything at all.

'Where do you want me to start?' I look around the room, see a map pinned to the wall opposite the screens. 'This our area?'

'Yeah. That's your place in the middle. I've made a start marking the camera locations. We could really do with a couple of dozen folk working on this.'

I can't argue with that. But for now at least it's just the two of us. Staring at the map, I picture the area I've lived in for years, trying to remember the major flows of traffic, pedestrian and vehicular. The lane at the back of my block opens up onto a main road at one end, but the other's a less-frequented residential area. Following that route is the quickest way to the park where the last dead body was found, but there's no way someone with injuries as bad as those inflicted on Dan Jones could walk all that way. Even if he was on some powerful narcotic. And if I remember rightly, there's a small cluster of local shops and a kebab place at the road end.

'He had to have come either this way or that.' I point out the lane ends. 'There's a post-mounted CCTV camera there.' I stab the main road entrance. 'You want to scan that from the feed, and I'll see if we've got anything from Shami's Kebabs?'

Karen doesn't even try to hide the sigh from her voice. 'Already watched and re-watched the playback from all the public feeds. There's nothing around the time you found him, or for about four hours beforehand. I'll push that back a bit further, but it's unlikely he walked there in daylight without anyone noticing him. Door to door's not turned up anything either.'

Of course it was never going to be that easy. I go back to the boxes and start hauling out the tapes, discs or whatever it is they're recorded on. At least they're all labelled, and it doesn't take too long to find the tape from the kebab shop. There's another from the corner store too, although whether either camera will give a view of what's going on outside is unlikely. They're two different formats, too.

'VHS first, or CD-Rom?' I hold them up like Christmas presents. Karen points at the chunky black plastic rectangle. 'Shami's it is, then.'

It takes the better part of an hour to get the elderly video cassette recorder working properly, and I try playing an old tape I found in the same cupboard as the machine first before trusting it with Shami's security footage. One of my abiding memories as a child is my father recording rugby matches from the BBC on to these old cassettes, and the number of times the tape got eaten was remarkable.

The quality of the image, once we get the thing to play

properly, leaves a great deal to be desired. I wonder what Shami, if that's really his name, was thinking when he installed the camera, as the out-of-focus picture, taken from a spot high in the corner opposite the entrance, makes it almost impossible to identify anyone coming or going. All we can see as we peer at the screen is the tops of people's heads, and the occasional full face as someone notices the camera and gurns at it.

I'm surprised at just how busy the place is. For all it's only a few hundred metres from my flat, I've only been in a handful of times over the years. The kebabs aren't bad, I seem to recall, and you get plenty in them, but I always find the raw onion repeats something awful. Waking up with the feeling that something's crawled into my mouth and died in the night usually puts me off going back for a few months. I've never had a dodgy stomach after eating one of Shami's kebabs, but they're not a patch on Mrs F's curry.

'We any idea if that timestamp's accurate?' Karen asks after we've both been watching for half an hour. It's something that's been bothering me too, although the time of evening would fit in with a steady stream of customers. My main focus is the not very clear view out through the window to the street beyond, improved a tiny bit every time someone opens the door. Against all the odds, it shows the opening to the lane, directly across the road and lit by a working street lamp.

I'm concentrating so hard on the scene outside, I don't at first notice much about the figure who comes in as the time scrolls past half ten in the evening. I'm more grateful for the clear view of the street I get for a short moment before the door closes. It's only when he goes straight back out again that something registers in my brain, and I scramble for the remote to pause, then click back.

'What is it?' Karen asks, but paused the image is even worse.

'That guy doesn't buy anything, see?' I scroll back a bit further until he's disappeared, then hit playback at half speed. The door opens again, he steps up to the counter and speaks briefly to the man serving, who shakes his head. Then the man doing the asking looks briefly up at the camera, swiftly away, and walks back out through the door. Not more than twenty seconds in total, blurred, and the briefest full-on view.

'Guess he wasn't hungry.'

'No, he was asking something, see?' I point at the black greasy hair of the server as he shakes his head again, then hit pause as the young man looks up at the camera. It's not a good image, but it's good enough. And the clothes he's wearing are another unsettling clue.

'We got the footage from the shop next door? That's a CD. Might be a better picture.'

Karen fetches it from the console desk, slots it into a different player and takes a minute or two to work out how to show the image on another screen. When it finally appears, I'm pleased to see it's much sharper, and the camera's been set up to show the faces of people as they come into the shop. I fast-forward to the time shown on Shami's video, then let it run at double speed until the same figure walks in. It's much easier to see his features here, and now I'm certain.

'Someone you know?' Karen asks, but I've already got my phone out, placing a call. DCI Bain's mobile goes straight to voicemail, so I leave a message asking him to call me, then try another number. This one's answered almost immediately.

'Hey, Con. How's it going?' DC Harrison's Edinburgh accent is soothing compared to Karen's East-London tone.

'Not bad, thanks. Listen, Janie. Is DCI Bain still up there? Only I can't get him on his mobile.'

'He's in a meeting wi' the boss man. I'm keeping well away, ken?'

I've met her sergeant, so she must mean someone higher

up the food chain. It would make sense that Bain would be liaising with someone senior, maybe another DCI. 'You couldn't do us a favour, then, could you? Might work out well for your investigation too.'

'Oh aye?' Such sarcasm in one so young. 'What you wanting?'

'I need a mugshot of the dead man you showed me. You can just text it to my number if you want. If he's dry, so much the better.' I can only remember him lying where we found him, skin glistening with rain, thin hair plastered to his face. Eyes closed.

'Mortuary photos should do you. I'll have to run it past Grumpy Bob first. You going to tell me why you want it?'

Grumpy Bob? He seemed quite cheerful when I met him. For a Scotsman. 'Think we might have a sighting of him down here from a week or so ago.'

'Have we any idea who he is?'

DCI Bain's face fills most of a screen screwed to the wall of the conference room at the back of the station. I've never much liked videoconferencing, but with Bain and DS Latham still in Scotland it's the easiest way to get most of the team up to speed. I've no idea where Diane Shepherd is, although Karen's tried to get in touch with her. Something about a meeting with the deputy commissioner.

'Nothing from facial recognition yet, but then that'll have been done at your end anyway, won't it?'

'Things move at a different pace up here. But so far his mugshot's not pinged on any of Police Scotland's databases. NCA might have a bit of a wider scope, so keep on it.'

I glance at the printout of the image DC Harrison sent me, alongside stills taken from the two security videos. It's easy enough to tell that they all show the same young man. Unless he has an identical twin, of course.

'You said you thought you might have a lead, Fairchild. Care to let us in on it?' DS Latham's voice is all sneer. He's not exactly pleasant to Karen either, so it might just be old-school misogyny that fuels his hatred. Bain notices it too, giving his underling a withering glance that goes unnoticed. The two of them look somewhat less comfortable than Karen and me, crushed into a small booth somewhere in a police station in Edinburgh.

'The clothes he's wearing in the security footage. I've seen them before. It's kind of a uniform.'

'Uniform?' Bain looks down at his own copies of the printouts, showing off the bald spot on the crown of his head. 'Looks like smart casual to me.'

'It could be, which is why I'm not a hundred per cent. The more I think about it though, the more I reckon I've seen him before. Here, in London. What he's wearing there, that's what triggered the memory. It's kind of a uniform, only not. It's what the followers of the Church of the Coming Light wear.'

'Church of the what?'

'The Coming Light. Surely you've heard of it. Reverend Doctor Edward Masters?'

The blank looks from Bain and Latham suggest that they haven't. It's possible that I'm seeing patterns where none exist, of course. It might just be a coincidence that this young man was wearing clothes similar to the ones I saw on the group working Euston station.

'They were up in Edinburgh the same night this body was found. Masters was conducting a prayer meeting or something.' I hold up the photograph; dead man, not living.

'And you know this how?'

I'm tempted to ask Latham why it matters, but he's a sergeant and I'm still just a constable. 'There was a bunch of them at the park, taking the Spice addicts off to their shelter, remember? And I saw them at Euston when I was heading out of town. Handing out leaflets, chugging the commuters, talking to some young rough sleepers. That's pretty much what they do, if you believe what they say.'

'And what, you just happened to recognise him from a chance encounter over a week ago?' Latham is sneering again. It's not pretty, and not particularly helpful either.

'He shoved a leaflet in my hands. I remember faces. Particularly ones linked to specific incidents. Don't you?'

Bain is either telepathic or used to dealing with Latham. He cuts in before we can start shouting at each other. 'What's your play here, then, Fairchild? We can't exactly go knocking on some church door based on your hazy recollections from a week ago.'

Actually, that was exactly what I'd been thinking of doing, just as soon as I worked out where the church was based. But then I remember Masters and the aura of power about him. The very fact of him being at my brother's wedding suggests he's well connected, and there's the court case that was dropped suddenly too. Going in unprepared could be a big mistake.

'I think following up on this lead as carefully as we can is the best option. Let's see if we can't get an ID on the guy, then see if it links back to the Church.'

'Agreed.' Bain looks down again and I get a second glimpse of his bald spot. 'We're going to be here another couple of days sorting things out with the locals. You two keep going through the CCTV, and we'll pull everything together at the end of the week, OK?'

It's nice that he makes it a question, but I'm not so stupid as to miss that it's an order.

'Yes, sir. We'll keep you up to speed if there are any developments.'

'You do that, Fairchild. I'll speak to you soon.' He hits the button to kill the conference call before we can descend into awkward 'bye bye's.

'Well, that was short and sweet. Nice to be congratulated on our hard work,' Karen says.

'You'd best get used to it. Praise is rare in plain clothes, although blame tends to get spread around a bit more.' I pull the photographs into a small pile and tidy them into an envelope. Nobody wants to stumble across a photograph of a dead man, even in a police station.

'So what next? We just head back to that stinking room and work our way through all the rest of the tapes?'

Put like that it's about as enticing as spending an afternoon with my mother. I look at Karen, think about the mountains of surveillance footage still to watch and how little chance we have of finding any more clues. CCTV is fine up to a point, but nothing beats getting out on the streets and asking questions.

'Fancy a kebab?'

37

Shami's Kebabs is unhelpfully closed when we get there, a sign in the window telling me it won't be open again before eight. I tap on the door, just in case someone's preparing food in the back, but there's no response. Nothing from the buzzers at the door leading to the flats above the shop either.

'Nobody home?' Karen asks, as if it was necessary. I shrug by way of an answer, and point to the road end.

There's more life in the corner shop. I don't know the name of the old lady behind the counter, although she's served me enough times over the years. Milk and bread, emergency bacon, that sort of thing. This shop has just about everything you could need, and it's not all that much more expensive than the supermarket. The sell-by dates on most of the processed stuff don't bear too close scrutiny, although the fruit and veg stacked up outside the door looks fresh enough. It just needs a thorough wash to get rid of the London grime.

'Can I help you with anything?'

I'd been hoping to speak to the middle-aged man who's usually working here when I come in, but I guess I'll have to take what I can.

'We're following up on the incident a week or so ago. The young man found in the alley over there.' I point in the general direction. 'You very kindly gave us some video footage from your security camera. I was wondering if I might talk to whoever was working in here that night?'

I've probably never spoken as much to this woman before, but she smiles at me in a friendly way before saying, 'You are the posh cop, aren't you? You live just over there, no?'

I can hear Karen stifling her laughter, and decide it's probably best not to turn and face her.

'Yes. That's me in the papers. But you know what they're like, eh? I'm not that posh really.' I wait just a couple of seconds, rolling up my sleeves slightly to reveal the twirling patterns inked into my forearms, then add, 'Were you working here that night?'

Whether it's the sight of the tattoos, or something else unrelated, she turns from smiling to serious in an instant. 'I'll go get my son,' she says, then disappears through a bead-curtained doorway behind the counter. A few moments later the man I was hoping to speak to arrives.

'Detective Constable Fairchild. How can I help?'

At least he's not sniggering about my press coverage. 'You handed over some CCTV footage to constables going door to door. I was wondering if you remembered anything about the night in question. In particular, this man?'

I have the still photographs taken from the footage in an envelope. The one of the man dead is in there too, so I take a moment to choose the right ones before placing them down on the counter.

'Doesn't ring any bells.'

'He was in the kebab shop first, asking questions, not buying. We think he might have been trying to find the same young man we found. Only I don't think his intentions were quite as noble as ours.'

He frowns, picks up the clearer of the two pictures and squints at it. Then he turns and shouts 'Mother,' followed by a string of words in a language I neither recognise nor understand.

The old lady comes back through, trailing her hands in the beads behind her, and then they both enter into what sounds very much like an argument over the picture. I let them take their time; the longer they study the image, the more chance they'll remember something about the man. Finally she turns away, flipping her arm at him as she goes back through into the room behind the shop. He turns to me, and places the picture back down on the counter.

'Mother says she thinks she might recognise him. There was someone that night asking around, but then there were police officers asking around as well. This is a good neighbourhood. You know this. Not like the estate with all its drugs and violence.'

'The man though.' I put a finger in the middle of the photograph, aware that this conversation could very quickly turn to a general complaint about the lawlessness in the area, the lack of bobbies on the beat or any other grievance this pillar of the community has.

'I think there was a man asking questions, yes. And this could be him. But he wasn't alone. There was a woman with him.'

'A woman? There's nothing on the tape.'

'That's what Mother says. She was a smart one. Young, but she knew where the camera was. Like she had been here before. Or maybe just observant.'

'Did she say what this woman looked like, your mother?' I nod my head past him at the bead curtain, half expecting the old woman to come back out again.

'She did. Said she was young. Still a child really, but she dressed like a grown-up. Too much make-up, making her face all pale like a ghost.'

A horrible feeling creeps into my mind, and I have a suspicion I know exactly who they're talking about. 'Was she Asian? About so high?' I hold my hand at about my shoulder height. 'Surly. Won't look you in the eye.'

'Sounds like you know her,' Karen says as the shopkeeper nods his head. She's not laughing any more when I face her.

'The young girl who visited Dan Jones in the hospital. Anna, she said her name was.'

'You sure it's her though? From a description like that? Could be anyone.'

'Could be, yes. But my gut says it's her. There's a logic to it, too. She's connected to him, after all, otherwise why go see him in the hospital? What if she helped him escape wherever it was he was being held?'

Karen lets out a slow breath that accurately pictures her doubts. 'It's a bit thin, isn't it?'

'Paper thin, but I know someone who might be able to shed a bit of light on it.' I can't believe that I'm even contemplating it.

'You do? Who?'

'The only man I know who's got anything on the Church of the Coming Light.' God help me, I'm going to have to speak to the press. The gutter press. 'Jonathan Stokes.'

Meeting on neutral ground makes me feel like a cold-war spy. The café's almost equidistant from the corner shop and the offices where the paper Stokes works for spews out its hateful bile. Transport links are better in my direction though, so I arrive before he does, and get to choose the best spot for our meeting. Karen wanted to come with me, but I managed to persuade her this was a job best done alone. The less attention from the press she gets, the better.

I've got my back to the wall and a good view of the exits when he arrives.

'Fairchild.' He shrugs off his dirty-old-man overcoat, its shoulders damp with rain, and hangs it over the back of the chair opposite me, then waves at the waitress for coffee before taking his seat.

'Mr Stokes. How did you enjoy the wedding?'

He cocks his head to one side at that, staring at me with his rheumy eyes for a while before breaking into a smile that shows too many yellowed and broken teeth. 'You were there, weren't you. Sneaky.'

'I saw the papers. Hard to miss them. It really is a slow news week when you go with a minor celebrity wedding for the front page, isn't it?'

'On the contrary. Charlotte DeVilliers is big news, especially after what her father did. What you did to him, too.' He reaches into his jacket pocket, pulls out an old-fashioned spiral-bound notebook and a biro. Its end is badly chewed, which might explain the broken teeth. 'Mind if I take some notes?'

'Sure. I'm not here to answer questions though. Not about Charlotte or her father, anyway. I'm more interested in asking questions.'

That gets me another cock of the head, a bit like a confused puppy, only the opposite of cute. 'And what's in it for me?'

'Strange how that never seems to come up when the roles are reversed, isn't it? I don't seem to recall there being any upside to my talking to you about my family background. Just endless nasty columns about posh cops and privilege. Yet as soon as I want something from you, it's "How much?"' I rub fingers and thumb together in front of him suggestively, but his annoyance is cut short by the arrival of coffee. It takes a while for him to pour in milk and add at least five sachets of sugar. Another explanation for the broken teeth. Only once the ritual has been completed and he's had a drink does he look at me again.

'OK. So what is it you actually want to know?'

'Edward Masters.'

Two words, and the transformation is instant. The blood drains from his face, his weather-beaten red turning to pasty grey. The hand holding the coffee mug starts to shake, and he rattles it on the tabletop as he puts it down.

'Masters?' He almost chokes on the name. 'What the fuck is this about, Fairchild?'

'I was hoping you could tell me. You know he was at the wedding, right?'

I can tell from the look on his face that this is news to him. Maybe the reverend doctor only attended the reception afterwards, and he could easily have been driven to the hall without any of the press at the church door noticing.

'Fuck's sake. Why?' Stokes takes another drink from his coffee, managing only to spill a little down his chin. I can tell that he'd rather it was laced with something stronger.

'Apparently my mother invited him. Wanted him to bless the union, too, but my brother threatened to call the whole thing off.'

'At least someone in the Fairchild family's got some sense, then. Jesus. Edward fucking Masters.'

'So what can you tell me about him? I saw your name on a lot of the bylines back when that court case was going through.'

'The case was dropped. No story there.' Stokes picks up his notebook and shoves it back in his pocket, fishes around for some change and rattles it onto the table. I can tell a man who's getting ready to leave easily enough.

'Is that why you're a hack now? Preying on vacuous celebs and hanging out with your pal Chet?'

He pauses, half twisted in his seat to retrieve his coat. I've hit a nerve, time to press it harder.

'I've read some of your pieces from a few years back, Stokes. The investigative stuff. You blew that environmental waste scam wide open. People went to jail. Now you spend your time trying to wheedle out the unimportant secrets of pathetic people. Secrets that don't even shock anyone any more.'

For a moment I think he's going to leave anyway. He stares at me, still poised, for a count of maybe ten seconds that feels like an hour. Then he sits back down squarely, rubs at his face with both hands.

'I knew this would come back to haunt me. Just goes to show, really.'

'Show what?'

'It doesn't matter. You want to know about Masters? Let's start with the fact that he's not a doctor, and as far as I'm aware the only church he's ordained in is the one he created.'

'The Church of the Coming Light?'

'The same. I take it you've met them?'

I pause a moment, not wanting to tell him exactly why I'm interested in Masters. At least not yet. I'd need to run it past both Bain and the team at Police Scotland anyway. Talking to the press in the middle of an investigation is frowned upon.

'Euston station. A bunch of them were mobbing commuters for charitable donations. I got the impression they might have been recruiting, too. They shoved a leaflet at me, got in my face, so I looked them up. Wouldn't have known Masters from any other religious nutjob otherwise.'

'Religious. Heh.' Stokes laughs without mirth, then thumps his chest when it turns into a cough. 'It's a front. A cult. Oh, I'm sure they do some good stuff. Take a few kids off the street and help clean 'em up. Just enough to keep the politicians happy, senior police off their backs. But the main reason they help waifs and strays is so that Masters can indulge his more unsavoury habits.'

I'm a bit concerned for Stokes now, which isn't something I ever thought I would be. The cough punctuates his words, and the colour that drained from his face when I first mentioned Masters is coming back now, darker and redder than before.

'You OK? Here, let me get you some water.' I stand up, intending to go to the counter, but he reaches up as I pass, grabs me by the arm. There's something very wrong with him now.

'Talk to Polly. Polly Cho.' The name means nothing to me, but it only seems to make his choking worse. He pulls himself up, still half doubled over so I have to bend to hear his rasping words, each one broken by a laboured intake of breath. 'Just. Be. Care. Ful.'

Then his grip fails and he collapses to the floor, writhing and choking, his hands grasping at his neck. He's going from red to purple as I drag the chairs away to make space for him, shout at the stunned waitress.

'Call an ambulance. Now!'

38

'Honestly? He's lucky to be alive.'

I'm not sure what's happened to the time, but I can see through the hospital window that it's dark outside. I came here in the back of an ambulance, holding on to the hand of a man whose death I'd have probably joked about as being a good thing. Had I not been there to witness it almost happening.

'Any idea what it was?'

The doctor shrugs. Like everyone else who works here, he looks tired. 'Best guess is his heart gave out when he got something stuck in his throat. Whoever gave him CPR saved his life though.'

Twenty minutes of intermittent mouth to mouth with a sleazy tabloid journalist while we waited for the paramedics to arrive. I shudder at the memory, want to go and wash my face, gargle salt water, maybe disinfect myself with malt whisky. I settle for wiping my lips with the back of my hand.

'I first learned how to do it at school. Hoped I'd never have to use it. Will he be OK?'

'Early days. But we've got him stabilised. Don't think he's going to be walking out of here any time soon. And no, he's not fit to talk to anyone either.'

I'd not really been intending to ask, but the doctor's words are enough to let me go. I stand up slowly, tired from a long day and the effort of all that CPR. 'I'll call by, see how he's doing tomorrow. Maybe Wednesday.'

'He'll be here.'

Outside, the sky's cleared, the earlier drizzly rain giving way to the closest approximation to a starry night you ever get in the city. I'd catch a bus back to the station, but it's near enough shift end to make the journey pointless. Karen knows about Stokes, so hopefully she'll let the relevant people know what's happened to him. The hospital is closer to my place, and it's early enough for there to be plenty of people about, so I decide to walk even though the memory of being attacked is still raw. There's a lot to mull over, and I've always thought best on my feet.

I've not got far up the road before my phone rings in my pocket. Pulling it out, I see a number I don't recognise. Probably someone calling to tell me I've been in an accident that wasn't my fault. I'd ignore it, but that's something detective constables don't have the luxury of doing.

'Yes?' I keep walking as I talk, phone clamped tight to my ear to block out the traffic noise.

'Constance. Hope you don't mind. I bullied your brother into giving me your number.'

Alex Fortescue. Not a cold-caller then. 'Hi, Alex. Thought you were heading overseas today.' A half-remembered conversation from the wedding reception left that particular nugget of information behind.

'Yeah. Op's been postponed, so I'm at a loose end for a couple of days. Wondered if you fancied a drink?'

I know better than to ask what the op was, and given the day I've just had, a drink sounds like a splendid idea. 'Sure. Whereabouts are you?'

'Charlotte's, actually. Izzy let me in.'

I stop walking, much to the annoyance of a few pedestrians behind me. Alex is a nice enough chap, but I'm not really looking for that kind of relationship right now. On the other hand, if he's at the house already it's kind of difficult to make excuses.

'I'm on my way there right now, actually. Half an hour, forty-five minutes. Unless you want to meet at the pub down the road? Can't imagine making small talk with my half-sister's easy.'

His laugh is genuine, friendly, warm. 'You're not wrong. I'll get the first round in. What's your poison?'

There's nothing odd about the question, the way it's phrased. I've probably asked the same of people a thousand times and more. Something about it gives me pause though. Poison. Might that be what did for Jonathan Stokes? The doctor said his heart gave out after he choked on something, but I cleared his airway and there was nothing blocking it. He wasn't wearing a tie, so that's not it. I play the sequence of events back in my head, and there's really no good reason for him to have started coughing, except that he'd taken a drink of his coffee a few moments earlier. But that doesn't work either. If you're going to choke on a drink it tends to happen straight away. I was sitting opposite him; I'd have ended up wearing most of it.

'You still there, Constance?' Alex's voice on the phone breaks my train of thought.

'Sorry. Just had a thought about the case I'm working on. Pint of whatever IPA they've got on tap will do me fine.'

'Pint?' There's a momentary hesitation, the faintest question in his voice. 'OK. See you in a bit.'

'Yeah. See you. And, Alex?'

'Yes?'

'It's Con, remember? Only my mother calls me Constance.'

I hang up before he can say anything more, shove the phone into my pocket and set off towards the pub.

Maybe it's the promise of a drink, but I make good time across town, and it's only half an hour after the phone call that I step from the cold night air into the warm fug of the pub. I take a moment to compose myself, unzipping my coat and unwrapping the scarf from around my neck. My hat I keep on, at least until I've satisfied myself that there are no paparazzi in here.

Alex's slumped in a corner seat, a half-drunk pint of something dark in front of him. Across the table from it, a full glass of IPA sits waiting for me. The glistening beads of condensation on the side, and still-tight head suggest it's not long poured. It doesn't take me long to neck it down to the same level as his, either.

'Cheers. I needed that.'

'Clearly.' He leans forward, picks up his glass and takes a more measured gulp while I shuck off my coat and dump it on top of my bag. Woolly hat removed, I scratch at my short hair in a vague attempt to make it presentable. It doesn't work.

'No wig today, I see.'

'Didn't think I'd need it when I left this morning.' I proceed to tell him all about my exciting afternoon at the hospital, and by the time I'm done so is my pint.

'And I thought my life was complicated. You want another?' Alex indicates the empty glass.

'It's OK. I'll get them.' I start to stand, but he's on his feet in an instant, grabbing the glass from the table before I can reach it. Impressive, given how much closer I am than he was when he started.

'I insist.' He's gone before I can protest, and who am I to complain about free beer anyway? It doesn't take long for him to be served. Monday nights are quiet here.

'So this reporter fellow. He going to be all right?' Alex asks when he returns.

'Who knows? Not sure I much care, to be honest.'

'I'm surprised you did what you did. After all the stuff he's written about you.'

If I wasn't a suspicious sod, I might have missed the subtle warning hidden in Alex's words. I told him Stokes was a reporter, that he was at Charlotte's wedding, but I'm not sure I've mentioned quite how much the man's been fixated on me and my family since I ruined Roger DeVilliers' life. 'All the stuff he's written about you' might be innocent enough, but it sounds to me like somebody's been google-searching my name. Alex is nice enough, but I don't know much about him beyond age sixteen or so, and I didn't exactly fancy him then.

'I couldn't let him die. Imagine how much fun the tabloids would've had with that.'

He shrugs to concede the point.

'So what about you, then?' I ask, keen to shift the conversation. 'Any idea when they're going to ship you out?'

'If you're that desperate to get shot of me, you can just say, you know?' Alex feigns being upset with a little too much enthusiasm. Or am I just looking for excuses? It's been a while since I chatted over a drink with someone like this.

'Actually, it's only a day's grace,' he says just in time for me to regret my thoughts. 'Can't tell you what or where, obviously, but I'll be gone in the morning.'

'You need to work a bit harder on your chat-up lines, Alex.'

A light flush creeps up his neck and into his cheeks, followed by a wistful smile that sits well on him. 'I wish.' He glances at his watch. 'Gone as in another country. I've got to report in, oh, about two hours from now.'

'On a couple pints of beer?'

'A couple of pints of low-alcohol beer that's better than it sounds but still not as good as I'd like.'

Now I feel bad for thinking he was angling for something more. The guy's just lonely. And that's when it hits me. He might be one of Ben's oldest friends, but he's not got anyone else outside of his unit. No wife, no family. He has parents at least, I remember him telling me 'Mrs Fortescue' was his mum's name. I don't exactly see eye to eye with mine though, so maybe he's cut ties with his. It occurs to me that when he was told not to report for duty for another twenty-four hours, he genuinely had no idea what to do with himself. And I thought *I* was married to my job.

'That's a shame. But, you know, you can always call me up next time you're in town. Maybe we could go have a meal or something.' Christ, I sound like a teenager again.

'Next time. Yeah. That'd be nice.'

The conversation peters out for a while after that, neither of us really sure what to say. Eventually, just as I'm about to come up with some vacuous small-talk platitude, Alex leans forward again, his voice low.

'Met your new boss today.'

He can't mean Bain, so that must mean Shepherd. Who was in important high-level meetings about something we're not allowed to know about. 'Diane?' I ask.

'Brigadier Shepherd, I think you mean.' Alex's mortification is a sight to behold.

'Brigadier? I thought . . .' But then I never thought at all. She told me she'd been army, and that superintendent was the nearest pay grade, or at least her level in the team pecking order. Brigadier sounds much more important and twirly moustache.

'She thinks very highly of you. Reckons you'd have made a good soldier.' He's smiling again now. 'Can't see it myself.'

'So what were you doing with Diane, then? Other than talking about me, that is.' I emphasise Shepherd's first name, just to tease.

'Nothing much, just catching up. She might be a civilian now, but she was my commanding officer a while back.' He drains the last of his low-alcohol beer, then sets the glass carefully down on the table before speaking again. 'Word of advice, Con. If you're open to it?'

Now I'm nervous. 'Always open to advice, Alex. Doesn't mean I'll follow it.'

'Sensible. But you'd be wise to listen when I tell you to trust Brigadier Shepherd. She might seem a bit chaotic at times, but it's an act. She doesn't take fools kindly, and she's got one of the sharpest strategic minds I've ever seen.' Alex shrugs again. 'And she likes you. That's worth more than gold.'

39

Karen's already at work when I arrive at the station the next morning, which is just as well as I still need someone to buzz me in. The sooner Bain is back and can get the paperwork signed off the better. It's bad enough that most of my old colleagues either actively hate me or wish I wasn't here. An official transfer to the NCA would mean I could get out of this godawful building once and for all.

'Any news on Stokes?' she asks as we walk the corridors to the back of the station and the CCTV viewing room.

'Not that I know of.' I've not spoken to anyone at the hospital since I left yesterday evening. Karen's question reminds me I've not spoken to anyone at the paper either, which probably means that's going to come back and bite me in the arse sooner rather than later. 'I'm sure if there was bad news it would've caught up with me by now.'

Karen raises an eyebrow at that, but says nothing.

'He did say something though, before he collapsed,' I add. 'Well, a name actually.' I fill her in on the details of the incident, firmed up by my going over them again and again in my head as I stared at the ceiling in Charlotte's spare bedroom. It's probably just as well Alex had to ship out, otherwise I might have forgotten the all-important bit.

'He said I should ask Polly Cho. At least that's what it sounded like.'

'Who's Polly Cho?'

'I have no idea. Not the young woman whose case against Masters' was dropped. She was called Sarah Gentle, I think.' I pull out my notebook and flip back to the scrawled notes I took on the train from Euston what feels like a lifetime ago. 'Yeah. Sarah Gentle. No idea what happened to her either.'

'And I suppose you want to find out, rather than, say, viewing all this security camera footage.' Karen nods at the box still half full of assorted different format recordings.

'Half an hour on the PNC should do it. If the name doesn't bring up anything, then at least we've tried.'

She looks at me as if trying is the last thing we should do, then shrugs and heads over to the nearest workstation. 'You could do this yourself, you know?'

'Not until I've got all my security clearances back. Believe me, I've tried logging on and I get bounced out quicker than you can say "password not recognised". It's bloody frustrating.'

'I can imagine.' Karen taps away at the keys, logging in and bringing up the search page, then types in the name 'Polly Cho'. I stare at the screen as the hourglass spins, and then let out a disappointed sigh when it shows no results.

'Different spelling, perhaps?' she asks.

'It's possible, I guess. Stokes was pretty out of it when he told me, and he didn't write it down. Not sure how else you can spell Polly though.'

And then it hits me with a horrible, hollow feeling in my gut. Can it be that simple? 'Try Pollyanna. Or just Anna.'

Karen doesn't ask why, just types in the full name. This time it comes back with a hit. Pollyanna Cho, sometimes known as Anna. She's barely sixteen, but there's a string of cautions. Most of her record is inaccessible because she's underage, but there's a photograph.

'Christ, I can be slow sometimes.'

'This is her? The young woman the shopkeeper saw?'

'This is Anna, the girl in the hospital. We need to find her fast. Bring her in.'

'For questioning?' Karen bends down to the computer again. I suspect she's checking the date of birth.

'For her own safety. She knows Dan Jones. Probably helped him escape before he could end up like the other victims.' I stare at the image on the screen, my thoughts tumbling like the levers in a lock. So many things slotting together. I should have seen it days ago. 'What address have we got for her?'

'You know she's hardly likely to be there, right?' Karen clicks away with the mouse until the relevant page comes up. Another piece of the puzzle falling into place. Of course she comes from the Danes Estate.

'We'll still need to follow it up though. You couldn't get on to the local station, could you? I don't fancy going in there without some uniform backing me up.'

Karen nods. 'You going to tell the boss first?'

I pull out my phone, flick through the contact list for DCI Bain. 'I'm going to try.'

Somebody must have thought the Danes Estate was a good idea, sometime back in the sixties or seventies. Centred around a quartet of concrete towers, it's criss-crossed with elevated walkways that provide great cover for drug dealers, rudimentary shelter for the homeless and multiple escape routes whenever there's a police crackdown. Not all of it's bad. The local community trust do their best in the face of deprivation and joblessness, but it's gained a reputation down the years that's proven hard to shake. Rumour has it the local authority want to bulldoze the whole thing and sell the site to a private developer. I kind of agree with them on the first part, the second not so much.

The address we have for Polly Cho is a top-floor flat in one of the lower buildings that squat around the towers like feral children. It's not that much different from my own apartment block, a mile or so away, except that this one's still in council ownership and could do with a bit of TLC. There's no lift, so Karen and I climb the concrete stairs, leaving our uniform escort to keep an eye on the car that brought us here.

I've barely had time to raise my hand and knock on the door before it's yanked open. The woman behind it is tiny, but fierce.

'I said no. Why you not understand? No. I don't want buy your shitty insurance.'

'That's good, because we're not trying to sell you any. Mrs Cho?'

The tiny woman goes from angry to suspicious in an instant, one hand still holding the door to slam in our faces should the need arise.

'Who are you?' She looks from me to Karen and then back again.

'Detective Constable Eve, ma'am.' Karen holds out her warrant card for inspection, and I feel a momentary twitch of jealousy. 'This is my colleague, Detective Constable Fairchild.'

Something changes in the woman's face as she hears my name. 'Posh cop!' Her face breaks into a smile. 'I see you in papers. Come in. Come.'

Karen gives me a look as we follow the woman into the flat. I shake my head, ever so slightly, to warn her not to mention it. Not here, and certainly not back at the station. We're both led into a small living room, its window affording a fine view over the nearby rooftops and on towards the distant skyscrapers of the city.

'You not sell insurance, so why you here then?'

'Can I confirm that you are Mrs Cho?' I ask.

'Miss Cho. Not Mrs.' She shakes her head and then smiles

again. She's old enough to be Anna's mother or grandmother, it's hard to tell. There's something of the moody young goth's features about her face, too, although she's the better part of a foot shorter. Small in all dimensions, like a child grown old without actually growing.

'We have this as an address for Anna Cho. Is she here?'

I can tell before the old woman answers that it's going to be no. She stiffens in her seat, the smiling eyes going hard again. More of the fierceness from when we first met her.

'I not know where she is. She never come home no more.'

'When was the last time you saw her?'

'I not know. Month maybe? Six week? What she do this time?'

There's a weariness to Miss Cho's question that suggests we're not the first police officers to have this conversation about her daughter.

'What about her father? Might she be with him?'

'He die long time ago. Promise me everything. Leave me nothing. Nothing except Pollyanna, and she only trouble.'

It's beginning to look like a dead end. 'So you've no idea where she might be?' I ask.

'Not on Danes Estate. I know if she were.' Miss Cho shakes her head. 'Maybe go ask those people she know. At the church.'

'The church? The Church of the Coming Light?'

Miss Cho's puzzled expression suggests it's not going to be that easy. 'I not know whose church it is. Big building. Over on Hatfield Street. It is youth centre now. Nobody pray there any more.'

I know the place she means, and from what little I know of her daughter, I can't think of anywhere less likely for Anna to hang out. It's probably the best we're going to get from Miss Cho, though. I stand up, Karen copying me a moment later.

'Well, thank you for your time. And if Anna does come home,

can you ask her to call us? It's very important we speak with her.' I put my hand into my jacket pocket, where normally there'd be a card with my contact details. Except that I've not had to carry one for months, so there's nothing but lint in there. It's far too long since I did any proper police work.

'Here.' Karen doesn't have cards yet either, but she's organised enough to tear a strip from her notebook and scribble down a number. 'This'll get you through to either of us.'

Miss Cho stands up and takes the piece of paper. She places it on the mantelpiece, then bends down and fetches something from a small table beside her chair. My heart sinks when I see what it is. A tabloid newspaper with my face on the front.

'You sign for me?'

40

'Don't say a word. You even breathe about this I'll . . .' I run out of steam. There's nothing I can do about it, and Karen's far too amused to let it lie.

'Autographing your photo on the front page of a tabloid. That's not something I ever thought I'd see someone do.'

Fair play to her, she shuts up about it by the time we've reached the ground floor and our waiting escort. A small crowd has gathered to see what all the fuss is about. Children who really ought to be in school, mostly.

'You know the old church they turned into a youth centre?' I ask of one of the uniform constables as we all climb into the car.

'Saint Jude's? Yeah. Been there a few times. Community policing and all that. Why?'

'Girl we're looking for used to hang out there, apparently. Might as well go and have a look, since we're in the neighbourhood.'

'Sure.' He starts the car and pilots it gently through a crowd not all that keen on getting out of the way. 'What's it like?'

'Eh? What's what like?'

'Seeing your face in the papers? The paps chasing you around? I've seen some celebs getting right narked about it.'

I'm about to protest that I'm not a celeb, when it occurs to me that's not what he meant. For the first time since I gained my unwanted notoriety, here's someone who's genuinely interested to know how I deal with it. Not enjoying my discomfort or mocking me for my background.

'It's weird. And unhelpful. Gives me a tiny bit of sympathy for those folk tripping out of nightclubs at three in the morning. We've all been there, right? Mostly nobody gives a fuck though.'

I catch his grin in the rear-view mirror as we speed up the road towards the traffic lights. Clearly posh cops don't say fuck.

The church is as I remember it, a fairly typical blackened stone building with a chunky tower and short steeple. If it ever had a graveyard the inhabitants have long since been moved on so that property developers can use the space to squeeze in more shops and cheap housing. There's a double yellow line outside the front entrance, but we're in a patrol car so park there anyway.

'Probably won't be long,' I say to the driver as Karen and I climb out. At the top of a short flight of narrow stone steps, the iron-studded wooden door is shut, but there's a light on beside it and more showing through the grimy stained-glass windows. When I try the door handle, it turns easily, the door opening on silent hinges.

'Can I help?'

I've barely had time to take in the hall, much bigger on the inside than the outside might suggest, when a young man is approaching us. His face is a picture of concern, and behind him I can see a group of teenage girls, still sitting in a circle but all turned to see who has interrupted whatever it was they were doing.

'Detective Constable Eve.' Karen is obviously relishing her new role, brandishing her warrant card like it's a backstage pass at Glastonbury. 'This is my colleague—'

'We're looking for Anna Cho. Sometimes calls herself Polly, or even Pollyanna.' I interrupt before she can tell them my name. I don't want to be signing any more newspapers today.

'Polly?' The young man looks surprised. 'Not seen her in months.'

'But you know her?'

'Yeah. She used to be part of the group. Maybe a year back, bit more.'

'The group. Sorry. Who are you and what do you do?' I can see his audience beginning to fidget, distracted by our presence.

'Pete. Pete Oldman.' He holds out a hand, so I shake it. 'I teach drama. Get these kids interested in something other than drugs and booze.'

'All girls?'

He looks around to the group in their circle, holds a hand up that seems to calm them. 'This class, yes. We have some mixed ones too, but the boys can get a bit disruptive sometimes. You know what it's like. Showing off, trying to impress their mates.'

'Yeah, I get that. But Anna – Polly. Can you tell me anything about her? We've spoken to her mum, but that didn't get us very far.'

Pete looks at me nervously. 'She's OK, though? Not in any trouble?'

'We need to talk to her, and urgently. She might be in trouble, but not with us. Least, not at the moment.'

'Well, like I said. I've not seen her in a while. I can ask the girls.'

'If you wouldn't mind.'

I follow him into the hall, noting that this time Karen stays by the door. The class is a mixture of all types, reflecting the multicultural make-up of this area. It occurs to me that some of the girls might be here because it's part of a community service order or similar, but none of them seem anxious to leave. From the layout of the hall, the way they're all seated in a semicircle, and the mixture of photocopies and dog-eared books they're all holding, I'd guess they're reading for a production. I can't see what it is though.

I keep my distance while Pete talks to some of his class quietly. I notice he doesn't approach all of them, and I'm sure he has his reasons. He's not quite done when the girl sitting closest to me says, 'You're the posh cop, aren't you?'

It had to happen, I guess. I shrug by way of an answer, hoping that's enough. It isn't.

'Is it true you're a millionaire, then?'

'Dressed like this and working as a cop? What do you think?'

That makes her frown. 'But the papers—'

'Are full of shit, mostly. Yeah, I grew up in a big house and went to a posh school, but I wanted to be a police officer and my dad didn't like that. So he cut me off without a penny.'

That takes a while to sink in. Then she mouths a silent 'Wow', and says nothing more.

'Jen reckons she saw Polly last week. Out with some of those weird cultists. You know, the Church of the Golden Shower or something.'

The girl nearest me lets out a shriek of laughter at that, and I almost join her. Pete looks bemused, although I find it hard to believe someone working on the Danes Estate could be so innocent.

'Church of the Coming Light,' I correct him. 'They're on the high street, right?'

'Yeah. Turned an old bank building into a shelter for the homeless. Seems vaguely ironic, don't you think? The temple of high finance now used to feed and house its victims.'

I say nothing to that, keen to get away from this place. There's only so much earnest community welfare officer my cynical heart can take. But as I'm leaving, my young admirer speaks up.

'They the ones who kidnap all those Spice addicts and stuff?' Her cynicism is more my level.

'In a manner of speaking. Why?'

'Saw a bunch of them coming out of that old club a fortnight ago, din't I. You know. Used to be Ritzy's only it got closed down. All boarded up now.'

'This whole area's due to be demolished soon. Local housing association's going to be putting up a couple of blocks of flats, but mostly it's executive homes for a million quid a pop.'

Our police constable driver double parks at the end of a quiet street, not even bothering to undo his seat belt, let alone get out of the car and give us a tour.

'In this part of town?' I peer out of the window at the dereliction, before opening the door to climb out.

'Yeah, well. That's what I heard. Been a while since anything's happened, so there's probably some action group or something holding it all up.'

I think I might have been into Ritzy's nightclub. Just the once, mind you, and many years ago. It was one of those places that even students would find hard to love. If memory serves, the owner lost his licence and the place was shut down by health and safety after it was found that the fire escape doors had been screwed shut to stop people sneaking in without paying. Either that or there were too many rats in the toilets.

The windows are all boarded up, front door locked with a heavy-duty vandal-proof hasp and padlock of the kind you'd expect to see on building sites. Around the back it's much the same. No way in without a key, or possibly several. Judging by the posters pasted to the boards, advertising gigs from years ago, nobody's been here in a while, so I guess the information my young thespian friend gave me was dud.

'Nothing happening here,' I say to Karen as we stand on the pavement and stare at the lifeless building.

'Nothing happening anywhere. This place is dead.'

She has a point. The road used to be busy, but now all of the local shops are boarded up much the same as Ritzy's. There's a pub a few hundred metres away at the other end of the street, a couple of hardy smokers leaning against the wall outside its front entrance. Past it, I can see the towers of the Danes Estate rising into the afternoon sky, their grey concrete cladding merging almost seamlessly with the cloud.

Even the church next door to the nightclub looks disused. It claims to be St Martin's but if that's the case then Martin's forgotten all about it. The gate at the bottom of the steps leading up to its entrance is locked with a rusty padlock and chain. There's no light from the stained-glass windows, and one panel is missing a lot of its glass. The paint has mostly peeled from the noticeboard just behind the railings, but I can make out a phone number with too few digits to be less than ten years out of date. Like Ritzy's and the shops, it's abandoned, and as I look around the area it's clear that nobody even lives here any more. I'd expect there to be temporary fencing up, security patrols and a site office for what is obviously soon to become another development. The lack of anything here, including people, suggests our driver is right about the development having stalled.

'This is a dead end. She's not here, and neither are those creeps from the Church of the Golden Shower. Let's get back to the station.' Karen strides back to our waiting patrol car, but I pause a moment, looking at the church again. There's something about it that doesn't quite sit straight, something that bothers me, but I can't put my finger on what.

'You coming? Only it's a long walk.'

Not to my flat it isn't. I could be there in five minutes from here, taking the shortcuts and back lanes. Just a pity the station is on the opposite side of London. One last look at the church, the nightclub and the surrounding abandoned buildings. Still whatever it is my subconscious is trying to tell me hasn't broken through. It'll come to me in time, I guess. Probably wake me up in the middle of the night and I'll wonder why I couldn't see something so patently obvious.

'Least we tried to find her,' I say as I climb into the car. 'Just hope she finds us before it's too late.'

41

It's late by the time I let myself in the front door to Charlotte's house. Heat washes over me, a sharp contrast to the evening chill outside. More wonderful still is the smell of cooking, and I follow it through to the kitchen at the back of the house. I can't see anyone about, but a pot is simmering on the hob, little gusts of steam escaping from the lid with a clatter. When I peer inside, the smell intensifies. Someone's cooking a curry that, while probably not as good as Mrs Feltham's, is certainly better than the takeaway pizza I'd been contemplating.

'It's not ready yet.'

I turn to see Izzy standing in the doorway, a look of irritation on her face that is so like my father's standard expression I almost laugh. She's dressed in baggy jogging bottoms and a hoodie, bare feet showing nails painted in a variety of different colours. The scared, abused and frightened teenage girl is still in there, but she's grown up over the past few months.

'Sorry. Smells good though.'

'Didn't know what time you'd be back, so I cooked something that could just sit and wait. There's naan to go with it, and the rice is in the steamer.' Izzy points at a stainless steel machine with glowing LED lights over on one of the polished stone counters. I don't think I've ever encountered a rice steamer before, but this one looks like it could mine bitcoins in its spare time.

'You don't need to feed me, Izzy. Not that I'm complaining, mind.'

'I know.' She heads over to the fridge, an enormous thing you could hide several bodies in. 'Beer?'

It's very tempting, but I need to sort some stuff out first. Not the least of which is fetching clothes from my flat. I've got the things I bought in Edinburgh, but if I'm going to stay here for any length of time I'll need clean underwear at the very least. There's a week's worth of post piling up, too. I'd have picked it up earlier, but I daren't run the risk of bumping into Chet Wentworth or any of his pals. Not with Stokes still in hospital.

'Maybe later.' I glance at my watch, aware that there's not a lot of 'later' left. 'I need a shower, and then I'll have to be Jennifer Golightly for a while.'

By the time I find a parking space within reasonable distance of the apartment block, I realise I'd have been quicker walking from Charlotte's place to my flat. But I didn't fancy carrying everything I need all the way back. And my stomach's full of incredibly good curry, too, which makes the thought of walking a mile or so each way less than appealing. I'll have to ask Izzy where she learned to cook; it's not something they covered much beyond basic baking skills when I was at St Humbert's.

There's always a risk that any paparazzi lurking around my place will recognise my car, of course. It had been parked in Charlotte's garage alongside her rather more elegant Tesla, and I almost contemplated borrowing that instead. I'd have been spotted for sure though, and driving something that cost more than the chief commissioner's annual salary wouldn't help to dampen the posh cop image.

Jennifer Golightly, with her frumpy clothes and mouse-brown shoulder-length hair flecked with grey doesn't attract the attention of the bored-looking pair of ne'er-do-wells lurking on the pavement near the stairs up to my level. I catch a snippet of their conversation as I walk past them though, and it doesn't inspire me with confidence.

'. . . Stokes in the hospital. Heart attack, they reckon. Massive one.'

'Stokesey? Bloody hell. Thought he was fit.'

'Yeah, well. Word is she was there, right?'

'Who?'

'Her. The posh cop. Fairchild. Way I heard it she just stared at him like she wanted him to die. Maybe even slipped something in his coffee, right?'

'Why was he even with . . .'

I move on as swiftly as I can without drawing attention to myself, even though I'm desperate to find out more. Too much to hope that my role in saving Stokes's life might be the news. I guess it doesn't fit the narrative of spoiled little rich kid just playing at being poor.

It still leaves me rattled, which is probably why I don't notice the figure lurking just beyond my front door until it's too late. I've already got the key in the lock when it steps out of the shadows.

'Nice wig. Might have to get me one of those.'

I almost jump out of my skin, even as my brain parses the voice, recognises it, and damps down the adrenaline rush.

'Anna?' I look at the short, young woman, her face mostly shadow, goth-black clothes perfectly suited to lurking. 'Or should I say Polly?'

'Just not Pollyanna, OK? Fucking hate that name.'

'What are you doing here?' It's a stupid question, really, but it's out of my mouth before I can stop myself.

'Heard you was looking for me, right? Well, here I am. Now can we go inside? It's fucking freezing out here.'

★ ★ ★

If Anna thought getting inside was going to help warm her up, she's sorely disappointed. If anything, the temperature in my flat feels colder than outside. It's damp, too, which makes it even worse.

'Jeez. You forget to pay the gas bill or something?' She stomps her feet, hugs herself tight, then walks past me into the narrow hall. She peers first through the door to the kitchen, then to the lounge.

'I've not been home. Hounded by the press, remember?' I point at my wig.

'Where you staying then?'

It's an innocent enough question, but I'm not about to invite her back to Charlotte's. 'Could ask the same of you. Your mum's not seen you in weeks. Drama club miss you too.'

'Drama club? Jesus. You have been doing your homework.'

'I'm a detective. It's my job. At least, it would be if I could persuade the tabloids to leave me alone.'

'Got anything to eat?' Anna walks into my kitchen as if it's her own, over to the fridge. Light spills out of it onto her face, showing a puffy eye, badly concealed with make-up. The faint whiff of decay spills out too, taking a little longer to make itself known.

'Eww. What died in here?' She slams the door shut with a little more force than strictly necessary, then starts going through the cupboards until she finds a packet of biscuits.

'Help yourself. You want a cup of tea to go with that?'

'Got anything stronger?'

'No. And I've no milk for tea either. Sorry.' I pull out a chair from the narrow table, sit down and watch as she munches through the biscuits. They've got to be past their sell-by date, but at least the packet hadn't been opened. Until now. After a while she pulls out the other chair and sits down too.

'So what you wanna see me about?'

Direct and to the point, I guess. I might as well respond in kind. 'Dan Jones.'

Anna stops chewing, and puts down the half biscuit still in her hand. 'What about him?'

'How do you know him?'

'He was nice. Didn't stare at us girls like we was asking for it, like? Think he was a bit scared of us, you know.'

'Is that why you helped him?' I study her face as I ask the question, looking for any tell. She's so heavily made-up it's not easy to see anything, except for her swollen cheek and bloodshot eyeball. 'That why someone hit you?'

'Fell down the stairs, din't I.'

I'd laugh were the situation not so serious. 'Look, Anna. You were seen the night we found Dan round the back there.' I chuck a thumb in the general direction of the bin store. 'You and another bloke who I'm fairly sure shoved a leaflet into my hand at Euston station just a few days later. Bringing us the gospel courtesy of the Church of the Coming Light. You got anything to do with that? The Reverend Doctor Edward Masters?'

She's good, I'll give her that much. The flinch when I name the church is almost imperceptible. But when I mention Masters she twitches, covering it up by snatching the half-eaten biscuit from the table and shoving it in her mouth. She grabs the rest of the packet with the other hand and is on her feet before I can react.

'Shouldn't've come here,' she says through a spray of crumbs. She's quick, too, halfway to the door before I'm on my feet. If my flat were any bigger, I'd probably not be able to catch her, but I get a hand on her arm and hold on tight.

'I'm trying to help you, Anna. Stop running away, OK?'

The life goes out of her, but I'm too seasoned a copper to fall for that old trick. I keep my grip as tight as ever. 'Look, I know you've got yourself into something bigger than you thought. I mean it when I say I can help.'

She stares at me with that venom only teenagers can truly muster. At that moment I'm sure she hates me more than anything in the world. It doesn't last though, and this time when she shakes my hand away, I let go.

'The young man you were with that night, asking questions in the shops and the kebab place. What's his name?'

'I dunno. Reverend calls him Tim. Not seen him around for a few days now.'

Something about the way she says it tells me she knows exactly why Tim's not around any more. 'You're part of the church, aren't you. That's where you've been staying, right?'

The nod is barely there, but it's enough to open the floodgates. 'I was sleeping rough when they found me. Proper messed up. You any idea what it's like growing up on the Danes looking like me? And no dad either?'

I shake my head. It's as far from my own upbringing as it's possible to get. And my father might be a prize arsehole, but at least he was there throughout my childhood years.

'Bad enough being called chinky and slit-eyes in Primary. It only gets worse when you get older. But the Reverend, he don't stand for none of that shit. We're all the same on the inside, that's what he says. God's beautiful creatures.'

It sounds idyllic, but I can't quite square that with the dead man in a dirty close in Newhaven; the body thrown out in the square not a mile from here; Dan Jones with his tongue ripped out and bollocks cut off. 'There's another side to it though, isn't there. Something you didn't find out until it was too late, right?'

There's a long pause before she speaks again, and I can see the emotions playing across her face despite her heavy white concealer. 'I can't say. You don't know him. What he can do.'

I think of Tim in an Edinburgh back lane, the nameless young man in the park, Dan Jones hiding under the garbage. 'I've a good enough idea.'

'No. You really don't.' Anna takes a deep breath, as if trying to focus herself. 'He has this power. He . . . controls people. Makes them do things. Terrible things.' She looks at her hands as if she is one of those people and can remember all the terrible things she has done.

'Hey, it's OK.' I reach out and lay my fingers gently on her shoulder. She shudders at the touch. Where before she'd avoided my gaze, now she looks straight at me.

'It's not OK. You can't help. It's too late for me.' She shakes my hand away. 'I shouldn't have come here. Shouldn't even have followed you that day. It hurts just to talk to you. You know that? He has that power.'

As if to illustrate her point, a great spasming cough shakes her to the core. I have a sudden vision of Jonathan Stokes choking, collapsing to the floor, unable to breathe. Anna has that same look of fear in her eyes just now, her face beginning to redden even underneath her heavy make-up.

'Please. Don't make me stay.' Her words are barely a whisper, her breath catching as she tries to speak. I lean in the better to hear, and she shoves me, hard. Caught off guard and off-balance, I flail for the doorframe, miss and land on my arse in the kitchen. By the time I've clambered back up onto my feet, she's out of the front door and away into the night.

42

'I'd like to go and speak to them. The Church of the Coming Light.'

Wednesday morning and I'm in early, another video conference with DCI Bain. This time Diane Shepherd is in on it too, although where she's called in from I've no idea. I've brought them up to speed about Anna, AKA Pollyanna Cho, and all the things she told me last night. I'd expected to get a telling-off for not bringing her in, but Shepherd cut Bain off before he could get started on that.

'D'you not think we'd be better off getting a warrant, raiding the place? Do we even know where they're based?' DS Latham's sneering face looms into the camera feed from Edinburgh. I don't want to think why the two of them are still up there.

'A little groundwork wouldn't hurt first, would it? We go in heavy handed and shut down an outfit with their public profile, it could blow up in our faces very quickly.'

'Public profile?' Shepherd asks.

'They run soup kitchens and homeless shelters all over north London, ma'am. Their drug intervention work has the support of several local MPs. The Reverend Doctor Masters is well connected, and he's a favourite talking head on some of the late-night news programmes. I think I'd be happier checking that all out before accusing him of murdering and butchering young men.'

There's a pause while they all digest this information. Eventually Bain speaks. 'How are you planning on talking to him?'

'I don't know where he is, currently. But there's a shelter not far from my flat. That's pretty close to where we found Dan Jones, and where the body was left in the park. I figured I could just go and talk to whoever's there about what they do, maybe try to get a tour of the facilities. If I can speak to some of the homeless folk too, so much the better. That's not going to happen if the place is swarming with uniforms.'

'What do you think, Karen?' Shepherd asks. Beside me, the detective constable startles, surprised to be involved in the conversation.

'I . . . I think it makes sense, ma'am. We've got a good relationship with the local police up there. Get a couple of community support officers to come with us. People who know the church – who the church know, more importantly. We don't want to alarm anyone, just put out a few feelers.'

'Why haven't we spoken to them already? If they're that close?' Finally DS Latham says something that's helpful, sort of.

'It's a good question. I've no idea what the answer is, but it gives us an excuse, wouldn't you say?'

The screen freezes with an image of Latham's sneering face on it. For a moment I think it's something wrong with the system, but then it dawns on me we've been muted while the established team can discuss the case between themselves.

'You reckon they'd notice if I scribbled a moustache and specs on that?' I ask Karen. She's still giggling when the screen unfreezes.

'We'll be back in town this evening.' Bain's face magically appears where Latham's was a moment ago. An improvement, but disconcerting nonetheless. 'Go speak to this Church, find out what you can. But tread carefully, OK? I don't want this spiralling out of control.'

★ ★ ★

From the leaflet they pressed upon me at Euston station a week ago, I might be forgiven for thinking the Church of the Coming Light were based in some exclusive rural campus, surrounded by nature and where the weather was always childhood-holiday summer. The nondescript building on the corner of the high street and one of London's busier arterial routes could hardly be further from that image.

From the front it looks old and dirty, rising three storeys and a fourth in the roof with dormer windows that might have a half-decent view of the nearby Danes Estate. The front entrance is ornate, pink granite steps climbing up from the pavement to a carved, arched doorway wide enough for two men to walk in abreast, and tall enough for them to keep their top hats on while doing so.

Our uniform escort is nowhere to be seen when Karen and I arrive, which gives us a chance to observe the place from across the road. If I was hoping to see a steady stream of down-and-outs filing in, I'm sorely disappointed. Nobody comes or goes in the five minutes before a squad car pulls up outside.

'You know this place does a lot of our work for us?' the friendly constable says by way of greeting after we've fought our way across the busy road.

'Hopefully it can keep on doing so. I'm not here to cause trouble if I can help it.'

He says nothing to that, and neither does his colleague, but I can see by their expressions that I'm treading on sore toes here. I know exactly how stretched budgets are, and how big the interlinked problems of poverty, homelessness, and drug abuse. It hasn't escaped me that I've been suspended from duties but still on full pay until very recently, which won't have endeared me to the hard-pressed bobbies on the beat either. Time to be tactful, Con. If you can manage it.

At the top of the steps, only one half of the heavy wooden double doors is open. As we approach it, there's little to suggest this is either a soup kitchen, a shelter for the homeless or a church of dubious provenance. The only clue it's a place that welcomes all is a handmade sign on the closed door that reads 'Food Bank. Hot Meals. Shelter.' That and the little church logo I last saw on the leaflet, reproduced here on a small plaque.

Inside, it's a different matter. We go through a narrow corridor into a much larger open hall, rising up through all four storeys to a glass cupola overhead. It reminds me curiously of Rose's place in Edinburgh, which is built on much the same scale. Where that house is full of clutter and cats, however, this one is filled with rows of chairs, and people.

'How the hell?' Karen voices my own thought. Neither of us saw anyone come or go, and yet the place is a bustle of busyness.

'Folk tend to use the back door.' Friendly Constable points to the far side of the hall, where a serving hatch is doing steady business doling out meals. Alongside it, another more modern pair of double doors sees a stream of people coming and going.

'Is there anything I can do to help?'

I turn at the question, see a young woman coming towards us, her eyes glancing nervously at the two uniform constables. She obviously recognises them when they face her, as her shoulders slump a little in relief. She's still wringing her hands like she's anxious to go off and pray somewhere though.

'Detective Constable Eve.' Karen has the patter down nicely now, showing her warrant card only briefly. 'This is my colleague—'

'Well, if it isn't Lady Constance Fairchild.'

43

The voice is so deep, so loud, I almost jump in surprise. A split second later I know who it is; we've met before, after all. Coming from a door off to one side of the front entrance, the Reverend Doctor Edward Masters is trailed closely by two of his security acolytes.

'Mr Masters. We meet again.' I hold out my hand as he invades my personal space with all the subtlety of a Russian oligarch.

'Reverend Doctor, actually.' He takes my hand in one enormous paw, bringing the other one around to make sure I can't escape. 'I was disappointed not to see you at your brother's wedding. Your mother tells me you chose not to go.'

His gaze is how I imagine a lion sizes up a gazelle. There's something deeply unsettling about him, not helped by what Anna has told me. It's all part of his act though, along with the too-long handshake.

'I didn't want to spoil his big day. Been getting a lot of attention from the press recently, and you know what they can be like.'

'A most noble sacrifice. Although there were members of the press at the wedding after all.' Masters finally releases me from his grip. I fight the urge to massage my hand or even wipe it on my trousers.

'Well then, Detective Constables. I don't suppose you're

looking for a hot meal or a bed for the night. What can I help you with?'

'About a week ago, the body of a young man was found in a park not far from here. We've been having some trouble confirming his identity, which suggests he might have been homeless, maybe an immigrant. The sort of person who'd likely turn to a place like this if things got very bad.'

A flicker of something like annoyance tightens his eyes for a moment, and then he beams a smile that is all impossibly white teeth. 'Of course. Of course. Terrible that a man should die in the cold, unnamed and unloved. If there is anything we can do to help the police with their enquiries, we will be happy to do so.'

'Perhaps I might speak to some of the volunteers who help here? Show them a picture?' I turn away from him and wave a hand across the crowd, aware that it's smaller now than when two uniformed police officers entered a few minutes ago. 'I wouldn't want to upset the—' I'm momentarily lost for what to call them. 'People?'

'They are most certainly people, Lady Constance. Not as fortunate as those born to the manner, perhaps. But we are all people. I do what I can to help, where others would simply turn a blind eye.'

I've heard sales pitches before, and his is certainly persuasive. Unless you know as much about the man as I do. 'And where does God fit into all of this?'

'God?' Masters lets out a low rumbling sound that I realise after a moment is a laugh. 'God opened my eyes. He came to me when I was weak and helpless, and He showed me a path to redemption. This is it, my ministry, my task on this earth. To give succour to the poor and the needy.'

'It must cost a lot of money. Not that these people don't need it spent on them.'

'You would be surprised at how generous people can be, given the right encouragement. The Church of the Coming Light has many benefactors. Lady Angela herself has recently made a most generous donation.'

'I'm sure she knows what she's doing. My mother and I rarely speak, as I'm sure you know. She disapproves of my life choices.'

Masters shrugs. 'It is a shame when families fall apart, but the calling you have chosen is noble. Given time, Lady Angela will come to see that.'

I'd say that ten years and counting was more than enough time to come to her senses, but I get the feeling it would be lost on Masters. I've also spent more time in his presence than I would like, but at least our conversation has taken us across the hall to the serving hatch. Karen is busy talking to some of the faithful, and our uniformed escort are keeping out of the way as best they can. Even so, the clients of this place – the homeless and poor and just bloody unlucky people – are drifting away. So much for neighbourhood policing.

'How many meals do you serve here? On a normal day.' Looking through the serving hatch, I can see a well-laid-out kitchen beyond. It wouldn't disgrace a top restaurant closer to the city centre.

'I have no idea. As many as are needed, I suppose. We would never turn someone away.'

'And you have accommodation here too? You take people off the streets?'

'"Take" makes it sound like they don't want to come with us. I can assure you, Lady Constance, we only offer assistance. We do not force it upon those not yet ready to accept it.'

Nothing he has said is in the least bit suspicious, nothing I've seen so far. And yet I know with a deep-rooted certainty that there is something very wrong going on here.

'Perhaps you might answer a question of my own,' Masters

says, and put like that it's very hard to refuse. Especially when Bain insisted we keep things friendly.

'Of course.'

'Why is it exactly you're here? I mean, we always welcome the police. We work closely with them. But we don't often see detectives here.'

Masters stares at me with the singular intensity of an unfed toddler as he awaits my answer. There's something of the baby about his round, podgy face too, but his eyes are dark pits.

'Like I already told you, a young man's body was found in a park nearby. Our initial investigations suggest he might have been homeless, sleeping rough, possibly taking drugs. I had hoped to circulate his picture, see if anyone recognised him.' I look around the now almost empty hall. 'But your customers seem to have other ideas.'

Masters breaks into a smile that's all shiny white teeth. 'What can I say? They maybe do not like the sight of a police uniform quite so much.'

'Well, I'll leave the photograph here anyway. Maybe it'll jog a memory, a name?' I take out the picture and hand it to Masters, studying his face as he looks at it. There's no sign of recognition, no sign of anything in the second it takes for him to scan it and hand it to one of his acolytes.

'I will see that it is circulated, and if anyone recognises the poor fellow we will let you know.'

'Thank you, Reverend Doctor.' I put on my best St Humbert's smile and don't even grit my teeth as I say it.

'Please, call me Edward. And for Lady Angela's daughter? It is no trouble at all.'

None of us say anything as the squad car drives us back to the local station. I don't think our visit has soured the relationship between the police and the Church of the Coming Light, but neither has it exactly achieved anything. I've no doubt whatsoever that the photograph we left behind is now in a bin, if it's not passed through a shredder first.

'They're not so bad, really.' The uniform constable who's been our driver for the past couple of days chimes in with his helpful opinion. I wish I could remember his name.

'How do you mean?'

'It's not easy round here. You know what the Danes is like, right? And that's only the half of it. Austerity's hit people hard. The Church picks people up when they're down, and the way I hear it they don't come on too preachy either. Not if you don't want it.'

I stare out of the window as we drive slowly through the part of London I've come to know as home. It's true the number of rough sleepers has increased steadily over the past few years, with small businesses closing down, shops boarded up, derelict buildings, drugs. Even the streets are more untidy, fewer sweepers and bin collections, more urban foxes spreading the rubbish around. It's like somewhere along the line people just stopped caring.

'That's the point though, isn't it? We shouldn't need that kind of charity. And what happens when we're so dependent on it we can't even investigate them when something goes wrong?'

There's a long silence after that, which I hope means they're thinking about it, but probably means they think I'm a weirdo. Soon enough we arrive back at the local police station.

'You needing anything else from us?' our driver asks once we've all climbed out of the car. I can see his appointment with the canteen written large across his face. It's getting past lunchtime so I can hardly blame him.

'No. We're good, thanks.' I shoulder my small rucksack and slam shut the car door before remembering my manners. 'And thanks for driving us around, too. Can't be much fun having to babysit a couple of junior detectives for a couple of days.'

'Beats patrolling the Danes,' the driver says with a smile. 'See you around, eh, Posh Cop.'

He and his colleague walk off towards the back door to the station, leaving Karen and me to stare at each other and try not to laugh.

'I think he fancies you,' she says after a while.

'Maybe. Not sure he's my type though. And in-work relationships are the worst.'

'Well, you can have him if you want him. Not my type at all.' Karen sets off towards the main street and the Tube station that will take us back across town.

'No?' I ask as I catch up and fall into step with her long strides.

'Yeah. Too eager for one thing. Too male for another.'

I can be slow on the uptake sometimes, so it takes me at least three seconds to work out what she's just said and what it means. Not so much the fact of her sexuality as that she's prepared to share that with me. The police might be a big happy family according to all the publicity, but it's still full of people who'd make your life a misery for something like that. Bad enough her having to put up with all the usual racist crap black officers endure. No wonder she's so keen to move to plain clothes.

'So, what's next?' Karen asks, changing the subject as swiftly as she brought it up.

'Well, the Church of the Golden Shower was a bust. Still reckon they're dodgy, but it's going to be a tricky one to prove.'

'I guess it's back to the CCTV footage then.'

The viewing room with its unpleasant, stagnant air. Endless hours of staring at screens that will show us nothing we want to see. Such is the life of a detective. Nothing at all like the cops on the telly.

'CCTV it is.'

44

I walk from Charlotte's back to my flat this time. The evening's dry, the air beginning to warm with the coming spring. It's good to get out on my own for a change. Working with Karen's fine, up to a point, but I've grown used to my own company. I'm not so good at being part of a team. Sharing a house with a teenager is a struggle too. Even one who's as skilled a cook as Izzy.

Jennifer Golightly's hair bobs against my shoulders, a reminder of a time when I was younger. I was never mousy brown, always dark, angry red, but I once wore my hair even longer than this. That was before I grew tired of my father's constant, unwitting misogyny and my mother's utter indifference to it. There are so many reasons why I left home, but her coldness is high up on the list of them.

It shouldn't bother me what she does any more, least of all with her money. I've convinced myself I was done with caring about that sort of thing. But as I walk the dark streets towards my apartment block I find myself thinking I'd rather she left it all to the local cat sanctuary than give a single penny to Edward Masters.

There has to be a reason for it, beyond his obvious ability to sniff out a fundraising opportunity and maximise its potential. How they even crossed paths is beyond me. Theirs are surely two completely different worlds. And yet something has brought them together.

As if on cue, my phone buzzes in my pocket. Incoming text. I take it out and peer at the screen, confused by the message and who it's from. How did she know my number? How did she know I was thinking about her?

Will be in London this evening. Understand you are staying at Charlotte's. Will meet you there at 8.00 p.m. Something important we need to discuss. Mother.

No 'love', no indecisive number of Xs, just 'Mother'. I'm surprised she has a mobile phone, let alone knows how to text. A quick glance at the time tells me I've an hour yet, and Izzy will be there to let her in if I'm a bit late. I can't deny the message has grabbed my attention though. Something so important my mother needs to talk to me in person? And yet it can't involve any other member of the family, or Aunt Flick would have called.

I'm still pondering the puzzle, staring at the screen and wondering if I should respond, when a voice interrupts my train of thought.

'Excuse me, miss? You live here?' I glance up to see people hanging around outside Mrs Feltham's front door. They're dressed for the cold, and at least one of them has a camera slung around his neck. Overweight, bobble hat to stop his bald head getting chilled.

Chet Wentworth.

He's the one who's spoken, and he takes a step closer, his camera coming up in what must be a reflex action. Get a shot, doesn't matter who it is. You can always delete it if they're nobody. That's the joy of digital photography. I click off my phone, slip it into my pocket while at the same time shaking my head. No words. I don't owe these ghouls anything. A shame they feel they're entitled to a response anyway.

'Come on, love. You must know the posh cop who lives

upstairs, right?' This from one of the reporters. I don't recognise his voice, and make the mistake of looking up at him to see who he might be. At the same time, Wentworth's flash explodes in my face. Way too close for comfort. Blinded and angry, I lash out on instinct.

'Get away from me, you bastards. Leave me alone.'

It's probably just bad luck, or maybe karma, but my hand catches something as I swing around. Vision coming back in a blurred and starry mess, I realise it's Wentworth's camera, and once more something cracks as I tug hard.

'Hey. That's—'

Expensive, by the sound it makes hitting the pavement. I push through the gathering crowd, knocking the nearest reporter aside in my haste to get away from them. I'm really not in the mood for this.

'Fuck's sake.'

'Hang on. It's her, isn't it.'

'Bloody—'

More reporters appear from the concrete steps leading up to my flat, no doubt alerted by the commotion. I'm stuck between two groups of them, a parked van blocking my escape route to the street.

'Is it true you were with Stokes when he had his heart attack?'

'Did you want him dead? Maybe slipped something in his tea?'

'Why are you trying to hide from us, Connie? Something you don't want us to find out?'

They're everywhere, surrounding me, shoving cameras and microphones in my face. Grabbing hands pluck at my coat, and for a moment I fear for my life.

'Get the fuck away from me.' I push through a tiny gap between two reporters with such force they both tumble to the ground. It's a lucky move, because their tangled limbs make it difficult for the rest to give immediate chase. Their blood is up though, and now I know how the fox must feel when the hunting horn sounds. Nothing else I can do, I put my head down and run.

My first thought is to get back to Charlotte's as quickly as possible, lock the door and hide. I can hear footsteps behind me though, and the last thing I want to do is lead them to where I'm staying. Where Izzy's staying too, and where my mother's due to arrive soon. I've an advantage over the reporters in that I've lived here for years, know my way around the back streets and alleys. With luck I can lose them.

A quick glance over my shoulder shows at least some of them following. There's a car keeping pace with me along the street too, even though the traffic is clear for once. They'll have a hard time following me in that as I turn down a short passage that runs along the back of the shops on the high street. Halfway along it, another even narrower passage winds past wheelie bins and rubbish before opening up into a quiet close. The first of my pursuers appears as I am ducking down the lane opposite, and his cry of 'Over there!' makes me speed up. It's dark at the far end, so they won't be able to see which way I go next.

I'm in pretty good shape after a few months of living in the wilds of Perthshire, but I'm not running fit any more. Luckily for me, my pursuers are more given to the beer and fags exercise regime, and one by one they give up the chase. I've cut a zig-zag path across this part of town, and I'm further away from Charlotte's place than when I started, but finally I feel safe to pause.

Still keeping to the shadows, I gulp down breaths of cool night air for a few moments, then start to take in my surroundings. I shouldn't be surprised to see where my feet have brought me; I knew where I was running, after all. And yet somehow the sight of the boarded-up Ritzy's nightclub and St Martin's abandoned, derelict church give me pause. Was there more to coming here than simply getting away from the press?

Running and adrenaline have made me sweaty, and I start to shiver in the chill night air. There's a pub a hundred metres down the road I could go to, but if memory serves it's not the sort of place a lone woman would be wise to enter after dark. Or indeed at all. Too close to the Danes Estate, and frequented by its more unsavoury residents. Glancing up over the church spire, I can see the four towers, lights speckling their sides in random patterns.

A noise close by grabs my attention. Light spills across the street from an open doorway, voices raised in angry shouts. Two men tumble out of the pub, their argument threatening to turn violent. I shrink further back into the shadows, hold my breath for a moment, hoping they'll go the other way. One of them shouts a stream of abuse, then stumbles away down the street. The other lurches towards the church and nightclub, then swings around and stares at his companion's retreating back. For a moment I think he's going to run at him, attack from behind unsuspected. In the end he simply yells 'Fuck you!', and then goes back into the pub.

As the moment passes, I force myself to relax a little. I slip out my phone, thinking about calling the police. It would be simple enough to ask someone to go and remove the reporters from my front door, but the request would come back to haunt me in more ways than one. From my short but painful experience, I've learned that the paparazzi take exception to having the cops called on them. And my fellow officers in uniform are not all as friendly and helpful as the young constable who's been driving me and Karen around for the past couple of days.

I could call her, of course. Get her to sort out my problems. Yeah, that sounds like a great idea, Con. I tuck my phone away and tip my head back until it bumps gently against the door behind me.

Which is when I see the light shining out of the church window.

For a moment I think it must be street lamps reflecting on the stained glass. Or maybe the lights from the Danes Estate towers shining right through the building. But it's too bright for that, and gently flickering as if it were fire somewhere inside.

I sniff for any scent of smoke, but I'm too far away. There's no chance I'd hear anything over the dull roar of the city either. I check the road, seeing nothing at this end where it's all boarded up and ready for demolition. Is this someone taking a shortcut with the planning department? Are they torching the church so they can get on with building expensive executive homes here?

It's not hard to keep to the shadows as I cross the road to the church. Closer in, I still can't hear anything crackling away, and the air is unusually crisp and clean for a change. The padlock and chain on the front gates don't look any different to yesterday, the door at the top of the steps the same. I make a slow circuit of the building, staring up at the blank windows, but there's no sign of any light from them this close in.

I check the three open sides before reaching the dark lane that runs between the church and Ritzy's. The fire doors open onto here, although I can't see in the gloom whether they're screwed shut or not. I can just about make them out as I walk quietly past, although most of my attention is on the church. It has a side entrance here too, locked and barred as firmly as the front. The wind-blown rubbish piled up around it suggests nobody's been this way in a long time. As I stare up at the windows to either side, I catch that light again, the faintest of flickerings. Not a roaring. A candle. Someone is inside, but I can't see how they can have got there.

It's nothing to do with me. I should leave well alone, head

back to Charlotte's, where my mother will surely be waiting for me by now. If I'm really bothered about it, I can just make a report in the morning. This isn't my problem. It isn't even all that suspicious. Churches and candles go together like Christmas and overcooked Brussels sprouts.

It's only when I turn from the door that I see the man, standing a few metres away. There's not enough light in the lane to make out his features, but there is enough to see his clothes. One of the acolytes of the Church of the Coming Light. Or rather, one of the hired guards who pretend to be acolytes while looking after the reverend doctor. I can't get past him, can't hope to overpower him, so I turn swiftly to run in the other direction.

Which is when I see he has friends.

45

I can't work out where they've come from, but the lane is suddenly full of people. They surround me before I can make a run for it, boxing me in with military precision. And then I see the fire door to the nightclub swing open again, more bodies rushing out. Strong hands grab me before I can take more than a couple of steps. My arms are twisted up behind me and the first man I saw steps up close.

'Who are you? Why are you here?'

He doesn't recognise me, and I'm still wearing Jennifer's frumpy clothes and wig. I stare at him through the slightly smeared non-prescription lenses of my mother's spectacles and say nothing.

'Search her.' The man steps back and a couple of his companions take his place. They frisk me, take my phone and keys out of my pocket, pull my small backpack off my shoulder and rummage through it. For about the first time since it was taken from me, I'm glad I don't have my warrant card. There's still a slim chance I might be able to blag my way out of this. Very slim indeed.

'Nothing.' One of the two men who frisked me hands what he's found to the acolyte who seems to be in charge. He looks at my meagre possessions with a scowl of disappointment.

'Take her inside.'

I'm frog-marched towards the nightclub fire door. There's a

female acolyte standing beside it, and she thumps hard on the metal as I come near. Someone inside pushes it open, then I'm hustled inside, along a short corridor stacked with the kind of supplies you'd expect were the place still licensed and operating, and out into the dance hall. The change in light levels hurts my eyes. It's bright in here, unlike the dark and sweaty nightclub I remember. Blinking and squinting, I vaguely recognise it from my one bad experience here, but the floor has been filled with chairs, arranged in rows and all facing a lectern. It looks more like a church hall than a place to score cheap drugs or a knee-trembler in the bogs.

Lead acolyte pushes past me, carrying my belongings to another man standing at the lectern. My eyes are adjusting now, but it still takes me a moment or two to recognise him. No idea what his name is, but he's the one who chased me all the way from the prayer meeting to the pub in Edinburgh. The one who took my photograph through the open door as I sat at the bar. He's wearing more fancy robes than the others, so is probably in charge.

'Found her sneaking around the church,' the bodyguard says. The senior acolyte looks across at me, no immediate sign of recognition on his face. I have to hope they won't realise I'm wearing a wig.

'And you didn't think to just scare her away? You had to bring her in here to see what we're doing?'

'I thought—'

'No, that's the whole point. You didn't think. And you're supposed to be the bright one.' He's rifling through my things as he speaks. My phone won't unlock for him unless I give him the pin code, but my driving licence and credit cards are in my backpack. Fuck's sake. How could I be so stupid?

'Oh Jesus. This is bad.' He looks at me more carefully now, one hand holding a slim rectangle of plastic. There's a moment where it could go one of two ways. Or at least that's what I tell myself. Then he pulls out his mobile phone, taps the screen, swipes and swipes again. I can't see it, but I know exactly what he's doing. He holds the phone up so that it's in line with my face, looks from one to the other and back again.

'Take off her glasses,' he says, and then does it himself when no one leaps to obey. I know what's coming next, and even though it's not my own hair, I still tense for the pain when he grabs the wig and pulls it off. He brings the phone up again, and lets out a quiet 'Fuck' as his shoulders slump. I know how he feels.

'Shove her in the storeroom. Someone on the door at all times. I need to speak to the boss.'

At least I'm out of the cold. That's what I tell myself as I sit in the corner of the almost empty storeroom and wait for whatever happens next. They were kind enough to leave the light on, and they've not tied me up, but this room has no window I can escape through. There's a rack of industrial shelving along one wall, a few cardboard boxes stacked up in the corner. Nothing I could use as a weapon, even if I thought fighting my way out of this situation was anything other than a really stupid idea.

They took my watch, as well as my phone. Maybe someone thought it was one of those fancy smartwatches, or something out of *Dick Tracy* that I could use to call in reinforcements. It wasn't. It was nothing more sophisticated than a cheap Swiss disposable my brother gave me for my sixteenth birthday. Of all the things I've lost, that's probably the worst. Phones can be replaced, credit cards can be cancelled, but that watch and me have history. It keeps pretty good time, too, whereas I've no idea how long it's been since I was captured, and only a vague idea of what time it was when that happened anyway.

Pacing doesn't help, and I've explored everything in the room there is to explore, so I sit with my back against the wall and stare at the door, rubbing nervously at my wrists. For a while after they shoved me in here, I could hear noises. People talking in low whispers, the sound of footsteps in the hall, the occasional squeal of chair legs pushed backwards, distant chanting. That went on for quite a long time, but now I can't hear anything. Maybe they've all dispersed from whatever nefarious and clandestine activity they were engaged in.

And what, exactly, was that? Being caught, bundled inside, identified, all happened swiftly, but I saw enough to know there were at least fifty chairs set out. Were there that many people? Hard to tell in the mêlée. Enough of them came out into the lane that I had no chance of escape, certainly. And there must have been more inside. But what were they doing here?

My first thought is some kind of prayer meeting, but that doesn't make much sense. These are people from the Church of the Coming Light. There's no need for them to meet in secret like some sinister evil society planning the overthrow of civilisation, surely?

Except that there is, if I allow my mind to wander down the worst corridors of conspiracy theory. If I join up the dots, link together the clues I've uncovered so far, then it leads to a horrific place. And if I dwell too long on what Anna told me, what happened to Jonathan Stokes, then being locked up in this empty storeroom is not good at all.

I'm on my feet again, pacing, before I know it. I need to be calm, focused, rational. All the things the police have taught me over the years. Jumping to conclusions helps no one, Con. You're better than that. You can get out of this.

I laugh at myself, and the noise helps. It's too quiet in here, too bare. I don't want to be left alone with my thoughts, when they keep drifting back to Dan Jones, the young man in the park, the body in Edinburgh. Dan got lucky, if only having your tongue ripped out and your bollocks cut off can be considered lucky. If he hadn't escaped – if Anna hadn't helped him escape – he'd have ended up like the other two. Sacrificed. That's the word I've been skirting around ever since they locked me up in here. Those are the stakes. I might take solace in the fact that all the dead bodies Bain and the team have been looking into have been young men, the kind of bullshit bush magic that takes hearts and tongues for their owners' strength tends to look down on the weak female form. It's not much of a silver lining.

I'm walking back to my spot opposite the door when I hear a commotion outside. Scuffing feet as someone hurries to do something, a click of a key turning in the lock. The door swings inwards, no light spilling from outside. There's no room in the narrow corridor for it to pass the looming figure that fills the doorway, and his ominous presence draws all the shadows towards him anyway. I knew he was coming, of course. But seeing him there is still a shock. The Reverend Doctor Edward Masters is an impressive figure in public. Here he seems like the very devil himself. He has my wig in one hand, my mother's old spectacles in the other.

'Well, well, well.' Even his voice is deeper, more threatening. His smile the grin of a hyena. 'If it isn't little Miss Jennifer Golightly.'

46

'Take her to the crypt.'

The crypt. If one word was guaranteed to turn my knees to jelly, that would be it. There's a crypt beneath the church in Harston Magna where generations of Fairchilds have been laid to rest. I remember sneaking down there with Ben, a dare when we were still kids. There was no electricity, no lights, so we took torches that weren't particularly bright, stole the key from the vestry, and snuck in as the day was fading to evening. I don't scare easily, but something about the low vaulted ceiling, the damp, the cobwebs and the utter silence got to me. Then there were the coffins, stacked one atop another in alcoves that had maybe been intended for one or two, but now were filled beyond capacity. Death doesn't frighten me any more, I've seen far too much of it in my line of work. Back then, though, it looked as if the dead were trying to break out of their cracked and woodworm-infested prisons. When the first rat scuttled over my foot, I turned and ran, Ben screaming behind me.

All of these memories and more flood my mind as two men step past Masters into the room and approach me. Far from adding to my fear though, that incident from my childhood gives me a certain strength. When the men try to take my arms, I shake them away, step towards their boss.

'I don't need to be carried. Just show me the way.'

It's false bravado, of course. They hold all the cards here, and

I've no doubt they intend to kill me. I just need to find a way of stopping them.

'Such courage.' Masters tries to sneer. I hold his gaze, chin up, until he looks away. 'It will not go to waste. The crypt.'

Not quite sure what else they should do, the two men usher me out of the storeroom. One leads me down the corridor, the other follows closer behind than is polite. Past the door to the dance hall, another one opens into a small office. Like everything else in this building, its window is boarded up. No clue here as to what time it is. Must be getting on for midnight though. I wonder what my mother will make of my not showing up. Most likely she'll just put it down to my typical bad behaviour. Izzy will worry, though. But if she tries my phone it'll go to voicemail, and she'll probably think I'm at the pub. Or maybe gone off with Alex Fortescue. Will she try and call him if she can't get hold of me? Does she even have his number? It's all academic anyway. No one knows where I am. They're not all going to come riding to my rescue any time soon.

'Mind your head.'

It's a curious thing for someone to say when they're intending to kill you, but I'm grateful nonetheless. There's a hatch in the floor on the far side of the office, stone steps leading down into darkness. This would explain how they could get into the church without opening any doors, I guess. As I descend, someone flips a switch and bare bulbs light up a narrow passage not unlike the crypt at Harston Magna. Damp, vaulted ceiling. Cobwebs. The flagstones underfoot glisten with oily moisture, and wobble as I tread on them.

At the end of the passage, a heavy wooden door reveals more steps down. At least the ceiling is a little higher here. I'm not as tall as the two men leading me, and I've had to crouch a little. Now I can stand without worrying about getting my hair full of grit from the ceiling. It's a small comfort.

The crypt, once we reach it, is larger than my family's resting place. The centre of the room is filled with a stone sarcophagus that looks to be far older than the church rising up above it. Alcoves line the walls, but they are all empty as far as I can tell. Except for the fat tallow candles that burn in each one, giving the room a low orange light that dances with the shadows as we disturb the air. Aside from the sarcophagus, which doesn't really count, the only piece of furniture in here is a stout wooden chair. It looks like something you might find in a late nineteenth-century American prison, and with wires attached to the local grid. As we approach I can see it's bolted to the floor. There are thick leather straps, padded with wool, on the arms and front legs. No guesses where I'm going next then.

'Sit,' the larger of the two men orders. I hesitate, looking around the room in the vain hope there might be some kind of escape route. The only way in other than the one we came through is an ornate iron gate, beyond which I can see more stone steps leading upwards into the body of the church.

'Sit!' This time the command is backed up with force. The other man grabs my arms and shoves me down into the chair. I put up a bit of a fight until he smacks me hard enough across the face to make my eyes water. The momentary shock is enough for them to pin my wrists and tighten the straps around them. They don't bother with my legs.

'Don't go anywhere now.' One of the men has a sense of humour. I glare at him, doing my best to memorise his face. You're going to get out of this, Con. You're a fighter. A survivor.

Even I don't believe myself, but I need to try.

They leave me alone, going out the way we came in. I test the straps, but they're stronger than me, and too tight to slide out of. My chair faces the sarcophagus, a gap between it and me of maybe a couple of metres. The gate and steps out into the church are on the other side. The ceiling rises to a point above me, shadows twisting in the candlelight. Stone carved faces leer at me, some devils, some green men, some creatures of nightmare. What is this place? Older than the church, sure. Older than the religion the church was built to serve.

Something moves at my feet, and I look down to see a lone rat sniffing around the chair legs. That's when I notice that the floor here is discoloured, the stone of the sarcophagus too. Stained dark by the blood of the poor bastards who've sat here before me. Dan Jones, the acolyte whose first name was Tim, the unnamed body in the park, the victims I saw in Bain's folder, their bodies dumped all over the country. How many more were never found?

Oh fuck. This is bad, Con. This is very bad.

'You are blessed, my child. Few ever see this place. Fewer still will know the bliss of becoming one with God here.'

Edward Masters emerges from the shadows, his eyes glinting in the flickering light. He was wearing his suit when I saw him before, bursting out of it as ever. Now his chest is bare, his dark skin slick and sweaty despite the chill air of the crypt. I had thought him fat, but his bulk is all muscle, pumped up like he's on steroids. He doesn't approach me at first, keeping the stone of the sarcophagus between us as if he's somehow frightened of me. That distance is reassuring, if nothing else.

'Who are you?'

It's maybe not the most obvious question, in the circumstances, but it's the first one that comes to me. Masters stops, his head tilted to one side as if he's considering his answer.

'I am the high priest. The giver of life and the bringer of death. I hold the power of God in my right hand.' He holds it up, clenching massive fingers into a fist just in case I don't know what he means.

'What is this place?' I strain against the straps holding my wrists, but they might as well be made of steel. Relaxing my arms, I nod at the sarcophagus. 'Whose coffin is that?'

'Coffin.' Masters echoes the word, not quite a question this time. Then he laughs a deep belly rumble that could be a bus passing by in the road, a Tube train down below. 'No coffin could hope to contain the spirit that sleeps within.'

'What is it, then? Dracula's last resting place?'

Masters unclenches his fist and lightly strokes the stone top of the sarcophagus. Anger blazes in his eyes now. I didn't like him calm, but I'm not sure this is an improvement.

'This tomb was here before London rose from the swamps around the Thames. It was built by the Roman invaders led by Julius Caesar himself. They brought this casket with them, all the way from Africa.'

I look at the unexceptional stone sarcophagus again. There really is nothing all that special about it, although it certainly looks old. And it's made of different stone to the rest of the crypt, which would suggest it's not local. Of course, it might just be that Masters is a madman.

'I thought you were a Christian. Isn't that what your church is all about?'

'God takes many forms, child.' Masters moves out from behind the stone and I see now that his legs are bare too, and his feet. I'm shivering with cold and I've got clothes on. How can he be sweating in nothing more than a loincloth? 'Before Christ came into the world, He was Yahweh, Jehovah, Ahura Mazda. To the Romans who brought Him here, he was Mithra. Many names, one God.'

Now I know he's mad, but that doesn't exactly help.

'And this God of yours, he likes human sacrifice, does he?'

Masters looms in close, his face mere inches from mine, massive hands easily enclosing my wrists and the straps that bind them.

'You cannot begin to understand his ways, child. You do not even believe. God cares nothing for those who cast Him aside, but there is power in their lives, just there for the taking. Power that can be used to help those more deserving than you.'

I open my mouth to say something pithy, but before I can even think of anything he grabs my face, squeezes my cheeks between thumb and forefinger with one hand. With the other he reaches in and grabs my tongue.

'Take a man's tongue and you gain the power of persuasion.'

He lets me go. It's all I can do to stop myself from gagging for a moment. Saliva floods my mouth and I spit out the taste of him as best I can. It spatters the floor beside the chair, soaking into the soft stone and highlighting the dark stains. I've barely recovered my composure when he grabs my crotch, pushing me back into the chair as he squeezes hard. Nothing sexual at all about the action, this is pure violence.

'Take his manhood, and you will be fertile in all your endeavours.'

I try to hold back the scream, but it escapes from me anyway, even as I stare deep into his mad, bulging eyes. He holds my gaze again, for long, drawn-out seconds. And then he releases me, steps back, breathing heavily as if he's just run here from the other side of the Danes Estate. He stalks away, hand resting on the stone lid of the sarcophagus, and as he goes I can see his shoulders heaving. His back is a mess of scars, raised out of his ebony skin like cords sunk into his flesh. His slow circum-navigation of the tomb takes long enough for my pain to subside, but I know this isn't over yet. Not by a long chalk. When he finally comes back to me, it's in a rush, his hand pressing hard against my breast, crushing it underneath his palm.

'Take a man's heart, and you gain all of his strength. All of his life.'

I can't breathe. He's so strong, so massive, my lungs are

useless. Is this how women accused of witchcraft felt, when the stones were piled on top of them? Not choked, not strangled, but crushed. Still bearing down on me with all the weight of the world, Masters once more leans in close.

'You are not a man, so none of these things are yours to be taken. None are mine to gift to those who might better use them. Your death will not be in vain though. It will let someone else live. Someone who deserves God's grace far more than your uncaring soul.'

I kick out with my feet, take a little satisfaction as he grimaces when my boot catches his shin. But my efforts are weak. I'm desperate for air, squeezed against the back of the chair, the pressure on my chest crushing my ribs, threatening to break them into shards that will pierce my lungs, pop my heart. I kick again, and this time he barely notices. I have no strength, no fight left in me.

The candles are growing darker now, shadows creeping out from the carved monsters on the ceiling as my vision begins to tunnel. I can see only that face, mad staring eyes, bulging with exertion. They are yellow, not white, the pupils tiny despite the lack of light in here. Thin capillaries snake over the surface like rivers of blood, glistening. This can't be how it ends, it's so stupid. Chased from my home by a bunch of third-rate hacks and wannabe YouTube stars. What a fucking epitaph.

'Good, good. I can feel your life in my hands now. Rejoice in the knowledge that it goes to one far more worthy than you. I will take your vitality and use it to heal.'

I barely hear the words. I can't feel anything but the pressure in my chest. Not my arms, my legs. My head is a heavy weight my neck no longer has the strength to hold upright. Nothing left at all, I surrender to the blackness.

And at that last moment, he releases me. My lungs suck in air on reflex, a deep, noisy gasp. I'm too far gone to notice Masters as he brings his other hand around, open, directly in front of my face. He leans close, lips pursed as if to kiss me. Only then do I see, through the unfocused fog, a small pile of powder on his palm.

'God be with you, Lady Constance.' He breathes the words, and his breath blows the powder into my face. It stings and numbs, filling my nose, my mouth, my throat.

And I am gone.

47

Am I dead?

It's dark as pitch, but I don't feel dead. There's too much pain for that. My chest throbs like I've been in a car crash. Every breath hurts, but at least I'm breathing. That's important, even though I can't think why. My brain feels like it's grown too large for my skull, a pressure in my sinuses and behind my eyes like the worst migraine. Hard to think with that pulsing, flashing light. Where am I? What's going on?

For a long time I can't remember anything. I know who I am, but my name eludes me. This should be more worrying than it is, but that's something else that I can't quite muster, the energy to be worried.

There's an itchy spot on the side of my nose, but when I try to raise my hand to scratch it, I hit something hard and rough. Stone directly above me, maybe no more than six inches away. Part of me knows this should be a reason to panic, but right now I'm calm. The pain in my chest is intense, but I can angle my arm, reach my nose. Getting rid of the itch is a small release.

The pulsing in my head begins to subside, and as it goes so I begin to remember things. My name's Constance. Con. It seems stupid that I would have forgotten that. Who forgets their own name?

I'm lying on my back. Not sure how I didn't know that before, but like my name it's obvious once I realise. Lifting my head hurts, and when I rest it back again, I feel hard stone beneath me. Where the fuck am I? What happened?

Flashes of memory begin to form into a more coherent picture. Being captured, strapped to a chair. Edward Masters crushing my chest. Well, at least that explains the pain. He blew some powder into my face. I couldn't help but inhale it. I still don't know what happened after I blacked out, where I am.

And then it dawns on me, in a flurry of cascading images. The crypt with its candle-lit alcoves, monstrous carvings writhing like shadow snakes on the ceiling, the chair bolted to the flagstone floor, stains all around it where countless victims have been butchered. And there, in the middle of it, like some prop from a bad horror movie, the ancient stone sarcophagus.

Fuck.

I'm inside it.

Panic batters at me from all sides. I lift both hands, heedless to the pain in my chest as I push against the solid rock on top of me. It's rough on my palms, cold and unyielding. I push harder, lungs screaming, but it doesn't budge. I bunch my hands into fists and hammer against the stone. Might as well try to punch through a cliff. There's no escape.

How long I lie in despair is anyone's guess. I can only take shallow breaths, the pain in my chest worse after my brief attempt at escape. I'm fairly sure at least a couple of my ribs are cracked. How strong was Masters that he could do that with one hand? How mad? In the darkness I can see his bulging eyes, hear his insane words about tongues and balls and hearts. Thank Christ I'm not a man, or he'd have cut me up like all the others. But what did he mean by it all?

I will myself calm, or at least as calm as it's possible to be, trapped in a stone coffin that was ancient when the Romans brought it here over two thousand years ago. Or maybe was hacked out by some incompetent mason a few years back when the good reverend doctor lost the last of his marbles. Muti. That's what Bain was talking about. I know the basics of it, faith healing and shamans. A bit more honest than homeopathy, and just as effective. It begs the question why Masters has been doing it though. Not for himself, that's for sure. If he's taking tongues and bollocks, hearts and God knows what else, he's got a market for them. Peddling cures like the best snake-oil salesmen. And just how much would a suspicious banker pay for good fortune in all his endeavours? How credulous would you have to be?

I have another small panic attack, smacking at the stone lid until I can feel my hands turning sticky with blood. Brilliant, Con. That's really helped. At least the pain in my knuckles distracts me from the pain in my ribs. I steady my breathing as best I can, try to relax even as the panic edges around me.

Masters' words echo in my head as I lie here helpless and frustrated. 'Your death will not be in vain though. It will let someone else live. Someone who deserves God's grace far more than your uncaring soul.' What the hell did he mean by that? I have a horrible feeling I know, at least what he intends. Even if it's all bollocks anyway. I'm distracted though, by two things. First, it occurs to me that sealed in a stone sarcophagus, even breathing shallowly due to cracked ribs, I ought to be running out of air by now. The other is that as the pounding in my head clears and the flashing in my vision subsides, I realise it's not completely dark in here. I can see the rough carved marks on the rock a few inches above me.

Gently, I bring one hand up in front of my face, then the other. My fingers are caked in blood and sand. I can see them move as I flex them. Light is getting into the sarcophagus from somewhere. I just need to find out where.

I can't move my head much. Whoever this thing was built for wasn't all that much bigger than me across the shoulders. They were taller though, or the stone was carved with space for a few keepsakes to take over to the other side. Tilting my head back, I can't see anything but darkness. I shuffle a bit, then twist as much onto my side as I can, grunting in a very unladylike fashion at the pain that jabs through my chest. It's agony, but I can see light past my feet. And not just any light. It's the orange flickering glow of one of the candles. There's a crack in the end of the sarcophagus big enough for me to see out through.

I'm too far away from it, but a few minutes of agonised shuffling has the soles of my boots pressed lightly against the stone. I draw my knees up towards my chest as far as I can, then kick down.

The pain drags a scream from my lungs, which only makes it worse. Stars flash across my vision, and the pounding starts up again in my head. I wait until it subsides before peering down at the crack. Is it bigger now? Did anything move?

Another kick and another wave of nausea. This time I don't wait for it to pass before kicking again. The lid of this coffin might be too heavy for one damaged woman to lift, but the sides are surely weaker. Again and again I kick out, convincing myself that the stone is giving way. Any moment now Masters and his acolytes will come running, stop me breaking their sacred relic, pull me out and kill me like they killed the others. But at least I won't die helpless, alone.

They don't come. No one comes. I kick and I kick, ignoring the pain, desperate and angry and frightened. Each time my feet hit the stone, the jarring sends shockwaves up my legs and spine to the base of my skull. The headache grows brighter and brighter. And then, with a noise like the gods at war, the end of the sarcophagus explodes outwards.

I am free.

I can't move for a long time. I'm too exhausted, too relieved, in too much pain. Only the nagging fear that Masters and his acolytes will be back gets me moving, and even then slowly.

It's not easy to slide and shuffle your way out of the end of a stone sarcophagus that's sitting about a metre off the ground. Even less so when your ribs are cracked and bruised. I manage eventually, sliding to the floor in an ungainly heap. The room is much as I remember it from before, although some of the candles have burned themselves out. I've no idea what time it is, how long I was unconscious, or how long it took to escape my prison. Half-escape, I should say. I'm still in the crypt, still in mortal danger.

The door to the tunnel they brought me in through is locked. Given the solid wood and iron nails of its construction, I don't think I'm going to break through there any time soon. Across the other side of the crypt, the iron gate is also locked, but the gaps between its ornate bars are wide enough for someone desperate to squeeze through. I never appreciated just how painful cracked ribs could be until I was that desperate. It's just as well I'm not as busty as my aunt.

The steps from the crypt bring me up into a small vestry to the side of the altar. I'm surprised to see pale daylight filtering in through the grimy stained-glass windows as I emerge into the main hall. How long have I been here?

It's clearly been a while since anyone worshipped in this church. Half the pews are missing, and of the ones that remain, most are on their back, broken. I know how they feel. St Martin's is similar to dozens I've been in down the years, a central nave, big stained-glass window over the altar, pulpit accessed by a narrow wooden stair. I can even see the wooden plaque with its slots for the hymn numbers, although what 146, 246a and 42 are, I've no idea. Singing was about the only thing I enjoyed about going to church, but I've managed to live without it for a good few years now.

The pain in my chest has been joined by a deep ache in my legs now. I push through it, limping to the main doors even though I know they'll be locked. Unlike a normal person's house, God's is kept secure with a heavy key that the vicar takes away with him. No lifting the latch from the inside here.

I work my way around to the side door but it's just the same. No easy way out, I might as well still be stuck inside the sarcophagus. I search through the vestry in the vain hope there might be a key hidden in some cupboard, or something as sophisticated as a phone. All I get is the chance to look up those hymns in the *New English Hymnal*. 'Holy! Holy! Holy! Lord God Almighty!', 'Holy Father, cheer our way', and – my favourite – 'While shepherds watched their flocks by night'. Or, as we used to sing it at St Humbert's, 'While shepherds washed their socks by night'.

No closer to escape, but with the image of a bar of Sunlight soap in my mind, I'm searching around the altar and pulpit when I hear a shout. It takes a second one for me to realise it's coming from the stairs down to the crypt. The third sends a chill through me that has nothing to do with my exhaustion.

'Where is she? Find her and bring her to me!'

Masters. Angry.

I look around the dilapidated church, desperate for escape or at the very least somewhere to hide. There is only one other door, leading to the tower and steeple and hanging half open. I don't want to go there, don't want to be trapped, but the noise of the gate to the crypt being unlocked spurs me on. I make it just in time, slipping through the gap and pulling the door silently closed as the first acolyte appears from the vestry. At least the steps upwards are stone, so my feet make no sounds as I climb. I'm all too aware that I'm dead if they find me though.

And then I see it. The windows are leaded panes coated with years of city grime and coal smoke. In the body of the church they were too high to reach, but here the steps climb past them. I remember now, looking from the outside when I was here with Karen yesterday. One window broken, some of the glass missing, the lead twisted and bent. Where was that window?

Noises from the hall filter up to me. They're searching methodically, trying the obvious exits first to make sure I've not escaped. It won't take them long to realise I couldn't have opened either of the church doors. I climb higher, racking my aching brain for any small details from yesterday. That window has to be somewhere near, surely?

I see it at the same time as I hear the door below being pushed open. No time to think, or worry about the consequences. The gap is big enough to fit my head through, and pushing at the leaded glasswork makes it bigger. I'm too high off the ground, but there's an old drainpipe I'd trust far more with my life than the Church of the Coming Light. I raise a small prayer of thanks to whoever designed this place, and the men who built it, as the pipe wobbles under my sudden weight, but stays put. Adrenaline lends me strength and makes the screaming pain in my chest and hands bearable as I inch my way down the tower. I drop the last metre, rolling as I hit the ground. Looking up, I can see faces in the broken window staring back. Then they disappear, indistinct cries coming from within the church.

Climbing the railings almost defeats me. My strength is running out fast, the pain threatening to overwhelm me. Somehow I manage, spurred on by the sound of hands pounding on the locked front door. I stumble on the pavement, hobble across the road towards the line of empty shops and houses. Do I try the pub down the road, call for help there? Will there be anyone about at this early hour? How long will it take my kidnappers to realise it's quicker to go back through the tunnel to the nightclub, come out the way they went in? What chance have I got if they see me and give chase?

The answer to that last one's easy enough. In my current state, fuck all.

Time to get the hell out of here.

48

I've no idea what time it is, or indeed what day. I can only tell it's early by the dawn light and the fact nothing is open.

The half hour it takes me to limp, stumble, fall and crawl back to my apartment block is the longest of my life. Every moment I'm certain the cry's going to go up, the hounds will fall on me and rip me to pieces. Each breath is an agony, ribs screaming at me to stop moving, rest, sleep. My hands are raw and bloody, and my head is at once sharp with fear and fogged with pain.

It's only as I stumble into the alley where I found Dan Jones lying amid the bin bags that I start to regret my decision to come here. I couldn't go back to Charlotte's, it's true. Izzy's there, and the last thing I want to do is lead anyone to her. I can't get into my own flat because they took my keys along with everything else, but there must be someone I can turn to, even at this hour.

There are no reporters or paparazzi photographers anywhere to be seen when I limp the last few dozen metres to the front of my apartment block. Even the cars parked either side of the street are empty, which is a shame. For once I'd have welcomed Chet Wentworth and his broken camera. Angry as he no doubt would have been, I don't think he'd have sold me out to the Church of the Coming Light. And he'd have had a working mobile phone to call the police, too. Where is everyone?

I knock lightly on Mrs Feltham's door, praying for a swift answer. I'd knock more loudly, but it takes all the strength I have left just to stay standing up, leaning heavily on the doorframe for support. No answer, no sound from inside that I can hear. Not that I can hear much over the noise in my head. How long I stand there waiting is anyone's guess, but it's obvious she's either fast asleep at the back of the flat or not in.

Struggling away from my support, I look around the street that's been my home for years. It was never the busiest of places, but now it's as if I've strayed into a movie about the apocalypse. There's nobody anywhere, no welcoming lights in any windows. Nothing.

And then I spot it, so far away the hundred-metre walk will almost certainly kill me. The corner shop is open, same as it was when Karen and I came here two days ago. I have no idea what I look like, but judging by the expression on the face of the old woman behind the counter it's not pretty. She stares at me for perhaps two seconds before turning without a word and disappearing through the bead curtain into the back room. Moments later her son appears. He has a napkin tucked into his collar, the stain of his breakfast marking the white cotton like blood. Suddenly I feel both faint and sick.

'Detective. What has happened?'

'Please. Call 999.' I don't recognise my voice. It sounds hoarse, alien, the words of another person. 'Tell them Detective Constable Fairchild has been attacked.'

His eyes go wide, but I see him take out his mobile phone. Then the world turns upside down and I'm crashing to the floor.

The first thing I see when I wake is a dark face looming over me. For a moment I think it's Masters, and I'm captured, done for. Then my eyes focus, see the different shape to the face, the hair that tumbles to the shoulders in curls more grey than black, the look of genuine concern.

'Con, girl. What happen to you?'

More awake now, I struggle to sit up and take in my surroundings. Mrs Feltham crouches in front of me, and behind her I can see the shopkeeper and his mother. I appear to be lying in a pile of cheap DVDs, and a tiny part of my brain remembers the cardboard promotion stand by the counter.

'Police?' It's all I can manage to say.

'Mr Patel has called them, like you asked. They're on their way. But come, let's get you up, child.'

Mrs Feltham holds out a hand, and when I don't move to take it she leans in and grabs me under both arms. I let out a little-girl squeak of pain as she hauls me upright.

'Ribs. Think I've cracked some.' Despite the agony, it feels better standing than lying on the floor. I look at the shopkeeper. Mr Patel. How many years have I been buying emergency supplies in here and never knew his name? 'Sorry about the mess. I'll pay for any damage.'

'Is not a problem.' Mr Patel waves his hands, palms towards me in a gesture I can't quite read. 'Would you like me to call an ambulance too?'

'I'll be fine. Thanks.' I shake my head, then wish I hadn't. The world spins around me, and only Mrs Feltham's swift reactions stop me collapsing to the floor again.

'Think we better get you checked over.' She stoops low, carefully looping one arm under mine, and steers me towards the door. 'Come with me, child.'

There are few people I'd put up with calling me child. I'm thirty years old, after all. Mrs Feltham's as ancient as the hills though, so I let her get away with it. I'm in no fit state to object to anything at the moment. I thank Mr Patel and his mother once more, then allow myself to be led out of the shop. A few more people are about now, as if the spell that was keeping them hidden from me has broken. Some give me strange looks as I limp past, but most ignore me like they would ignore a homeless person begging for change.

'Thought I heard a noise earlier, but when I came to the door there was nobody there.' Mrs Feltham guides me inside her ground-floor flat, then carefully closes and locks the door behind her. She leads me through to the kitchen, sits me gently into an old wooden chair at the formica table. Before doing anything else, she goes to the stove where a pot is sitting, pours dark liquid into a mug and brings it over along with a carton of milk. There's a bowl of sugar in the middle of the table, and although I wouldn't normally dream of adding it to something so fine, I heap three teaspoons in before taking a sip.

The coffee is every bit as magical as I remember. It's at the perfect temperature for drinking, and soothes my throat even as it begins to clear the fog from my mind. I don't expect it to heal my cracked ribs, but it somehow dulls that pain too. By the time I've drunk half of it, Mrs Feltham has returned with a large bowl full of steaming water, a clean white flannel floating on the top. I don't say anything as she takes first one hand, then the other. The water stings as she cleans away blood and grit.

'What have you been doing, Con?'

'Trying to break out of a stone sarcophagus.' For some reason I can't help myself telling Mrs Feltham the whole story. It takes a while, punctuated by the short breaths that are all I can take right now. At the back of my mind I wonder why it's taking so long for anyone to arrive following Mr Patel's 999 call, but it's a small worry easily swamped by the relief of being somewhere warm and safe.

'Mercy, but you find yourself in the strangest of circumstances. And that poor boy you found around the back. This is all to do with him?'

'I reckon so. Masters. He's been sacrificing homeless folk, runaways. People who probably won't be missed. Taking parts of them to give himself strength.'

Mrs Feltham pours more coffee, hotter this time, and sits down opposite me. 'Not for himself, no. This is old magic, dark magic. It is evil, but powerful. And it is others who benefit from it, not Masters. If that is even his true name.'

I drink more coffee, without sugar this time. The hot liquid is working its magic on me now, the sinus pressure in my head almost gone. I can think more clearly, but I can also feel the pain in my ribs, my hands, and the ache in my feet and shins from where I kicked my way out of the stone sarcophagus. Everything has gone from once removed to sharply focused. Even Mrs Feltham's words.

'You think he's an imposter?'

'Do I think he is not a real preacher? Well, he doesn't worship the God he claims to. I think you know that too. You have seen what he does, have you not.' The old lady stares at me, her eyes clear for all that she wears spectacles as thick as bottle ends. I lift a hand up to my face, but my mother's false glasses are gone, as is the wig. I'm still wearing Jennifer Golightly's dour clothes though.

'There. I think it's wearing off.' Mrs Feltham reaches forward and snaps her fingers in front of my face. I recoil instinctively.

'What?'

'He worked a powerful glamour on you, child. It was eating away at your soul. Would have devoured you entirely if I'd not found you when I did. You would have been his to command, to do with as he pleases.'

'I . . . ?' I'm not at all sure what to say, but before I can gather my wits, there's a knock at the door, loud enough to make me jump.

'That will be your friends now.' Mrs Feltham gets to her feet and sweeps out of the room in a manner that reminds me surprisingly of Rose. For all their obvious differences, the two have exactly the same aura of all-knowingness about them.

Wearily, and with much ah-ing at the pain, I get up too, follow her out into the hall, arriving just in time to see her open the door. DCI Bain stands there, Karen beside him, and behind them a pair of uniformed constables. He looks at me in much the same way I might look at something that's been left at the back of the fridge to rot for months.

'Jesus Christ, Fairchild. You look like shit. What the fuck have you been up to?'

49

Bain wants me to go to hospital, but I'm not having any of that nonsense. Not now. I need to see this finished, even if my whole body feels like it might simply shut down at any moment. We take a squad car to the church and Ritzy's nightclub, while a second team heads over to the shelter. DS Latham's in charge of that, and I could see the mixed emotions on his face as the DCI gave him his orders. He doesn't like being sidelined, but neither does he want to be in a car with me if he can possibly avoid it.

'What's up with Latham?' I ask as we get close to the church. I'm not happy about the number of trucks going that way, or the ones coming back laden with demolition waste.

'How do you mean?' Bain says. 'He can be a bit prickly, but he gets the job done.'

'He hates even having to breathe the same air as me, sir. Every time you mention my name he breaks out in hives, and I don't even know what hives are.'

'He has his reasons. He'll get over them.'

I'd push the matter further, but we've arrived back at the church. Only now the road's been cordoned off, and a huge caterpillar tractor is hacking away at the walls of the nightclub. A corner of it's gone already, bent reinforcing bars poking out of broken concrete like metal bones in a fatal wound. I'm in no fit state to run anywhere, but the DCI proves himself fitter than he looks, and more spritely than I'd have given a man of his age credit for.

He's out of the squad car before it's completely stopped, dodges under the swinging arm of the caterpillar and leaps up to the driver's door. There's a moment when I think he's going to fall off, get himself crushed under those enormous steel tracks, but the engine dies away to a slow tickover instead. I'm too far away and the noise is too loud to make out the words exchanged between the two of them. It's clear after a tense twenty seconds or so that Bain has won. The driver kills the engine, climbs out of the cab and jumps down to the ground.

'Reckon someone was in a hurry to cover up the evidence,' Karen says from the other side of the squad car. I watch as the dust begins to settle, the haze that was obscuring the damage parting to reveal far less than I'd feared. Ritzy's nightclub might have been a dive, but it was built well enough to survive a nuclear strike.

'Done us a favour though.' I nod towards the corner of the building that's been ripped away. It includes the locked front door, now lying face down in the road a good ten metres away. 'Not going to need a big red key to get in now.'

The site foreman insists on hard hats, even though beyond the initial damage to the front corner of the building, nothing has changed in the nightclub save for a thin layer of dust over everything. My ribs still hurt like hell, but I keep my wincing to a minimum as we pick a route through to the main dance hall. It's still laid out with chairs and a lectern, and my first thought is one of relief. Until that point I'd not been able to quell the niggling thought that I might have somehow hallucinated the entire night's events.

Finding first the storeroom in which I was held, then the small office at the end of the corridor, helps to cement the reality of it in my mind, while at the same time reinforcing just how surreal the whole situation was, and continues to be. I can't bend down to move the rug that's been hastily thrown over the trapdoor, and Bain is clearly far too senior to do such menial tasks, so it's left to Karen to reveal the stone steps and passageway through to the crypt.

There were lights the last time I came this way, but now the electricity has been cut. I stand in the dark tunnel, trying to remember all the details while we wait for torches to be brought from the squad car. The two uniform constables accompany us on the short trip to the far end of the tunnel, perhaps because they're nosey, but just as likely because they don't want to lose their precious torches.

I was worried that the door might be locked, but when we reach the crypt it's wide open. The candles have all been extinguished, only the sour smell of burned wax tainting the air. That and something else that sparks a memory I can't quite pin down.

'Over there.' I point towards the sarcophagus, still sitting in the middle of the room. A beam of light cuts over it, and something looks out of place. It's swept past before I can see what, resting instead on the chair where Masters almost squeezed the life out of me. It's empty now, but the stains show up even worse under the harsh white electric light. Spatter patterns that would make a forensic pathologist rub their hands with glee. People have died here. Messily.

'Jesus.' Bain steps out into the crypt, his feet echoing on the flagstones. I'm not sure I really want to go back in, now that I'm here. After what happened before, and Mrs Feltham's strange words, the stone closes around me like a tomb. I can remember all too well the feeling of being trapped inside that narrow sarcophagus. And now I realise what it was that I saw, what sparked that memory.

'The stone top.'

Nobody pays me any attention, so I grab the torch from the nearest constable. He'd been shining it at the carved grotesques on the ceiling, and gives me a short 'Hey' of complaint. It dies on his lips as I direct the beam where I want it.

The massive stone slab that I couldn't lift when I was trapped inside the sarcophagus now lies across it at a sharp angle. As if whoever was putting it back on again was in too much of a hurry to do the job properly. I can imagine the panic, the anger, the frustration when they realised I'd escaped. The rush to destroy as much evidence as possible before I brought police and forensics experts here to start pulling their vicious little cult apart.

I move the torch to the end where I escaped, and sure enough the broken pieces of stone are still strewn about the floor. I step into the crypt, gasping in pain as I catch my foot on an uneven flagstone. Something is drawing me to the hole at the end of the sarcophagus. Some combination of half-remembered words, observations, things I don't want to think about. I shine the light on the floor, mostly so that I don't stumble again, but also because whilst I need to look inside the coffin, I really don't want to. But finally I am there, at the end, standing where I fell not more than a few hours ago. I turn slowly, playing the light on the damage my boots did, and there, inside, are another pair of feet. Another person.

'There's someone here.' My voice is so quiet nobody seems to hear, so I say it again, louder this time. 'There's someone inside.'

That gets their attention. Bain hurries over to where I'm standing, kicking stones aside as he does. Karen moves more carefully, but soon the both of them are bent low, peering into the sarcophagus and the figure lying within.

'We need to get the lid off,' Bain says, then directs the two constables to help. It was too much for me, but the three of them make light work of it. I don't see where they put it down, don't hear it clink against the floor. I can't even breathe as I step forward and play the torchlight over the small, thin figure lying in repose. Part of me knew this was how it was going to end, even though the rational part of me can't even begin to say how I knew.

'Oh my God. Who is she?' one of the constables asks. Bain knows. All he says is 'Oh shit.'

They've folded her arms across her chest, put her false spectacles in one hand. She's even wearing my mousy-brown wig with the grey highlights, but I'd still recognise my mother anywhere.

50

The day passes in snapshots of activity and pain. I'm more tired than I've ever been, but there's no way I can sleep. For one thing, my cracked ribs make any movement difficult, despite the painkillers. For another, while a number of the acolytes of the Church of the Coming Light have been rounded up and brought in for questioning, Masters remains at large.

I should go home, get some rest, practise sleeping in a more or less upright position. Instead I mope around the station and the conference room the NCA team have taken over, waiting for updates. If I leave, they'll most likely not let me back in again. So I stay.

'Why are you still here?'

I must have nodded off briefly, as the voice startles me. So does the jolt of pain through my chest when I twitch awake. I turn more slowly to see Superintendent Shepherd standing in the doorway. Except that she's not a superintendent, is she. She's a brigadier.

'Ma'am?' It's all I can think of to say. My brain's not working at full capacity right now.

'Honestly, Fairchild. Any other officer would have taken the rest of the day off. The rest of the week. At least tell me you've been to A & E for a check-up.' She bustles into the room, more like a mother hen than someone given to barking orders she knows will be carried out without question. I struggle slowly to my feet.

'I'm fine.' I'm not fine. Her hand at my elbow is all that stops me from planting my face on the carpet tiles.

'Sit,' she orders, lowering me back into my chair. 'I'll get us some coffee.'

There's a pot on a side table, and I watch as she pours coffee into two mugs and then spoons sugar into one of them. I thought it was for her, but I'm grateful for the sweetness and energy when I find out she's given that one to me.

'Ed's filled me in on what happened. I'm sorry about your mum.'

She looks it, too. I'm still finding it hard to process. 'We weren't close, but thanks anyway.'

'You have a certain knack for getting into trouble. I had a young captain under my command much the same. You remind me of him.'

'That's right – you're not a super, you're a brigadier.'

Shepherd raises an eyebrow at that. 'Not common knowledge. Especially in these parts.'

'Any particular reason you keep it secret?'

'Much the same reason you don't tell people you're Lady Constance, I'd guess.' Shepherd pulls out one of the chairs and sits in it so close our knees are almost touching. 'It's a distraction. And I got bored of all the *Doctor Who* jokes.'

'What happened to him? Your captain?'

'Afghanistan happened.' It's all she'll say on the matter. I can tell by the way she gazes off across the room to the whiteboard. 'So what exactly is the deal with the Reverend Doctor Edward Masters? And how is it that a church in north London has an undocumented late-Roman crypt underneath it?'

I'd shrug, only I know just how painful that would be. 'I can't begin to understand what drives him, but it's basically dark muti, like DCI Bain thought. Human sacrifice, taking the best bits to give strength or other desirable traits to whoever commissioned him. I suspect that's where a lot of the money for his church comes from. Wealthy businessmen with an unhealthy dose of superstition.'

'I've seen some awful things in my time, but . . .' Shepherd grimaces. 'Sooner we catch the sick bastard the better.'

'How's it going? Must be every copper in the Met out there looking for him.'

'And more. We've put out an all ports, and Interpol are on it too, just in case he's slipped through the net. We'll get him, have no worry about that.'

'Easy for you to say. You're not the one whose ribs he broke.' I shift in my seat and reach for my coffee, then regret it when the pain stabs me again. And the mug's empty.

'OK. Enough's enough. I'm going to get Karen to take you home, and you're staying there until we come for you.'

I'm about to say 'Who are you now, my mum?' when it hits me that I don't have a mother any more. I wonder if anyone's broken the news to my father. I should call Aunt Flick. What about Ben and Charlotte, though? They've only just set off on their honeymoon. Should I call them and ruin that?

'You'll be fine, Con. I'll put a security detail on your door if you want.' Shepherd mistakes my silence for fear, although to be fair I'm happier in here surrounded by police officers than I would be out there with cracked ribs. I don't even have my can of mace spray; nobody's been able to find my backpack or coat yet. That makes me feel more vulnerable than anything, knowing that Masters has my phone, my keys, my sense of security. Damn him for taking that. I won't give him the satisfaction. I try to sit a little more upright in my seat, ignoring the pain that I'm going to have to get used to for a while anyway. My resolve doesn't last long.

'OK. I'll go home. But you let me know the minute we have any leads on Masters, right?'

'Deal.' Shepherd stands up, holding her hand out, fingers splayed, to stop me from following. 'Stay there. I'll go and find Karen.'

She walks to the door, then turns back to me before leaving. 'Welcome to the team, Con. I think you'll fit right in.'

There are no reporters outside my apartment block when we arrive, no paparazzi photographers lurking behind the concrete pillars. Not for the first time, it occurs to me that they would never just camp out here at all hours and in all weather. Not for me, however much they thought the story had all the right ingredients for a good dose of moral outrage. And yet far too often over the past few months they've been waiting for me when I came home. How did they know? It doesn't take a genius to see they must have been tipped off by someone, and the list of people who would know my movements that intimately is not long.

Karen follows me up the stairs, even though I'm quite capable of climbing them unaided. I reckon she'd give me a lift back to Charlotte's if I asked, and it's tempting. I can't get in right now, though, and Izzy's gone back to Harston Magna for her own safety. It's just as well I gave Mrs Feltham a spare set of keys to my flat. I'll have to change the locks again, but at least I can get in, have a shower and put on some clean clothes.

'Want a cuppa?' I ask as I walk through to the kitchen. 'Actually, scratch that. I've no milk. Might have some beer though.'

'I could nip down to the corner shop and get some milk. It's probably not good to mix beer with those painkillers you've been taking all day.'

'You sure?' I start to walk over to where my bag would be

hanging, if it hadn't been taken off me last night, along with all my money and cards. Karen seems to understand my predicament before I do.

'It's OK. You can owe me. Anything else you might need?'

'Milk's fine, thanks. I'll have to see about getting some cash in the morning. What a nightmare.'

'We'll get through it though. Back in five, OK?' Karen disappears into the hall. A moment later I hear the jangle of keys as she takes them from the sideboard. The door closes and the lock clacks into place. I shuffle painfully about the kitchen for a moment, then cross the hall to the living room. It's easier to stand, or to sit fairly upright. Moving between the two is agony, so bending down to grab the remote control for the telly is fun.

I've hardly got the thing switched on when I hear a light tapping sound at the front door. That was quick, maybe too quick. And anyway, she took the keys with her didn't she? Ten years in the police has made me wary, the last twenty-four hours more so than ever, so I check the spyhole to see who's there. It's not Karen bearing gifts. Of all the people it might have been, this one is perhaps the least expected. I slide the chain off and unlock the door, half opening it to reveal Anna Cho. She's been caught in the rain, her hair bedraggled, coat dripping. I look a bit closer. That's my coat. And that's my small backpack slung over her shoulder.

'Din't know where to go, like. It's all gone to shit, right?'

There's something about her that feels all wrong. She looks like she's not slept in days, probably not eaten either. But it's the deadness in her eyes that sets me on edge. If I could, I'd turn her away. I don't want anything to do with her. But she needs to come in for questioning, at the very least. And I'd like my things back too.

'You'd better come in.' I open the door wider, stand aside to let her enter. She hesitates for a moment, eyes darting to the side in a manner I'm too tired and too slow to pick up on. It occurs to me too late that there's only one way she could have got hold of my coat and backpack. She was there, at Ritzy's.

'I'm so sorry. He made me . . .'

Which is when Edward Masters steps into view.

51

I couldn't stop him from barging in even if I wanted to. He's twice my size, and he hasn't got cracked ribs. The two of them are inside, the door slammed shut behind them, before I can so much as shout. How the fuck did he get up here past the squad car parked across the road?

'Come to give yourself up, have you?' I try to sound brave, but probably fail. How long have I got before Karen comes back? Can I shout and warn her, or will he let her in and then have two of us captive? I'm not going to let that happen.

'What is that you say?' Masters pushes past Anna, shoving her so hard that she falls back into the jumble of boots and other rubbish by the front door. My old golfing umbrella is there, but I can't reach it to use it as a weapon. There's nothing else I'd fancy my chances with. Not in this small flat.

'You are a thorn in my side, Lady Constance Fairchild. An irritant like a mosquito buzzing around my ear. But like the mosquito, I will swat you away. First though, you will give me what you should have given your mother.'

He reaches towards me in much the same way as he did back in the crypt, as if he's conjuring some invisible force between us. If there is such a force, it's insubstantial too, and there's something about the way he says 'mother' that brings my anger to the boil. I've heard men like him use the same sneering tone when they say 'woman' or 'girl' too. There is not one scrap of respect in it, only contempt. And a flickering doubt in his face, too. He curves his fingers in towards his palm, pulling his hand as if tugging on reins tied around my neck. I feel nothing, which is hardly surprising given I'm not really into that kind of kink.

He throws his hand in my direction and pulls it back again, dark brow furrowed as his frustration turns to swift fury. I would laugh, but I've seen what he can do with those hands.

'How is it you are not helpless now? Who are you who can throw off such powerful magic without a thought?'

Magic? Is that what this is? But then again he must believe in his muti, otherwise why do it? And why toss the dead bodies aside as if they mean nothing to him.

'I don't believe in fairies, Masters. Well, not that kind anyway.' I make a small shrug with my shoulders, and the fact it only hurts a lot, rather than unbearably, gives me a kind of rogue strength. I'll taunt him, keep him occupied, and soon enough help will come.

'You have no idea what forces you are messing with, child. This one knows.' He turns away briefly to where Anna cowers in the corner by the door. With his other hand, he makes the same pulling motion, and I can see the struggle in her face as she tries to stop herself coming to him. It's futile though. Step by pitiful step she inches closer until he can wrap his giant hand around her neck.

'Leave her be.'

'Or what?' He squeezes until Anna's eyes bulge, her cheeks turning red under her thin white make-up. And yet she doesn't fight him. Her hands hang at her sides, one with fingers loose, the other clutching something.

'She is mine. Completely. Mine to give life to, and mine to take it away.'

Anna lets out a slow gurgling whine, and yet still seems unable to fight back against Masters. I can only watch as he slowly chokes the life out of her.

And then I realise that I can do far more than watch.

'Enough of this shit. Put her down.' I step forward as I speak, pull back my arm, make a fist and punch him as hard as I can. Right in the face. One arm occupied, Masters is too slow to parry with the other, and I feel the satisfying crunch of cartilage as his nose breaks. His head snaps back and blood spurts across his cheeks. For a moment I think he might go down, but he shakes off the blow like a terrier killing a rat. Then my ribs remind me of what he did to them earlier.

'You dare!' He roars like an angry bear, as much affronted as in pain. I don't care, all I can feel is my chest on fire, and curling up against the agony only makes it worse. I fall to my knees as Masters rises up, both hands huge boulders almost grazing the ceiling before he brings them down for a killing blow. I tense, resigned to it but still willing to fight to the end. If I'm going to die, then I'll look death in the face, spit at it if I can.

There's an oddly faint 'pock' noise, and everything changes. Masters' eyes, bulging and mad with fury, go wide, then roll upwards into their sockets. His fists fall from the sky like meteorites, but at the same time he crumples like a concrete tower when the demolition explosion goes off. It's all I can do to scramble out of the way as he crashes to the floor in an unconscious heap. I stare at him for long moments, and then up at the space where he had been standing. Anna looks back at me with wide eyes, my golf umbrella in both hands, bent with the force she used bringing its handle down on the back of his head.

We're still staring at each other a minute later when the key clicks in the lock and the door opens to reveal Karen Eve with a carton of milk in one hand. It's to her credit that she doesn't drop it.

'The fuck?'

52

I'd hoped to avoid hospital, but sometimes you just have to accept the inevitable. The pills the nurse gives me don't really take the pain away, but they do make me not care so much about it. Each breath is an interesting adventure though. Too deep and my vision starts to darken, too shallow and I risk having to take a deep one or pass out.

The hardest thing is getting dressed. They put me in a gown, the easier to X-ray and scan me, prod me and poke me. Now I've been left in a little cubicle with the pile of grubby clothes I came in wearing. At least they're Jennifer Golightly's unfashionable garments; it's far easier to put on a blouse than a T-shirt, less painful to climb into a sensible-length skirt than jeans. I struggle a bit with my boots, but only because bending is inadvisable if I don't want to end up on the floor. Dammit, Con. Why do you have to be so stubborn? You could milk this situation for all its worth. Get yourself a private room and round-the-clock care for a day or two.

Not that I ever would. There's others far more in need, and I don't much like hospitals anyway.

I should leave, out through the front door to the nearest taxi and a ride home. But do I go back to my crime-scene flat, or Charlotte and Ben's house? With Izzy back at Harston Magna, there'll be nobody there to help me convalesce.

Instead, I take the lift to the sixth floor, struggle along the familiar corridor until I reach the ICU. Dan Jones still lies in his bed, the pillows slowly digesting him. He looks thinner, greyer, even less alive than the last time I was here. It's the next room along that I'm more interested in though.

'Wondered how long it would take you to get here.'

A lone figure sits on one of the plastic chairs across the corridor from the observation window. Diane Shepherd stands as I approach, head tilted slightly to one side as she takes in my appearance.

'You look like shit, Fairchild.' She sniffs the air like a hound. 'And you don't smell much better. Go home, for God's sake.'

Given that describing her as dishevelled would be kind, I think Shepherd's words are a bit rich. I can't deny that I'm slightly whiffy though, a mixture of all manner of unpleasant things and fear.

'I just wanted to see him.' I turn towards the observation window on to the next room in the ICU. It's almost identical to the one where Jones lies, only the figure in this bed is altogether larger. The Reverend Doctor Edward Masters is hooked up to a breathing tube, a saline drip and several monitors. His head is wrapped in a soft bandage, swollen like a rotting carcass. Nobody has tried to set his broken nose, although they've cleaned the worst of the blood from around his mouth. 'I didn't realise he was so bad.'

'Doctor says he's lucky to be alive. Not sure lucky's the word I'd use. What did you hit him with?'

'My fist.' I look down at my hand, wary of lifting it lest the pain in my ribs flare. 'And a lot of rage.'

Shepherd makes a sound that's halfway between a cough and a laugh.

'Anna whacked him on the back of the head pretty hard with my umbrella, too,' I add.

'You make quite the pair. If he's not seriously brain damaged it'll be a miracle.'

'How is she? Anna.' I look away from Masters, finding I don't much care what happens to him as long as it's permanent.

'We've got her in protective custody. She's a wild one, and we're treading carefully, given her rap sheet. It helps that she's of age. Just. She seems to think the world of you, too.'

'Can't imagine why.' I shrug, then immediately wish I hadn't.

'She's been telling us a lot of interesting things about Masters and his church. Claims she wanted to before, but couldn't because of the spell he'd cast on her. Reckons you broke his hold on her when you broke his nose.' Shepherd tilts her head at the window, but I don't look around.

'Even if I think his muti is bullshit, that doesn't mean others don't believe in it. They'd have to, otherwise how would he get away with it? I'm glad she's helping, but look after her, yeah? She's been through a lot of shit, and she saved my life.'

'She's going to be a key witness in any trial, so don't worry about that. She knows a lot about Master's inner circle. We've picked up most of his accomplices already, and once we start playing them off against each other the whole story will come out soon enough.'

Shepherd looks like she's swaying slightly as she speaks, and then it dawns on me that it's not her. She reaches out a gentle hand and steadies me.

'Come on, Con. It's time we got you home.'

'I knew she'd not been well, but your mother was never one to share. Especially not when it came to herself.'

I'd thought when Diane Shepherd had said she was going to get me home she meant a squad car back to my flat. Instead, she put me in the back of her Mercedes and instructed her driver to take me to Harston Magna. I'm not entirely sure how she could have known about Aunt Felicity and Folds Cottage, but I suspect Alex Fortescue might have had something to do with that.

However it was done, it was a kindness I'll not forget soon.

It's taken three days, but finally I feel awake, alive and comfortable enough to mix with people, and so I'm sitting in the kitchen, drinking tea and staring at the biscuits I know will be uncomfortable to eat. Who knew that cracked ribs could be so debilitating? Pain notwithstanding, it would be almost perfect. Were it not for the fact that my father is here too. He looks like he's aged ten years since Ben's wedding, although part of me wonders if that's because of the way his wife died, rather than any heartbreak at her loss. He's never been one to court that kind of publicity, and my mother's death is most certainly public.

'What was wrong with her?' The words sound crass, heartless even.

'According to her doctor, she had terminal cancer. It started in her breast, spread to her lungs and liver. She never told me.'

For the first time in decades I feel a certain sympathy for my father. He's a bully and a coward, an old-school misogynist who drove me away from the family with his calculating sexism. But in that moment he looks like a little lost boy.

'Was she not taking any treatment for it?'

'Apart from daily prayer?' His laugh is hollow. 'I spoke to our GP. Neither her nor the oncologist have seen her in over six months, although they both knew about it, which is more than I did. I've looked in the bathroom cabinet. There's nothing stronger than aspirin in there. She didn't say anything. Why didn't she say anything, Constance?'

Because your marriage failed the day you decided to have an affair with your best friend's wife? Before that? Even ten years ago you were living separate lives, in separate parts of the hall. Barely talking to each other and certainly not talking to me. I hold that piece of hard truth to myself.

'When did she first meet Masters?' I ask instead. My father's reaction is predictable.

'Who?'

'The reverend. That chap she invited to the wedding. Tried to kill me, remember?'

'Oh, him. I guess that was maybe six, eight months ago? Before all that nastiness with Roger, anyway. No idea how they crossed paths.'

'What about the money she gave him?'

That gets his attention, as I suspected it would. The worried frown answers my question for me. 'Money?'

'Mother made a donation to the Church of the Coming Light. I don't know how recently or how much for, but you might want to get on to her executors and see about that. He was playing her, like the conman he is. My guess is he promised her a cure. Just didn't say that it wouldn't work. And that it would involve sacrificing her only daughter.'

'Con, dear. Have you had your pills?' Aunt Flick interrupts before we can come to blows, but in truth I haven't the energy for confrontation.

'I'm fine.' I turn back to my father, say the words I never thought I would. 'I'm sorry. It's been a tough few days.'

He looks at me with an astonished expression, as if he's only just now understanding that I am a person, my own person, and not some object labelled 'daughter' he can order around as he pleases.

'Tough for us all, and there'll be hard times ahead.' Aunt Felicity has the truth of it, and possibly the solution. She hefts the old china pot into the air and waves it gently around. 'Who'd like some more tea?'

53

Two funerals and a wedding. I'd have been happy enough never to set foot in St Thomas's Harston Magna ever again, and yet here I am for the third time in less than a month. I'm at the front this time, couldn't really hide at the back without raising too many questions. There's no space anyway. For all my mother and I never got on, it looks like the whole village has turned up to send her off.

Glancing along the pew, I see my father staring at the coffin. We've not spoken since that morning almost a week ago in Aunt Flick's kitchen, but he looks a lot less harrowed than he did then. Maybe the fact that Margo DeVilliers is sitting beside him helps. Well, if that's where he wants to find solace, who am I to tell him no?

I follow his gaze as the vicar drones on about something worthy. I should feel something for the tiny woman lying in that dark and shiny wooden cage; she brought me into the world, after all. But I'm finding it hard to come to terms with the manner of her death. The post-mortem said the cancer was to blame, that she most probably died shortly after being placed in the sarcophagus, her body simply too weak to carry on living. The pathologist skirted over the reason why she was in there in the first place, but it doesn't take a genius to work it out. Masters promised her a cure, selling it with all his charismatic preacher skills. What I don't know – don't want to know – is whether she knew the price of that cure would be my life. I'd like to think that she didn't, but it's going to take some work. Does that make me a bad person?

The service is mercifully short. Mother would have hated that. She'd have hated that it was officiated by the local vicar, too. Most of all she would have shuddered at the thought of being taken down into the Fairchild family crypt, underneath the nave. Laid to rest alongside generations of stuffy aristocrats. As far as I'm concerned she's just an empty shell now, soon to be dust and bones. What does it matter where they lie?

I don't follow the rest of the family down there. For once I'm fine with letting the Fairchild men take on that responsibility. I just want to get outside, away from this place.

'How're your ribs holding up?'

Izzy's all dressed in black, which is more than I've managed. Dressing's still an exercise in pain management, and so I tend to go for things that can be easily pulled on.

'I'll live.' The words come out reflexively, before my brain's had time to parse them. At least no one else is in earshot to hear my faux pas. Izzy half grimaces, half smirks.

'You coming to the wake then?'

The wake, at the hall, where all the good people of the village will chatter and drink and eat disgusting canapés. A crowd of people, each one anxious to express sympathy for my loss when in truth I don't really feel one. Guilt, sure, but loss? No.

'Think I'll give it a miss. Head back down to London once I've spoken to Ben.'

We both look over towards the narrow entrance to the crypt, but there's no sign of anyone coming back out again yet. Behind us, the church has almost emptied, and by the time I've shuffled slowly to the door it's clear. Outside, a small group of photographers and journalists are huddling under a tree for shelter from the drizzly rain. I've almost grown used to them now, and if it weren't for the fear of pain, I might even raise a hand and wave.

'Weird how they've never really pestered me at all, but whenever you're around they appear.' Izzy gets to the heart of something that's been bothering me for a while now, and as I spot a familiar face in the small crowd of paparazzi, I feel it's time to sort things out once and for all.

'You might want to go back inside for a bit then,' I tell her. 'I'm going to see if I can't stir things up a bit.'

It takes me longer than I was hoping to cross the distance from the church entrance to the crowd of journalists. I can't imagine that photographs of me hobbling along the uneven graveyard path will make good tabloid fodder, but then I've never understood the prurient fascination with the lives of others anyway. Something about my determination must be having an effect on them, too. At the church steps, I was getting the usual catcalls of 'Give us a smile, Connie' and other similarly inappropriate suggestions. Once they realise I'm heading their way, the voices fall silent, and as I get closer quite a few of the photographers start to pack up, move off. By the time I'm at the point where they were all clustered, only one remains.

'Am I that scary?' I ask, nodding at the backs of the retreating press.

'Actually, yes.' Jonathan Stokes looks frail, thinner in the face than when I met him in a café just a week or so ago. His skin has taken on a grey pallor, and his hair hangs in damp rat tails over his scalp. 'And I asked them to go. Set them straight about what happened, too.'

'That's big of you.'

He shrugs. 'You saved my life. Didn't have to do that. I'm grateful.'

'What was I supposed to do, let you choke to death when I know CPR?'

'That's not what I meant. But I'm grateful for that too.'

I have a suspicion I know what he's talking about, but it's not a line of enquiry I really want to pursue. Better to put Masters and his perversion of muti into a box marked 'superstition' and leave it at that. And besides, there's something else I want to know.

'Here's the thing I never understood.' I shove my hands in my pockets, then regret it when my ribs complain. 'I can't believe you guys would stake out my apartment the whole time. I mean, a story's a story, but that's a hell of a lot of effort for very little return.'

'You know that's not how we work, right?'

'Yeah. That's what I thought. So if you weren't there all the time, you must have been tipped off I was coming. And the only people who could have done that are my fellow police officers. Feels good to be loved, doesn't it.'

'You pissed off a lot of people when you broke open Bailey's corrupt little clique. Probably more than when you put DeVilliers away, though that's why I was on your case.'

'Thought as much. Your paper's owned by one of Roger's old friends, isn't it.'

Stokes shakes his head at that. 'Not my paper any more. I quit.'

That raises my eyebrow. 'Do I see a conscience stirring?'

'Not really. Still only good for this kind of work. Embarrassing celebrities, raking muck.'

'So why'd you tell them all to leave me alone then?' I nod my head in the vague direction all the other journalists have gone. 'I don't do exclusives.'

'Ha. No. Wouldn't ask for one. This Masters thing's going to be big, and you're right in the middle of it. You and your family. Thought I'd give you a heads-up. And a bit of space to mourn your old mum even if you didn't exactly get on.'

'That's very noble of you, I'm sure.' I turn to walk away, but he reaches out to stop me. Not catching my arm this time, I notice. He's learning.

'That young copper who died last year. Dan Penny.'

An unwanted memory pushes its way into my mind. Gun to the back of the head, execution style. Swift and brutal. 'What of him?'

'He came up through training with a new friend of yours, Detective Sergeant Latham. Couple of uniforms in your local nick were good chums of his too.'

Stokes says nothing more. A quick touch of forefinger to temple by way of a salute, then he turns and walks away.

Acknowledgements

It's a bit of a minefield, writing acknowledgements at the back of a book. So many people help me in so many ways, it's almost impossible to know when to stop. There's always the worry that I'll forget someone, too.

Having said which, I owe a huge debt of gratitude to the team at Wildfire Books and Headline: Alex Clarke, Ella Gordon, Jo Liddiard, Jenni Leech, Siofra Dromgoole and everyone else who has worked so hard to make this book a thing. Thanks also to my copy editor, Jill Cole – yours is an essential job, but one which is often unacknowledged. I'm enormously grateful to Rose Akroyd, too, for bringing Con Fairchild to such brilliant life in the audiobooks.

I would not be in a position to write these stories without the tireless work and support of my agent, the effervescent Juliet Mushens. Thank you, Juliet, again.

These books look very nice on a shelf, but it's all you readers who make it worthwhile. Thank you for taking a chance on Con first time around, and if you've come back for this one then I must be doing something right. Here's hoping you all stick around for more.

And finally thank you to Barbara, who doesn't read crime fiction but does keep me sane. I couldn't do it without you.

If you loved this, don't miss

NO TIME TO CRY

the first book in James Oswald's

Constance Fairchild series

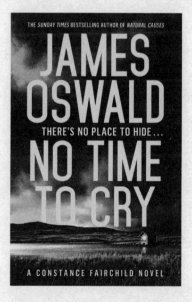